**Len**[...]ed in
Calliforn[...]
with he[...] AND NEIGH[...]
romantic suspense author, [...] a computer programmer.
A Romance Writers of America Golden Heart® Award
finalist, she has also won the prestigious Daphne du
Maurier Award for Excellence in Mystery/Suspense. To
get the latest news about Lena, please visit her website,
lenadiaz.com

**Cindi Myers** is the author of more than fifty novels. When
she's not plotting new romance story lines, she enjoys
skiing, gardening, cooking, crafting and daydreaming.
A lover of small-town life, she lives with her husband
and two spoiled dogs in the Colorado mountains.

# SERIAL SLAYER
# COLD CASE

## LENA DIAZ

# MISSING AT
# FULL MOON MINE

## CINDI MYERS

# MILLS & BOON

First Published in Great Britain 2022
by Mills & Boon, an imprint of HarperCollins*Publishers* Ltd
1 London Bridge Street, London, SE1 9GF

www.harpercollins.co.uk

HarperCollins*Publishers*
1st Floor, Watermarque Building,
Ringsend Road, Dublin 4, Ireland

*Serial Slayer Cold Case* © 2022 Lena Diaz
*Missing at Full Moon Mine* © 2022 Cynthia Myers

ISBN: 978-0-263-30330-8

0222

MIX
Paper from
responsible sources
FSC™ C007454

This book is produced from independently certified FSC™
paper to ensure responsible forest management.

For more information visit: www.harpercollins.co.uk/green

Printed and Bound in Spain using 100% Renewable electricity at
CPI Black Print, Barcelona

# SERIAL SLAYER COLD CASE

## LENA DIAZ

I couldn't live in my make-believe world, sharing my stories, if it wasn't for the support of so many people, including my family and these wonderful friends: Connie, Jan, Amy, Alison, Angi, Jean, Donnell and so many more! I love you all.

# Chapter One

Maintaining a white-knuckled grip on the steering wheel while negotiating the treacherous curves up Prescott Mountain on his daily commute was typical for Ryland Beck. *Smiling* while he resolutely refused to look toward the steep drop on the other side of the road *wasn't* typical. Nothing, not even his phobia about heights, could dampen his enthusiasm this chilly October morning. Today he'd begin his investigation into a serial killer case that had gone cold over four years ago.

Bringing down the Smoky Mountain Slayer was the challenge of a lifetime. No suspects. No DNA. No viable behavioral profile. In spite of the lack of evidence, Ryland was determined to put the killer behind bars. He wanted to give the families of the five victims the answers and justice they deserved.

Unfortunately, what he couldn't give them was closure. Closure, as he well knew, was a fictional construct. The death of a loved one would always leave a gaping hole in the hearts and lives of those left behind. But knowing the victim's murderer had been caught and punished would go a long way toward making the excruciating grief more bearable.

He continued winding his way up the mountain to-

ward UB headquarters as he considered the limited information he'd found on the internet about the killings.
The Slayer's *modus operandi* was consistent: all of his
victims were strangled, their bodies dumped in the woods
in Monroe County. But aside from them being young
women, the victimology was all over the place. Their
educational and economic backgrounds varied, as did
their ethnicity. Some were married, some weren't. Some
had children, some didn't. All of that made it nearly impossible to build a useful profile to help figure out who'd
murdered them.

The detectives from the Monroe County Sheriff's Office had deemed the case unsolvable. But here in Gatlinburg, Ryland had a unique advantage: an über-wealthy
boss who knew firsthand the suffering a victim's family
endured when a murder case went cold.

Seven years after his wife was killed and his infant
daughter went missing, Grayson Prescott had given up
on the stagnant police investigation. He decided to create a cold-case company called Unfinished Business.
Just a few months later, UB had solved the case. Now,
the thirty-three counties of the East Tennessee region
had formed a partnership with UB and were clamoring
for them to work their cold cases.

If those counties had the budgets they really needed
in order to do their jobs, they wouldn't have to contract
with a civilian agency to help them pro bono. Ryland had
faced that same issue during his past career with the Tennessee Bureau of Investigation. How many killers had
gone free because some bean counter valued money over
lives? How many of those killers went on to murder other
people? Those questions haunted Ryland. But his guilt
was easier to endure knowing that the only reason he'd

ever give up on a case at UB was if *he* decided it was un-solvable, not because of a lack of resources.

He rounded another sharp curve. A man was stand-ing in the middle of the lane. Ryland slammed on his brakes, wrenching the steering wheel hard to the left. The man dove to the right, toward the drainage ditch. Ryland's Range Rover skidded sideways. His heart was in his throat as he wrestled with the wheel, trying to steer away from the treacherous cliff. The huge tires grabbed, held, then shot him across the road to the other side. He braked hard and came to a rocking stop inches from where the man had been standing just moments earlier.

A pent-up breath stuttered out of his lungs. Nausea roiled in his stomach. His hands ached from holding the steering wheel so tight. For several seconds, all he could do was sit in shock, thinking about what had happened, what had *almost* happened. He'd nearly catapulted off the mountain to certain death. And he'd almost killed a pedestrian too.

Meanwhile, the man responsible calmly stood up about twenty feet away, on the other side of the ditch that he'd apparently jumped. He brushed off his jeans, then smoothed his smudged white shirt into place, seem-ingly oblivious to his close brush with death. And in spite of the chilly temps, he wasn't wearing a jacket. What was he doing out here, on an isolated mountain, miles from town?

When he finally looked at Ryland, there was no fear in his expression, and no trace of guilt over standing in the road around a blind curve. Then he did the oddest thing.

He smiled.

It was a feral-looking smile, one that had Ryland instinctively tucking the edge of his suit jacket behind his holster, just in case the guy was about to draw on him.

As if reading Ryland's mind, the man's eyes narrowed. He snaked his right hand behind his back. And waited. Was there a gun in his waistband? A knife? Why was he acting so odd? Had he meant to cause an accident and was disappointed that he hadn't? If that was the case, he was dangerous, and needed to be stopped.

That thought had Ryland glancing in his rear view mirror, realizing that if another vehicle came around the curve and he was still sitting here, they'd have to swerve to avoid him. And if they didn't have a road-hugging four-wheel drive, they might not be as lucky as he'd been.

He jerked the Rover as far to the shoulder as he could and put on his hazard lights. He hopped out and was just starting around the hood when the man stepped into the woods and disappeared.

"Hey, mister, wait!" Ryland hesitated at the edge of the muddy ditch, hoping to catch a glimpse of the guy. But all he saw were bushes and trees.

"Mister, come back. I want to make sure you're okay," he called out. Under his breath, he added, "And that you don't play God with someone else's life out here."

Silence was his answer.

After a baleful look at the muddy water in the ditch, he backed up and took a running leap.

# Chapter Two

Ryland shoved open one of the glass doors to Unfinished Business so hard it bounced against the doorstop and swung back at him. He managed to catch it just before it could slam into his face. He shook his head in disgust. A broken nose would have totally capped off this miserable morning.

His already painfully shrinking leather boots squeaked against the wood floor as he slogged to his desk in the cavernous two-story room to his left. All eyes turned to him, including Grayson and his wife, Willow, in one of the glass-walled conference rooms in the second-floor balcony at the far end.

Ignoring his audience, he yanked open his bottom drawer to get his go-bag of clothes and toiletries for unexpected last-minute flights or other emergencies. Today definitely qualified in the *other* category.

One of his fellow investigators, Adam Trent, stopped beside his desk. His lips twitched as he struggled to suppress a grin, and whatever sarcastic comment he was contemplating.

A fat blob of mud chose that moment to slide out of Ryland's hair and drop on the folder in the middle of his desk.

Trent eyed the mud, then Ryland, his mouth curving with amusement. "Did you visit Old MacDonald's farm on the way to work?"

"Not another word," Ryland snapped.

An even larger blob of mud splatted onto the floor.

Trent howled with laughter.

Ryland aimed some colorful phrases his way and grabbed his go-bag. "When you manage to stop laughing, make yourself useful. Tell security to be on the alert for a possibly armed, middle-aged white male roaming the woods just down the road. I'll alert Gatlinburg PD after I change clothes."

Since Trent was still laughing, Ryland wasn't even sure he'd heard him. He gritted his teeth and trudged past the entrance toward the bathrooms on the right. Every squeak of his ruined shoes was punctuated by laughter coming from the room he'd just left.

"Um, excuse me," a feminine voice he didn't recognize called out from behind him, near the entrance. "Can someone help me find Ryland Beck? I'm Detective Bree Clark with the Monroe County Sheriff's Office. I brought the boxes of files and evidence from the Slayer case."

"Yes, ma'am." Trent was still chuckling as he responded. "Hey, Ry, hold up. You've got a visitor."

Ryland whisked open the bathroom door and escaped inside.

RELIEVED TO HAVE finally finished transferring the physical evidence from the Slayer investigation into UB's evidence room, Bree Clark adjusted her skirt and sat in the guest chair beside Ryland Beck's desk.

Ryland, using the dolly Bree had brought in her police-issue SUV, deposited the last of the twelve boxes of case files on the other side of his desk, before taking his seat.

She was about to hand him the chain-of-custody forms, but hesitated when she noticed a mud-splattered folder in front of him.

He grimaced and tossed the folder into a drawer. "Is that the inventory list we were marking off earlier?"

"Yep." She set the papers in the spot he'd cleared. "Since you already initialed each item, all you have to do now is sign the first and last page, then verify the contact information. When you're ready, I'll brief you and your team like we agreed—"

"Ryland." One of the men several few desks away was holding up a phone and motioning toward him. "Gatlinburg PD has more questions about that guy you saw."

Ryland gave her an apologetic look. "Sorry. There was…an incident on my way here and I need to take that call. Be right back."

She nodded, wondering if the incident he was referring to explained the mud and tears in his suit when she'd first seen him. When he'd returned wearing jeans and an emerald-green shirt that emphasized the green of his eyes the muscular contours of his chest, she'd forgotten all about the mud. Instead, she'd focused on trying to act professional and not let him see how rattled she was.

Even now, watching him across the room talking on the land-line, it was hard not to stare. But no matter how well he filled out those jeans, or how impressive his biceps were, what really mattered, what had to matter, was whether or not he was the top-notch investigator she'd been told he was.

When her boss had informed her that Monroe County would partner with UB to have their cold cases worked, she'd been more than a little worried. It didn't reassure her that UB had been vetted by dozens of agencies, or that their investigators were all former law enforcement. Her concern was what they were now—civilians. Which meant they operated by their own rules, without the oversight she and her peers had. One wrong step, one illegal search, could lead to a judge throwing out critical evidence. A case could go from cold to un-prosecutable in an instant. It was her deepest fear that UB would accidentally destroy the chance of ever getting a conviction in the Smoky Mountain Slayer case.

Earlier, as she and Ryland had carefully checked off each piece of evidence and locked it up, there was no denying he *seemed* to know what he was doing. But it was still hard to take him seriously when he could have passed for a male cover model.

As if sensing her perusal, he glanced across the room and smiled. She smiled in return, then self-consciously turned her attention to the front wall of glass and the packed parking lot outside.

The dozen or so people in this massive squad room didn't account for the large number of vehicles. And since most of the walls were glass, she could see everything at a glance. Aside from the bathrooms and what appeared to be storage closets to the right of the main entrance, the building seemed to consist of this one large room and some stairs at the far end that led to a balcony of glass-walled conference rooms.

Maybe there was a basement and the drivers of the other vehicles worked there. One of the doors by the bathrooms could conceal another staircase instead of a closet. It certainly wouldn't be unusual in this area to have a basement. Most of the buildings were tucked into the sides of mountains, with a maze of support beams and stilts off the back, anchoring them into the bedrock. A lower level hidden from the front entrance would double the building's space. And it would provide spectacular views off the back.

"Sorry for the delay. You're probably in a hurry to brief my team and hit the road."

She turned in her chair just as Ryland sat at his desk, giving her another charming smile that had her pulse ratcheting up several notches. Good grief, he was sexy.

"No worries," she said. "I don't mind the wait." If it meant spending time with him, she'd be happy to stay all day.

"The Monroe County Sheriff's Office is in Madison-ville, right? About an hour and a half from here?"

"Closer to two, especially if there's traffic. But I'm not in a hurry to head back. Don't get me wrong. I love my job and wouldn't want to work anywhere else. But I'm excited to meet more members of your team and get a feel for how you're going to approach the investigation. This is Monroe County's first time working with UB."

"It's nice to meet someone who loves their job as much as I do. Wouldn't trade mine for the world. As for this being the first case UB has worked for your county, that's true for most of the thirty-three counties we support. We've only been open for a handful of months. Initially, we worked from my boss's estate at the top of this moun-tain. This new building has only been open a few weeks and we're still settling in."

"I can understand that. My boss couldn't believe his luck when we came up in the queue so quickly."

"No luck involved. One of the perks around here is

that each investigator takes turns picking a dream case to work. This was mine."

She stared at him in surprise. "Your dream case is the Slayer case?"

"Serial killer cold case. No DNA. No suspects. It'll be the most challenging investigation I've ever worked. What's not to love about that?"

She shook her head. "I hope you still feel that way a few weeks from now. Once you get to the point of giving up, no hard feelings. If you manage to develop even one promising lead, it's more than we have now."

It was his turn to look surprised. "I have no intention of developing leads and moving on without fully exploring each one. If this thing *can* be solved, I'll solve it. I'm in this for the long haul."

"Good intentions are great and appreciated. But I'm not convinced you'll get any further than we did. We put a ton of work into the investigation and came up empty."

He leaned back in his chair. "I get the impression you're not a fan of involving UB."

Her face grew warm as she thought about just how vehemently she'd argued against hiring a group of civilians to work her team's case. But she didn't shy away from the truth. "Can't fault your impression."

He smiled at that. "What's your homicide clearance rate, Detective?"

"I wouldn't know. Calculating stats is my boss's job."

"Humor me. Take a guess."

She leaned back in her chair too. "All right. I'll play along. Seventy-five percent."

"Not even close. UB calculates the stats for each county we work with. Considering only arrest rates for murder, regardless of whether there was a conviction, Monroe barely tops fifty percent."

She winced. "How do we compare to our neighboring counties?"

"They range from fifty to sixty-one percent."

"Sixty-one? That's the best?"

He nodded. "Now consider just the cold cases. Investigations that are technically open, but unless a new lead comes in, no one's actively working them. There are several hundred thousand in this country. Of those, how many do you think are ever solved?"

"No idea. Twenty-five percent?"

"Try one percent."

She stared at him, stunned. "That's awful."

"Agreed." He motioned around the room. "The team you see here is dedicated to changing that statistic, at least for East Tennessee."

She frowned. "Doesn't seem like a big enough team to have a goal that lofty."

"It's small by design, at least for now, while we're still new and learning how to work together to our best advantage. Aside from our boss—Grayson Prescott—his wife, Willow, who's a part-time investigator and part-time victim's advocate, there's a special agent on loan from the TBI who brainstorms with us and provides law enforcement oversight like when we need a warrant, and eight full-time investigators."

"Eight? How do you expect to solve more than a few cases a year with only eight investigators? My team has five and we couldn't solve the Slayer case after a full year of working on it."

"Keeping the core team small helps us work better as a cohesive unit. Each of us has our own cases, but we meet regularly to brainstorm on all of the open investigations. If we need additional expertise, we bring on temporary consultants. In spite of operating for only a few months, we've started investigating twelve cold cases and have already closed nine."

"Closed, as in solved?"

"As in presented our findings and enough evidence, in our opinion, to prosecute each case. Yes."

"Wow. That's, what, seventy-five percent? A far cry from the one percent you quoted earlier."

"Full disclosure," he said, "some of the cases were chosen specifically because they appeared to be easy solves, not that any of them are really easy. But there was evidence that, if tested or re-tested with today's better technology, we strongly felt could lead to usable DNA profiles and potential hits on the FBI's DNA database, CODIS. We needed those quick solves to garner confidence from the various law enforcement agencies we were trying to win over. It worked. Now they're clamoring for us to work their more difficult cold cases."

"Makes sense. I'm assuming you use all the latest forensic techniques, like culling public ancestry databases for DNA hits to come up with suspects?"

He nodded again. "Forensic genealogy is a favorite tool of ours. It was key to solving the first case we took on. Still a doubting Thomas about our abilities?"

She gave him a rueful smile. "I'm not quite ready to dust off my pom poms and cheer for UB. But at least now I understand why my boss was so excited about you working the Slayer case."

His eyes took on a teasing light. "Somehow I can't picture you as a former cheerleader."

She arched a brow. "I'm not sure whether to be grateful or offended."

He grinned. "Don't be offended. You've definitely got the looks for it." His face lightly colored. "My apologies. That was inappropriate."

She rolled her eyes. "I'm not someone offended by a compliment. That's what it was, right? A compliment?"

"Definitely."

"Then thank you. And you're right. I was never a cheerleader. I was one of the jerks making fun of the cheerleaders back in high school. Turns out they were smarter than me. A lot of them went to college on full cheer-scholarships. I had to flip burgers the whole way through."

"Guess we both learned the hard way. I stocked grocery store shelves during my college weekends and pulled occasional night shifts disinfecting a lab. But we'll keep that particular skill just between the two of us. I don't want the lab rats downstairs drafting me to help with cleanup any time soon."

"Downstairs? You have a lab onsite?"

"We sure do. The main lab's a few hours away. My employer funded an entire wing dedicated to processing our evidence before anyone else's. Here at UB headquarters, we have a much smaller annex. But, depending on the sample and types of tests appropriate for a piece of evidence, we can get DNA results back in days, or even hours, instead of months or longer in a typical overworked, underfunded state lab."

She groaned with envy. "Not fair. Are you hiring?"

He chuckled. "If or when we hire more investigators, I'll be happy to add your résumé to the hundreds we already have on file."

"Hundreds? Guess I'll keep my day job." She rested her forearms on the desk. "I'm truly impressed with what you're accomplishing here. And I'm actually starting to get excited to have you working on the Smoky Mountain Slayer case."

"Good to hear. I've been meaning to ask you why the killer is called the Smoky Mountain Slayer. I thought the Smokies didn't extend into Monroe County. But I'm a recent transplant from Nashville, so I don't know the eastern portion of the state all that well yet."

"I wouldn't know my way around Nashville either. But you're right. The Smokies aren't in my county. A reporter came up with the name and it stuck. I guess the Unicoi Mountain Slayer isn't as marketable as the Smoky Mountain Slayer." She shrugged. "Doesn't really matter. The Unicoi and the Smokies are both part of the same mountain chain, the Blue Ridge Mountains. And the first victim was found just inside our border with Blount County."

"And the Smokies *do* extend into Blount, I'm guessing?"

"They sure do."

"Whatever helps with news ratings, I suppose."

"I suppose. And believe me, the press in my county is notorious for gobbling up the smallest hint of a rumor and blowing it up all over the news feeds. They were broadcasting about the first murder before we'd even removed the body. AP picked it up, and it was sent all over the country."

He winced. "Makes it hard to keep details from the public during an investigation."

"No kidding." She motioned toward the dolly by the desk as she stood. "I'll return that to my SUV so I don't forget it later. I'm supposed to brief you and your team on the case, right? When is that scheduled?"

He grabbed the dolly's handle before she could. "I can get everyone together right after I put this in your vehicle."

"Did you forget I brought it in all by myself, along with the first load of boxes?"

"Only because I wasn't at my desk when you made that first trip. Please, I insist." He motioned for her to precede him to the door.

While she didn't need his assistance, it was nice being waited on for a change. The guys she worked with treated her as if she was one of them, which she appreciated most days. But being shown old-fashioned courtesy by a gorgeous and surprisingly smart man like Ryland was a true pleasure.

"Thanks. I appreciate it," she said. "And I just remembered there's a folder for you in the cab of my Explorer. It's got information you won't find in the official Slayer files."

# Chapter Three

They both donned light jackets before heading outside in the chilly mountain air. Bree went to the cab of her white-and-green SUV while Ryland loaded the dolly into the back. She grabbed the folder she'd forgotten to bring inside and turned around just as he joined her.

He eyed the inch-thick, accordion-style folder with obvious reluctance as he took it from her. "I thought you had something *unofficial* to share. That looks like a pile of paperwork for me to sign."

"I wouldn't be that cruel," she teased. "This is a copy of my personal folder on the Slayer. My contact information on the inside flap. You're welcome to call me anytime, day or night, if you have questions. Or if you just want to update me on the status of the investigation. I'd really appreciate that, if you don't mind."

"Of course. I'd want the same thing."

She smiled her thanks. "The folder is chock full of summaries and lists, lots of cross-references to the main files in the mountain of boxes by your desk. They should help you come up to speed fairly quickly. I included my personal notes too, for each of the five murders."

He leaned against the door, still not looking in the folder. "Personal notes?"

His wary look had her frowning in confusion. "Well, yeah. Didn't you include subjective notes on cases, your impressions, things that didn't seem to add up, when you were a special agent? You worked for the state police, the TBI, before taking this job, right?"

"You did an internet search on me?"

"Of course. I wanted to make sure the lead investigator working my case was well-qualified before I turned everything over."

He arched a brow. "*Your* case? I thought Detective Mills was the primary on the investigation. That's what Sheriff Peterson told me when I requested the evidence and files."

Her cheeks heated. "Mills ran things, sure. But I helped. Our whole team did."

"And you've taken a personal interest in the investigation."

"Okay, I'm not sure where this is going. But, yes, this case matters a great deal to me. Five young women were senselessly murdered in my county by the same killer. I take that very personally. Wouldn't you?"

"Absolutely." His tone was even, matter-of-fact. "I just wondered whether you have a personal connection to one or more of the victims."

"If I did, I'd have taken myself off the investigation because of the conflict of interest."

"Good to know. And in answer to your earlier question, no, the TBI did *not* allow us to keep personal notes on the side. Everything, including my notes, was part of the official record. We couldn't risk a defense attorney accusing us of a Brady violation, withholding evidence. That could result in a mistrial, or worse, having the case overturned on appeal."

Her face heated again. Even though his tone was respectful, it stung having her methods questioned. She'd spent thousands of hours and months of her life trying to figure out who the Slayer was so she could bring him to justice. Being second-guessed by someone five minutes after handing over the investigation had her bristling like a porcupine.

"Thank you for the lesson on evidentiary procedures, *Detective Beck*. Apparently I was mistaken thinking you'd want a copy of my personal case file. You're welcome to cull through the dozen boxes of files inside UB and come to your own conclusions." She held out her hand for the folder.

"I didn't say that I wouldn't appreciate your notes, *Detective Clark*. I just wanted to understand why they weren't in the files you already gave me." He pulled the stack of papers from the accordion-style folder and started to skim them.

She crossed her arms. "Maybe if I worked for the TBI, or UB, I'd have the luxury of doing things the way you do. But Sheriff Peterson doesn't want feelings, impressions, or conjecture put into the record. And I don't want to lose that kind of information. My notes help me remember what I was thinking during an interview, the tone of voice used, their attitude, that sort of thing."

He glanced up at her. "You don't record the interviews?"

"Well, of course I do," she snapped, too annoyed now to soften her response. "But if I'm canvassing a neighborhood, going door to door asking questions, I don't have the luxury of a video recording. Later, at the office, I type up my notes for the case file, leaving out the subjective parts, *as required by my boss*."

He nodded, seemingly unfazed by the annoyance she'd been unable to hide as he slid the stack of papers back into the folder. He hesitated, then pulled out the thick envelope she'd included. "What's this?"

She let out an impatient breath. "Pictures. And before you ask, they're copies. The originals, at least the ones relevant to the case, are in the boxes I gave you. I wrote the name of each person on the back of each photo."

He slid the stack out of the envelope and tucked the folder under his arm so he could shuffle through the photos. "If some of these aren't relevant, why include them?"

"Oh, for goodness' sake. You're like a dog with a bone. At least I know you were serious when you said you wouldn't give up on the investigation. You never let anything drop, do you?"

His mouth twitched, as if he was trying not to smile, which aggravated her even more. She motioned toward the photos. "I was trying to give you context, to put faces with the names you'll read in the reports. I included everyone at the sheriff's office, even the admins in case you need additional copies of anything or have general questions about how we do things."

"Great idea. I wouldn't have thought of that."

"Will miracles never cease," she grumbled.

This time he did grin, but he didn't look up. Instead, he slowly fanned through the photos, showing far more interest in them than he had with her cross-references and summaries. As he flipped one over and read the name on the back, he frowned. "Why is a junior prosecutor in here? I thought this never went to trial."

"It didn't. But it was high profile, so we gave regular briefings to the prosecutor's office, at the request of the senior prosecutor. He wanted to continually evaluate whether we had enough evidence for a grand jury."

"And did you? Convene a grand jury?"

"No. We never got remotely close to having a viable suspect in any of the killings." She motioned toward his still-damp hair. "My turn. Since we're playing *Investigator Jeopardy*, I might as well ask the question that's been eating me up with curiosity since I walked into UB. You were covered in mud and your suit was torn. Mind telling me what happened? Was that the so-called incident you spoke to the police about earlier?"

He flipped to the next photo as he answered. "It is. I asked the police to patrol the mountain road, not that they agreed. They said they'd get to it when they can." He pulled another picture out of the stack and turned it over to read the back. "As to what specifically happened, there was a man standing in the road when I came around a curve on the way here. Luckily he jumped out of the way. Even luckier, for me, after swerving toward the cliff's edge to avoid him, I managed to *not* drive off the side of the mountain."

"Oh my gosh. How scary."

"Terrifying. He acted rather odd afterward. I'm convinced he wasn't in his right mind. No jacket, no backpack, no car parked anywhere to explain why he was there. And I'm half-convinced that he tried to force me off the road on purpose."

She stared at him in shock. "Did he admit that?"

"Before I could get close enough to talk to him, he took off. I'm worried he had a knife or a gun. That's why I asked Gatlinburg PD to come out here to look for him."

She glanced past the parking lot and road to the thick

woods dotting the mountain side. "Was he right by UB when you saw him?"

"Close enough. About a half mile from here."

"And your torn, muddy suit? How did that happen?"

"When he ran into the woods, stupid me thought it made sense to go after him, so I hopped a ditch." He eyed her over the top of a picture. "My long jump skills haven't improved since high school."

She blinked. "You didn't make it across? You fell into the ditch?"

"Face-first."

She burst out laughing, then pressed her hand to her throat, heat rising in her cheeks again. "Sorry. I shouldn't have laughed. Couldn't help it."

"I don't mind you laughing. But if Trent does, again, I'll have to slug him. Or shoot him."

She chuckled, only half-convinced he was kidding. "Trent. He's one of the investigators I met while putting the evidence away, right? Someone you work with?"

"Unfortunately." His smile reassured her that he was teasing.

Some of the tension drained out of her. She hated that she'd been so aggravated with him earlier. Her temper rarely did her any favors. "What about the cuts in your suit? Did those happen when you fell?"

"My suit jacket caught on the bushes and tree branches when I tried to follow the mystery man into the woods. I only got a few feet in before I was forced to turn back. He seemed to know how to avoid getting skewered. I didn't."

The urge to laugh again was hard to resist. But she managed. Barely.

"The guy did me a favor in one respect," Ryland said,

as he continued to examine the pictures. "Ruining my suit gave me an excuse to wear jeans. I hate suits."

Too bad. He looked great in them. Then again, he looked great in jeans too.

"Son of a... *That's him*." He held up one of the pictures. "This is the guy, the one who ran into the woods."

When she saw who he was talking about, she shook her head. "No way. That's Dane Palmer, lead prosecutor for Monroe County."

He frowned and studied the picture again. "I didn't get a good look at his face until after I'd almost mowed him down. By that time, he was standing on the other side of the ditch. But I'm telling you, this is the guy I saw."

"Can't be."

"Does Palmer have an identical twin? A triplet?"

"Not a twin, triplet, or quadruplet to be had. He's an only child. Ryland, I don't think you understand the significance of what you're saying. Palmer isn't some half-crazed criminal skulking around Sevier County running out in front of people's cars. He's probably the best prosecutor Monroe County—heck, Tennessee—has ever had. He wins almost every case he prosecutes. He's practically a legend."

She started naming off some of the more memorable cases. "He put away Silas Gerloff, that guy from the road rage incident a few years back. He purposely crashed his car into another guy's car because he got cut off. Then he gutted him with a knife." She shivered.

"And Dan Smith, the businessman who took a gun to work and shot his boss and three other people because he'd been fired. His lawyer tried to get him off on an insanity plea, but Palmer convinced the judge not to buy into that. Smith is in prison for life, no possibility of parole. There's the pedophile, Liam Kline. No, wait, his conviction was overturned. But that's a rarity for Palmer. Oh, and Nancy Compadre. You must have heard of her, even in Nashville. She's the young mother who drowned her two sons when she drove her car into the river, then claimed two Black men were responsible. And—"

He held up a hand to stop her. "Okay, okay, I get it. Palmer has done a lot of good for your county. But that doesn't change what I saw. Your prosecutor is the guy who almost sent me careening off a cliff this morning, then smiled like a psychopath and acted like he was about to pull a gun on me. I got a really bad vibe off him. I honestly feel he's dangerous, which is why I asked Gatlinburg PD to look for him. Maybe he's a Dr. Jekyll, Mr. Hyde kind of guy and all you've ever seen is what he wants you to see."

"You feel that strongly that he's the man you saw?"

"I'd swear it on a Bible."

She blinked. "A Bible? Really?"

"A *stack* of Bibles. King James version."

"Southern Baptist?"

"Born and raised."

"Wow. You really are serious. Give me a sec." She stepped away to make a call. A few minutes later, she returned. "You probably should have your vision checked since I'm *certain* you're wrong. But I can't *prove* you're wrong. Palmer took a vacation day today. He didn't tell anyone where he was going, which isn't necessarily a red flag. But I asked one of his guys to call his cell. Palmer didn't answer."

"Does he have a wife we can talk to?"

"Divorced. No kids. Lives alone." She yanked open the door and hopped into the driver's seat. "Get in. Show me where you saw this mystery man."

# *Chapter Four*

Ryland held up a low-hanging branch so Bree's long blond hair wouldn't tangle in it. She passed beneath it, smiling her thanks as they followed the mystery man's trail. He felt that smile all the way to his gut. Bree Clark was incredibly appealing. And he couldn't really explain why.

She was pretty, certainly. And she had a knock-out figure that would make any man take notice. He'd practically drooled when he'd first met her and she stood to shake his hand, revealing sumptuous curves and gorgeous legs. But her appeal was so much more than that.

Maybe it was her fiery temperament, the confident, determined look in her hazel eyes, the impossible-to-hide honesty of her reactions. If she ever tried to make a living playing poker, she'd starve. Bluffing was a skill she didn't have.

It cracked him up how aggravated she'd been when he'd questioned her about her handling of the investigation. She'd obviously wanted to slug him. But she'd tried to pretend it didn't bother her, at least until she couldn't tamp down her anger anymore. It was refreshing to be able to trust someone's reactions. But her inability to conceal how she really felt was undoubtedly a challenge while interviewing suspects. He wondered whether her fellow detectives routinely made excuses to conduct interviews, rather than let her do it.

"Are you stuck in the bushes again, city slicker?" She glanced over her shoulder at him.

Realizing he'd slowed down while cataloging her finer points, he cleared his throat and jogged to catch up. "I'm doing just fine, forest girl."

She rolled her eyes and turned back, easily picking out a trail he'd never have seen on his own. And yet she followed it as if she'd been born with a special tracking gene. It was uncanny how she could spot a broken twig, a twisted blade of grass, a scuff in the dirt that could have been made by someone's shoe. Her ability to follow a trail was the only reason that Ryland hadn't insisted on leading the way. He'd much rather be the first one to encounter danger, but he'd lose the trail in about two seconds.

It shouldn't matter which of them went first. They both had law enforcement backgrounds and had their guns drawn in case the guy they were tracking really was dangerous and armed. But Ryland had been raised to be protective of women. It was practically killing him not to push her behind his back. Instead, he compromised by keeping watch on the bushes and trees they passed so he could jump in front of a bullet for her at the first hint of trouble.

Back in college, his friends had been well aware of his caveman protective streak and had teased him that he should go into the Secret Service. But since he wasn't willing to take a bullet for some *guy*, his potential career with the Secret Service had been doomed. Then again, if the president was a woman, maybe he'd sign up to be a human shield. He could think of worse ways to earn a paycheck.

They reached a clearing, and he finally was able to stand beside her instead of feeling like a heel following her. He was about to ask if she'd lost the trail when he noticed her face had turned ashen, her eyes haunted as she stared past his shoulder.

He whirled around, both hands tightened on his pistol as he swung it back and forth. But all he saw were the trees, deep in shadow since the thick canopy of branches overhead was blocking out the sun.

"Bree? What's wrong? Did you see him?"

"No. But I've seen *this* before." She motioned around the clearing.

He tried to see what she was talking about, but everything seemed...normal. Or, based on his limited experience, as normal as he thought a clearing *should* look in the middle of the woods. "You've seen *what* before?"

She jogged to a tree about ten feet away and patted the trunk. "North." She jogged to another tree. "East." Two more trees. "South, west. Do you see it?"

He was about to say no, but then he realized he did. "Four trees, forming a square if you draw a line around them. More or less."

"And each tree has some bark missing, a man-made mark showing it's part of the formation."

He looked again at the first tree she'd pointed to. Sure enough, there was a four-inch-long gash carved horizontally across the trunk about five feet off the ground, eye-level for someone Bree's height but a tad too low for him to have noticed at first glance. Each of the four trees she'd singled out bore a similar mark.

Tightly clutching his pistol, he scanned the forest around them again. "What do these marked trees have to do with the man we're looking for? Prosecutor Palmer?"

"He's not Palmer. You have to be mistaken."

He didn't bother arguing. She was still alarmingly pale. And since she refused to stand still, he was forced to follow her around the clearing, scanning the trees as he went.

"What are you doing now?" he asked.

She didn't answer. Instead, she paced off equal distances from each tree, finally stopping in the approximate center of the square they formed. Then she hiked up her skirt and dropped to her knees.

He swallowed, and tried not to stare at her glorious legs. Wasn't she cold? It had to be in the fifties up here. He was about to offer his jacket to put under her knees when she grabbed a stick and started digging.

He frowned. He didn't have a clue why she was digging. But he didn't like her being in such a vulnerable position when they still hadn't found the man they were searching for. He could be out here right now, hiding, watching, waiting for...something. Was he armed as Ryland believed? Dangerous? Maybe, maybe not. But Ryland couldn't shake the feeling that they weren't alone in these woods.

Leaving Bree digging, he walked the perimeter of the square, peering into the gloom, aiming his gun into nothingness. When he'd covered the entire area, twice, he relaxed, if only a little. In spite of his instincts screaming that someone else was out here, he hadn't found any evidence to back it up. There'd been no telltale flashes of jeans and a white shirt, no whisper of fabric as someone shifted position in some unseen hiding place. If there was someone watching, and he wanted to harm them, wouldn't he have done something already?

Heck, maybe the best strategy right now was to help

Bree finish whatever she was doing so he could hurry her out of here, back to the office where she'd be safe. He grabbed another stick and dropped to his knees to help her dig.

He shoved the stick deep and scooped aside a layer of mud and leaves. A sickening stench filled the air, a smell Ryland had encountered far too many times in his career. Bree shot him a startled look and coughed into her hand.

Two minutes later, they found the first bone.

## Chapter Five

Bree wrapped her arms around her waist and sent up a silent prayer for the victim and their family, while the Sevier County crime scene techs took pictures and placed evidence markers near the shallow grave that she and Ryland had discovered.

No matter how many murder scenes she'd been to, the senseless loss of life always hit her like a punch in the stomach. The usual heart-wrenching questions swirled through her mind. Did the victim know what was going to happen to them before it did? Was the end fast, merciful? Was it painful? Were they a husband, a wife, mother, father, sister, brother? How many others would suffer, their lives forever changed, because of this one person's tragic end?

She drew several deep breaths, fighting against the wave of anger and depression that threatened to drown her. This murder was hitting her even worse than usual, because it might have been committed by a killer she'd tried and failed to bring to justice. In a way, this person's death—whoever they were—could be, at least partly, her fault.

*Get your emotions under control and act like a professional. You're not going to help the victim unless you pull yourself together.*

Help the victim. Her internal voice was right. She needed to get a handle on her emotions. Only then could she work on figuring out what had happened, who'd done this, and stop them before they killed again.

Except that this wasn't her jurisdiction. And it wasn't her investigation. If this murder was linked to the Slayer case, UB would follow up with Gatlinburg PD, not her.

She fisted her hands at her sides, uncomfortable with her new role as a bystander instead of a participant. She watched the techs, the police milling around, the detectives pointing out things they wanted their techs to photograph and collect. Not offering her own suggestions, was one of the hardest things that she'd ever done. She wanted to explain to them, remind them, that one little fiber, one drop of sweat or saliva, could be the key to unraveling the Slayer's identity once and for all.

*If* this murder was the work of the Slayer.

Given what she knew about serial killers, it didn't make sense that he'd go outside his geographical comfort zone when all the other killings had happened in Monroe County. But other things about him had never made sense either, like his inconsistent choice of a particular victim type, other than that they were young females.

This current scene also didn't fit with his modus operandi about what he did with the bodies. He'd left all of them in the woods. But until this one, he'd never buried any of them. Why change that now? Was it because this was the work of a copycat, and he didn't realize the previous five victims hadn't been buried?

The answer to whether or not they had a copycat was critical to both the Slayer investigation and this new one. If they were related, then all the information on the Slayer's prior crimes would be combined with this murder to try to create a workable profile. If they weren't related, evidence from the Slayer murders had to remain separate and not influence the decisions and conclusions made by the detectives.

A mistake in determining whether the killer was the Slayer or a copycat could be devastating, resulting in false leads, invalid conclusions, the wrong pool of potential suspects. A mistake like that could mean both killers remained free and neither paid for their crimes.

She desperately wanted to lift the tape and at least look at the grave. Maybe she'd notice something she hadn't earlier. No one had even touched it since she and Ryland had pulled out that bone. They were all waiting for the Sevier County medical examiner and his team to arrive.

The ME would preserve trace evidence on the body, giving them a better chance at solving the murder. But even knowing that, she still wished she and Ryland had dug a little more before stopping and calling the local police. They'd followed protocol, preserved the scene. Training and experience had overridden their desires to hunt for clues. But now they couldn't even be sure whether they were dealing with a male or female victim.

If they'd uncovered the skull, they might have found some hair to tell them length and color. The pelvis could help them guess whether the victim was male or female. Remnants of clothing might match pictures from missing persons cases and provide a tentative ID. Since they'd done none of that, now they'd have to wait days, maybe weeks, for the ME to share their conclusions.

She sighed in frustration and glanced to her right, where Ryland stood several yards away, talking with the owner of UB and several of UB's investigators. It was only after they'd arrived that Bree had realized Ryland wasn't just one of them: he was their boss, UB's top investigator. He'd barked out orders, and the others had jumped to comply, securing the scene, stationing still more UB investigators at the road to direct Gatlinburg PD and the Sevier County Sheriff's deputies to the scene.

Her phone buzzed in her pocket. She pulled it out and checked the screen. Sheriff Peterson must have passed along the information she'd texted earlier about her and Ryland's discovery. This latest text was from Detective Mills, the lead over the Slayer investigation, back when there'd been an investigation.

How sure are you that the marks on the trees are the same as before? he texted.

As sure as I can be without a picture in front of me. Can you send one?

Hang on.

She would have sent him a picture to compare to the ones they had on file, but she knew better than to do that, and he knew better than to ask. Every picture taken of a crime scene had to be logged as part of the evidence. If someone saw her taking pictures, they'd confiscate her phone. Either with her permission, or courtesy of a warrant, they'd look through all of her pictures to make sure they retrieved the crime scene photos. They'd also look through her emails and texts to make sure she hadn't sent the pictures to anyone else. She'd be lucky if she got her phone back while it was still current technology.

The police weren't that strict in the past. But law enforcement had learned the hard way to be extra careful. As Ryland had reminded her earlier, anything a defense attorney could label as evidence could be used to work the system. A violent criminal could go free because of a legal loophole. She had absolutely no desire to be responsible for something like that.

Her phone buzzed again. She checked the screen and tapped the thumbnail image Mills had sent her. A close-up popped up of one of the trees she'd photographed, a picture that was already official evidence from one of the earlier Slayer crime scenes, so she wasn't violating any evidence protocols. She studied the image, then looked up at the nearest marked tree. Similar. But not a perfect match.

Then again, she didn't expect a *perfect* match.

Each gash was individually hacked and gouged into the trees. It would be impossible for them to be identical. But were they similar enough to conclude the same person had made both marks? She looked at the tree again, then the screen. Nothing jumped out as being all that different. But without being able to examine the tool marks, she couldn't be sure. Then again, maybe the Slayer had used different tools this time. He hadn't before. All the tool marks had identifiers that indicated they'd been made by the same tool—a hatchet, they believed.

Possible match, she texted back. Will try to get a close-up view again of one of the trees here to compare.

Three little dots popped up, indicating he was typing a reply.

Peterson just said not to spend more time on this. If copycat, not our jurisdiction. If it's the Slayer, UB can work on it. Brief UB, as originally planned, then come back.

She swore bitterly.

A few seconds later, as if he'd predicted her reaction, Mills texted one last word.

Sorry.

She couldn't help smiling. The two of them had worked together for years. He knew her well.

Not your fault. Will do. TTYL.

She shoved her phone in her pocket as Ryland walked up.

"Let me guess," he said. "Texts from the boss? Ordering you to back off?"

"One of my fellow minions, actually. But, yes, I've been reminded this isn't my case. I'm supposed to brief your team about the Slayer investigation, then head back to the office. Is the briefing still on? Given what's happened?"

"I'd still like to talk it out, if possible. But it might be a while. You and I will have to give written statements to the Gatlinburg detectives. And Grayson will want to compare notes with the rest of us. He's pretty ticked that someone else was murdered on his mountain."

She'd turned to watch the techs taking pictures, but Ryland's casual announcement had her whirling back to face him. "Someone else murdered on this mountain? This isn't the first body you've found here?"

He held up his hands in a placating gesture. "Take a breath and about three or four giant steps back from where that train of thought is taking you. The other Prescott Mountain murders have nothing to do with this."

She crossed her arms. "You haven't even read the Slayer files yet. You're not qualified to make the determination that these other victims you mentioned aren't his doing."

His jaw tightened. "Actually, I *am* qualified to make that determination. There was a serial killer operating up here in the past. That's one of the first cases that UB worked, and *solved*. There were no unanswered questions, no loose ends left to tie up. He had his own graveyard at the top of the mountain, in the woods outside of Grayson's personal estate. And his MO never wavered. The only thing in common with the Slayer is that both killers left victims' bodies in the woods, and they both buried them."

"I think you're making a judgment call you shouldn't, not until we get the evidence. But I'll drop it. For now. However, you're definitely wrong about one thing."

He arched a brow, his short-lived annoyance replaced with amusement. "What's that?"

"The Slayer didn't bury his victims."

He glanced at the shallow grave that was still waiting for the ME to arrive and finish uncovering its secrets. "Then either this isn't the work of the Slayer or he's changed his MO."

"Or neither of those alternatives."

He frowned. "You lost me."

"I've been thinking about how shallow the grave is. Maybe the body wasn't actually buried, not by human hands anyway. Falling leaves and other debris could have naturally covered it. Rain would make the remains sink into the ground."

"Fair enough. We'll have to wait for reports from the ME and the Gatlinburg detectives to see whether they agree with you. What's more important right now is figuring out the victim's identity, and how long they've been missing so a timeline can be established. Maybe things in Monroe County got too hot, forcing a switch in locations. Maybe your Slayer hasn't been dormant as long as you think."

She wrinkled her nose in distaste. "He's not *my* Slayer."

"Poor choice of words. Sorry about that."

She glanced around, then motioned toward the right side of the taped-off area. "Where'd your friends go? Back to UB?"

"Some did. The rest are hunting."

She blinked. "Hunting?"

"For the guy I almost ran over."

"I thought Gatlinburg PD was searching for him."

"They are. But my boss insists on helping with the search."

"Isn't he wealthy? Of the filthy rich variety?"

"If being a billionaire makes you filthy rich, then yes. Why?"

"I've never met a billionaire who risked his life searching the woods looking for killers."

"How many billionaires have you met?"

She chuckled. "You've got me there. But even not having met other billionaires, I'd be willing to bet your boss isn't like any of the others."

"Probably not. He's a brilliant businessman. But he's also a former army ranger. He's driven, tough, knows how to handle himself. And he's not the type to sit around and let others do the hard work when he knows he can contribute."

"Sounds like you really respect him."

"I do. He's a great guy, a really good friend."

"I'm surprised you're not helping him with the search."

He grinned. "You may have noticed that in addition to my poor long jump skills, I'm not exactly skilled in the tracking, hiking, or outdoor survival arena. The Boy Scouts would have fled in terror if I'd ever asked to join them."

"No camping out in a tent for you?"

"My idea of roughing it is a hotel with less than three stars."

She rolled her eyes. "I don't believe that for a second. You like people to underestimate you, don't you?"

He didn't deny it. Instead, he motioned toward the grave. "Since you said the Slayer never buried his victims in the past, what made you start digging?"

"The marked trees."

"Given his history of not burying bodies, you didn't think maybe he'd marked the trees in preparation for leaving a body here?"

She flicked her hair back over her shoulder. "That's a logical conclusion. But I've been so convinced he stopped killing four years ago that I assumed this was an old body dump site we hadn't discovered. Based on that belief, I figured the body could have decayed into the forest floor, that we might have to dig a bit to find it. Of course, given the state of decomp, we know it hasn't been years. It's more likely a few months. But I didn't know that when I started digging."

"I don't think it's been months." He motioned toward the nearest tree wrapped with yellow tape. "That gouge in the tree's bark isn't weathered with age. It's the color of a fresh two-by-four from a box store. This is a recent kill."

# Chapter Six

Bree shook her head. "I can't believe I missed that. Even with the awful smell when we opened the grave, I figured the body had been there a few months. Until the ME makes a determination, I guess we won't know for sure."

"What I want to know is how those overzealous reporters you described in your county held back the information about the marks on the trees. Or did I just miss that while surfing the internet?"

"The press never knew about it. By the time I figured it out, the Slayer investigation was already going cold. The press had moved on to something else. Unfortunately, they're on the scent again. Someone stirred them up and they're hounding us, following detectives every time we head to a crime scene."

"What do you mean, someone stirred them up?"

She moved back so a pair of uniformed officers could get past, heading toward the road. "Shortly after UB notified us a month ago that this case was bubbling up in the queue, rumors started circulating around town. We've had citizens calling, asking if the killer is active again. We were all told to keep it under wraps that UB was going to get involved, but somehow it must have gotten out."

He winced. "That might be our fault. Our victim's advocate, Willow Prescott, spoke to each of the victims' families to make sure they were informed and had a contact to reach out to if they had questions. We didn't want them hearing it on TV first or through some other means. But even though we asked them to keep the information confidential, it's possible some of them told others and it spread around."

She sighed. "That's probably what happened. I didn't know anyone from your company was speaking to the families."

"Your boss did. We cleared it through him first. It's standard procedure for us to send a victim's advocate out before we start a case. Peterson provided us with the contact information for the families."

She clenched her fists beside her. "He should have told me, should have told all of us."

"How'd you figure it out? About the trees?"

"Changing the subject?"

His eyes sparkled with amusement. "Trying to."

She blew out a long breath and forced her hands to relax. "Okay, I'll drop it. But I'm definitely having a heart-to-heart with Peterson about the lack of communication when I get back. As to your question, I discovered the *murder-square*, as I call it, by accident. I was re-visiting one of the scenes and braced my hand against a pine tree to step over a dead branch. That's when I felt the cut in the bark. It was too straight and perfect not to have been done on purpose. Then I realized other trees had similar markings, and I compared them with photos from the earlier crime scenes."

His brows raised in surprise. "Your people took close-up photographs of all the trees in the general vicinity of where the bodies were found? At every scene?"

"No need to sound impressed. They weren't *that* thorough. None of the pictures from the other scenes showed cuts on the trees. I went back on my own, to each dump site. Sure enough, there were four scored trees at every location, forming a square with the body in the center."

"And a 911 call always initiated the discovery of each victim?"

"Yes. But it wasn't the killer making the calls, if that's what you're thinking. We identified every 911 caller, ruled them out as suspects. Some of them discovered the bodies while hiking through the woods. One was camping nearby and heard some kind of noise, most likely an animal, and followed it to the scene. The last caller heard a dog barking and went looking for it."

His brow furrowed. "Did they find the dog?"

"No, and neither did we. The killer may have used a dog to lure the victim to him. Or just to ensure that someone discovered the body. Either way, that lead went nowhere."

They stood silently for several minutes, watching the organized-chaos around them. Crime scenes always reminded her of ants on an anthill. Watching everything as a whole made it seem pointless, like nothing was being accomplished. But watch one individual ant and it became apparent that he was accomplishing a specific goal, making progress that was otherwise hard to notice.

"Bree?"

"Hm?"

"If this recent murder was done by a copycat, they had to hear about the murder-square from someone. Who else knows about that?"

"My boss and the other detectives I work with. But if you're creating a suspect list in your mind, you can forget it. The guys I work with aren't murderers. What's more likely is that over the past four years, information about the crime scenes trickled out through innocent hallway conversations that were overheard. Or maybe loose lips at a party after a few drinks. It happens." She crossed her arms and leaned against the tree opposite him.

"It does. But let's assume that information didn't leak, that this latest killing is by the Slayer. That means the geographical area he prefers to kill in is much larger than once believed."

She briefly closed her eyes. "That idea has been eating me up since we found that bone. If true, it could mean there are more victims we haven't discovered."

"Maybe he only recently started up again, in this new location. He could have been incarcerated during the gap in the timeline and only recently got out."

"I prefer that scenario," she said. "Fewer victims that way. But I don't think it's likely."

"Why not?"

She turned to watch the crime scene techs as she answered. "His previous victims were always left where the likelihood of discovery was high. This place is remote, on a two-lane road up a mountain very few people have a legitimate reason to visit. It's not like Dollywood is at the top, or some other tourist attraction. The Appalachian Trail is miles away, so hikers aren't going to stumble across this place. And even if they did, without knowing about the murder square, they wouldn't know to scrape aside leaves and debris to look for a body. This screams copycat to me, a copycat who wasn't concerned about someone finding his kill."

"But he did want the body found."

She frowned and looked over at him. "What makes you say that?"

"Putting aside my belief that the guy we tracked to the grave is Palmer, and that Palmer is the killer, look at the logistics. The victim was left practically at the front door of the company where a group of investigators is about to begin work on the Slayer case. If the killer's from Madisonville, he probably heard the rumors, and that I'm the lead investigator. He deliberately targeted me, hoping I'd follow his trail, see the trees, and find the body."

"Even if that's true, all it does is confirm that the killer is likely from Madisonville. That doesn't exactly narrow the potential suspect pool."

"Then we start with the one suspect we do have—Palmer. We'll find out where he went today. And as soon as the victim's been identified, we'll work on a timeline of his, or her, last known movements, try to see if their path crossed Palmer's. We also have to dive into the original case files, review every Slayer murder from the beginning, look for new angles to explore." He gave her a sad smile. "Correction—*I* need to dive into the files. I keep forgetting you're not officially working on the case, that you have to go back to your job after we're done today."

She shook her head. "I wish I could stay and brainstorm with you. But I have orders, and a mortgage to pay, groceries to buy. Can't afford to just up and quit."

"Most of us can't." He gave her a sympathetic look. "I'll keep you updated. And when I interview your prosecutor as my number one person of interest, I'll keep you posted on his excuse for being up here, and whether he offers an explanation for how his trail could have led us to the kill site without him knowing about the body."

She chuckled. "You're not going to let that go, are you? You're positive we're after Palmer."

"I am until, or unless, I meet him in person, and he somehow convinces me that his doppelganger is running around Gatlinburg."

She laughed again, but her smile quickly faded. Everything they'd said was roiling through her mind. Several times she opened her mouth to speak, then thought better of it and kept quiet.

"You might as well say it." His deep voice was laced with amusement. "Whatever you're holding back is going to make you burst otherwise."

"That obvious, huh?"

"Completely. Go on," he said. "What else?"

"It's just that, well, when we made this discovery, I was convinced it was the Slayer's work. Everything points to it, so far anyway. If I assume he wasn't in prison and wasn't sick or anything, then I have to believe he just, what, decided to take a break? It doesn't happen. Serial killers escalate. They don't de-escalate. Maybe this really is a copycat. The what-ifs are driving me crazy."

His mouth quirked in a wry smile. "I'll play devil's advocate and argue with your scenarios. To start with, your premise that a serial murderer can't stop on their own is flawed because several have. I'm sure you've heard of Bind, Torture, Kill—the BTK Killer, in Kansas. After killing several people, he spent the next seven years focusing on playing husband and father before killing again."

"One exception doesn't destroy years of research into serial murder," she said. "Dennis Rader, the BTK Killer, is an aberration, an outlier. As serial killers go, the example he presents is extremely rare."

"I'll give you another one, then. The Golden State Killer. Raped and murdered dozens, then abruptly disappeared from police radar. He was caught over thirty years later, but to everyone's knowledge, had never attacked anyone again during the interim. Wasn't incarcerated, sick, disabled in any way."

She shook her head. "You know your serial killers. I'll give you that. I'd argue that both Rader and DeAngelo, the killers you've referenced, would have continued killing if their obligations hadn't gotten in the way. They were both leading double lives, preoccupied with earning a living and supporting their families and pretending to be normal. No doubt they still had their sick urges, but didn't have the time or opportunity to act on them. Regardless, I'm not trying to win serial killer trivia. I'm just saying that if the Slayer was still free and able to kill, it's hard for me to imagine him stopping for four years. He was in an escalation phase back then, his kills getting closer together. I'm back to thinking it's a copycat. And before you warn me about jumping to conclusions, consider the guy who jumped in front of your car. We assume he's involved but he may not be."

He shoved his hands in his pockets and settled more comfortably against the tree. "How do you figure that? We followed his trail to the grave."

"His trail didn't stop at the grave. We stopped, because I saw the marked trees. Maybe he's not involved in any way." At his disbelieving look, she held up her hands in a placating gesture. "Just give me a minute here. I'm pointing out your investigative bias because you consider yourself an expert on Prescott Mountain."

"I *am* an expert on this mountain. I travel the road out front every day."

"But there's not a fence around it or a gate at the bottom to keep the riffraff out. The road up here is probably publicly maintained, right? Open to anyone?"

"It is. But—"

"But nothing. Have you noticed how incredible the views are up here? When there's a gap in the trees, at least?"

He gave her an odd look, but nodded. "Sure. The views are…great."

"I'm telling you, these are some of the best views for miles around. A moment ago, I said it was unlikely that many people come up this mountain. But I'm rethinking that. Some hiker or casual sightseer has to have stumbled onto this place and discovered its beauty. It only takes telling one other hiker to start spreading the word. It's one of the highest elevations in the area. And it's not saturated with tourists like Clingmans Dome, which makes it more appealing."

He gave her a grudging nod. "Valid points. It's a wider mountain than where the Dome sits too, with a more gradual ascent. Easier to hike, I suppose."

She smiled. "Exactly."

He crossed his legs at the ankles and glanced at the crime scene techs several yards away. "Do you always argue a point then contradict yourself with the next one?"

She laughed. "Probably. I sometimes drive my team crazy with my what-ifs."

"You're not driving me crazy. I find your mind to be quite…fascinating. Beautiful actually."

She blinked, her whole body going warm. "I, ah—"

"I'll allow that someone might come up here for the views alone," he said, steering them back to safer territory and helping to settle the butterflies that had taken flight in her stomach. "There's not much traffic here normally. And I assumed no one would come up here at all unless they worked for UB or were employed on Grayson's estate. But maybe some do. It's not like I watch the road all day to notice which people come and go. Heck, half the time I'm not at the office. I'm out interviewing potential witnesses or in other counties talking to detectives about their cold cases. Like this morning, I got here several hours later than usual for that very reason. I was wrapping up another case." He raked his hand through his hair, making it stick up in spikes.

She stepped closer and reached up and smoothed it down, without stopping to think about it. At his questioning look, her face heated. "I should have asked first. Your hair was sticking up."

"Thanks. I think." He winked, which had those dang butterflies taking flight again. "As to everything we just said, remember Occam's razor."

She nodded. "The simplest explanation is usually the right explanation."

"Exactly. I'm more inclined to think that if this is the Slayer's work, the most reasonable explanation is because he was incarcerated for the past four years. I can get a list of ex-cons who've been released into this area recently and cross-check that against any names that come up during the investigation."

"That'll be a long list."

He looked like he was about to reply, but they both went silent as the medical examiner and his assistant finally arrived and picked their way toward the grave.

Their progress was slow. It was excruciating watching their painstaking work. But finally they pulled enough dirt back to fully reveal the skeleton—or what little Bree could see from her vantage point.

A commotion sounded from the other side of the clearing. Grayson, Trent, and two other men Bree had seen earlier at UB headquarters stepped out from the trees. When they spotted Ryland, they headed their way.

Trent gave Bree a polite nod, but addressed his comments to Ryland. "We followed the trail at least a hundred yards from here. But once we reached harder ground, we lost it. There weren't any more shoe impressions to find."

He was about to say something else, but stopped when two Gatlinburg police officers entered the clearing, escorting a man between them—in jeans, a white shirt and no jacket.

Bree blinked in shock. "Ryland, is that the man you saw earlier?"

His jaw was tight, his whole body tense. "No question." His gaze shifted to her. "Do *you* recognize him?"

Her whole body flushed hot and cold. "I want to say no. But I can't. That's Dane Palmer, senior prosecutor for Monroe County. And apparently, he's also the Smoky Mountain Slayer. I've been chasing the bastard for years and he was right under my nose the whole time. Those Gatlinburg cops have no idea who they're dealing with. They obviously haven't arrested him. He's not in handcuffs." She drew her pistol and started forward.

# *Chapter Seven*

It had been a close thing when Ryland grabbed Bree's gun and tucked it out of sight before the police saw it. Would she have shot Palmer? Ryland didn't think so. But she'd been so angry that he wasn't sure. At the very least, she'd have been arrested for brandishing a weapon at a prosecutor, effectively ending her law enforcement career. Grayson and the UB investigators had formed a circle around her, blocking her from sight until Ryland could calm her down.

Once she *had* calmed down, she was horrified over her behavior. She must have thanked him and the others a dozen times. He'd then reminded her that they didn't have proof the prosecutor was a killer, in spite of how bad things looked right now. And it was because of that lack of proof that he hadn't been arrested. Then one of the crime scene techs had stepped forward with a wallet the ME found while moving some leaves from around the remains. The driver's license inside left no doubt as to the owner.

Dane Palmer.

When confronted by detectives, Palmer had emphatically insisted that someone must have stolen his wallet. The police had asked him to come to the station for questioning. He'd looked around like a drowning man searching for a life preserver. That's when he saw Bree and smiled. He'd immediately agreed to an interview, *if she was the one who conducted it*. Apparently he'd assumed she'd be a pushover, that she'd lob softballs at him.

He'd also insisted he'd only answer questions at a neutral location. He was worried about potential damage to his professional reputation if someone at Gatlinburg PD alerted the public and they saw him being brought into the station. That's when Grayson had stepped forward and offered UB headquarters for the so-called meeting.

As Ryland looked down the long conference room table where Bree sat across from Palmer, he was certain Palmer was regretting the agreement. Bree most definitely was *not* a pushover. A quick glance at Grayson and Trent beside him, then at the two Gatlinburg detectives at the far end, confirmed they'd all arrived at that same conclusion.

"Let's see if I have this right." Bree flipped through her notes on the legal pad in front of her. "You took the day off to run some errands in Madisonville, then headed to Gatlinburg."

"That's right."

"Because you wanted to check out the antique shops."

"I already told you this, Detective. My mother's birthday is coming up, and I always go antique shopping in Gatlinburg for the occasion. She collects Depression-era glassware. I was trying to find something she doesn't already have, in the patterns she likes."

"Really? My mom collects glass too. What patterns were you looking for?"

He crossed his arms. "American Sweetheart in pink and Paden City Ardith in yellow." From the smug look on his face, and the disappointed look on Bree's, Ryland guessed those must have been valid glass patterns.

"Very nice," she said. "But how did you plan on shopping for Depression glass without your wallet?"

His mouth compressed in a tight line. "I didn't *know* that I didn't have my wallet until I saw a technician holding it."

"You didn't notice it was missing when you tried to buy something?"

He yanked a set of keys out of his jeans pocket and tossed them on top of the table. "See that miniature credit card on my keychain? I use that for most purchases. I didn't need my wallet."

"Easy enough to verify." She poised her pen to add more notes. "What's the name of one of the shops where you made a purchase?"

His gaze shot to the Gatlinburg detectives before he looked at Bree again. He cleared his throat. "I didn't buy anything."

She glanced up from the legal pad. "You didn't buy *anything*?"

His face reddened. "That's what I said, *Detective*."

"Why didn't you buy anything? You took the day off to shop."

"Obviously I didn't find what I was looking for."

"Right, okay." She set her pen down, a skeptical look on her face. "You don't have a receipt to prove you were downtown at the time when someone looking exactly like you, dressed like you, stood in the road and nearly caused Mr. Beck to drive off the side of the mountain?"

Ryland stared steadfastly forward, ignoring the look of concern Trent was giving him. It was damned inconvenient that Trent and all of his UB teammates had witnessed his height phobia first hand a few months earlier. With luck, that embarrassing episode would never happen again.

"Oh, for goodness' sake," Palmer said. "Jeans and a plain white shirt aren't exactly rare around here. And why would I stand in the road?"

"I can think of one compelling reason." Bree rested her forearms on the top of the table. "You wanted to toy with the UB team because you heard they were looking again at the Smoky Mountain Slayer cold case. You wanted to lead them to your latest kill and rub their noses in it."

His face turned so red that he looked in danger of stroking out. "You, Detective Clark, are way out of line."

"Just doing my job, sir. Asking questions that need to be asked."

He jabbed his finger in the air at her. "This isn't your jurisdiction. Don't tell me you're doing your job. Accusing a respected prosecutor of murder sure the hell isn't *doing your job.*"

She frowned. "Accusing you of murder? No, sir. Not at all. I was throwing out scenarios, hypotheticals in response to your question about why you'd be standing in the road."

He narrowed his eyes. "Are you trying to be funny? Because I'm definitely not laughing."

"Murder is never a laughing matter."

He swore and sat back. "My patience is wearing thin. We've gone over this already. I took a day off to shop, didn't find what I needed and was about to drive home when I heard on my scanner about police activity on Prescott Mountain. Out of curiosity, I drove up here to see what was going on."

"Do you realize how suspicious that sounds? That

you just happened to show up at a murder scene where someone fitting your description is a potential suspect for the murder?"

"Ask anyone who knows me. I always listen to the scanner. If there's something major going on, I like to check it out. It's a way of keeping tabs on what's happening in the community."

"In your own county, maybe, sure," she allowed. "Why here in Gatlinburg? Wearing shoes that, by the way, appear to have a tread pattern consistent with the trail we were following."

He gritted his teeth. "They're a common type of walking shoe with a non-skid grip. Everyone around here wears them. As to the rest of what you said, my mother lives in Gatlinburg. It's my duty as her son to keep up with what's going on, to make sure she's in a good place, a safe place. I've always kept an eye on what the authorities are doing around here because of her."

"Right." She let the word hang in the air like an accusation and took her time making some notes on her legal pad.

Ryland had to hold back a grin. She never raised her voice, never lost control. Instead, she was pushing Palmer's buttons, getting *him* to lose control. So much for being bad at interviews as he'd assumed earlier this morning. She was knocking this one out of the park.

She put her pencil down and calmly met Palmer's hostile gaze. "Where were we? Oh, yes. You drove up Prescott Mountain because you heard something going on over the scanner. Then what?"

He mumbled something under his breath that Ryland couldn't quite catch. He had a feeling that was a blessing.

"Sorry. What did you say?" Bree asked ever so politely.

He tugged at his shirt collar. "When I saw the police cars parked on the side of the road, I pulled over to ask what was going on. To my surprise, as soon as I got out of my car, two officers met me at my door. They said something about me looking like some guy the detectives wanted to talk to at a murder scene." He shook his head, clearly annoyed. "I graciously agreed to accompany them to answer any questions their detectives might have. Obviously if they wanted to talk to me about a murder around here, there was some kind of mistake. I was happy to clear it up. That's when that tech held up my stolen wallet." He looked toward the Gatlinburg detectives at the far end of the table. "Which, by the way, needs to be returned." He held out his hand.

One of the detectives shook his head. "Sorry, Mr. Palmer. The wallet was found inside a crime scene. It's evidence."

"That's ridiculous. At least give me my driver's license."

"You can apply for a replacement copy online."

Palmer glared at him and snatched up his keys. "If there's nothing else—"

"One more thing, if you don't mind." Without waiting for his response, Bree rushed to ask her next question. "How long has this day off of yours been planned?"

He frowned. "Like I said, I always take off right before my mom's birthday to shop for her gift. I do it every year."

"But when I called your office, they didn't know where you were."

He rolled his eyes. "A junior detective asks my assistant where I went on my vacation day, and you're surprised she didn't tell you?" He laughed. Bree's cheeks

flushed a delicate shade of pink. "*Now* are you finished
with your questions? Junior Detective Clark?"

"It's Detective, actually. No junior."

"If you say so."

A look of annoyance flashed across her face, but she
quickly schooled her features. "I just want to remind you
that you agreed to speak with me to allay suspicions, so
the detectives from this county can move on to other
potential suspects. Ending the interview now won't ac-
complish that goal. Perhaps you could supply us with a
quick timeline of what you did today? That would go a
long way toward alleviating any concerns."

The string of curses he let loose had even Ryland
wincing.

Bree handled it with remarkable poise. When the prosecutor stopped swearing, she asked, "Is that a no? Sir?"

"You need me to repeat it to make it more clear?" Sarcasm dripped from every word.

"If you choose not to provide a timeline, it could
prove...difficult...for the police to figure out when and
how someone could have stolen your wallet and left it
at a murder scene." She motioned toward the other end
of the table. "I'm sure these fine detectives are willing
to drive to Monroe County, if necessary, to partner with
us in clearing up any remaining confusion. Sadly, their
presence at your office will be noticed. And remarked
upon. The sheriff, maybe even the mayor, might have to
respond to questions from concerned citizens about why
their esteemed senior prosecutor is being investigated in
relation to a murder."

His eyes narrowed, but nothing could hide the look of
malevolence in their dark depths. Had she pushed him
too far? If he had nothing to do with this recent murder,

or any of the others, then she was making a powerful enemy who could likely hurt her career. If he was the killer they were after, it could be dangerous for her to confront him like this, especially since they had nothing to hold him on.

Ryland glanced at Grayson, who appeared to be just as worried as he was. Letting Bree question Palmer might have been a mistake after all.

"Mr. Palmer?" She rattled the bear's cage again.

Ryland cleared his throat. "Perhaps we should end the—"

Palmer held up a hand to stop him, his gaze never leaving Bree. "A timeline? To help figure out who took my wallet?"

"Exactly. If, as you say, someone took it, then we need to find out who that was. You were the victim of a crime, after all. And it would help prove you weren't the person Mr. Beck saw earlier this morning." She tapped her pen on the legal pad. "What time did you last see your wallet, before the tech held it up, of course?"

He eyed her a long moment. Ryland was pretty sure *he'd* be squirming beneath that gaze, squirming to *punch* the guy. But Bree simply stared back, her expression serene. Either she didn't realize she'd stirred a hornet's nest, or she was much better at bluffing than he could have anticipated.

"Now *this* sounds like something worth exploring instead of your other questions that were a complete waste of my time." Palmer's expression turned less hostile. Perhaps he believed she was finally going to lob those softballs now. "I headed out the door at my house at precisely seven o'clock. My wallet was with me at that time."

She wrote the time and a note beside it. "You're sure?"

"Positive. I'm a man of routine, Detective. I make sure I have my wallet and my keys just before I leave the house. And since I planned on stopping at the dry cleaners down the street right after they opened, I'm certain of the time as well."

She wrote down the name of the dry cleaners that he gave her. "Did you go back home after that?"

"No. The clothes are hanging in the back of my car, clearly visible through the rear windows." He glanced toward the detectives. "I assume one of you noticed the clothes?"

They both nodded. Palmer smiled. "Now that we have that *very important* question settled, what's next, Detective Clark?"

"Walk me through where else you went, and provide the approximate times, please."

He rattled off the names, approximate addresses, and times for several other places where he'd stopped, including the library to drop off books and a box store to pick up some headphones he'd ordered.

"After topping off my tank, I headed up US 411 toward Gatlinburg, eventually turning onto 441. It's not a complicated route. I'm sure you traveled here the same way this morning. The only difference is the few twists and turns in Madisonville from my part of town to the highway, as compared to wherever you live."

"Which gas station, please?"

"This is ridiculous," he complained.

She simply sat, waiting, with pen in hand.

Ryland quickly did the math in his head, starting from when Palmer said he left his house. On a typical morning, Palmer couldn't have done all of that and made it up Prescott Mountain in time to be the guy standing in the road when Ryland was on his way to the office. But today wasn't typical. Ryland had run some errands of his own this morning for a case he'd just wrapped up. He'd gotten to work several hours later than usual. Palmer could still be the man who'd nearly forced Ryland off the road.

So what did that mean overall? If Palmer intentionally meant to be in the road when Ryland came up the mountain, had he done some surveillance of ahead of time? Did he know that Ryland would be running late this particular day? Or was this a reconnaissance run, he saw Ryland's Rover heading around the curve, and took advantage of the opportunity?

Palmer finally gave Bree the name and address of the gas station she'd asked about.

"How did you pay for your gas?" she asked.

He opened this mouth to respond, but hesitated, frowning. Then his expression cleared. "Cash. Usually I'd charge it, but I had some cash and wanted to get rid of it. So I went inside and paid."

"You wanted to get rid of it? Why?"

"Too much cash makes a wallet bulky. It's not comfortable to sit on, especially for a long drive. That's why I had my wallet in my console, because I... Hey, wait. I'll bet that's it. When I went inside the station to pay cash, someone must have taken my wallet out of my car."

Bree arched a brow. "At the gas station in Madisonville?"

"Yes. That has to be it. I don't remember seeing the wallet after that."

"You're saying that someone stole it, drove two hours away, and dumped it on Prescott Mountain at a murder scene, where you just happened to show up later to check on activity you heard over your police scanner?"

His face turned a mottled red again. "Thank you, Detective, for going through the logistics. Hearing it all together does sound farfetched. My wallet must have still been in the console on the drive to Gatlinburg. At some point *after* I got here, it was taken. Why, I don't know. Or for what purpose. Apparently whoever this man is that Mr. Beck saw and thought was me is the one who stole my wallet, then headed up this mountain. Heck, maybe he stole it because the two of us looked alike and he thought he could pass for me, use my credit cards. But he got spooked, dropped it, ran."

Ryland glanced at Trent, who shrugged. That was the first explanation Palmer had given that actually sounded feasible. Maybe the guy in the road really did have nothing to do with the murder. He ran from Ryland after the near accident because he had a stolen wallet. Was it possible he just happened to run near the gravesite and accidentally dropped the wallet? Had he stepped on it so it got shoved under some leaves? Maybe. But there was one rather large hole in that scenario.

Bree tapped her pen on the legal pad. "I'm still trying to understand how you and this mystery man, who could be your twin, ended up in the exact same location."

Bingo. That was the part bothering Ryland the most. Even allowing for the distance between him and the man by the road, he felt he'd gotten a good enough look at the guy to identify him in a line-up. And the guy he'd have picked in that line-up was Palmer. So the guy he'd seen had to be Palmer. Didn't he?

Bree gestured toward Ryland. "Mr. Beck is certain that you're the man he saw."

"Mr. Beck is mistaken."

"He's a former special agent with the TBI. He's trained

to be observant, to notice the smallest details. He's prepared to swear under oath that you're the man he saw."

"Oh good grief. I'm an average-looking white guy wearing jeans and a white shirt. No tattoos, no distinguishing characteristics. Mine is not the kind of face that people tend to remember, Detective Clark. It's been the bane of my existence my whole life. In this instance, you're saying that because I'm an average Joe, and look like any other average Joe, I'm suddenly a killer? Give me a break. The whole idea is ludicrous."

Bree glanced at Ryland. The doubt he was starting to have was reflected in her eyes. She cleared her throat and gestured at the prosecutor. "Mr. Palmer—"

"No, stop. Not one more question. And just to be clear, I'll state this one more time. The first and only time I came up this mountain was when I drove up after hearing activity on my scanner. Since Gatlinburg PD was at my side from the moment I opened my car door, they can vouch for my whereabouts and the timeline of when I arrived. I would imagine that if they look through traffic video in downtown Gatlinburg, they'll see my car here and there to prove where I was and when." He motioned toward the media wall at the end of the room, dominated by a huge TV screen in the middle. "You'd think a company with access to the best equipment and technology money can buy would have better investigators. If they did, they'd know they're wasting your time, and mine, with this interview."

He shoved back from the table and stood. "This has gone way past the informal question and answer session that I agreed to. It's now harassment." He looked pointedly at the Gatlinburg detectives, then at Ryland and his team. "If anyone wants to talk to me again, they can submit a formal request to the prosecutor's office. And if you cause me any reputational damage, by the time I'm through, you'll all be lucky to have your jobs."

Bree's eyes widened, and she looked at Ryland again. He gave her a reassuring nod, but he didn't feel all that confident himself. Palmer wasn't like any prosecutor he'd ever dealt with. Ryland didn't doubt he meant every word of his threat to ruin their careers if they caused him trouble. While Ryland and his fellow UB investigators had nothing to worry about, Bree's situation was more precarious. She could lose her job over this.

Palmer motioned to Bree as if she was his assistant. "Drive me to my car. You can follow me back to Madisonville, and we'll head straight to the sheriff's office to see what he thinks of what you've done here today."

She made no move to stand. "My apologies, Mr. Palmer. I still have to provide a written statement about the discovery of the body in the woods. And then, per Sheriff Peterson's orders, I'm supposed to brief the UB investigators about the Slayer investigation. I'm sure one of the Gatlinburg detectives will be happy to take you to your vehicle."

He planted his palms on the table, leaning toward Bree. As one, Ryland, Trent, and Grayson moved to flank her.

"You need to leave," Ryland told him. "Now."

Palmer gave him a disgusted look and stalked out of the conference room.

# *Chapter Eight*

Bree struggled to maintain her poise as Trent and the detectives followed Palmer out of the conference room. With most of the inside walls being glass, he could see her if he turned around and looked up at the second floor balcony. Not wanting to give him the satisfaction of knowing how badly he'd rattled her, she pretended indifference. But as soon as he'd been escorted out the building's main doors, she slumped in her chair and clasped her hands together, trying to stop them from shaking.

Grayson took the chair across from her that Palmer had vacated, while Ryland sat beside her. He shocked her by taking her hands in his.

"You okay?" Ryland asked.

She glanced at his large but surprisingly gentle hands covering hers, giving her the anchor she desperately needed. Her heart seemed to lurch in her chest, and she couldn't help wishing he'd hug her instead of just hold her hand.

"Bree?" His voice was as gentle as his touch, and filled with compassion and concern.

She cleared her throat. "I'm, ah, fine. Or I will be. Just need a minute." She couldn't quite manage a smile. "That was intense."

"You handled him like a champ. If you were nervous, it didn't show." He gently squeezed before letting go and sitting back.

The loss of his touch had her clutching her hands together again, to keep from reaching for him. Good grief. Why was she so needy right now? This investigation was really rattling her. Or was it just Ryland?

Since he was waiting for her answer, she tried to remember what he'd said. That she'd handled Palmer like a champ? That had her sitting a little straighter, some of her confidence finally, blessedly returning. "You really think so?"

"Scout's honor."

She blinked, then glanced across the table at his boss, who was watching both of them with open interest. She cleared her throat again. "You, Ryland, were never a Scout."

He grinned. "Guilty."

She laughed, which was a small miracle given what had just transpired.

"Better?" he asked.

And then she realized what he'd done. He'd given her the strength she needed to move past her fears. Somehow he'd known exactly what to do, how to make her feel better. She unclenched her hands.

"I guess I am," she said. "Thanks to you. I'm feeling a lot better. In fact, I've gone from being totally freaked out to edging on furious. How dare a prosecutor treat me like that. *Junior* detective? *I'll regret this?* What the heck?"

"Is he always like that?" Grayson asked, reminding her again that it wasn't just her and Ryland in here, alone. And making her realize just how badly she'd like that—

to be alone with him. Which didn't make sense, and was all kinds of wrong right now.

*Focus, Bree. Focus on the case and answer the nice billionaire's question.*

She arched a brow. "You mean is Palmer always a jerk?"

Grayson's mouth twitched, but he didn't quite smile. "I would have said something a bit more...colorful. But yes."

"Pretty much. But this, this was different. I've never seen him so..."

"Angry?" Ryland offered.

"No. Not angry. More like...out of control. Nothing rattles him, ever. To get so defensive, especially in front of anyone outside of the prosecutor's office, or even the sheriff's office, is completely out of character."

"This was personal," Ryland said. "He felt threatened and lashed out."

"Detective Clark," Grayson said. "How long have you been working with Palmer?"

She thought about the question. "I can't remember the first time I met him, but he was a Monroe County prosecutor long before I became a police officer. My best guess would be close to when the Slayer murders started, about five years ago. Five victims were killed in a twelve-month time span, and then nothing. Even though we never had a suspect, Palmer took a personal interest in the investigation and held regular status meetings with our department."

Grayson glanced at Ryland. "Is that unusual, in your experience?"

He nodded. "It happens, but it's rare. Bree, do you

know why he was so interested in a case that didn't have any suspects? There was nothing for him to prosecute."

"He claimed he wanted to ensure we didn't make missteps that would jeopardize a conviction if it ever went to trial."

"Has he done that on other cases, before or after that one?"

She frowned, then slowly shook her head. "Not that I know of, no. But if we assume he's innocent, not involved in the murders, I can sort of understand his motivation. He's a politician at heart. His reputation to the general public and media is everything to him. Given how high-profile the Slayer case was, he may have genuinely been worried we'd make him look bad."

Grayson nodded in agreement. "While *I'm* not an investigator, I deal with a lot of different personality types in the business world. Based on that, and from what I just saw, I think your assessment is spot-on. Palmer seems driven by ego, not a sense of justice. His lack of empathy was clear when he never asked about the victim, and didn't even bring up the possibility that the Slayer might be killing again. Although, to be fair, being questioned as a potential suspect caught him off guard, put him on the defensive." He shrugged. "We could be placing too much importance on the interview. Hard to say. Ry, what's your take? Could he be the Slayer?"

Ryland leaned back in his chair, facing Bree. "He lied about being on the road when I came around the curve."

"We don't know that he did," she countered.

"I saw him. I identified him in the picture you showed me, then later in person when Gatlinburg PD escorted him to the crime scene."

"Eyewitnesses are notoriously unreliable, in spite of

what I told Palmer. Even trained observers often disagree about *what* they saw, or *who* they saw, when giving accounts about the same incident. That's been scientifically proven in studies, over and over. It's why we work to gather hard factual evidence. And it's the main reason that groups like the Oversight Project exist, to review convictions to see if innocent people have been wrongly put in prison. People, eyewitnesses, make mistakes that put innocent people away. DNA and other scientific evidence have shown that time and time again."

"She's right," Grayson offered, as he pulled out his phone to check a text message. "When Willow and I were gathering information to start Unfinished Business, we reached out to the Oversight Project to get their take on the handling of cold cases. If I remember correctly, they told us something like seventy percent of the people they exonerated were convicted largely based on misidentification by eyewitnesses."

Ryland held up his hands in surrender. "Okay, okay. I'm willing to admit that it's *possible* the man I saw this morning wasn't Palmer. But he still stays on my persons of interest list."

Grayson put his phone away. "That was Chief Russo from Gatlinburg PD. As soon as Palmer's wallet was found, Russo's team started trying to trace his movements in Gatlinburg courtesy of traffic camera video. None of the cameras downtown picked up the prosecutor's car." He held up his hands when both Ryland and Bree started to say something at the same time. "Giving him the benefit of the doubt, he could have parked in a lot a few blocks back from River Road and walked. A lot of people do. It would explain his car not appearing on video. However, if he was truly shopping for dishes, those are heavy, and fragile, not something you'd want to cart around. I sure wouldn't."

Ryland nodded. "Which likely means he lied. The question is why. Is he trying to cover up involvement in the murder? Or something completely unrelated? Bree mentioned he's consumed with protecting his professional reputation."

"You're thinking an affair?" Bree asked. "Maybe with a married woman? I can see him lying to cover that up. Most people would."

"Absolutely," Ryland said. "Maybe he intended to shop for his mother's present later today and didn't want to admit where he'd really been. But if I was questioned about an alibi for murder, I'd give up names left and right to make sure the investigation didn't focus on me."

Grayson shook his head. "I've met a lot of narcissistic types, like Palmer appears to be. They're hard to predict, because they consider themselves smarter than everyone around them. He probably felt safe not revealing his secret since there isn't any hard evidence against him for murder."

Bree leaned against the table. "Sounds like you're both thinking he's *not* involved in whatever happened up on the mountain."

Ryland answered her. "That's for Gatlinburg PD to figure out. I need to focus on your cold case and let the police work the active case, at least until we find strong evidence to support a link."

"The marks on the trees aren't enough?" Bree asked.

"They're enough to support that a copycat could be active. Don't get me wrong, I'm not ignoring what happened today. But the cold case is my primary objective."

She sighed. "I get it. And as far as Palmer's concerned,

in spite of how he acted in the meeting, I'm having a hard time seeing him as a violent offender. He may turn out to be, but in my experiences with him over the years, it doesn't feel right. Plus, there's another small thing that's been bothering me about him in relation to this case. It's, well, it's about the mud."

"Mud?" Ryland's brows shot up. "You mean, my muddy suit?"

"Kind of. You said the guy from the road jumped the ditch and took off into the woods. I know you were muddy earlier because you tried to hop the same ditch and missed."

He winced. "Thanks for the reminder."

She chuckled. "My point is that if the ground was so wet near there, with all that mud, how is it possible that Prosecutor Palmer's jeans looked clean, and there wasn't a hint of mud on his white shirt? Or even his shoes?"

Grayson sat back. "She's got you there, Ry. Didn't you tell me earlier the guy in the road had a smudged white shirt, as if he'd wiped dirty hands on it?"

He slowly nodded. "I sure did. I suppose Palmer could have a go-bag in his car, like we all carry. Heck, I've got one at home, my desk here, and my car. A lot of law enforcement does, in case they have to pull an all-nighter, or their clothes get messed up at a crime scene. Maybe Palmer realized he had mud on his shirt and exchanged it for a fresh one from his go-bag."

"Okay," Bree continued. "So then why cause that near accident, run into the woods, go back to his car, wherever it was, and change his shirt, then come back about two hours later when all the cops were on the scene? It sort of paints him as an idiot, taking all those risks.

And one thing for sure, Palmer is no idiot. He's cunning and smart."

Ryland tapped his hand on the table, a smile playing about his lips. "Maybe you should drop off your résumé after all, just in case a position opens up around here. Those are sound arguments."

A wave of pure pleasure had her stomach fluttering and her cheeks heating. If he'd told her she was beautiful, it wouldn't have made her go all mushy inside. But complimenting her brains had her wanting to melt into a puddle on the floor. "Thank you. So what do you say? Have we got one jeans-and-white-shirt guy or running around, or two?"

"I'm not ready to draw a conclusion," Ryland said. "But I'm leaning toward two. I'm also leaning toward my eyewitness account being far shakier than I'd thought. Hell, who knows? I certainly wouldn't swear it was Palmer I saw at this point."

Grayson stood. "If I'm not mistaken, that detective downstairs waving at us is the one who wanted you both to fill out written statements after interviewing Palmer. I suggest you do that as quickly as possible so we can move forward with the briefing about the Slayer case."

Bree and Ryland both turned to see the man he'd mentioned.

"I hate paperwork," she said.

"Necessary evil," Ryland teased as he too stood.

She started toward the door, then stopped when her phone buzzed in her pocket. She read the screen and groaned. "It's my boss. Palmer must have already bent his ear. I've been ordered to return to Madisonville, immediately."

# Chapter Nine

"Stay here much longer and I'll charge you rent."

The sound of his boss's voice had Ryland looking up from his desk, surprised to see Grayson in the aisle with his arm around his wife's shoulders. Clearly he and Willow were on their way out. Ryland glanced around the squad room, stunned to realize everyone else had left and the fading sunlight was casting long shadows in the parking lot.

He pitched his pen on top of some folders and rubbed the back of his neck to ease the stiffness. "Can't remember the last time you two left before me. Heck, I don't even remember everyone else leaving. I must have zoned out."

Willow waved toward the stacks of files. "Fascinating reading?"

"More like tedious. These are the Smoky Mountain Slayer files. Bree warned me her boss is a stickler for keeping the records objective, facts only, no impressions or theories. She wasn't kidding. It makes for some dry reading. I'm not getting a feel at all for what the detectives thought about the various witnesses or even what direction they might have wanted to take the investigation if they hadn't been forced to move on to other cases.

Willow smiled. "Are you sure that's the only reason you want to meet with Bree again? To get her perspective on the case?"

Grayson squeezed her shoulders. "Willow—"

She gave him an innocent look. "You did say they were holding hands in the conference room. Or did I hear that wrong?"

Ryland cleared his throat. "I, ah—"

"So you're heading to Madisonville to discuss the investigation, then," Grayson interrupted, giving Willow a frown that had her laughing. "How long will you be gone?"

"A couple of days, I imagine. I'll probably head there tonight so I can meet with her in the morning before she heads to work. It might be the only way she'll be able to carve out some time for me."

At Willow's wink, he rolled his eyes. As always, she was perceptive. There was no denying that his interest in Bree was more personal than it should be with him working a case for her department. But somehow he'd resist the temptation. He had to. He needed to focus and make sure the Slayer was brought to justice. And even if he didn't have the case to consider, the two of them lived a couple of hours from each other. That wasn't exactly a recipe for a successful relationship—especially since they both loved their jobs and neither was likely to consider quitting to move to the other's city.

And, good grief, he was taking leaps in thought that were ridiculous considering he'd only met her this morning. But it was hard not to take those leaps. It felt as if he'd known her for weeks, months, instead of only hours. The two of them just…clicked. Talking to her, brainstorming with her, felt so natural, so…right. And just thinking about her had his blood heating, his fingers itching to tangle in her hair and stroke her soft-looking skin. He'd have paid a small fortune to taste her lips, feel her curves pressed against him as he held her tight.

He cleared his throat, refusing to look at Willow for fear that he'd see his desires mirrored in her all-knowing eyes. Instead, he focused on Grayson to try to get the conversation—and his traitorous thoughts—back on track.

"Bree's boss had texted her to head back right after we spoke to Palmer," Ryland said. "But she stayed to provide that written statement Gatlinburg PD wanted. Unfortunately, her boss called again as she was heading out the door and was livid that she wasn't already on the road."

"Yikes," Willow said. "Sounds like a tough guy to work for."

He risked meeting her gaze again, but she seemed serious now, no longer teasing him about Bree. "I said the same thing. But Bree was quick to defend him, says he's fair and generous with praise and raises when they're earned. She claims he's just really particular and doesn't like surprises. She blamed herself, said she should have reminded him earlier that she was obligated to fill out the police report before leaving."

"Yeah, well," Willow said. "If my boss micro-managed me like that, I'd be out of there."

Grayson chuckled. "Since you have your boss wrapped around your little finger, I don't see that ever being a problem."

She grinned and stood on tiptoe to kiss him. It was

probably supposed to be a quick kiss, but Grayson had other ideas.

Ryland cleared his throat, loudly. "If this is going to be X-rated, I need to head downstairs to the break room and get some popcorn for the show."

Willow laughed as she extricated herself from Grayson's arms. "Save the popcorn for another day. Come on, husband of mine. We have bags to pack, hotel reservations to make."

He kissed her forehead. "How about warm up the car? I'll be right out."

"I've heard that before. Ryland, don't you dare let him look at those files. He's a total wannabe investigator, and I'll never get him out of here if he starts reading the reports. Promise me you won't let him."

"Scout's honor," he told her.

She lightly punched his arm. "We all know that carries no weight with you. I mean it. Don't keep him long. We have plans. Oh, and when you see pretty Bree again, do hug her for me, won't you?"

Before he could think of a snappy comeback, she hurried out of the squad room.

When the front door closed behind her, Grayson perched on the corner of his desk. "Sorry about that. She's a matchmaker at heart. I shouldn't have let it slip about you, ah, comforting Bree earlier."

"Willow mentioned hotel reservations and bags to pack. Is there something you want to tell your second-in-command?"

Grayson smiled at his unsubtle changing of the subject, but didn't remark on it. "As a matter of fact, there is. I'm briefing the team tomorrow, but it looks like you'll be in Monroe County, so I'll tell you now. We've been corresponding with Katrina's *adoptive* parents ever since you located them." He shook his head. "I guess I should start calling my daughter Lizzie since that's the only name she knows. Regardless, a few hours ago, her…parents… agreed to meet with Willow and me. We'll be in Poplar Bluff, Missouri, for the next few days to talk through this mess and figure out the next steps."

Grayson shook his head. "When my first wife was murdered, and our baby girl went missing, I never could have predicted that almost eight years later I'd be planning civilized conversation with the couple who took Katrina and raised her."

Ryland stood and clasped his shoulder. "I can't imagine how hard this is. But I admire the hell out of you for how you're handling it. Most people wouldn't care that the Danvers didn't know Katrina was stolen. They'd take them to court and wrench Katrina—Lizzie—away from the only home she knows. Are you going to meet Lizzie on this trip?"

He let out a ragged breath. "Not yet. She'll stay with a friend of the Danvers for the duration of our visit. We're feeling our way forward, figuring it out as we go. I want to be a part of my daughter's life, somehow. I don't want to traumatize her, though. It's not her fault what happened. But I'll be damned if she goes through life never being told who her real mother was. That wouldn't be fair to Maura."

"I'm sure you'll figure something out. You've got this."

Headlights flashed through the front glass walls. Grayson stood. "Looks like my time's up. Don't worry about anything here. I'll tell the team tomorrow about your trip to Monroe County. Trent can be my right arm while you and I are both away."

"Trent. Great. I'll have to clean up whatever mess he makes when I get back."

Grayson chuckled. "I'll be sure to let him know you said that."

"Please do. Go on, off with you before Willow comes in here packing a pistol."

"You too. Go home, Ry. There's nothing here that can't wait. See you in a few days." He strode across the room, and soon he and Willow were zipping out of the parking lot in his black Audi R8 Spyder.

Ryland grinned. He'd bought his Range Rover because it was like a mountain goat, with roll bars and a fancy, remote-controlled winch on the front in case he ever needed to pull himself out of an icy ditch once winter rolled around. Still, there was no denying the appeal of the sexy convertible Grayson drove. On a flat surface, it was probably a dream to drive.

After a frustrating search online to find a place to stay in Madisonville, he was forced to settle for an unappealing two-star motel in Sweetwater, about nine miles away. He sorted through the folders in the maze of open boxes beside his desk and pulled a few more out to add to the ones he'd already been reviewing. After topping off the stack with the folder Bree had made for him, he grabbed his go-bag of muddy clothes and headed out.

Rush hour was long over. Even stopping at his house first to pack a fresh duffel bag, he'd likely reach the hotel in less than two hours. It would be too late for a visit with Bree. But he could at least call her, see if he could bribe her with a free breakfast if she'd meet him before work in the morning.

It only took a few minutes to reach his cabin at the bottom of Prescott Mountain. He'd just finished packing and was heading through his kitchen toward the garage when his phone buzzed in his jacket pocket. As soon as he saw who was calling, he stopped and tossed the bag on the counter.

"Sheriff Peterson. How can I help you, sir?"

"Mr. Beck, Detective Clark didn't bother returning to work this afternoon, and she's avoiding my calls. I assume she's still with you at UB headquarters. Tell her if she doesn't call me in the next sixty seconds, she'll be suspended for a week without pay." The line clicked.

Ryland swore and immediately called the sheriff back.

Without preamble, Peterson said, "Bree? You using Mr. Beck's phone?"

"Sheriff, this is Ryland Beck. Bree isn't at UB. She left hours ago, right after filling out her written report for the police. Has anyone gone by her house to see if she's there?"

"What the… Are you sure? She left *hours* ago?"

He checked his watch. "It's seven o'clock now. Our interview with Palmer was over by two. It took both of us another hour, easy, to fill out reports and answer Gatlinburg PD's questions. By my calculations, she should have reached Madisonville a little after five."

"Well, I'll be damned. Hang on a minute."

Ryland leaned against the counter, tapping it impatiently as he waited. He didn't know Bree well enough to be sure how she'd react in various situations. But given her defense of her boss earlier, he was inclined to think she wasn't the type to ignore his calls.

He glanced at the digital clock on his stove. He'd been waiting for Peterson for at least five minutes. What was taking so long?

"Mr. Beck, you still there?"

"I am, yes, sir."

"I called Bree's neighbor, Mrs. Riley. She said Bree's police-issue Explorer isn't there, and her personal car's been in the driveway all day, as usual. Hasn't moved. Detective Mills contacted a friend at the phone company to ping her phone. They're double-checking, because they did this fast and might have made a mistake. But they gave me the GPS coordinates they triangulated based on the last time her phone pinged off any cell towers. I'm going to have my guys see if they can figure out the location."

Ryland was already bringing up a GPS app as he listened. "Can you give me the coordinates?"

"Texting them to you now."

Ryland checked his screen. "Got 'em. Hang on." He cut and pasted the data into the GPS app.

"I'll send someone by her house," the sheriff continued. "Just to make sure she's not there. Maybe her SUV broke down and she accidentally left her phone in it after hiring someone to drive her home. That's the most likely scenario. I imagine she's still ticked at me. Maybe she decided not to bother coming in after all that." In spite of his words, there was concern in his voice, as if he was trying, hard, to convince himself something bad hadn't happened.

Ryland watched with growing trepidation as the GPS blip moved across the map, then stopped. He felt the blood draining from his face.

Bree had never made it off Prescott Mountain.

# Chapter Ten

Bree's back ached from being jammed against the steering wheel. The pain was becoming so unbearable that she finally grasped the back of the driver's seat and pulled herself a few inches higher, shifting her position. The Explorer shuddered and rocked. She froze, not even breathing, until the movement stopped. Slowly, carefully, she let out a deep breath and reluctantly settled against the steering wheel again.

The irony of her current predicament wasn't lost on her. As a little girl, when she'd been in her dinosaur phase and begged her mom to let her watch a rerun of *Jurassic Park*, her mother said she was too young to see it. She'd worried that Bree would have nightmares about those "scary dinosaurs." Bree's dad didn't see it that way. And his soft heart couldn't deal with her tears when all her friends had seen the blockbuster movie and she hadn't.

He took her to the library on a Saturday morning, supposedly for some father-daughter time. After five minutes inside, so that he could honestly tell Bree's mom they'd gone, they took off down the street and watched a *Jurassic Park* classic-movie matinee at a dollar theatre. He'd been right about his tomboy daughter. She'd loved it. But her mother was right too. The nightmares were terrifying. She'd quietly suffered through them on her own, not wanting to get her daddy in trouble.

Now, here she was, a grown woman, living out one of the scenes from the movie. She was trapped in her crumpled SUV pointed nose-down toward the valley floor, suspended in the branches of some far too skinny-looking trees clinging to the side of Prescott Mountain. But unlike the little boy in the movie, she had no hope that Dr. Alan Grant was coming to her rescue.

No one was.

She'd accepted that depressing fact about two hours ago. That's when the battery had died, the post-crash alert system stopped flashing her emergency lights, and the horn stopped blaring.

With the pieces of her smashed cell phone sprinkled like glitter around the cab, the Explorer's 911–assist system was incapable of calling for help. And since her initial attempt to climb out the broken side window had sent the truck sliding down a good foot before jerking to a halt, she'd been trying *not* to move.

At some point, she'd have to accept that her only chance of survival was to leap out the window and pray she could grab a tree branch before the truck's downward plunge took her with it. But she hadn't quite figured out how to manage that.

She risked a quick glance over her shoulder where the windshield used to be. The view really was spectacular, with a full moon painting swaths of light across the valley floor. The trees were so far away that their autumn-dressed leaves sparkled like red and gold pixie-dust against a black velvet canvas. It was a lot like when her mom had taken her to the top of the Empire State

Building. Except this time, she was about two Empire State Buildings up with no elevator to take her to safety.

The one blessing about her current situation was that if the seemingly inevitable happened, at least her parents wouldn't suffer, hearing how their only child perished. Bree had been their "surprise" baby late in life after they'd given up on being able to have children. Strangers had always assumed her mom and dad were her grandparents. It had bothered her, but they'd just smiled and never corrected anyone. They honestly didn't care. They were so grateful to finally have a baby that they didn't mind being the oldest parents at every birthday party or school event. Her mom had passed several years ago after a massive heart attack. Daddy died a few months later, supposedly of the same thing. But Bree had always felt he'd died of a broken heart.

She blinked away the tears tracking down her face, not daring to move her hand to wipe them away. And then she smiled, a bittersweet smile, as she thought about her one big regret—that she'd never get the chance to tell Ryland Beck she had a mad crush on him.

Was he attracted to her too? She thought he probably was, based on some heated, appreciative glances he'd thrown her way. And those sexy, charming smiles he'd gifted her with. Plus the incredibly sweet gentleness in his touch as he'd consoled her in the conference room. But she'd probably never know for sure.

In the short time since meeting him, she'd vacillated between wanting to drool all over him and wanting to yell at him. She couldn't remember the last man who'd gotten under her skin like that. It was maddening and exciting at the same time. Finding out whether the sparks between them would have led to fights or some really hot sex, and maybe something far more lasting and special, would have been fun. But even the possibility of exploring a potential relationship with him, after the Slayer case was over of course, had been eliminated in the span of a few seconds and one wild, terrifying ride over a cliff.

She shuddered, then bit her lip when even that slight movement had the truck bouncing in its precarious perch. When it didn't fall, she slowly inhaled, exhaled, no sudden movements.

And remembered.

She'd been driving down Prescott Mountain, rounded one of the crazy treacherous curves, then *bam*. A vehicle had slammed into the back of her Explorer. She'd been so busy fighting the skid, the last thing on her mind had been to glance in her mirrors and see who'd hit her. It had all happened so fast, a matter of seconds. It was impossible to regain control. And the guardrail, rather than stopping her two-and-a-half-ton truck, had acted like a ramp, sending her airborne.

As the truck somersaulted over the cliff, she'd screamed and twisted around, clinging to the seat back. For one millisecond, she'd glimpsed another vehicle up on the cliff's edge. It was a vehicle she recognized. After all, it had been in the city's parking lot every day since she'd joined the Monroe County Sheriff's office. The reserved spot had an elegant gold-and-black sign, declaring the name of the driver allowed to park there.

*Prosecutor Dane Palmer.*

Ryland had been right to suspect him of being up to no good.

A cool breeze blew through the holes where the windows used to be. Metal creaked and moaned. A loud crack sounded from the passenger side of the SUV. She looked on in horror as one of the branches snapped and fell away. The truck shuddered, then started turning and sliding sideways.

Bree grabbed the seat back and screamed.

# Chapter Eleven

Ryland turned the Rover around at the top of Prescott Mountain, in front of the security gate that Grayson had installed several months earlier at his estate.

"Any luck?" Trent asked through the Bluetooth connection in the Rover.

"Zilch. I'm outside Grayson's place now. Didn't pass a single vehicle on my way up. All the guardrails are in place. Nothing broken that I could tell. Maybe the GPS coordinates Peterson gave me were wrong."

"Or maybe her phone battery went dead, or the phone quit working as she was heading down the mountain."

Ryland blew out a breath. "If that's the case, she could be anywhere between here and Madisonville, broken down, stranded. Do me a favor and call Peterson again, see if he can verify the cell tower information. And let me know what his people are doing on their end to find her."

"Will do. What about Gatlinburg PD? Did you call them already?"

Ryland made a disgusted sound. "They're the first ones I called. They gave me the standard answer police always give someone when they want to report an adult missing. Wait a few days and see if they show up. Without evidence of foul play or suspicious circumstances, they go with statistics, that the adult decided to take off on their own and will most likely show up again unharmed."

"Can't really fault them there. Most supposedly missing adults do show up, right as rain, nothing sinister to it. Maybe she was ticked at Peterson, like he said, and went somewhere to cool off before heading back."

"Come on, Trent. She's a police officer. She knows better than to worry someone like that. She'd have told Peterson where she is, even if she was too mad to head to the office."

"You're really worried about her, aren't you?"

He glanced past the guardrail, at the lights of Gatlinburg far, far below. His stomach knotted at the thought of her having gone over, plunging down into the valley.

"Ry?"

He shuddered and focused on the road. "Yes, I'm really worried about her."

"Well, she is kind of hot. She's got killer legs, a tiny waist, an impressive set of—"

"Grow up, Trent."

He chuckled. "Just keepin' it real, Mr. Doom and Gloom."

"Call Peterson back, all right? Get me new coordinates. I'll head down the mountain and take another look."

"Okay, okay. I trust your instincts. Something's really wrong." Worry and concern had replaced the humor in his voice. "Instead of calling Peterson, I'll get one of my contacts at the phone company to double-check everything. And I'll get some of the team on this to help with the search."

"Thanks, man. I appreciate it."

"Ry?"

"Yeah?"

"We'll find her. My ETA's fifteen minutes. Callum and Faith live fairly close. I'll get them out here quick, right behind me."

He tightened his grip on the steering wheel. "Let's hope I'm ruining everyone's evening for nothing. Thanks for having my back."

"Always. Talk to you soon."

Ryland headed down the mountain, creeping along with his headlights on their brightest setting, occasionally shining his flashlight out the side window. Whereas before he'd focused on the guardrails, this time he kept his gaze mostly on the asphalt, looking for skid marks.

The idea of anyone plummeting down the side of the mountain had his stomach knotting. But Bree wasn't just anyone. There was something captivating about her, something…special. The idea of something happening to her had his chest seizing up. She was so smart, sassy and full of life. And sexy as hell. His granddad would call her a spitfire, the ultimate compliment in his grandfather's opinion. She was definitely that, and more. Bree was a free spirit with a tenacious desire for justice, which was the ultimate compliment in *his* opinion.

*God, please let her be okay.*

He was halfway down the mountain when his phone rang. He pushed a button, answering through the truck's Bluetooth speakers again to leave his hands free.

"Ry, it's Trent. Those GPS coordinates haven't changed. But I did get more clarity around them. In this area, with spotty cell coverage, the coordinates are more of an approximation. Better than a guess, but way less accurate than they'd be in town."

"Well, that's something. Helps explain why I haven't

found anything so far. How inaccurate are we talking? Miles off?"

"More like half the length of a football field, in any direction."

The hope that had flared inside Ryland disintegrated. "Then she still has to be on this mountain." He swallowed hard and glanced toward the nearest guardrail.

"I'll be there soon. I've got flashlights in my emergency kit. Faith does too. She's a couple of minutes behind me, Callum not much farther."

"Sounds good. When I finish this pass, I'll head up the most likely route she would have taken to Madisonville, just in case those coordinates are more off than your person at the phone company thinks they are. *Hold it.* I've got some skid marks here."

"Where? What's your location?"

He braked and leaned forward, peering through the windshield. "A little over halfway down. Give me a sec. I'm getting out for a better look." He shoved the truck into Park and hopped out with his flashlight, shining it on the dark marks on the pavement. Definitely fresh, and too far down to be the ones he'd made this morning.

Turning in a circle, he shined the light toward the ditch and the trees that went up that side of the mountain. Nothing. No trenched grass or broken limbs to indicate a vehicle had crashed through there. The shoulder on the opposite side was generously wide, with enough space for someone to pull over if they wanted to snap a picture or change a flat tire. Some of the skid marks led toward the guardrail, but it was intact, nothing to indicate a driver had lost control and gone over the side.

Something flashed in the light. He narrowed his eyes, carefully shining the light along the railing. One section, about ten feet long, reflected the light a little differently than the rest.

*Because it was bent.*

He ran toward the railing and stopped in front of the dented portion. Two of the posts in the middle had been snapped in half. But they were being held in place by the horizontal strip of metal. If he hadn't shined the flashlight just right, he'd never have even noticed it. All the other posts were intact.

His hand shook as he ran it across a streak of white on the metal above one of the broken posts. White flakes shot in the air like dandelion seeds. It was paint, white paint. The same color as Bree's police-issue SUV.

He aimed the flashlight over the railing, past the cliff toward the valley below. His knees nearly buckled when he realized what he was looking at.

About thirty feet down was the twisted wreckage of a green-and-white SUV with the words Monroe County Sheriff on the tailgate and the driver's side. The truck was pointed hood down, but tilted toward the right. The only thing holding it up were the branches of some trees growing out from the side of the mountain under the cliff where he was standing.

His hands shook as he shined the light toward the driver's window, or where the window used to be. The truck suddenly shifted. Metal screeched. It slid down several inches before slamming against another tree branch and stopping again.

A scream filled the air.

His heart nearly leaped in his throat. "Bree?" he called out. "Bree? Are you in there?"

"Ryland! I'm here. Help me!"

The truck jerked again, sliding sideways a few more

inches. *Crack.* A branch gave way, slamming against another one.

"Ryland!"

"Don't move, Bree!"

"It won't hold much longer. Please, help me!"

"Don't move," he repeated. "I'll be right back!"

"Don't leave me!"

The panic and fear in her voice cut him like a knife. But he couldn't waste another precious second if there was any chance of saving her. He sprinted for his Rover and hopped behind the wheel.

"Ryland? What's going on?" Trent called out. "Did I hear someone screaming?"

"She's here, Bree. Call 911. Get the fire department up here. Somehow her truck flew *over* the guardrail and landed in some trees below the cliff. It's pointing nose-down and slightly sideways, barely holding. It'll go any minute." He slammed into Reverse and wheeled the Rover around to face the guardrail, then shot forward, skidding to a stop inches away.

"Are you kidding me? The car's in a freaking tree?"

"I'd try to attach my winch to the bumper of her SUV, but I don't think it would work. The truck's too heavy. It would pull mine down with it. Tell them to bring grappling hooks, a helicopter, hell, I don't know. Hurry!"

He grabbed the remote control for the winch and shoved it in his shirt pocket, buttoning it closed so it couldn't fall out as he ran to the front of the Rover.

"Ry, talk to me," Trent yelled through the Bluetooth speakers inside. "I'm calling 911 right now. Wait for the firefighters to get there. Don't do something stupid."

"I can't do nothing and let her die," he yelled back.

"If by doing *something*, it means climbing down a cliff

without safety equipment, then you dang well better wait. Don't get yourself killed trying to do the impossible. It's too dangerous. Ry! Ry? Are you listening to me?"

"I'm a bit busy here. Did you call 911?"

Trent swore. "Wait right where you are. Calling them now." The line went silent.

Ryland pressed one of the buttons on the winch remote through his pocket. The engine whirred, feeding out steel cable. He pressed another button, stopping it, then grabbed the hook on the end. Now what? He needed some way to tie the cable around himself without it sliding up his body and him falling.

After a few agonizing seconds of pondering the problem, he threaded it tightly around and between his thighs, then attached the hook back around the main cable, forming a chair of sorts. He made it as tight as he could, hoping it couldn't slip off him even if he flipped over.

His stomach roiled. He squeezed his eyes shut, taking deep breaths, fighting back the darkness that threatened.

"Ry?" Trent's voice called out again. "Firefighters are on the way with a ladder truck. Wait by the road to flag them down."

He forced his eyes open and turned around to face the guardrail.

Big mistake.

The moon was bright tonight, bright enough to show him just how far down the drop was. Sweat ran down the side of his face in spite of the cold air. A buzzing noise sounded in his ears. Images flashed through his mind.

A cable car, high above the snowy mountains.

His father's face in the window, showing his disappointment that his spoiled teenaged son thought riding in a cable car was lame and had refused to get on.

Beside his father, his mom blowing him a kiss, forgiving him as she always did.

The cable car jerking, making an odd thumping sound, then climbing, sliding up the cable, higher and higher, farther and farther away.

A sickening screech of metal on metal. A pinging sound as the cable began to separate, flinging bits of metal out into the open air. Another jerk, the car swinging wildly. Screams of terror. A glimpse of his parents' ghost-white faces in that split second before the cable snapped and they plunged to the valley floor below.

"Ryland!" Trent and Bree both called out at the same time, snapping him back to awareness. He shook his head, desperately trying to clear the buzzing from his ears.

"ETA five minutes!" Trent's voice sounded from the speaker in the cab. "You there, buddy? Talk to me."

Bree didn't have five minutes.

He could do this. He *had* to do this. He drew several deep breaths, offered up a quick prayer and climbed over the guardrail.

# Chapter Twelve

Bree clutched the driver's door, desperately trying to hold on as Ryland winched himself down the cliff face toward her. The truck's awkward downward and slightly sideways angle now was making it nearly impossible not to pitch out through the hole where the windshield had once been.

The truck wobbled and bounced, creaking and moaning as if in pain. The remaining branches wouldn't hold much longer.

She didn't know whether to thank God that Ryland was trying to save her, or curse him for risking his life. Could he even reach her once he was level with the truck anyway? The cliff face was at least ten feet away. If he thought he could climb onto the trees holding the truck, she'd have to warn him away. That kind of movement would send the truck crashing down, possibly pulling both of them to their deaths.

*Creak.* The truck jerked.

She let out a small cry, unable to stop herself. When Ryland didn't look down at her, she let out a ragged, relieved breath. His situation seemed almost as precarious as hers. She didn't want to distract him.

He was facing away from her, rappelling down in

some kind of chair he'd fastened with the cable. His shoes scrabbled against the cliff face as he tried to keep himself from scraping against it.

Another creak. She squeezed her eyes shut. This was it. The truck was about to go. She didn't want to see the end coming.

*Breathe in, breathe out. God, please let it not hurt. Make it quick.*

"Bree, open your eyes. Look at me."

Her eyes flew open. She gasped in surprise when Ryland swung out from the cliff, into the open air just past the truck door.

"Get ready," he yelled. "I'm going to reach for you. I can only use one arm or I'll tip over. You'll have to grab my hand."

He swung back toward the cliff. Hot tears coursed down her cheeks. What was he saying? Give up her hold on the truck and grab at him as he swung by? Impossible.

He swung out toward her again.

"Bree, I can't get any closer. Do you understand? On my next pass, grab my hand and I'll pull you onto my lap." He swung back toward the cliff. "Next swing," he called out. "That last branch is bending and cracking. It's not going to hold. It's now or never. Reach for me, Bree."

He pushed off from the cliff again. He swung out toward her, closer, closer.

"Now, Bree. Grab my hand!"

She shoved with her feet, throwing herself out the opening toward him, a scream in her throat as she fell into open air, arms flailing. She missed! Impossibly, his arms wrapped around her, yanking her to him. The cable jerked. She was falling! She screamed. Another hard jerk knocked the breath out of her.

"I've got you. I've got you. Hold on. Grab hold, Bree. Wrap yourself around me. Do it!"

She was wrapped in an iron-tight bear hug against his chest. His legs were wrapped around hers. They were both hanging upside down, suspended from the cable.

"Grab me. Hurry! Before we hit the cliff!"

She squeaked in terror, wrapping her arms around his neck, holding him as tight as she could.

*Crack!* The shriek of metal filled the air. *Scrape, crack.*

"Hold on, hold on!"

She sobbed against his neck, digging into his jacket, pulling his hair, whatever she could to keep from falling.

A tremendous rush of air shot out at them. Something sharp slashed across her arm. More cracks, popping noises, then…silence, for the space of a heartbeat. An incredibly loud bang sounded from far away. The world tilted crazily. The cable jerked and spun.

"Almost there, just a few more seconds."

Almost *where*?

"Hold on, Bree. Don't let go. I have to turn us or the guardrail will chew us up. Hang on."

The guardrail? She jerked her head around. They weren't upside down anymore. Somehow he'd flipped them over. She looked up just in time to see the flash of metal coming at them, fast. Or were they coming at the metal? She let out a small cry, certain it was about to slice into her arms around his neck.

His powerful thighs jerked beneath her. The cable whined and spun. His feet were braced against the side of the cliff just below the guardrail. His left arm remained tightly around her like a vise. He reached up and grabbed the railing with his right hand, jerking them against it.

The winch stopped. Everything stopped. She stared at him in shock, his eyes inches from hers.

"Hard part's over, Bree. I need you to grab the railing. These posts in this section are solid. Climb up and over. You can do it. I've got you. I promise I won't let you fall. Hurry."

There was something odd-sounding in his voice, something...off...that had her grabbing for the railing in spite of her terror that she'd fall if she did. She needn't have worried. He never let her go. He gripped the back of her skirt, steadying her, helping her until she scrambled over the top and fell down onto the other side.

Seconds later, he landed on the ground beside her, the cable whistling as it coiled on top of his chest. He lay there gasping for air, eyes closed.

Bree clutched his hand as they lay beside each other on their backs, a hysterical laugh bubbling up in her chest. It came out more like a whimper than a laugh, though.

His hand tightened around hers. "It's okay. You're okay."

"You saved my life, Ryland. I can't believe you did... whatever you did. But you saved me. Oh my God. What just happened? I can't believe any of that just happened."

She stared up at the canopy of trees overhead, trees that were safely anchored into the ground, not sticking out like bony fingers from the side of the mountain, cracking apart and slowly releasing their hold on her truck, on her. "I'm guessing that last bit of noise was my SUV plunging to the bottom of the mountain."

She drew another shaky breath. When he didn't say anything, she rolled her head to the side, looking at him. His eyes were closed, his face deathly pale.

She scrambled to her knees and leaned over him,

searching for injuries. "Ryland? Ryland, are you hurt? Answer me."

"I'm. Okay." His voice was a thready whisper. Sweat poured off his face.

"Frankly, if he did what I think he did," a man's voice said as footsteps came toward them, "he's probably on his way to being catatonic."

"Shut up, Trent," Ryland whispered between clenched teeth, his eyes still closed.

Bree frowned in confusion as Adam Trent rounded the Rover and crouched beside his friend.

She looked down at Ryland. "I don't understand. What's wrong with him? I don't see any cuts anywhere."

"Just. Need. One. Damn. Minute," Ryland choked out, eyes squeezed tightly closed, his breaths growing ragged, strained.

Trent shook his head. "Ryland's got a bit of a fear of heights. We're talking full-blown clinical phobia, the kind where you get light-headed. Sometimes you throw up, sweat and eventually lose consciousness."

"Shut. Up." Ryland rasped, his voice barely audible now.

Bree stared at Trent, horrified. "Are you telling me he not only risked his life to save me, he lowered himself down a cliff knowing he could faint at any moment and fall to his own death?"

Ryland groaned.

"That about sums it up." Trent sounded ridiculously cheerful given the circumstances. "Wait for it. Wait for it. There he goes, folks."

Bree jerked back toward Ryland just as his arms fell to his sides and his jaw went slack.

# Chapter Thirteen

Bree paced back and forth in Ryland's kitchen, talking to Peterson on the phone on what was turning out to be the longest day of her life. And it wasn't even eleven pm yet.

Ryland and his UB teammates waited in the family room. They'd all come to see him, to make sure he was okay after he'd refused to go to the hospital, like Bree. The only people who hadn't come over from UB were Grayson Prescott and his wife, Willow. Apparently some trip they were going to take tomorrow had been unexpectedly moved up, and they'd had to fly out tonight. But they were keeping tabs on what had happened and had been assured that Ryland was okay.

"Yes, sir," she said, in response to her boss's latest question. "I'm fine. I promise. Just like I told you the last six times you asked." She paused by the archway between the kitchen and family room, catching Ryland's questioning look from the couch. She gave him a helpless gesture and continued her pacing.

Peterson was still making sure she knew he wasn't pleased with her. "You should have gone to the hospital, Detective. At the very least, you need an MRI or whatever scan they do these days to check out head injuries."

"I didn't hit my head or ever lose consciousness. If I

had, I assure you I would have gone to the hospital. But I didn't. Nothing's broken. Just a few bumps and bruises. It was the scariest experience of my life, but thanks to Ryland, at least I still *have* my life. Another few seconds and I'd have been compost at the bottom of the mountain." She shuddered. "Have you located Palmer yet?"

"We spoke on the phone. He's decided to stay in Gatlinburg to visit his mom for a few days before heading back."

"What? You didn't send someone up here to arrest him?" Ryland, Trent, and a few of the others looked at her through the archway. She mouthed a silent *sorry* for being so loud and paced the other way as she listened to her boss's lame explanation.

Stopping her nervous pacing, she leaned against the counter and stared out the back door. Ryland's yard was flat, with thick trees surrounding it, blocking any potential view of the mountains when the sun was up. Pretty unusual around here, where most people kept at least part of the brush and trees cleared so they could look out at the Smokies. But after learning about his phobia about heights, she could certainly understand why he didn't want the views. She was shocked he'd ever accepted a job where he'd have to drive up and down one of the highest mountains in Gatlinburg, given his fears. She was grateful he'd taken the job, though. Otherwise she wouldn't be here anymore.

When Peterson paused for a breath, she said, "Basically what you're telling me is that you don't believe me that he's the one who bumped into my SUV and sent me careening off a cliff. He's developing a pattern now. First Ryland, now me."

"We don't know that for sure."

"Don't we? The evidence is stacking up against him."

"You're jumping to conclusions. I can't speak to what Beck saw or didn't see. But what you saw was a car that looked like Palmer's. But you didn't actually see the driver. Unless you've thought about it and changed your mind?"

She clutched the edge of the counter in frustration. "No. I didn't see the driver. But what are the odds after everything else that happened today, with us knowing he was in the area, that someone driving a car exactly like his tried to kill me, without it being him?"

"Slow down, Detective. You're making assumptions without facts to back them up. I'll send Detective Mills up there in the morning to work with Gatlinburg PD to investigate the accident—"

"It wasn't an accident, sir. The guy pulled right up to the guardrail to gloat about what he'd done. If it was an accident, he'd have gotten out of the car and called down to me, asked if I was okay, called 911. Instead, he drove away. Like the coward he is."

"I'll agree they were a coward, whoever was in that car. But you don't know that it was Palmer. It could just have easily been some teenager who accidentally bumped your SUV. When he saw the aftermath, he was scared and took off. A hit and run. That kind of thing happens all the time."

"You're not even going to pursue Palmer, are you?"

He sighed heavily. "Yes. We're going to talk to Palmer, investigate what happened, see if he was involved. The truth will come out. And if I have to call the mayor to pressure Palmer to come in for an interview, I will. We'll get him on video and ask the hard questions. And I'll ask

Gatlinburg PD to do a courtesy check on his car tomorrow, see if there's any damage."

"Tomorrow? Why not look at it tonight? You could ask Gatlinburg PD to go to Palmer's mom's house right now. We can't risk him fixing it if you wait. Or switching cars to conceal what happened."

"Are you listening to yourself right now? If he hit you as hard as you said, his bumper will be damaged. He can't fix and repaint something like that overnight. As for switching his car, come on, Bree. Gatlinburg PD will verify the VIN number against his insurance. This isn't their first gig. You're tired and not thinking straight. You've suffered a traumatic event. You're reacting like a victim instead of a detective."

"Yeah, well, there's a reason for that."

He chuckled. "I'll give you that one. Hang loose for a little while longer. You said you're at Beck's place right now. Where's it located? I can send one of our guys out there to bring you home. Obviously you won't be driving your police-issued SUV."

"No kidding." She speared a hand through her hair and shoved it out of her face. "His cabin's at the bottom of Prescott Mountain. But I don't see any point in making someone drive almost two hours to get me and two hours back. It's already late. Ryland said I can use his guest room. And Faith, one of the UB investigators, was nice enough to pick me up a couple of outfits to choose from and some toiletries from an all-night box store over here. She even got me a phone since mine was destroyed. I'll be fine until Mills comes up tomorrow to investigate what happened. He can take me home when he heads back."

"That works. We'll talk again tomorrow. But don't plan on working for a while. I mean it. You don't come back to the office until you take a minimum of a week off. And when you come back, you'll have to meet with the department's shrink and get a note to return to active duty."

She clenched her hand into a fist. "I don't need to take a week off, or even a day. Physically, I'm fine. And I'm not suffering from PTSD. I have work to do."

"No, Detective. You don't. We'll divvy up your cases to the rest of the team, share the load. Can you imagine what a defense attorney could spin for a jury if he found out you worked on his client's case after a traumatic event, without taking some downtime and seeing a therapist? That reasonable doubt threshold would be gone. I'm not taking any chances. One week and a doctor's note. If the doc won't sign off after a week, you stay gone however long he thinks you need. I mean it."

"Sir—"

"No more arguing. That's an order. I don't want you calling for updates on the investigation either. As far as I'm concerned, you're a civilian right now. Rest, relax, no working on the case. And if something changes with your situation, if you even have a twinge of a headache or a weird pain somewhere, go to the hospital. Understood?"

Her shoulders slumped in defeat. "Understood."

"Good night, Detective."

"Night, sir."

"Oh, and Bree?" His voice softened. "I'm glad you're okay."

The emotion that leaked through his tone had her throat tightening. "Thank you, sir." She ended the call and shook her head.

"I take it that didn't go the way you'd hoped."

She turned to see Ryland, standing by the sink about

five feet away. Her mouth went dry. Her arms ached to wrap around his waist, hold him tight. He'd saved her. Worse, he'd almost died doing it. What kind of man risked his life like that for a woman he'd only just met? She already knew the answer: a special, amazing man. A man she selfishly wanted to save her again, from the sea of emotions threatening to drown her.

He frowned with concern. "Bree?"

Reminding herself there was a roomful of people on the other side of the wall, she tamped down her emotions and put on a brave front. Or tried to.

"The call definitely didn't go the way I wanted. My *hope* was that my boss would take me seriously and go after Palmer. But he wants to take it slow and easy. Examine his car tomorrow, ask him to come in for an interview."

"What would you do in his situation?"

She was about to say she'd arrest Palmer, but instead of flippantly answering his question, she took a moment to think it through. She gave him a reluctant smile. "Honestly, without allowing emotion to cloud my judgment, I'd do the same thing as Peterson. Investigate. Gather the facts. Then decide on a course of action."

"Now there's the savvy investigator I met this morning. Although, after what we've been through together, it feels like we've known each other for years. Like we went through a war together and lived to tell the tale."

"Survivors," she whispered, barely able to force out the word. "We're survivors." The horror of everything that had happened slammed into her, leaving her shaking. To her shame, a tear rolled down her cheek. She wiped it away and drew several deep breaths, fighting to glue the pieces of her composure together before she completely lost it.

Suddenly his arms were around her, pulling her against his chest. "It's okay, Bree. Everything's going to be okay. You're safe. No one's going to hurt you here. Take it one step at a time. We've got this. Us survivors."

She threw her arms around his waist and melted against him, hugging him tight. If anyone else had offered her sympathy right now, and a safe place to land, she'd have broken, shattered into a thousand pieces beneath the weight of what had happened tonight. But somehow, Ryland's arms around her were the strength she'd needed to keep holding on. And she instinctively knew, no matter how hard things got, that he'd always be there for her. They'd formed an unbreakable bond tonight. And here, in his arms, she finally had what she'd been needing, the knowledge that she was safe.

A few moments later, the muted sound of someone laughing in the family room had her reluctantly pulling out of his arms and stepping back. She hastily wiped at the tears on her cheeks, her face heating.

"No rush," he told her. "We can stand here all night if that's what you need. Or I can hold you again, if that's what you want. Everyone else can wait."

She let out a shaky breath. "Careful what you offer. I was already crushing on you before all this, so it wouldn't take much to tempt me back in your arms."

A slow, sexy grin curved his mouth. "Consider me warned. Notice that I'm not running. I'm staying right here, with you. My offer's still open. And if you're not ready to talk about what happened, I can send everyone else home. They can come back tomorrow, or the day after that. Or never. You don't have to talk to anyone until or unless you're ready, and you want to."

She stared at him, slowly shaking her head. "You're an amazing man, Ryland."

His gaze locked on hers. His Adam's apple bobbed in his throat as he swallowed. Then he slowly closed the distance between them again. "Bree—"

She side-stepped him, her emotions too ragged to risk him touching her again, even though she wanted it, needed it, so badly she ached. Before, his touch had given her strength. Now she was afraid if he touched her, she would break.

He frowned and leaned back against the nearest counter.

She wrapped her arms around her waist. "Your friends have been patiently waiting for me to get off the phone. They care about you and deserve to know the details about how you almost got killed."

His eyes widened. "This isn't about me."

"It's your team. Of course it's about you. I'm happy to tell them everything I can about tonight."

He frowned. "I don't think you understand why they're—"

"It's really okay. After we talk, I'll catch some shut-eye, then head to Madisonville tomorrow when one of my teammates picks me up. I'll be out of your hair, and you can get back to your usual routine." She headed toward the archway and into the family room.

# Chapter Fourteen

Ryland recognized the signs of fatigue in Bree's posture as she curled her legs beneath her on the couch beside him. She was being incredibly patient, answering his team's questions, repeating the details as many times as needed. He filled in what he knew, trying to help. But she was the only one who'd been there when she was run off the road. And she'd been stranded for hours before he'd come along.

When Trent started to ask another question, Ryland held up his hands. "Enough. Let's stop the inquisition for the night. Bree needs to rest."

Her eyes widened. "No, no, it's okay. I don't mind answering more questions."

"I mind. You're exhausted. And to be honest, so am I."

"Whoa," Trent said. "You're not going to pass out again are you?"

Ryland narrowed his eyes. "Just remember, I'm the one divvying out assignments."

"Assignments?" Bree asked. "Are they helping you look into the Slayer case?"

"Sort of," Ryland said. "Chief Russo called me after you left UB earlier and updated me on the ME's findings. The murder victim we found has already been identified.

Her name was Patricia Rogers. She was white, twenty-eight years old—"

"Wait," Bree said. "Patricia Rogers from Monroe County? *That* Patricia Rogers?"

"She's from your county, yes. I don't know if there's more than one person with that name there. Possible friend of yours?"

She scoffed. "Hardly. If she's who I think she is, I arrested her several years ago for attempted murder—of her five-year-old daughter. Palmer did everything he could to put her away, but the charges didn't stick. Not enough evidence to convince the jury. But she definitely did it. Thankfully, family services was able to terminate her parental rights and rehome her children with loving families."

"That's the basic background Chief Russo gave me, so I'm guessing the victim is the woman you arrested. I'm surprised your boss didn't mention it when he was talking to you earlier."

"I'm not. He's forced me to take a week off from work. He probably didn't want to tell me anything that might get me more interested in this recent murder investigation, emphasis on recent. I'm pretty sure I've seen Patricia around town at least a few times over the past month."

"That's spot-on with what the ME said. He figured one to two weeks. Gatlinburg PD is reaching out to an entomologist to try to narrow down the time of death estimate even further."

"Did he weigh in on whether he believed the body was intentionally buried, or it was concealed naturally, by falling leaves?" she asked.

"I haven't heard anything about that yet."

Trent cleared his throat. "Mind if I jump in here?"

"You already have," Ryland said drily.

Trent grinned. "Then I'll keep going. There are only so many coincidences that can happen before we agree they can't be coincidences. Palmer's name has come up too many times. The fact that he has a link to this latest victim seals the deal. He's involved in all of this, some-how. I'm inclined to side with Bree that he might be the one who forced her off the cliff."

She winced.

Ryland put his hand on hers. She gave him a grateful smile. But when Faith arched her brows from the other couch across from him, he cleared his throat and pulled his hand back. "Let's wrap this up. Bree, the main rea-son everyone is here tonight isn't to check on me. It's be-cause when Grayson called earlier for a briefing on what happened, and I updated him on the ME's findings, he gave us a new directive. We're putting all of our other casework on hold so we can look into this latest murder, and what happened to you tonight, as well as the Slayer case to see how it relates to everything else going on."

Bree blinked in surprise. "Why would he do that? I thought you have to work cases for all the other counties."

"We do. Believe me, it's going to be a royal pain ex-plaining to everyone that we're not actively working their investigations. But Grayson doesn't care. As he put it, he wants to make sure that no one else loses their life on his mountain ever again."

Ryland arched a brow at Trent. "That plays directly into your first assignment. You're in charge of guardrails. You get to head up a construction project to put a bet-ter safety barrier in place to help ensure another vehicle doesn't go off the side of Prescott Mountain."

Trent groaned. Everyone around him laughed.

Ryland continued divvying up assignments. "Lance, Faith, Asher, you'll shadow Gatlinburg PD on the investigation into Patricia Rogers's murder. Be sure to offer our lab's assistance. Nicely but strongly encourage them to allow an Amido Black test on the victim's skin for the killer's fingerprints. Obviously that's a long shot since the ME's report said very little skin remained on any of the remains. But if there are any testable areas, we want to do it. Make sure you let them know if they do end up getting fingerprints on the skin that way, there's a program the FBI has that can identify the victim's skin pattern and remove it from a picture, hopefully leaving just the killer's fingerprints. Our FBI contacts should allow them the use of that program.

"I'd also like you to try to figure out the identity of the man who was in the road this morning near where we found Rogers's grave. He looked like Palmer to me, which is really weird if he's not Palmer. Whoever he is, we need to know why he was standing in the road."

"You got it," Faith said.

"Trent, I'll give you a break even though you don't deserve it after teasing me. Have Brice help you with the guard rail project. You can both do some real investigating on the side. I want you to find out who clipped Bree's bumper. Make sure you personally see Palmer's car and can verify whether it's been in an accident."

"Trent," Bree said. "Palmer's still here, in Gatlinburg. My boss should be able to provide his mother's address. Supposedly that's where he's staying, and where his car will be."

He nodded his appreciation, then gave Ryland a grateful look. "Thanks for letting me in on the investigation, in spite of the teasing."

"Don't be so quick to thank me. You and Brice have one of the hardest, most important jobs. We need to find out whether someone was specifically targeting Bree or not. If they're targeting her, we need to know why, and we need to know ASAP. If they tried killing her once, they'll try again."

Bree tensed beside him, her face going pale.

Ryland gave her a reassuring smile. "We're on it, Bree. Don't worry."

She nodded, but couldn't manage an answering smile. Ryland was getting more and more worried about her. He had a feeling she was near a breaking point.

"We really need to wrap this up," he said, noting how pale she looked. "The Slayer case, and any ties to the most recent crimes, becomes our main focus now. Ivy and Callum, starting tomorrow, you're going to live and breathe the Slayer cold case."

"And me," Bree said. "I can help too."

Ryland frowned. "You're supposed to be recuperating, not working. Your boss—"

"I'll deal with my boss. And I'm not about to sit around and do nothing while you're running the overall investigation. We both went through the same ordeal."

"Hardly. I didn't take a terrifying ride over a guardrail and hang in a tree for hours. My involvement was next to nothing compared to what you went through. You need to take it easy."

Her jaw tightened. "Not happening. If you don't want my help, I'll dig into this on my own. If it wasn't personal before, it is now. Don't try to shut me out."

"She has a point," Faith said. "I vote she gets to work on it."

"This isn't a democracy," Ryland said. "You don't get to vote."

Faith rolled her eyes.

Ryland shook his head. "Why do I get the impression none of you are nearly as intimidated by me as you should be?"

Faith grinned. "He caved, Bree. You're in."

Bree glanced back and forth between them. "He did? I am?"

Ryland sighed. "You are. For now. We'll see how it goes."

Faith gave Bree a thumbs-up.

Ryland couldn't help laughing. "All right. Everyone remember, even though we're splitting the team between two active case investigations and one cold one, we still follow standard procedures." He motioned to the dark-haired man sitting next to the very blonde Faith. "That means keeping our resident TBI liaison, Rowan, informed and involved in all decisions that can impact the future ability to prosecute any suspects we identify."

He checked his watch. "It's, good grief, almost two in the morning. Everyone get some sleep."

Everyone stood to go. Faith hesitated, glancing at Bree. "Are you sure you're okay staying here? I've got an extra room if you prefer to crash there."

Bree blinked. "I, ah—"

"She's staying here," Ryland announced. "Good night, everyone."

Faith's brows raised. She looked at Bree, waiting.

"I'll stay here," Bree told her. "But thanks for the offer."

"Anytime. Take care."

Soon, Ryland was locking the front door behind the

last of the investigators. His shoulders slumped with exhaustion as he headed back into the family room. It was empty. Bree was gone.

"Bree?" He called her name and checked the kitchen first. Empty. "Bree?"

"In here."

He followed the sound of her voice down the back hallway to the guest room at the end. She was standing in the doorway, her face still alarmingly pale.

She gave him a tentative smile and motioned toward the bedroom. "I appreciate you letting me stay here tonight."

He hooked his thumbs in his belt loops. "You're welcome to stay here as long as you want."

Her eyes widened. "Did you forget my warning in the kitchen earlier?"

"If you're trying to scare me away, telling me you have a crush on me isn't the way to do it."

"That doesn't scare you, huh?"

He slowly shook his head. "Not even a little."

Her stomach jumped nervously. "Ryland, why do you have such a phobia about heights?"

He stiffened.

She stepped into the hallway and put her hand against his chest. "I'm sorry. I shouldn't have asked. Don't be angry."

He sighed heavily. "I'm not angry. Just…tired. Some other time, okay?"

He fingers flexed against his chest. "Of course. Ryland?"

His pulse thudded in his ears at the feel of her hand. "Hm?"

"I never got to thank you for saving my life. Do you mind if I thank you now?"

"You don't have to thank me, I—"

"I want to. Please."

"Ah, okay, sure. But I—"

She stood on tiptoe, then reached up and pulled his head down toward her. By the time he realized what she was going to do, she was plastered against him and kissing him the way he'd craved since the moment he'd seen her at UB headquarters.

She kissed him with wild abandon, stroking his tongue with hers, making him groan deep in his throat. He speared his hands through her long hair, turning and pressing her against the wall. Every nerve ending inside him was on fire, for her, as he took control of the kiss. It went on and on, until they finally broke apart, panting, gasping for breath, staring at each other in wonder.

Her passion-glazed eyes searched his, her lips slightly parted as she struggled to steady her breathing.

He was in even worse shape. There was no denying what that kiss had done to him. And when her gaze dipped down, her eyes widened, clearly seeing his predicament.

"Wow," she said. "Impressive."

He laughed. "Wow yourself. Feel free to thank me any time you want."

Her lips curved in a sultry smile. "I'm not warning you again. When this case, these cases, whatever—when it's over, maybe we can—"

"Oh. Yeah," he said. "Definitely."

She swallowed, then drew a ragged breath. "But right now, as much as I'd like to, we can't…you know…because, well, while we're working together in any capacity, even if I'm basically on leave, I should focus, you should focus. We can't…until…" She drew another ragged breath. "Good night, Ry."

He was careful to hide his disappointment as she turned back toward the bedroom. "Good night, Bree."

The door closed.

He stood there a long moment, still trying to get his breathing under control, not to mention the rest of his body.

Suddenly, climbing down a cliff didn't seem like such a big deal anymore. Not if it got that kind of reaction from Bree. He wondered if she'd still be interested in him if she realized just how hard he was falling for her. She'd no doubt been considering an affair, something short term. It would scare her right back to Madisonville if she realized that he was already envisioning a possible future with her.

A future that would be dang near impossible since they lived two hours away from each other. Of course, that hurdle paled in comparison to the real problem.

Someone had tried to kill her today.

And they might try again.

He clenched his fists and headed down the hallway to his own bedroom. From here on out, he was sticking with Bree, whether she wanted him to or not. At least until they caught the guy who'd sent her over the cliff. Because even though it defied belief, she already mattered to him more than any other woman ever had. And he wasn't about to stand by and let some maniac hurt her.

# *Chapter Fifteen*

Bree had originally refused when Ryland encouraged her to stay at his cabin while on leave from her job. But the appeal of him having her back if the man who'd forced her off the cliff came after her was too hard to resist. Especially since the identity of that man was still in question. According to Gatlinburg PD, Palmer hadn't gone to his mother's house as he'd told Sheriff Peterson he would. No one knew where he was right now. Which meant no one had seen his car, and whether or not it was damaged.

Bree, of course, believed Palmer had disappeared so he could get the damage fixed. All she could do was hope that once he finally reappeared, an expert would be able to determine whether the vehicle had been repaired. Of course, if it hadn't been repaired, then she was back to having no clue who was trying to kill her.

For the past few days, Bree and Ryland had spent their time mostly at his cabin, discussing the ongoing investigations and fielding calls from the UB investigators—with the exception of Ivy and Callum. Those two preferred to review the Slayer files on their own first, without being swayed by Bree's opinions or perspective.

Even though Bree longed to be officially back at work, it was no hardship waking up to gorgeous Ryland every day. Of course, waking up to him in the same bed as her would have been far better. But they were keeping things professional, or as professional as they could in spite of the undercurrents of attraction sparking between them. The memory of that earth-shattering kiss was never far from the surface. Pretending it had never happened was becoming more and more difficult. So when Ivy finally asked Bree to come to UB headquarters to give her perspective on the Slayer killings, she and Ryland had jumped at the chance.

Bree lined up five photos in the middle of the conference room table. "Now that I've provided the overview on the murder scenes and what we did to investigate the crimes, let's take it back to victimology. These are our five victims, during happier times obviously. Ada Cardenas was a single mom, never married, with one child. Tammy Wilcox was also single, but no kids." She pointed to a third picture. "Robyn Morton, divorced, no kids. These two at the end are Candy Morrison and Joanna Sanford, the only victims who were married. Joanna had kids. Candy didn't."

Ryland looked across the table at Ivy and Callum. "The victims couldn't be more different physically either. As you can see, their hair varies from blond to dark brown, short to long, straight to curly. They're all relatively young, but there's still a variation in their ages. The main thing they seem to have in common is that they're attractive females."

Ivy idly tapped the table. "That's what Callum and I concluded too. What about geographical similarities? I don't know your county, Bree, so that's hard to glean just from their addresses."

Bree arranged the pictures into three groups. "These

two lived in sparsely populated rural areas. This one lived in town just a mile from the Madisonville Sheriff's office. While she—" she pointed to the picture of Candy "—lived in the suburbs. And the very last one, Ada Cardenas, was actually the first victim. She's the one we found near the border with Blount County, in the foothills of the mountains. Of course, regardless of where they actually lived, their bodies were discovered outdoors, in wooded areas."

Callum shook his head. "Their educational backgrounds are different too. Four of the five were college-educated, middle class. But one never finished high school and lived in poverty, relying on social safety nets to help her make ends meet."

"Occupations are inconsistent too," Ivy said. "They were all paid by the hour as opposed to earning a salary. But some had blue-collar service jobs while others had white-collar office jobs." She sat back in her chair.

Bree crossed her arms on top of the table. "You're starting to run into the same roadblocks my team ran into. We couldn't find any ways where these five people's paths might have crossed. They didn't know each other. They didn't date the same people or have the same friends. They didn't even shop at the same grocery stores. While that makes it hard to figure out how they were targeted, it does reinforce the idea of a stranger as their killer. Our working theory was that these were randomly chosen victims of opportunity."

"No foreign DNA was found," Ryland said. "At any of the murder scenes, right?"

"Right."

Ivy blew out a breath, obviously frustrated. "I don't like assuming these are all done by the same killer without forensic evidence to tie them together. But seeing the similarity in how the bodies were dumped, where they were dumped, and the fact that they were all strangled is certainly compelling."

"Did you notice the medical examiner reports?" Bree asked. "All of their fingernails were cut short, and bleach was used to wash their fingertips."

"Bleach." Ivy leaned forward, resting her arms on the table. "I totally missed that."

"Twelve boxes of reports are a lot to go through in just a few days." Bree smiled.

Ivy returned the smile. "Did he wash any other part of the bodies in bleach?"

"Just the fingers. Some of the victims had bruises on the sides of their rib cages. All of them had bruising on their necks. Our working theory was that he had each victim on their back and straddled them, his thighs pressed against the sides of their ribs as he strangled them. The bruising indicates he used his hands."

Callum straightened. "Were the necks swabbed for DNA?"

"They were. None was found."

Callum settled back in his seat, looking disappointed. "He wore gloves."

"Most likely. And his victims fought him, probably scratched him, which explains the clipped and bleached nails."

Callum slowly nodded. "Years ago, we would have profiled him as a cop or someone in law enforcement because he knows about forensics. He murders them somewhere else, then takes them to a dump site, minimizing the amount of forensic evidence we might find. Especially in the woods, where the elements and wildlife are likely to scatter and destroy anything of forensic value. And he uses bleach to destroy DNA."

"Years ago," Bree said. "But not now. Because everyone who has a TV knows about basic forensics."

He smiled. "Exactly. Really makes our jobs harder."

"It certainly does," she said. "There are more specific similarities in the autopsy reports, such as ligature marks and the types of bruises they exhibited. Again, working theory is that he abducts them, probably at gunpoint or knifepoint to get them to comply. Then he takes them to the primary site, which we believe might be his home, perhaps rural, isolated from anyone who might hear them scream. He ties them upright in a chair—based on the ligature marks—and, although he doesn't sexually abuse them, he does torture them. He has a fondness for knives, to cut, not to stab."

Bree looked at Ryland. "Has UB received a copy yet of the ME's report on Patricia Rogers? Did she have similar injuries?"

He shook his head. "Other than Chief Russo's phone call about the victim's identity, there hasn't been anything further yet from the medical examiner. Unless Callum or Ivy heard something I haven't?"

"No," Ivy said. "But we hope to have the report soon. Bree, I haven't gotten a good feel for how long he holds each victim before he kills them. Seems to vary quite a bit. But I need to review more documents to be sure."

"Based on the timelines we constructed, it appears that he holds them for less than a day. In one case, as little as four hours. Another, it was almost twelve."

Ryland pulled the five pictures toward him. He carefully studied each one. His eyes held a mixture of sadness and anger when he slid the pictures back to the middle.

"I know you collaborated with the FBI on this. But the profile I saw was woefully inadequate."

"The FBI was pretty slammed and couldn't devote the resources we needed. Although we were told if we got another victim, to contact them again and they'd re-evaluate their case load."

Ryland's jaw tightened. "How nice of them."

She shrugged. "To be fair, they were in the middle of a terrorist investigation at the time. I think they did the best they could. We sent information to them and worked with a special agent remotely, through emails and over the phone. He studied the case files and provided suggestions of how to proceed. The seemingly-generic profile they gave us will probably match the suspect once we figure out the killer's identity. But as an investigative tool, it's pretty much worthless."

"Can I see it again?" Ryland asked.

She stood and walked up and down the table, checking the labels on the various boxes and folders, before sorting through one of the boxes at the far end. She pulled out a slim manila folder and gave it to Ryland before resuming her seat.

He pulled out the profile and set it on the table. Ivy and Callum leaned in on either side of him, skimming the contents.

"White male, twenty-five to thirty-five," Ryland said. "That describes about ninety percent of serial killers ever caught."

Bree nodded. "Kind of my take on it too. Since the victims vary in race, I don't even put much stock in the assumption that the killer is white. I think that was a guess, more than anything, based on most serial killers being white males. We should keep an open mind on the killer's race."

She motioned toward the folder. "The profile says he's an organized killer, which again is no surprise since he was meticulous about leaving no forensic clues behind."

Ryland handed the profile to Ivy, who moved to sit beside Callum to read the rest of it.

"Any more questions?" Bree asked. "I think I reviewed all the main points."

"Not yet," Ivy said, "but I reserve the right to ask more as I dig further into the files."

"Of course," Bree said. "I've got time off right now, whether I want it or not. Happy to help in any way that I can."

"Normally," Ryland said, "with cold cases like this, where a serial killer is suspected, we'd try to disprove that the victims are linked. But since the FBI reviewed the case and doesn't dispute the link, we'll accept that premise. Agreed?"

Callum and Ivy, who had finished reading the profile, both nodded.

"Any suggestions you want to offer?" Ivy asked him.

"Re-visit each crime scene as if this is day one and it's a fresh murder," Ryland said. "Focus on victimology. Start with family then build a list of everyone the victims knew—friends, enemies, where they worked. Re-interview key people. Begin to build a timeline. Use the original case as a skeleton but understand some of the bones may be missing or belong to another skeleton altogether. Check cell phone records. Get an expert to perform tool mark analysis on those marked trees, at every scene—including the current one if we can get access to it. Look for the victims' diaries, appointment books.

Go through the evidence locker for that and see if their families have old calendars or something that was the victim's that might have more timeline information on them. Even though it doesn't seem useful, go ahead and perform geographical profiling, inclusive of the latest murder. Maybe we can gain an understanding of why the killer may have moved, if it is the same killer."

Bree's head was spinning, listening to everything he was saying. But Ivy and Callum nodded as if it was all part of their normal routine—and maybe it was. They both took notes, just the same.

"Set up social media sites to stir interest by the public," Ryland continued. "Use the Smoky Mountain Slayer name. Sensationalize it. You'll generate a lot more hits that way. Encourage comments and posts of any information about the victims. Oh, and you might want to submit the cases to the Project Cold Case website."

"Project Cold Case?" Bree asked.

"It's a website that encourages people to upload information about cold cases, to get more eyes on it. You never know when a helpful tip will come along."

She nodded, amazed that he knew about things like that. She'd never heard of it. And she hadn't used social media the way he was describing it. During her time on the Slayer case, she'd searched social media to learn about the victims, not necessarily to generate leads. Ryland was constantly impressing her.

"Callum, let's see if our lab can extract a usable DNA profile from the evidence in all five killings. Work with Rowan to maintain chain of custody and move the evidence to the lab for testing. Technology changes all the time. Maybe samples were too small to test four and five years ago when the victims were murdered. But touch

DNA technology is incredible these days. We might get lucky."

"I'll text him now. We'll start with the first victim since killers tend to make mistakes early on before they perfect their craft. Odds are better that if there's some DNA to be had, it'll come from that evidence."

"Good thinking," Ryland said. "Ivy, I'd like you to work with one of our profiler consultants to get a fresh profile, one that includes the latest murder, and one that doesn't—since we don't know yet whether this latest one is related. Maybe our profiler will have better luck at providing something useful. You can compare the profile with any names that come up while looking at each of the victims. Hopefully we'll generate at least a few leads that way."

"You got it." She added to her list on the computer tablet she was using.

"Let's get the team to start reporting status daily, end of day," Ryland said. "And since the team is scattered around, from here to Monroe County, we'll do the status meetings via computer. Callum, can you set the meetings up for, say, the next week, and send the links to everyone?"

"I can get that out before lunch," he said.

"Great. Thanks. Oh, one more thing. This is a side item I'm curious about but really doesn't further our efforts to solve the Slayer case or the recent events. Still, it's bothering me, so I'd appreciate it if one of you could get the ball rolling, maybe pull in Brice or someone else if you need to."

"Of course." Callum said. "What do you need?"

"Palmer has a near-perfect winning record with his prosecutions. We're talking unheard of percentages, suspiciously high. I want to know what he's doing to make that happen. Maybe pull in a private investigator local to Monroe County who can plug into the town gossip and do some digging. If Palmer's on the up-and-up, fine. If not, I want to know what's going on. If it's something nefarious, I'll present the information to Sheriff Peterson and let him decide what to do about it."

Bree touched Ryland's sleeve. "I appreciate you doing that. It never occurred to me to look into those numbers."

"It's been bugging me since you mentioned it. Might as well see if there's a reason for that."

"I'll take care of it," Callum said. "Anything else?"

"No. I think you and Ivy have more than enough to do right now. Take it a step at a time. If it gets to be too much, ask someone else on the team for help or bring in a consultant to do legwork.

"Bree," Ryland continued, "you'll notice that I allocated our team mostly toward current events. Lance, Faith and Asher are working Patricia Rogers's murder. Trent and Brice are splitting their work between shoring up the safety system on the road out front and working with Gatlinburg PD and your office to investigate how your SUV went off the mountain. And Rowan, our TBI liaison, is working mainly with both of those teams. That's six people working the active investigations, while only Ivy and Callum have been assigned to work specifically on these cold cases." He motioned toward the pictures of the five victims.

"I did notice, actually," she said. "But I'm not complaining. The Rogers murder does appear to be the work of the Slayer. So it makes sense to focus on the one with the freshest evidence. And I appreciate your team trying to find out who ran me off the road and endangered you.

If it was on purpose, I want to ensure no one is targeting me and will make another attempt at trying to kill me." She gave a nervous laugh, but no one else laughed.

"That's my number one priority," he said. "I'd like you to continue to stay with me until we figure out who might be after you."

She stared at him, surprised. "I have to go back home soon. My job won't wait forever."

As if on cue, Ivy and Callum moved to the far side of the table and began pulling more files out of the boxes.

Ryland leaned forward, resting his forearms on the table. "I'd prefer you continue to stay with me. It's safer. I can escort you home to pack a bag, if you want. Or take you to a store here to get more clothes. But I really don't think you should be alone. It's too dangerous."

She blinked, not sure what to say. Part of her longed to stay in his cabin, to see him every day. But how much longer could she do that and keep her heart intact? He seemed so perfect for her, in every way. But there was no forever for the two of them. There couldn't be, not with their separate careers two hours apart. And every day they were together would just make it that much harder to leave.

He was watching her intently, waiting for her answer.

She cleared her throat. "I, ah, I'm not sure that—"

His phone buzzed in his pocket. He frowned and checked the screen. "Sorry, I have to take this." He punched the button. "Trent, what've you got?"

By the time Ryland ended the call, Ivy and Callum had moved back to stand with Bree, expectantly watching him. The look on his face and the tone of his voice had alerted all of them that something important had happened.

He closely watched Bree as he updated them. "Trent's

in Madisonville. He's been staking out Prosecutor Palmer's house, waiting for him to finally return home. Palmer pulled into his driveway about an hour ago. Bree, he didn't fix his car as you'd feared. The right front part of his bumper is messed up. And there's a white streak of paint across it."

"Son of a… I knew it," Bree said. "I knew he was the one who ran into me." She headed toward the door. "We need to head to Madisonville. I want to be there when Peterson arrests him and—"

"Bree. There's more."

The tone of his voice had her turning around, a feeling of dread shooting through her.

He followed her to the door and stopped in front of her. "Your boss had someone performing surveillance too, one of your detectives. They had Palmer in handcuffs the second he pulled up. Of course, when they showed Palmer the damage to his car, he acted shocked. He claimed someone must have hit it while it was parked on the street. But since he hadn't gone around to the other side, he hadn't noticed the damage."

"Of course he'd say that," Bree said. "I'm just relieved that Sheriff Peterson stepped up. He must have believed me after all to have put Palmer's house under surveillance. Where has Palmer been hiding out all this time?"

He glanced at Ivy and Callum before answering. "I don't know for sure. He claimed he was stressed out over everything that was happening and drove around Tennessee, staying at hotels here and there. Peterson is verifying that. But, Bree, they didn't arrest him because of the bumper. They arrested him because a few hours ago, they found another body in the woods, in Monroe County. And this time, they have video. It shows Palmer driving his car into those woods, then hightailing it out of there just before someone discovered the body. He's been arrested for murder."

Moving to the nearest chair, she slowly sat, nausea making her stomach churn. "Someone else has been killed?"

His eyes were sad as he nodded, then motioned toward the media wall at the end of the room. "Ivy, since you're the closest, would you mind turning on the screen and opening the video link that Trent just sent us? He said the story's blowing up the airwaves in Madisonville right now. Bree, you weren't kidding when you said the press had been stirred up in your county. They're all over this."

The screen turned on. Seconds later, Ivy had the news feed from Madisonville tuned in. The conference room was silent except for the reporter's voice, sensationalizing every little piece of information they had, accurate or not. And behind her, a video kept looping of Prosecutor Palmer being hustled out of a police SUV in handcuffs at the back of the police station.

"I'll hand it to your sheriff," Ryland said. "He did try to keep it quiet. He took him around back instead of doing a perp walk out front."

"He's not the type to do a perp walk, says it's undignified for law enforcement to put someone on parade that way." She shook her head. "Any idea how the reporters got wind of this so fast? Even knowing our press people the way I do, I'm surprised they were at the police station and got those pictures."

"Trent said they…" Ryland motioned toward the TV. "Looks like they're showing that part right now."

They watched in silence as another reporter interviewed the owner of a gas station. He pointed to the woods behind him and told the reporter about a body being found there early this morning, saying that he was in early working on repairs and looked outside.

"He's describing Palmer's car," Bree said. "He was there when it drove into the woods. Is that what happened? He called the police because he saw a suspicious car?"

"That's the story, Trent said. Looks like they're going into those details now."

They watched the rest of the broadcast. When it started over again, as "breaking news," Ivy shut down the feed.

"They didn't mention the victim," Bree said. "Other than that they found a body. Was Trent able to get any information on who was killed? And how?"

"That information has been withheld and Peterson hasn't spoken to him yet."

"At least the family won't hear about their loved one on TV. I hope the autopsy can help ID the victim fast and the family is notified before anyone else figures out who was killed. Do we even know whether it's a male or female?"

"No clue at all."

She stood. "What a mess. My fellow detectives are going to be bombarded by reporters and all kinds of false tips will be called in. It's like the original Slayer case all over again. I need to be there to help them."

Ryland crossed his arms. "I don't suppose I can convince you not to go? To lay low at my place like I was saying earlier? It's better not to take chances with your safety."

"While I appreciate that you want to protect me, I'm not the delicate flower you seem to think I am. I'm going to Madisonville, with or without you."

"Your purse is at the bottom of the ravine, along with

your credit cards and ID. That will make it impossible for you to rent a car."

"Blackmail, Ryland? Really?"

"I prefer to call it protection detail. If Palmer isn't the one who tried to kill you—"

"His car is damaged, with white paint on it. He's the one who hit my SUV."

"If he's not," he repeated, "you're still safer staying here. With me."

"Safer or not, I'm not hiding out when my team needs me. And you don't hold all the cards like you think you do. Faith not only brought me clothes and toiletries the other night, she brought me a phone and a UB credit card in case I needed anything else. I've got my personal car at home, with an extra set of keys, cash, and an emergency credit card. I'm all set. I just need a ride to get there. I've already got an account with a driver service. I can call them to pick me up and use my card that's on file." She pulled out her phone as if ready to call for a ride. "Or you can drive me to Madisonville and beg my forgiveness the whole way for trying to dictate where I go and what I do."

Callum laughed, but quickly sobered when Ryland shot him an aggravated look.

"Put the phone away." Ryland's mouth curved in a reluctant grin. "You win. I'll drive you. But I won't be begging your forgiveness. I'll be talking your ear off, trying to talk some sense into you, the whole way there."

# Chapter Sixteen

Telling Bree that he'd "talk some sense into her" had apparently not been a good strategy. All Ryland had managed to do was rile her up even more so that the first half of their trip to Madisonville was spent in stony silence with her refusing to say anything.

The second half of the trip, they'd had a vigorous discussion about the case and her role in it. He'd finally gotten her to agree that it made sense for her not to go directly to the sheriff's office to demand an update on the interrogation of Prosecutor Dane Palmer. Of course, that was partly based on him refusing to drive downtown.

Her personal car was in her garage. And since she'd gotten her spare key from her neighbor, there was nothing else Ryland could do to force her to not destroy her own career. But he'd used psychology to stall her for at least a few more minutes. He'd convinced her that if she wanted her boss to take her seriously and not fire her on the spot for ignoring his orders, she might want to change her clothes. Although she certainly looked great to Ryland, he doubted the T-shirt and jeans that Faith had brought her would add much weight to her argument that she was ready to get back to work.

As soon as Bree had disappeared into her bedroom,

Ryland had been on the phone with Trent. He'd gotten to Bree's house in record time, probably breaking all the speed limits between the sheriff's office and her home. He'd managed to get here before Bree had come back out. Now he was sitting in the family room, giving Ryland an update.

And the information he had changed everything.

A door closed down the hallway. A few moments later, Bree rounded the corner into the family room, looking even better than the first time Ryland had seen her, which didn't seem possible. Her incredible figure was impossible to disguise, even with loose pleated pants, a dark blouse that covered any hint of cleavage, and a navy-blue blazer that screamed professional businesswoman. It almost made him think he should have put on a suit instead of jeans. Almost. He really hated suits.

She'd done something with her beautiful blond hair too. It was tamed into some kind of fancy braid. And her fresh makeup emphasized her intriguing hazel eyes and plump pink lips. She was absolutely stunning.

"Hi, Trent." She glanced curiously back and forth between them as she handed the UB credit card to Ryland. "I've grabbed my second set of keys, some cash and my emergency backup credit card from my safe. I don't need the UB card now." She moved past him and sat in the chair facing him and Trent on the couch. "What's going on? Trent, are you heading downtown with us?"

"No. He's not," Ryland said, finally finding his voice. "We're not going downtown."

"I'll, uh, just head out," Trent said. "I've got a few more things to look into."

"Text me any updates," Ryland told him. "If I don't

hear from you, I'll see you on the video chat at tonight's status call."

Trent nodded. "Bree, I'll see you around."

With that, he was gone. Bree turned a puzzled look to Ryland. "What's going on? I don't want to miss Palmer's interrogation."

"Your boss ordered you not to even think about the case. It's better to let him wonder whether you're following orders rather than show up and prove you're not. You did say you wanted to keep your job. Has that changed?"

She frowned. "What's changed is that the man who tried to kill me has been arrested. I want to see him, ask him that all-important question—why."

"Maybe he was mad about how you interviewed him at UB headquarters. Or maybe he was worried you were too clever, that you knew the Slayer cases so well that having Palmer as the primary suspect would make all the puzzle pieces come together in your mind. Or maybe he'll never answer that question. Regardless, it's not like your boss will give you a chance to ask him. You're the victim. Victims don't interrogate the people accused of hurting them."

She started to argue again, but he held up his hands in a placating gesture.

"You asked me why Trent was here. He just came from the sheriff's office and managed to get one of your coworkers to give him some information. I really think you want to hear this before risking your career to demand an audience you're not going to get."

She let out a frustrated breath. "All right. Update me on whatever Trent found out. Then if you don't want to go with me to the office, I'll take my own car."

He motioned toward the couch.

She rolled her eyes and sat. "Okay. What's this important information I need to know?"

He sat beside her, facing her, resting his right arm across the back of the couch. "The story that Trent got is that Palmer insists he's not the one who drove into the woods this morning where the body was found."

"Well, of course he's denying it. But he's on video. The gas station owner on the newscast said he saw him, that it's him on camera."

"You're right. His surveillance camera clearly shows the license plate. It's been verified with the DMV records. Since your boss was already on the alert about Palmer coming back, when the plate was run, he was called. That's how this all came together so fast."

She frowned. "And Palmer? The witness didn't mention him. Was Palmer on the video?"

"The driver is captured on the video. I'm told he looks like Palmer."

"*Looks* like him? They aren't sure?"

"The video quality isn't that good, bad enough to potentially give a jury reasonable doubt. They need more evidence."

"Okay, well, the bumper damage is evidence of what he did to me. And they should be able to work up a timeline of when he left wherever he's been staying versus when he got to his house."

"I'm sure they will. Trent's trying to get that information to work the timeline from our end."

She thought about it a moment. "The proof is in the license plate. It's on video. And since it was Palmer who was driving his car when he got home this morning, not someone else, he's the killer."

"Back up a minute," he said. "It sounds damning. But

if someone had told you a week ago that Palmer was a murderer, and that he'd try to send someone careening over a cliff, what would you have said? Honestly. After knowing him for years."

She stared at him a long moment, then looked away. "I'd have said they were crazy. But that doesn't change the facts. How many people are shocked when they find out their next-door neighbor, the nice, quiet guy, goes on a rampage and takes out a bunch of people at a shopping mall with an AK-47? It happens."

"You're right. It absolutely does. And I'm not saying that Palmer is innocent. But what if he is?"

She slowly turned to look at him again. "Innocent until proven guilty is the most basic principal in our justice system, and I think it's the most important guiding principal we have. I'd rather a killer went free than send an innocent person to prison."

He smiled and took her hand in his. "I'm with you on that. It's the core belief that guides everything I do in my job. So with that in mind, I'm going to throw out some what-ifs. Okay?"

She crossed her arms, obviously not happy, but she was trying to keep an open mind. And he loved that about her. "Go ahead."

"What if Palmer's wallet really was stolen from his car? What if he really did go to Gatlinburg to buy his mother a birthday present, but never found what he wanted, so he didn't realize his wallet was stolen? What if he really did hear the police chatter on the radio when you and I discovered the body, and he came up Prescott Mountain out of curiosity and maybe even ego, thinking he might be able to offer theories or suggestions? What if it wasn't his car up on the mountain, and he's not the one who slammed into your bumper?"

Her mouth tightened, but she didn't say anything.

"And finally, what if he really did go straight home from wherever he was staying this morning and didn't stop off in the woods to dump a body? If everything I just said is true, then what conclusions does that lead you to make?"

She shook her head. "That he'd be the unluckiest guy in the world, which of course is ludicrous. Someone else would have to have a car just like his and is driving it around to the same places he's going, making it look like he's a killer. But that's not possible since the video shows his car in the woods. Same make, model, color, and with his license plate. Don't forget that part."

"I haven't." He pulled his phone out, punched up the picture that Trent had sent him, and handed the phone to her. "Swipe to view the last three pictures on my phone."

She took it and studied each of them. "It's Palmer's car."

"Are you sure?"

She frowned and studied the pictures more closely. "Same make, model, color. The front bumper is mangled with white paint streaked across it. Is this plate the same as Palmer's?"

"It is."

"Okay. Well, then, it's definitely his car. But I don't recognize the surroundings. That dilapidated wooden fence behind the car isn't the brick fence that surrounds Palmer's neighborhood. Where was the picture taken?"

"A junkyard outside of town."

Her gaze shot to his. "When?"

"This morning, shortly after Palmer was arrested.

Trent found it. On a hunch, based on some past experiences with other cases, he called around to all the junkyards in town to see if the car had been taken there. One of the owners checked and called him back."

She shook her head. "I don't understand. Peterson would have had Palmer's car impounded downtown, not sent to a junkyard."

"Palmer's car *was* impounded. Still is. Trent verified it. He checked the VIN on both vehicles and they're different. This isn't Palmer's car."

"I don't...that doesn't make sense. Palmer's car was damaged when he pulled up in his driveway. That has to be his car."

"Remember he said it was parked on the street. It is possible that someone damaged it while it was on the street, and he never saw it."

"He'd have heard it. Or someone else would have. It takes a lot of force to crumple a bumper."

"Good point. Maybe our copycat stole the car while Palmer was sleeping, drove it somewhere else, took a sledgehammer to it and painted the bumper white. Then he brought it back and parked it right where Palmer had left it."

"Sounds really farfetched."

"And yet, it's the only way I can think of to explain how we have two different cars that look identical and have the same damage."

"I'm open to someone framing Palmer," she said. "But I'm trying to understand how that would work. Let's say the guy who jumped in front of your Rover wasn't Palmer. How did he know to wear jeans and a white shirt the same day Palmer did?"

"Maybe he keeps surveillance on him. He may have

been in Palmer's house to find out what outfits he has, and he's bought the same for himself. So every day, he dresses however Palmer does that day. And every day, he's trying to do something to make Palmer look bad. Maybe most of the time, there isn't anything he can do. But he's patient, and sticks to the plan."

She rubbed her hands up and down her arms. "Okay, that's super creepy, sneaking into his house, copying his wardrobe, and following him around for days or weeks, maybe longer."

"Imagine the kind of person who would do all that? If he does exist, and he's been keeping an eye on Palmer and mimicking him and has this disguise to look like him, it becomes plausible that he decides to plant the wallet and hopes to lead people to the grave at some point."

"Not just some people," she said. "He was counting on it being an investigator familiar with the case. He would have assumed that you knew about the gouges on the trees."

"Right. I can't imagine him planning for Palmer to show up in the woods the day we found the grave. The killer lucked out when that happened. But he planted the wallet, regardless, to throw suspicion on Palmer whenever the body was discovered."

"I guess that would work." She sat there a few moments, then clasped her hands tightly in her lap. "There's another option." Her voice was quiet, reserved.

"What would that be?"

"Back to the theory that everything points to Palmer because he *is* the Slayer, not because someone else is framing him."

"But the duplicate cars—"

"I'll get to that. Hear me out. There's no DNA, a lack

of forensic clues in any of the original five Slayer killings. That's not an easy feat. It had to be done by someone who is smart, cunning, controlled, and plans everything out. Like Palmer. Maybe the gap in the killings is because the Slayer—Palmer—felt the heat of the investigation and was worried we might catch him, so he backed off. But he's a sociopath, so he can't stop forever. When he heard that Unfinished Business was going to look into his killings, his ego wouldn't let him ignore that. He wants to prove he's the bigger, badder guy, that he can outsmart UB. So he starts killing again both to confuse UB and to provide a diversion, to give investigators an alternate theory about what's happening. He's taunting UB. But he also wants to make a statement, let Monroe County know they can't catch him. So he tries running me off the cliff, as a message, basically, that no one can catch him."

"Bree, this is really elaborate pie-in-the-sky stuff. It doesn't make sense."

"What part of being a sociopath makes sense?"

He shrugged. "I don't see how you can argue any of this. It's based on conjecture, not facts."

"I think we've already established that you and I look at investigations differently. That doesn't mean a theory I come up with isn't ultimately true."

"You're right, and I don't mean to say that my way is the only way—"

"Really? You sure about that?" she teased.

He grimaced. "Sorry. I can be a bit overbearing sometimes, my way or no way. I'll allow that your way of investigating can be just as valuable as mine, all right?"

"Can I get that in writing?"

He laughed. "I just want to mention the two cars again. How does your theory explain that?"

"Alibi. Think about it. It's brilliant, really."

He stared at her a long moment, then nodded. "I think I know where you're headed with this. But go ahead."

"All right. Assuming Palmer's the killer, he left the wallet at the grave to make it look like someone is framing him. And he stored a second car, just like his, in the back of a junkyard in case he needs a way to point to someone setting him up. I'm guessing he used the backup car for hauling bodies, so a cadaver dog wouldn't get a scent hit on his own car. That's probably the original reason he got two cars."

"Ah. Good theory there. That would make sense, if he's setting up an elaborate alibi. Keep going."

"Okay. Where's the junkyard in relation to where he dumped the body?"

"Not far. Maybe a quarter mile," he said.

"He dumps the body, switches cars so he's in the clean car. When the second car is discovered, cadaver dogs will indicate that's the car that hauled bodies, not Palmer's car. As you indicated, the vehicle identification number proves which car is his personal car. I'm guessing the second car was stolen at some point?"

"Trent is trying to find out. But I certainly can't see someone leaving legit registration back to themselves, so stolen works."

"No one is ever going to believe that Palmer would steal a car and kill someone, not without hard evidence. We're talking DNA. It's like a get-out-of-jail-free card. He can do whatever he wants, setting himself up to look like someone is out to get him. And I'll bet the only DNA the police will find is in that second car, which isn't Palmer's car. With his reputation, his standing in the community, there just might be enough reasonable doubt to get him off."

"Are you playing devil's advocate?" he asked. "Or do you honestly believe everything you just said actually happened?"

She held her hands out and shrugged. "Doesn't matter what I believe. The facts are what matters. All I'm saying is that the facts can be interpreted in two completely different ways. Either Palmer is sadistically smart and playing with everyone, having a grand old time to prove how he can outsmart them, or he's truly innocent and someone else is setting him up, as you said. Keep in mind, if I can come up with a complex yet explainable alternative to Palmer being the killer, so can a defense attorney."

Ryland swore. "You're right about that. And I told Trent to let Peterson know about the second car. So if Palmer is using the two cars as a way to cast reasonable doubt that he's being framed, we just did half the work for him by alerting the police."

They both sat in silence for a few moments. Then Bree said, "We need more facts to point us in the right direction. The question is, where do we get those facts? What do we do next in order to figure out whether Palmer is innocent or guilty?"

"Old-fashioned investigative work. We need to really dig into Palmer's life, past and present. We need to find out if there's anyone who hates him so much that they'd resort to murder and a frame-up to destroy his life. Knowing him, is there anyone you can think of who might fit that category?"

She chuckled. "You're kidding, right? Try everyone he's put in prison over the years."

"I'm not sure I agree with that. If someone's trying to

frame him, they're risking everything to do it. And they have to be willing to kill other people, collateral damage, just to frame Palmer. I doubt the vast majority of people he's put away fall into that category. We'll have to talk to family, friends, coworkers, anyone we can to build a picture and come up with those potential names. And we check with Palmer himself to see if anyone has ever threatened him, someone he takes seriously and was or is concerned about. It could very well be someone he put in prison, who has since gotten out and blames him for whatever they lost while in prison. A lot of those guys lose everything, even with a short stint behind bars. Their families abandon them. Possessions get confiscated, sold. Houses are foreclosed on. The careers they've built are destroyed. Especially if, God forbid, they were innocent and sent to prison. That's enough to warp anyone's mind."

She arched a brow. "And turn them into a killer?"

He shrugged. "I suppose it's possible. But once again, we're making leaps. Let's start at the source."

"Palmer."

He nodded. "Somehow, I've got to get your boss to let me question him."

She slowly shook her head. "No. He won't let a civilian near him. I have to question him."

"Peterson ordered you not to work any cases. We have to find another way to get the information that we need. You know how things work at the sheriff's office. And you know the people who work there. How can you get the information from Palmer without sacrificing your career to get it?"

# Chapter Seventeen

The bell tinkled over the doorway to the little café, causing Ryland to look toward the door from the booth he and Bree had chosen at the back. A young woman with auburn hair stepped in, looking around as if she was trying to find someone.

"Is that her?" Ryland asked.

Bree glanced up from her menu and looked over her shoulder. "Ah, no. Melanie's closer to forty than twenty, and she's got brown hair."

"Are you sure she's coming?"

"I'm sure. She's wanted this for a long time."

"This? What are you talking about?"

"In exchange for getting us the information we needed, I made a deal to…" The bell tinkled again. She looked back and waved. "That's her."

The woman started down the long aisle toward them.

"I don't think you mentioned which detective she's dating."

"And I won't. The fewer people who know, the better. I don't want to get him in trouble." She rose as Melanie stopped beside their booth. "Mel, hey. This is investigator Ryland Beck. He works for Unfinished Business, like I told you."

He stood and shook her hand. "Ms., ah, I don't think I got your last name."

"Her name is Mel. That's all you need to know," Bree said. "Ignore him, Mel. He's not comfortable not knowing every little detail. Thanks so much for agreeing to help. Have a seat." She slid across the booth to make room.

Melanie gave Ryland an uncertain smile as he sat across from her and Bree. She warily glanced around the café. "I'll just leave this with you. I have to get back to the office." She took a manila envelope out of her purse and set it on the table. She leaned in close to Bree. "The interview was on the record. Peterson had no problem with him going in and asking Palmer your follow-up questions. I only printed out the transcript of the part you asked about."

Bree squeezed the other woman's hand. "Thank you so much, Mel. This will really help with our investigation."

"I still don't know why you aren't working it officially with the others. But I won't pry." She looked around, as if searching for something. "Where is it?"

Ryland frowned. "Where's what?"

"It's on the back porch, wrapped up and safe. The gate's unlocked."

Mel's face flushed with excitement. "I can't wait. I'll stop by on my way back to the office. I don't want to risk someone else discovering it outside. Thanks, Bree. You don't know how long I've wanted this."

Bree's expression was a bit pained. "You have great taste. Hope you enjoy it."

"Oh, I will, I will. Good luck with your investigation. Nice to meet you, Mr. Beck."

"You too, Ms...."

"Holland." She put her hand on her mouth. "Oh, oops.

It's so hard to keep a secret. Forget I said that." She hurried down the aisle and out of the café.

"Why did you do that?" Bree asked. "You knew she wanted to remain anonymous, or as much as possible anyway."

He rolled his eyes. "She works in the sheriff's office and dates one of the detectives. She has access to the records and can print transcripts of interrogations. Five-four, a little on the heavy side, about forty, with shoulder-length curly brown hair. Oh, and her first name is Melanie but I'm assuming that everyone calls her Mel, since you do. With all that, do you honestly think I couldn't have figured out her last name? Asking was easier, and it worked. Besides, her picture's probably in that stack of photos you already gave me, with her name written on the back."

She laughed. "You're right. It is. So much for *me* keeping secrets." She took a sip of her Pepsi.

"At least now I know why you took that painting down from over your couch before we left and set it on the back porch. What I don't understand is why you agreed to give it up in exchange for information from Palmer. We could have gotten it another way without you losing something you so obviously loved."

"You could tell I loved it?"

"Are you kidding? There were tears in your eyes as you told her it was on the back porch. It's not too late. We can head over there, stop her before she takes it. I've got access to a substantial petty cash fund at UB. Grayson would consider it payment for services rendered if I bribe your friend to forgo the painting."

"Ha. Trust me. That wouldn't happen. She's wanted that since the day she came over for a dinner I put on for us detectives and their significant others. She's an art lover, like me. And almost drooled on my floor wanting it. I consider it a small price to pay if it helps us figure out what's going on."

"What's so special about the painting? I mean, it's pretty and all. But it's just a landscape."

Her eyes widened. "Just a landscape? That's like saying a Lamborghini is just a car."

He grinned. "Consider me schooled. This is where I admit I know close to nothing about art."

"I won't waste our time trying to go into the history of the painter and that particular painting. Suffice it to say it means a lot to me. I practically starved for a whole year to save for it because it was coming up at auction. The fact that I got it was a small miracle. What made it more special is that it was a gift to my mom, who absolutely cherished it. I inherited it after she and my daddy passed within a few months of each other. It always reminds me of them, and makes me smile when I see it." Her mouth tightened in a firm line. "Or it did. It's going to be hard to get used to not seeing it hanging over the couch anymore."

She grabbed the manila envelope and worked at opening the seal.

"I'm sure I can buy it back—"

"Let it go, Ryland. Consider it my first real contribution to the case. Let's see if it was worth the sacrifice." She pulled out the small stack of papers that were inside. "Six pages. That's a lot of names to have to look into." She quickly scanned them. "Double-spaced. That helps. Fewer names to whittle down." She shook her head. "Still a lot to dig through. Looks like Palmer rambled a bit. He listed fifteen or twenty people who might want to frame him."

"Can I see it?"

She handed him the pages and took another sip of her drink.

Ryland snapped pictures with his phone's camera as he scanned the interview excerpt, singling out the names Palmer had mentioned.

When the waitress stopped by to see if they needed anything else, Bree thanked her and said their lunch was delicious and they'd be leaving soon.

As the waitress moved to another booth, Ryland attached the pictures to a text.

"What are you doing with those?" Bree asked. "Sending them to someone else?"

"Callum. I asked him to do a quick check on the names, see if he can get addresses, or at least last known locations."

"How many names did you find in the transcript?"

"You were close. Sixteen. Those are the only people. Once we interview Palmer's family and friends, we may add a few more people who hate him to that list. But it's a start. Are you ready to go?"

"Definitely. Where to? Back to my place?"

"Until we solve this thing and can be sure who rammed your SUV, I still think you should stay with me in Gatlinburg. So, yeah, let's head back so you can pack a suitcase."

"Works for me. Now that I have this information from Palmer, I'm okay not sticking around in Madisonville. Especially since I'll be with a man who risked his life, in spite of his phobia about heights, to save me. I'll never be able to repay that debt. Thank you, Ryland."

He grimaced at the mention of his fear of heights as he escorted her outside. "Stop thanking me. That would be a great start at repayment. Unless you want to thank me the same way you did at my cabin." Although he was teasing, he wouldn't stop her if she wanted to kiss him again. *He* sure as hell wanted to kiss *her*.

Bree's face flushed and she cleared her throat. "Um, we can explore that later, after the case is resolved." She glanced up at him. "And then maybe you'll tell me what happened."

"What happened?"

"To make you afraid of heights."

His throat tightened. "One day. Maybe." But he doubted it. That wasn't something he liked talking about to anyone. The only reason his teammates knew about it was because they'd all been together when he'd fainted once before. And then Trent had dug into his background to find out the cause of his fear. He'd hated Trent for it at the time. But they'd gotten past that and had become the very best of friends.

He and Bree had just pulled into her driveway when his phone buzzed. He cut the engine and checked the screen. "That was fast. Callum already found six of the people on the list. They're all in the same place."

"Madisonville, I'd imagine."

"The Riverbend Maximum Security prison in Nashville."

"Oh. Well, we can mark those six off since they couldn't be involved in framing Palmer." She grabbed her purse, ready to get out of the car.

"Actually, I'd kind of like to talk to them."

She settled back against the seat. "Why?"

"He put them away. They've got strong motives to

hate him. And he obviously agrees or he wouldn't have mentioned them. There are plenty of cases where people in prison masterminded murder outside the prison walls. We can explore this first group fairly quickly, see if there are any red flags that go up. If one of them seems to be hiding something, we can dig deeper and see if they could be involved, see who their contacts are. All it takes is one good friend or a family member outside of prison to carry out their plans. We just have to follow the bread crumbs."

"Okay. Not something I'd have necessarily thought to do," she said. "But I'm game. Send me the six you're talking about and I'll notify the prison, find out if or when we can have access to the prisoners. If they're due in court for an appeal or something like that, they might not be available for an interview. But I'd think at least one or two should be capable of accepting visitors, today if the prison will be flexible since I'm law enforcement. Family or press would never be able to do a last-minute visit. It usually takes weeks to get permission for a visit to someone like these on the list, the maximum security prisoners."

"Sending you the list now." He pressed some buttons on his phone. "Done."

When she read all of the names, she grimaced. "Never thought I'd apply to visit any of these creeps after what they did. Silas Gerloff, that road rage guy I told you about. Dan Smith, the workplace violence guy. Wait, why is the child murderer, Nancy Compadre, on this list? The profile says the killer is a man."

"The profile of the original Slayer murders. We don't have a profile yet for these most recent murders, and I don't feel we're in a situation where we can cross someone off our potential suspect list without talking to them first. Or at least speaking to someone who knows them."

"Point taken. She stays. Let's see, oh, this one isn't in prison, unless he was sent back for something else."

"Who?" he asked.

"Liam Kline. He's the pedophile I told you about earlier. Well, at least, he was convicted as a pedophile. But his conviction was overturned. He was released about a year ago."

"You never told me why his conviction was overturned. Do you know?"

She grimaced. "Mistakes were made with the handling of evidence. Kline was convicted of possessing child pornography on his computer at work. He was originally sentenced to twenty years. Kline's lawyer appealed and argued that the prosecution had exculpatory evidence that proved another guy at his workplace had access to his computer. And he's right. The guy did have access. But Kline didn't know that, certainly not during the original trial. The second guy was a janitor working night shift. He was also a pedophile, with a prior conviction, easily found if you search the state's sexual predator database. Kline couldn't adequately explain the porn on the computer in his office since he didn't know of anyone who could access it. It was only through discovery after the conviction that the lawyer working on the appeal was able to find out the prosecution team had all of that information and never gave it to the defense."

"Are you saying that Palmer knowingly convicted a man he knew was innocent?"

"No. That's what Kline's lawyer says. My view is that Palmer had too many cooks in the kitchen. The junior prosecutors each had a little piece of the overall puzzle in their files. But they didn't put it together and realize what they had. The evidence wasn't logged properly and wasn't given to the defense during discovery."

"I find that hard to believe," he said. "As organized as you say Palmer is, how could he make a mistake like that?"

"He didn't. His team did. Big difference."

"Okay, okay. I see your point. Maybe Palmer didn't convict an innocent man on purpose. But that doesn't make it any less devastating to the guy who was labeled a pedo. How long was he in prison?"

She cleared her throat. "Three years."

Ryland swore. "Okay. We definitely need to talk to this Kline guy. He's got motive and opportunity since he's a free man. I don't know if he has the money to purchase a look-alike car and buy elaborate disguises to make himself look and dress like Palmer, but—"

"Oh, he does. He took the city, and Palmer, to civil court. And won. Millions, although I'm not sure of the exact amount."

"That probably went a long way toward making amends. Three years, millions of dollars. A lot of people might think he got a good deal. We should look into him anyway. What happened to Palmer? Did he get some kind of reprimand on his record? Have to pay civil fines to Kline?"

"I honestly don't know. If he did, it was kept hush-hush. If you can trust the news reports, Kline signed some kind of nondisclosure agreement where he couldn't say anything about the exact amount of the settlement or any repercussions to the prosecutor's office. The only reason I know the amount was in the millions is because of scuttlebutt at the office. One of the clerks involved in typing up the agreement told a friend who told a friend."

He smiled. "Kind of like Mel Holland. Secrets aren't easy to keep. They always come out."

"Seems that way. Let's head inside. Submitting this request to visit the five others in prison is too hard to do on my phone. I'll use my laptop."

"While you're doing that, and packing a suitcase, I'll see if I can get a current address for Liam Kline."

# Chapter Eighteen

For Ryland's sake, Bree wished the ex Mrs. Kline would have asked her and Ryland into her Gatlinburg mountain home. But instead, she'd invited them to sit at the table on her wraparound porch—a porch that had an excellent view of the town of Gatlinburg, a few thousand feet below. The few times that Ryland had made the mistake of glancing toward the railing, he'd quickly looked away, his face going pale. Now he steadfastly focused on whoever was talking, or tapped notes into his phone app.

"Thank you again for agreeing to meet with us," Bree said. "It wasn't easy finding you since you've changed your last name and moved to Gatlinburg. I'm so grateful that your husband's lawyer was able to give a message to your lawyer and that you called me back. If we have follow-up questions after today's visit, I hope you won't mind if Ryland or I call you directly? We've both saved your number in our phones. But if you'd prefer we go through the lawyers again, we'll delete your number."

"You can call me all you want. As to whether I'll answer next time, we'll see. You said you're working on some type of investigation and needed to talk to me about Liam. That got my curiosity going. I can't imagine him being in trouble again. What's going on?"

"We just need to talk to him about a case."

"I told you over the phone that I don't know where he is."

Bree nodded, not willing to admit that she and Ryland were skeptical of that claim. That's why they were here. To try to pressure her for his address. The lawyer route, trying to get his address that way, had gone nowhere.

"Understood," Bree said. "We'll try contacting him through his lawyer, like we did you. But we'd like some background information for our discussion with him. Can you tell me how long you've lived in Gatlinburg?"

"I sure don't see where that matters. But I didn't understand the odd questions the detectives asked me when Liam was arrested either." She shrugged. "I guess my kids and I have been here a little over three years now. It was impossible to stay in Madisonville. The press wasn't exactly kind to my family after Liam was charged, even worse during the trial. They speculated, openly, that maybe I'd known what he was doing and had covered for him. My children were bullied at school. All our friends turned their backs on us. I tried to be the supportive wife, to believe in my husband and protect my family as best I could. But the things that came out during the trial..." She shook her head. "It was awful. Once the verdict came in, and he was found guilty, I started looking for a new place, landed here."

Her hand shook as she pushed her light brown bangs out of her eyes. "Liam appealed, of course. He sent me letters from prison, proclaiming his innocence. But I... I didn't believe him. It's horrible to not be able to believe in your own husband, even more horrible years later when his appeal wins and the new evidence proves, beyond any doubt, that he was innocent all along."

Her eyes were bright with unshed tears. "My husband deserved my support and got none. It's a regret I'll have to live with the rest of my life. But there's no fixing it now. Once that pedophile label is put on someone, it sticks. There are people who will always believe he's guilty, that he got off on a technicality, without even looking at the evidence and realizing he was exonerated. I remember what it was like for me, for my boys, to live under that stigma. I'll always love Liam. But I can't live like that again. I just can't."

Bree gave the woman what she hoped was a commiserating look. But even though she could empathize with what she and her children had gone through, she felt even worse for what Liam Kline had suffered. The people he loved the most in this world, the people he desperately needed to believe in him, didn't. They'd turned away, leaving him completely alone as he was sent to prison, knowing that the pedophile label put him in terrible jeopardy with other inmates and would likely force him to be in solitary for his own protection.

Ryland gave her a sympathetic look too and rested his forearms on the table. "Are your sons still here with you?"

Her expression brightened. "Oh, yes. Larry and Lyle are too young to be on their own. Although, hard to believe, Larry just started high school this year. Lyle's still in middle school. That's where they are right now, at school. I'm fortunate to work from home. That's why I was able to meet with you after you called." Her smile faded. "I'm sorry I can't help you as far as giving you an address for Liam. I truly don't know where he's living now. You should work with his lawyer to get that information."

"We will, for sure. He didn't contact you when he got out of prison? Does he not know where you live?"

"I've never revealed my new name or address to him. But he still contacts me, through our lawyers sometimes as I already said, but mainly through email. I use a new account for my other correspondences. But I've kept my old account open, for Liam's emails. I don't have the heart to shut it down completely. But I quit reading and responding to him long ago. It's too depressing."

"What about child support?" Bree asked. "It's rumored he got millions in the civil case he won against the city. Did you get a judgment against him for support?"

She raised her chin. "I did. I know it sounds bad that I don't communicate with him but I take his money. But they are his children. They deserve some of the good things in life too, and he can afford it."

"No judgment here," Bree said. "But if he's paying child support, how does that money get to you?"

"Wire transfer. Our lawyers set it up."

"And visitation? How is that handled? A third party? Supervised by the courts at a neutral location?"

Her face reddened. "There is no visitation. I've been fighting him on that for the past six months. When he first got out of prison, he didn't talk about shared custody. But now he's going after me in court, trying to force me to let him see them. There's no way I'll ever let that happen. I have to protect my sons."

Bree straightened in her chair. "Protect them? Are you afraid of him, Mrs. Kline?"

Her hesitation told the story. The woman was definitely afraid of her former husband. What Bree wanted to know was why.

"Mrs. Kline?" she pressed. "Did your husband ever hurt you or your children?"

"What? No, no. Of course not. Liam was a good man,

a good husband and father. It's just…" She twisted her hands together on top of the table.

"I know this is hard," Bree said. "But it's important."

Her eyes narrowed. "I don't think you ever explained what case you're working on. You said you had questions about Liam, that he might be able to help you. But I don't see how. What's this about?"

Bree didn't want to say that Liam Kline was a potential suspect in some murders. He'd been falsely convicted once, and lost his family, his livelihood, his reputation— everything—because of it. She couldn't risk telling his ex-wife about their investigation without also risking that rumors would spread and his name would be whispered about as a suspect in serial killings. Without hard facts to implicate him, they were simply on a fishing expedition. And there were plenty of other names on Prosecutor Palmer's list of people to look into. Bree gave Ryland a *help me* look.

He smiled at Mrs. Kline. "It would be unethical to discuss the investigation. But I assure you, we're hoping Mr. Kline can help us. His name came up with several others as someone who may be able to point us toward a suspect."

Bree nodded, impressed with how he'd framed it. Everything he'd said was true. But he made it sound as if Kline wasn't under suspicion in any way.

Mrs. Kline relaxed against her chair, apparently willing to accept Ryland's explanation. "I really can't help you with an address. But you can get a message to him through his lawyer. Obviously you already have *his* contact info. I sincerely hope Liam can help you, but I wouldn't count on him wanting to. Liam is…different than he used to be. He's changed. That's why I don't want him to visit with the children."

Bree stared at her, well aware that Ryland seemed just as surprised as her. It sounded as if Mrs. Kline had contradicted her earlier statement that she hadn't seen Liam since his conviction.

"Liam is different now?" Ryland asked. "What makes you say that? I thought you hadn't seen him in years."

She stiffened. "I didn't lie, Mr. Beck. I haven't seen Liam since the day they took him out of the courtroom in chains. But I read enough of his emails in the beginning of his prison sentence to see him…change. He was such a kind, sweet, handsome man. Everything I'd ever wanted. Even knowing he was guilty…"

She cleared her throat. "Even *believing* he was guilty, in the years before his appeal proved his innocence, I had a hard time ignoring him. Love isn't a faucet you can just turn off and on. It broke my heart reading about his suffering, the horrible things that happened to him in prison. What they did to him, well, it would break anyone. It certainly broke Liam. He became harder, more… coarse. There was a darkness in his words. Hate. That's what scared me, Detective Clark. Realizing the man I'd loved was gone, and in his place was a bitter stranger. It got so bad I had to stop reading his emails. And that darkness is why I'll fight to my last breath to keep custody of my kids, and make sure they never see the man their father has become. I'd rather they remember him the way he was."

Bree leaned forward. "You said what happened to him would break anyone. What did you mean?"

As if looking deep within herself, she stared out over the mountains, a faraway look in her eyes. "My lawyer explained to me that pedophiles are often placed in solitary confinement for their own protection, or even in a special ward in the prison to keep them away from the general population. I guess the inmates have some kind of twisted code. You can rape and murder all day long and they treat you like a hero. Harm a child, and you've crossed some kind of line. I don't know why Liam wasn't immediately put in solitary. Maybe it was an honest mistake, an oversight. Or maybe the guards wanted to see first whether he'd be okay without separating him from everyone else. They put him in a cell with a killer. He was attacked before the end of the first day."

She ran her hands up and down the light jacket she was wearing. "My lawyer sent me a picture, an update on what had happened. I guess he felt I should know since Liam doesn't have any family besides me and the kids." She shivered, swallowed. "I told him not to share anything else about Liam again. I couldn't handle seeing anything that…awful. It still gives me nightmares."

When she went silent, Bree glanced at Ryland. He shrugged, not sure what to do either. Finally, Bree cleared her throat, to get her attention. "Mrs. Kline—"

"His face looked like it had been put through a meat grinder." Mrs. Kline continued to stare out past the mountains, but her entire body was shaking. "The things they did to him." A single tear slid down her cheek. "It's a miracle he survived. But after…after what they did, he didn't even look…human."

"I'm so sorry about your husband," Bree said. "For what he suffered."

She turned to look at Bree, a single tear rolling down her cheek. "*Ex*-husband. I'm sorry, but I can't help you.

We're finished here." With that, she went into the house, closing the door behind her with a loud click.

Bree and Ryland didn't speak again until they were sitting in his Rover. He started the engine and got the heater running, but instead of returning to UB headquarters where they'd been earlier, setting up the meeting with Mrs. Kline, he seemed lost in thought, staring out the windshield.

Bree sat back too, grateful for the reprieve. She wasn't ready to face anyone else at UB just yet. She felt too bruised, raw, and terribly sad.

Ryland was the one who finally spoke. "She said her husband was broken, filled with hate. If anything could turn a good man bad, what Liam Kline suffered would do it. We have to keep him on our potential suspect list."

"You're right," she said. "He seems like our most likely suspect at this point. But I hate it. I hate that an innocent man had his life ruined, his face…the person he sees in the mirror every day—destroyed. And we're going to make it worse by asking him if he's the guy killing people. And trying to frame Palmer." She shook her head. "It's awful."

"It has to be done. We can't ignore him because we empathize with what he's been through."

"I know," she said. "I know. It just really sucks."

"I won't argue that." He glanced at the digital display in the dash. "It's not time yet for the status call, and we still have plenty of daylight. Have you heard back from the prison yet about our request?"

She pulled out her phone and scrolled through her emails. Most were junk mail, but one had an official look about it. It was from the prison.

"We're in luck. Two are available today, the others

are available tomorrow. I just need to confirm what time we'll get there so they can prepare."

He glanced at the clock again. "Riverbend's about four hours from here, give or take. We'd arrive after dark. Will they let us interview them that late?"

"Only one way to find out." She called the number from the email. A few minutes later, she ended the call. "Since it'll be so late, they're limiting it to one today. But we can still interview the others tomorrow, starting bright and early at eight. My suitcase is still in the back, but what about you? Do we need to go to your house first and get you a suitcase?"

"My go-bag's in the back. I'm all set." He pulled out onto the road. "Which dirtbag do we get the pleasure of talking to tonight?"

"Silas Gerloff. The road rage killer."

# Chapter Nineteen

The sound of chains rattling in the outer corridor was soon followed by the sight of four prison guards escorting Silas Gerloff toward the interview room. Ryland noted the shackles on Gerloff's ankles and wrists and the heavy length of chain connecting them. He glanced at Bree, who was wide-eyed and appeared to be just as surprised as he was.

He leaned in close. "That's a lot of guards and chains for a guy who murdered one person in a road rage incident."

"I was thinking the same thing. Maybe he's done some really bad things inside the prison walls that we don't know about."

"Here he comes."

"Mr. Beck, Detective Clark," one of the guards called out. "Back up against the wall. Do not approach the prisoner."

Bree hesitated.

"Come on," Ryland whispered. He took her hand and pulled her with him about ten feet from the table where they'd been sitting in the middle of the room.

"Clear," the guard called out. "Open the door."

An electronic buzz sounded, and the heavy barred

door slowly slid back, metal screeching as it cleared the opening and sank into a slot in the wall.

"Guard number two, see to the chairs."

One of the guards hurried into the room. He picked up the chair that Ryland had been sitting in and placed it in front of him, then did the same with Bree's chair, leaving only one chair at the heavy steel table, which was bolted into the floor.

"Ready, sir," the guard said, waiting beside the table.

The lead guard, standing behind Gerloff, barked out another order. "Prisoner, move forward. To the table, then halt and sit. No sudden moves."

Gerloff shuffled forward in his orange jumpsuit, chains clinking and swaying. Ryland was amazed he could even walk beneath their weight. There certainly wasn't any danger that Gerloff would make a sudden move. The dark-haired man couldn't be more than five and a half feet tall, and probably weighed about a buck forty. But he looked solid, his muscles well-defined, at least what muscles Ryland could see beneath his tattoos. They covered every inch of his arms, even the backs of his hands and knuckles. But they stopped just beneath his chin. There were none on his face.

"Clear," the lead guard called out again. "Close the door."

The door slid closed with a solid clang. Apparently at least one more guard was watching and listening from some control booth.

The lead guard stood with his back to Ryland and Bree, giving more orders as the other three fastened Gerloff's chains to a massive steel loop in the tabletop. Once that was done, they attached his ankle chains to another thick loop on the floor underneath the table.

The three of them stepped back, behind Gerloff. "Prisoner secure, sir," one of them called out.

The lead guard circled the table, tugging on the chains. He leaned underneath it, tugging on those too before backing up. Apparently satisfied, he stepped back. The other guards backed away from the table too, spreading out around the room, all facing the prisoner.

The head guard finally turned toward Ryland and Bree. "You may not approach the prisoner. You're to sit in your chairs and remain there until the prisoner has been removed from the room. You have one hour, not a minute more. Questions?"

"Are you all staying for the interview?" Bree asked.

"Yes, ma'am. For your security."

Ryland motioned toward the table, and Gerloff, whose dark eyes were locked on him and Bree. "Do you secure every prisoner here the way you've secured Mr. Gerloff?"

"I can't discuss security protocol, sir. Please consider prisoner Gerloff to be exceptionally dangerous. Is that clear?"

"Clear. Thank you."

The guard waited until they'd taken their seats. Then he moved to stand about six feet behind the prisoner.

"Fifty-nine minutes," he called out.

"O…kay," Bree said. "Mr. Gerloff, thank you for agreeing to meet with us. This is Ryland Beck, former special agent with the TBI, currently an investigator with UB. I'm Detective Clark from Monroe County, and we—"

"I didn't agree to meet with anyone, lady. I agreed to see who wanted to talk to me, and then I'll make up my mind whether I'm going to answer any questions." Gerloff's gritty voice filled the room, its deep tone seeming to echo off the walls. He raked a glance across Bree, and then, as if dismissing her outright, focused on Ryland. "What's UB, TBI guy?"

Bree pursed her lips but remained silent.

Ryland started to lean forward in his chair, but the quick shake of the lead guard's head had him sitting straight. In all his years in law enforcement, he'd never once seen security this tight. It was bizarre, to say the least. But he wasn't going to question it. They obviously knew far more about their prisoner than he or Bree did. Something he'd remedy as soon as they were out of here. He was now extremely curious about Gerloff's background, especially since becoming a prisoner at this facility.

"UB stands for Unfinished Business. That's cop slang for a cold case. We're a civilian company that partners with law enforcement to try to solve cases that don't seem to have any leads."

"Unfinished Business," he mumbled, as if testing the syllables on his tongue. "I like that. Cold cases, huh? If you're here to ask me about some of those, trying to pin something on me, then we're done. I ain't talkin'." He yanked his arms, rattling the chains against the table.

The lead guard started forward, as if to end the interview.

"Wait," Ryland called out. "Please. We're not here to pin anything on you, sir. We're hoping you can help us with a current case involving Prosecutor Palmer of Monroe County, the county where you were arrested for your road rage…incident."

"Hold up," Gerloff said, raising a hand to signal the guard.

The guard stopped, his right hand poised on his baton as he waited.

"Palmer, huh?" Gerloff asked.

"Yes," Ryland confirmed. The light of interest in Gerloff's dark eyes told Ryland he'd stumbled onto the key that might get him to talk, so he went with it. "He's been arrested for murder."

Gerloff chuckled, his mouth curving in a chilling grin, gold flashing on the few teeth he still had. He glanced over his shoulder at the lead guard. "Cool your jets, Morris. I ain't talking to the female. But me and this UB fella have some things to discuss."

Bree stiffened beside Ryland. He wanted to reassure her, but he didn't want to do anything to change Gerloff's mind about the meeting, so he sat and waited.

The guard's face reddened slightly at the casual use of his name, but he stepped back, remaining several feet behind the prisoner.

"Palmer," Gerloff spat out. "Now there's a guy who deserves every bad thing that could possibly happen to him. Just look at me. I don't even have a record. Or, I didn't, until that guy cut me off on the highway." He shrugged, chains rattling. "Stuff happens, you know? But Palmer goes for the maximum penalty, convinces the judge I'm a 'danger to society.'" He held his fingers up, making air quotes, as he spoke. The chains rattled and clomped when he rested his arms on the table again. "Not surprised he snapped and killed somebody. The guy's not right in the head, you know. Who'd he kill?"

"We don't know that he killed anyone. He's been arrested, but the case against him is far from solid."

He frowned. "Why not? Aren't there witnesses who saw him? Who can swear he was there, where the bodies were found? I'll bet his car was seen in the area. Am I right?"

Ryland drew a slow, deep breath, careful to keep his expression blank. He hadn't said there was more than one murder, but Gerloff said *bodies*, plural. It sounded as if he knew about the murders. Was that because he'd seen news coverage? Or because he had insider knowledge? And him mentioning a car had Ryland especially suspicious, although that too may have been mentioned on the news.

"There are witnesses, yes," Ryland told him. "I'm one of them. I saw him on a mountain road a short distance from where Detective Clark and I discovered one of the bodies."

His gaze flicked to Bree, then back to Ryland. "Discovered? How? What made you look for it? Was it hard to find?"

"Detective Clark and I went into the woods to find the man I believed was Prosecutor Palmer. She saw some things that made her suspicious, and is the one who actually found the grave."

He frowned and finally gave Bree his full attention. "What was suspicious?"

She looked at Ryland. "Should I tell him?"

Gerloff pounded his fist on the table. "What was suspicious?"

"The prisoner will keep his hands down and not hit the table," the lead guard said.

"Shove it, Morris. Tell me what was suspicious or this little visit is over."

Guard Morris turned a light shade of red again, but remained silent.

Ryland nodded, letting Bree know he felt it was okay to share the information. It seemed important to Gerloff. And Ryland wanted him to keep talking.

"There were gouges on the trees, one in each corner of the glade, marking off the points of a compass, north, south, east, west. It made me think there might be a body buried in the middle."

He pointed to Ryland. "You answer this time. What do you mean, buried?"

Red alarm bells were going off inside Ryland's mind. Gerloff seemed surprised the body was buried. Why would he be surprised? Unless he knew the body wasn't supposed to be buried? Why would he know that? And why would he care? Unless... He looked at Bree and could tell by her expression that the same red flags were going off for her as well.

She cleared her throat, getting the lead guard's attention. "Sir, I need access to my phone. They made me lock it up with my purse and keys outside."

He frowned. "That's against protocol. You don't get your personal belongings back until you're outside of the prisoner area."

"It's really important. I just need to look up something on the internet. Please?"

"That door doesn't open during the interview. However, I can get another guard to look up what you need. Will that work?"

"Yes. Thank you."

He radioed for another guard. A moment later, the guard appeared in the hallway. He motioned to Bree and she hurried over, telling him what she needed.

Ryland continued the discussion with Gerloff, deciding to bluff and see what happened.

"Yep. We've got a copycat killer running around, trying to pass off his kills as if he was the Smoky Mountain Slayer. But he keeps screwing up, doing things wrong that make it obvious he's not the Slayer. Like burying his bodies instead of leaving them out in the open the way the Slayer did."

Gerloff stared at him, his eyes narrowing. "Is that right? He buries each one, does he? How many?"

"Two so far. But we intend to stop him before he kills again."

"You already have. Palmer's been arrested. I mean, that's what you said."

"Oh, we know that's not going to hold. The copycat has made some big mistakes. We're on his trail. Or, I should say, the police are. Detective Clark and I are following up with anyone who might have a grudge against Palmer, who might be working with the copycat on the outside to try to frame Palmer. That's why we wanted to talk to you, since you're one of the people Palmer told us might have a grudge against him. Your name was on the list he gave us of people who might be trying to frame him."

His face reddened. "Thought you weren't here to pin something on me."

Ryland shrugged.

Gerloff's face got even redder. But he was obviously wavering between cutting the interview short and satisfying his curiosity. Finally, he said, "Who else is on the list?"

Ryland barely managed not to grin. Gerloff's curiosity had won out. He told Gerloff the first name.

"Never heard of him. Keep going."

Ryland gave him another name. Gerloff made a comment that the guy was an idiot who couldn't tell his left shoe from his right.

"Nancy Compadre."

"A woman? Are you kidding me? Keep going."

Bree's back stiffened over by the bars. She was obviously listening to Gerloff, even as she continued to speak to the guard who was radioing to someone else what she wanted.

"Let's see. Dan Smith."

"The office killer?"

"He shot his boss and three other people, yes. He's at this same prison."

"Well, I ain't ever seen him here. Who else?"

"Liam Kline."

Gerloff stared at him a long moment. "Who else?"

Bingo.

Kline was the only one he hadn't said anything about. There was a connection there.

"Have you ever met Kline?"

"Nope. Never heard of him."

Bree turned around and jogged to her seat beside Ryland. She gave him a subtle nod, before facing Gerloff. "You're lying, Mr. Gerloff. Liam Kline was your cell mate. I just confirmed it. He was your cell mate from day one until he was released a year ago. Is he the one who's framing Prosecutor Palmer? Did you put him up to that? So you can get your revenge?"

He stared at her, his eyes darkening with anger, so dark they appeared black. Then he raised his arms, chains rattling, and held them out in front of him like claws, squeezing them in the universal sign of someone choking someone.

Ryland jumped to his feet. "We're done."

Morris ordered him to sit, but Ryland ignored him. He grabbed Bree's arm and hurried her to the door. "Let us out. Now."

Ten minutes later, they were sitting in the parking lot in his Rover.

He gently clasped her shoulder. "Are you okay?"

She gave him a grateful smile. "Thank you for getting us out of there. I've never felt so uncomfortable in my life."

"Well, I sure as hell wasn't going to sit and let him make threats. You said he and Kline were cell mates. What else did you find out?"

"It's more like what did your team find out. I texted Trent and asked him to give me everything he could find on Gerloff. One of the very first things he found out was that he was Kline's cell mate. As soon as I saw Kline's name, I knew we were on to something. Here, let me try to summarize what Trent sent."

She pulled up the email on her phone as Ryland headed out of the parking lot toward Gatlinburg. "Let's see, okay. We already know from Mrs. Kline that Liam was brutally attacked the first day he was in prison. I got the impression she thought it was his cell mate. But it wasn't. Some of the other prisoners ganged up on him in the prison yard. They got a huge group of inmates to crowd around, blocking the camera views. No one would admit to seeing what happened. No one was brought up on charges. Then, once Liam recovered, he was placed—not in solitary, as he should have been—but right back in the general population, with Gerloff as his cell mate. Apparently, Gerloff killed his previous cell mate, before Kline."

He glanced at her, stunned. "Sounds like someone wanted Kline dead."

"The warden thought so too. There was an investigation, and five guards were fired. But when the warden was going to move Kline to solitary for his own protection, he refused, saying he wanted to stay with Gerloff."

Ryland shook his head, steering around a slow-moving car. "Why would he do that? Doesn't make sense."

"In hindsight, it does. No one touched Kline again after the attack. He never had to be locked up in solitary for protection either. And there were some mysterious deaths after that, five prisoners killed in various ways. Low-key. Quiet. No witnesses. No one brought up on charges. But get this. All five were in the prison yard the day that Kline was attacked."

Ryland nodded. "Okay, now it makes sense. For some reason, Gerloff takes a liking to Kline and offers his protection. He's got some kind of reputation in the prison. Other guys are scared of him. He takes out the ones who hurt Kline, and makes it known that if anyone else touches him, they'll be killed too. The only question is, what did Gerloff promise in return?"

"If you're thinking something sexual, I don't think so. Gerloff is completely homophobic. He's attacked guys if they just looked at him wrong."

"Gerloff hates Palmer. That was obvious back there."

"So does Kline. Maybe that's what drew them to each other, what they both had in common," she said.

"Where does that leave us? Kline was a decent guy before prison. Loses everything he cares about, including his looks. Then shares a cell with a scary, evil guy for three years, probably egging each other on over their mutual hatred of Palmer. Is that enough to turn Kline into a killer? Is he the guy I saw on the road, with a disguise that could fool a Hollywood makeup artist?"

"Are we completely giving up on the theory that

Palmer did it? That he planned everything out to take suspicion off him?" she asked.

He blew out a deep breath. "It just feels too far out there to think he'd do that. I suppose it's possible. But I'm not putting my money on it."

"Me either. It's the whole KISS principle."

"Keep it simple, stupid?"

She laughed. "Exactly. Or Occam's razor, if we want to keep it a little more professional. The simplest explanation is usually the right explanation. Something along those lines. Although there's really nothing simple about any of our theories."

He chuckled. "Definitely not."

"Can you handle me making a theoretical leap here? I don't want to offend your investigator sensibilities by suggesting a theory without the facts to back it up yet."

He rolled his eyes. "I think I can handle it. Heck, I've been proposing wild theories all day. Go for it."

"In that case, I'm going to say the obvious and simplest answer seems to be that, yes, Kline is the copycat. He picked a case he knew Palmer was involved with and used it to try to frame him. He pretended to be Palmer and killed two people. The first one is someone Palmer knew was guilty, but got off on a technicality. I'll bet when we get the ID on the latest victim, they'll be in that same category—someone Palmer prosecuted but got off, someone guilty. The setup is that Palmer felt justified in killing them because they were guilty. And he resented they'd damaged his nearly perfect prosecutorial track record."

"And Kline? What does he get out of this? The satisfaction that Palmer goes to prison?" He blinked and glanced at her. She looked just as stunned as he felt.

"Ryland—"

"Give me a second." He pulled to the shoulder and put the Rover in Park before turning to face her. "Do I say it? Or you?"

She smiled. "It's your turn."

"Gerloff and Kline both hate Palmer and want him to pay for putting them in prison. They fantasize together for years about how they'd destroy Palmer if either of them ever get out. Then Kline's appeal is successful. But even people who are exonerated are rarely released the day the judge rules on the case. Paperwork has to be filed, plans made. He could have spent another day, a week, maybe even a month in prison if things went slowly. Knowing he was going to be set free, he makes a plan with Gerloff to get even with Palmer. Maybe in the beginning it was about Kline filing the civil suit alleging prosecutorial misconduct. But Palmer never had to publicly admit to any misconduct, and he didn't lose his job. Maybe Plan B all along was to frame him. Gerloff advises him on how to kill. He's obviously killed far more people than the one road rage victim. And you can tell he's a sociopath just by looking at him. I'll bet that road rage incident was one of many murders even before Gerloff went to prison."

"More guesses, without facts, Ryland?" she teased.

"You've ruined me. What can I say?"

"I think you were going to say what we've both figured out, the Plan B goal in all of this."

He nodded. "Prison has been the ultimate punishment for Gerloff and Kline, hell on earth. They want Palmer to experience that kind of hell. Kline is framing Palmer so he'll go to prison. And by ensuring he's framed for heinous crimes, he'll be sent to maximum security, the same prison as Gerloff. That's the payback to Gerloff for saving Kline's life. Palmer suffers the indignity of going to prison. And Gerloff gets to do whatever he wants to Palmer."

# Chapter Twenty

Ryland and Bree sat at the small desk in the two-bed-room hotel suite he'd gotten them so they could share his laptop for the impromptu meeting with the UB team. They'd just finished updating the team on everything that had happened. Their law enforcement liaison, Rowan, was now calling Sheriff Peterson and Chief Russo to provide them with updates. No doubt one of them would issue a BOLO soon so that law enforcement in the area would be on the lookout for Kline, using the picture that Faith had managed to get from the prison while Bree and Ryland gave their update. It was the picture the prison took the day he was being released, and Kline's face was just as ravaged as his ex-wife had described. Seeing him like that had cemented Ryland's belief that Kline really could be their guy, that a once good man could turn bad when everything he cared about had been taken from him.

Brice and Asher gave their updates about the Rogers case, including that she'd been visiting Gatlinburg dur-ing the time she was killed. It certainly seemed like a glaring coincidence that Palmer was also in Gatlinburg at the same time.

Palmer's alibis for the times of both recent murders couldn't be corroborated. He'd taken vacation days both times.

"Did Gatlinburg PD agree to let our lab run the Amido Black test to look for fingerprints on Rogers's skin?" Ryland asked.

Lance motioned to get everyone's attention. "I'll take that one. The police here have been extremely cooperative and gave our lab techs full access. Our people performed the test at the morgue, rather than bring the body to UB, per the medical examiner's request. Unfortunately, no fingerprints were found. It's possible the killer wore gloves, but given the decayed state of the body and small of amount of skin available for testing, it may just be that any fingerprints are long gone."

"It was worth a shot," Ryland said. "Any luck finding potential suspects who look like Palmer and have been seen in the area?"

"I've got that one," Faith said. "I hit the pavement downtown with Palmer's picture. Went to all the antique stores and restaurants. Talked to a gazillion people, and quite a few remembered seeing him downtown. But there's no way to know if it was Prosecutor Palmer or someone disguised to look like him. The timing lined up with what Palmer said, so it's possible he was in town antiquing at the time he said he was. Kind of hard to prove either way. I was hoping to find witnesses who think they saw Palmer when he wasn't supposedly in Gatlinburg, but that was a bust."

Bree sighed heavily. "Sounds like you guys and gals are working hard, but we've got a long way to go to get enough facts to move forward."

"We've only been at this a handful of days," Ryland

said. "Considering what we started with, I think we're on track. We'll get it done. Don't worry."

"Oh, I don't doubt it at all. It's just been incredibly stressful and I was hoping for a miracle, I suppose, like some real forensic evidence that could act as a flashing neon sign for us."

"Even with a lab on site, forensics can take a bit of time. And I gave Ivy and Callum a huge list of things to work on, maybe too huge. Did either of you get anywhere with looking into the cold case aspect of all this?"

Ivy motioned at Callum, who was with her at UB headquarters in a conference room for the meeting. "You've talked to the families of two of the Slayer victims so far, right?"

"Right. Just finished up with Sanford, and I spoke to the Cardenas relatives earlier this morning. Tomorrow I've got Morrison and Wilcox lined up. The Morton family is out of the country on vacation. I'm working through the time zone differences with them for a conference call, possibly later tonight. Or, rather, really early tomorrow morning, like around two. I was able to revisit the body dump sites of all five victims, but nothing struck me that wasn't already covered in the original reports. As to Sanford and Cardenas, I've got a lot of information on their friends, families, where they liked to shop, eat, things like that. And I'm building a timeline of their last days. No overlap between them, though, not that I've found so far. Oh, and no ties to Palmer that I've been able to find."

Ivy chimed in. "I'm going to help him with all that eventually. For now, I've been working on a lot of the other things you wanted, like getting the Slayer cases uploaded to social media sites and websites devoted to bringing public awareness to cold cases. I've submitted requests to obtain cell phone records from their respective carriers. Oh, and when Callum visited each of the dump sites, he got me some great pictures and measurements of the marks the killer made in the trees. I took pictures and measurements at the site up here, where Rogers was found. All of it's been sent to a tool mark analysis expert to see if the same tools were used for all the murder scenes."

"That's great," Ryland said. "You've got the ball rolling on a lot of analysis. That should really help when we start getting the results back."

"Thanks, but I'm not done. Let's see, what else..." She swiped through several screens of notes on her computer tablet. "Okay, here we go. I've hired a geographical profiling expert to compare all the cases. He's new to us, but Trent recommended him from a case he worked before coming to UB. And I got in touch with the original special agent who did the profile for Bree's office when she was investigating the Slayer. I know we want a different profiler this time, but I also didn't want to insult the original agent and cause UB any problems in the future. So I very nicely and carefully explained that we were looking for fresh eyes on this and had a new case to consider as well, the Rogers case. And of course the newest one that just happened, but I don't have solid information on that one just yet. It went pretty well. He gave me another contact, and that guy has a lot more experience. I'm hoping for a profile in the next few days. Well, two profiles, actually, as you requested. One without the Rogers case and one with." She swiped through her notes, then sat back. "I've got a lot more to look into but that's it so far."

Bree laughed. "Ivy, I think you got more done in a few days than I'd get done in a week. I'm super impressed with you, with all of you. Thank you so much for your hard work."

"Of course," Ivy said, smiling. "Happy to help."

"Thanks Ivy," Ryland added. "I agree, everyone's done a tremendous amount of work. I think the elephant in the room that no one has mentioned yet, though, is DNA. I was hoping the evidence from the Slayer cases would be re-tested, and that Gatlinburg PD might allow our lab to test for DNA on the Rogers murder. Has anyone had any traction with that?"

Trent, who'd been typing on his computer for most of the call, waved at the camera. "I can speak to that."

Ryland sighed heavily. "Honestly, I think your report on guardrails can wait."

Several of the investigators laughed.

Trent made a wounded look. "I'm shocked you don't find my construction bidding process to make travel safer for all of us riveting. But I'll forgo that report today. You were asking about DNA. I'm your man. Everyone else was socked with work, so I volunteered to work with Rowan to get the evidence to the lab, and I checked in with Chief Russo about the Rogers case. The Rogers case is still being looked into by the medical examiner, and they're not ready to send samples over. But they will. As for the rest, I literally just got a report in my email on that. Hold on to your seats, folks." He cracked his knuckles like a major league pitcher getting ready to throw a fast ball.

"Hold it," Ryland said. "Does this mean you didn't look into what happened with Bree's SUV being forced over a cliff?"

"I hate to save him from a thrashing," Brice spoke up. "But I took point on that, and there really isn't a lot that he could do that I'm not doing. I'm actively working with Gatlinburg PD but don't have anything yet."

"Hey, hey, hey," Trent said. "Ivy reached out to me for help. This is legit."

Ryland arched a brow. "Ivy?"

She held her hands out in a helpless gesture. "You did tell Callum and me that if we ended up needing help to ask someone else on the team. I asked Trent."

Ryland groaned.

Ivy grinned.

"Before you guys duke it out," Faith spoke up, "I forgot to tell you as part of my report that I called the Monroe County medical examiner's office to check on the latest murder victim. Sheriff Peterson has a standing order for everyone to share information with UB, so that really helped. The victim who was killed late last night, or early this morning, however you look at it, was Stephanie Zimmer."

"I should have guessed," Bree said.

"You knew her too?" Ryland asked.

"Knew *of* her. Another one of those rare cases Palmer lost. And like Rogers, she was obviously guilty. She poisoned her husband. A search warrant issue had key evidence in the case thrown out. There wasn't enough evidence after that to get a conviction, so she walked."

"Bree," Trent said, "I really like you, but you're on my time right now. I've got important stuff to say."

She laughed at his teasing. "My apologies. Go ahead."

"Hold that thought." This time it was Callum who spoke up. "Ryland, that side research into Palmer's prosecution win percentage is shaping up. There's definitely something going on there, and it's not just what happened to Liam Kline. I should have the final report from the private investigator in Monroe County by the end of this week."

"Thanks, Callum."

"Enough. I'm not kidding." Trent sounded exasperated. "I just got some information and, trust me, you really want to hear this."

Ryland glanced at Bree before looking back at the computer. "All right. What do you have?"

Trent leaned toward the camera. "This literally just came through. Our lab was able to find DNA on two of the Slayer's old cases. Thanks to the Monroe County Sheriff's Office, the evidence was perfectly preserved, and the DNA wasn't degraded. Ladies and gentlemen, we have the DNA profile of the Smoky Mountain Slayer."

Bree pumped her fist in the air. "Yes! All we have to do is put it into CODIS and hope there's a hit—"

"That would take days, maybe longer. I went on a hunch, based on what you and Ryland have been telling us. I specifically asked for a comparison with a specific person. I was right. We have a match."

Bree stared at the screen in shock. "Are you telling us you know the identity of the Smoky Mountain Slayer?"

He smiled in triumph. "I certainly do. His name, ladies and gentlemen, is Silas Gerloff."

## Chapter Twenty-One

Nearly a week later, Bree was cursing beneath her breath and trying, without any luck, to get comfortable in a hard plastic chair at the Monroe County Sheriff's Office.

Ryland chuckled beside her. "You're not big on waiting, are you?"

She shifted again. "These chairs are awful. I can't believe my boss is making us sit in the public waiting area until he's ready to meet with us."

"Maybe it's his way of reminding you that you're officially on leave, essentially a civilian. I'm sure he's not happy that you were involved in the investigation with me."

"I'm not on leave anymore. My week has been up for several days."

"I seem to remember a requirement about meeting with a doctor before you came back."

"Pfft. I'm sure he's not going to enforce that. It's silly. I'm obviously fine. Besides, we solved the Slayer case for him." She motioned toward the TV on the opposite wall, with a banner scrolling across the bottom. "It's all over the news. The way you and Grayson spun things, it gives most of the credit to the Monroe County Sheriff's Office. Peterson should be thrilled about that, and that Gerloff has been charged. Plus, it's only a matter of time before they catch Kline. Thanks to your lab finding DNA at the two most recent murder sites, and comparing it to the profile on record with the Tennessee violent offender database, we have a match. Kline is the copycat."

She looked up at him. "The part that sucks is that Palmer's in the clear and has been released. I would have preferred he experience the hospitality of the county jail a little longer. That file you've got with you proves everything Kline was trying to prove, that Palmer cared more about his winning percentage than whether someone was innocent."

He tapped the folder on his lap. "Don't worry about Palmer. When Peterson sees this, his days as lead prosecutor are numbered. He'll probably be disbarred and likely come up on charges."

She motioned toward the news report on the TV. "I just wish we could tell that to the media. It would be nice to get all the fawning over Palmer off the news and tell people what he's really like, that he doesn't deserve their sympathy. He may have been Gerloff's and Kline's victim as far as setting him up, but he did far worse to so many people."

He put his hand on top of hers where it rested on her chair. "What's really bothering you? Everything's working out. Peterson may yell a little, or a lot, to make sure you know he's still the boss. But he's not going to fire you. After everything you've done to close the Slayer case, as well as the copycat case, he wouldn't dare. So what's the real problem?"

She looked at his hand on top of hers and had to blink back unexpected tears. The problem was that she didn't want to ever let go. She'd finally found what she really wanted—him—and now they were about to go their separate ways. Him to Gatlinburg, her to her house ten minutes away. There weren't any more excuses for her to stay at his house.

And there wasn't any point in trying to explore this… whatever it was between them. A long-distance relationship wasn't an option when neither of them wanted to give up their respective careers. And driving two hours to work each day and two hours home? That would get old fast, wearing both of them down.

"Bree? What's wrong?"

Dare she tell him? She looked up into his handsome face, those gorgeous green eyes riveted on her as if the only thing in the world that mattered right now was finding out what was bothering her. He cared about her. No doubt. But did he care as much as she hoped?

She had to take a chance. If she didn't, she'd regret it for the rest of her life. There had to be a way to overcome the distance between them, literally, the two-hour commute. She didn't have a clue what the solution might be. But at least if she told him how much she cared about him, how desperately she wanted to explore a relationship with him that didn't involve bad guys and flying off cliffs, he'd know how she felt. And then he could let her know if he felt the same. Even rejection, as much as it would devastate her, was better than not knowing.

She drew a steadying breath, then slowly turned her hand palm-up, threading her fingers with his.

His brows rose, and his gaze shot to their joined hands. His Adam's apple bobbed in his throat. "Bree? Is there something you want to tell me?"

"Yes. There is. I—"

"Detective Clark, Mr. Beck, the sheriff will see you now," a voice called out.

Bree groaned at the sight of Peterson's administrative assistant in the waiting room doorway, motioning for them to follow her.

Ryland squeezed her hand, then stood, pulling her with him.

"I don't want to go," she complained.

He laughed. "You can't put off talking to him forever. It's the only way to get reinstated at your job. Besides…" He held up the folder. "Justice awaits."

SHERIFF PETERSON GLANCED up from his desk as Ryland and Bree walked into his office. If Bree didn't know him better, the thunderous frown on his face would have scared her right back to the waiting room. But he was all bark, very little bite, as long as he respected you and trusted you. And she'd never done anything to make him not trust her. Well, except for not following his orders about not working the case. And she hadn't gone to the therapist. She bit her lip. Maybe she should be worried after all.

"Close the door," he ordered, his voice gruff.

Ryland closed it, then shook hands with him before taking a seat across from Bree in front of his desk.

"Good to see you again, Sheriff," Ryland said. "Under much better circumstances than when UB discussed taking on the Slayer cold case six or seven weeks ago."

Since her boss was glaring at her until Ryland started talking, she gave Ryland a grateful look for drawing his attention.

"Yeah, well," Peterson said to Ryland. "Things turned out much better than I ever anticipated. We're building a strong case against Gerloff for the Slayer killings. The DNA evidence your company was able to get seals the deal. It's a huge relief bringing this to a resolution and getting justice for the victims and their families."

"Unfinished Business isn't done yet. Aside from Adam Trent working with your detective team, I'm happy to bring more investigators here if you need them. In Gatlinburg, two of them—Ivy Shaw and Callum Wright—are supporting what Trent's working on here, chasing down loose ends, hunting for more evidence. We'll follow your lead at this point and transition to a background role. We won't quit until you've got everything you need for the prosecution of Gerloff, and Kline as well, once he's located."

"Much appreciated. I know Detective Mills has been grateful for the help from that Trent fellow. As for the Rogers and Zimmer murders, your work on that has helped us avoid those becoming cold cases too. Without your lab's touch-DNA tests proving Kline was at both crime scenes, I don't know that we could have gotten him on those. He really knew what he was doing, wearing gloves and keeping the bodies so pristine and devoid of forensic evidence. I hear the DNA you found was on some of the leaves and debris in both locations that you got after performing a follow-up CSI collection at both sites. And that the DNA you collected is most likely from sweat that dripped off Kline's forehead as he dumped the bodies. It's amazing you were able to key in on that." He frowned. "Of course now it's a matter of finding him. Kind of hard to find a guy when the only picture we've got is over a year old. And we don't know if he's still using his Palmer disguise."

Bree sat forward in her chair. "At least the public has

been alerted that if they see someone they believe is Palmer, that they should be careful, and of course look for the telltale signs of a mask. Up close, it should be easy to tell the difference. Not that we want anyone that close to him."

He slowly turned to face her, his expression hardening. "What part of me ordering you not to participate in the investigations and to get some rest did you not understand?"

She blinked. "I, ah, I did get some rest. Sort of. And—"

"From what I hear, you've been poking that nose of yours into all things Slayer-related from the moment Mr. Beck rescued you from that cliff. Why are you even here? You should be home right now."

"My week is long up. I even went several days past that. Now I'm back, ready to help Mills and the rest of the team wrap up the loose ends on the investigations."

"Oh, well, in that case. Just hand me the doctor's note and I'll let you be on your way." He held out his hand and arched a brow in challenge.

"You, ah, weren't really serious about making me see a shrink, were you?"

He crossed his forearms on his desk. "You don't seriously want us to lose a case, and let a bad guy go free because you were too selfish to follow protocol and get cleared to return to duty, do you? I warned you about what defense attorneys would do if you aren't cleared."

She crossed her arms. "You're not playing fair."

He rolled his eyes. "Bree, I appreciate everything you, Mr. Beck and UB did. More than you can possibly imagine. But I don't make these rules just to hear myself talk. It's important. PTSD is nothing to joke about.

Call the doctor. Make an appointment. Until then, you're still on leave."

She grumbled beneath her breath.

"What was that? Were you thanking me for not firing you for insubordination? Is that what you were saying?"

She forced a smile. "Of course. Yes, I was thanking you. Sir."

"You're welcome. Now, if there's nothing else—"

"Actually," she said, "there is one more thing. It's about Palmer. I heard he's been released. Is he back at the office? Is he in today?"

"He's been released, but unlike you, he has enough sense to follow protocol. He's on administrative leave and has already been seeing the therapist over the stress of everything that's gone on."

"Leave it to Palmer to make me look bad."

"Don't blame Palmer for your actions. Why are you asking about him anyway?"

She was still stinging from his rebuke, but supposed she deserved it. "We want to interview him."

He straightened. "Interview him? About what? The man was framed for murder. What do you want to talk to him about?"

She motioned to Ryland. "You want to answer that one?"

He tossed the folder on top of the desk. "When we believed that Palmer might be a killer, UB dug into every facet of his life. One of the items that came under scrutiny was his incredible winning percentage as a prosecutor. I've personally never heard of any prosecutor with a percentage that high. And there's a reason for that. It's not legit." He motioned toward the folder. "What you'll find in there is evidence of gross prosecutorial misconduct on many of his cases. Bree and I wanted to ask Palmer some questions about all that. But since you're making her continue her administrative leave, I'm happy to turn the information over to you to do with as you see fit. And I'll be glad to drive Bree home."

She frowned at him, but when she would have complained, Peterson flipped open the folder.

"Gross prosecutorial misconduct, huh? Can I assume you mean he withheld information from the defense that could have been exculpatory, like what happened in the Kline case? He purposely allowed defendants to go to prison, even though he had evidence that might exonerate them?"

"Yes sir. Exactly that. There's a pattern, too much of a pattern to be an accident, as was argued in Kline's civil case."

He sat back. "I should have argued harder with the mayor after that civil suit. I told him he should fire Palmer. But the mayor wanted to give him another chance, in case it really was an accident."

Bree leaned forward again. "You really did that? Argued to fire him?"

"You and Mr. Beck aren't the only ones to be suspicious of that winning percentage. I imagine some of the cases I've questioned over the years are in this folder. But getting the mayor to let us look into it is a whole other matter." He tapped the folder. "Thank you, Mr. Beck. I don't think the mayor can ignore this now. Not after Kline went on a killing spree because of Palmer's actions. And not with the evidence you've got in here. Palmer's days around here are numbered."

Peterson stood. "If that's all, I've got another meeting to get to. And you, *Detective* Clark, need to go home. I'll set up an appointment for you at nine tomorrow to see the doctor. If she gives you the all clear, consider yourself reinstated."

"Oh, thank you, sir. I really appreciate it."

"Go on. Before I change my mind." He softened his order with a smile.

Bree smiled back, and headed out of his office with Ryland.

# Chapter Twenty-Two

"Here we are again," Bree said, as Ryland pulled his Rover up to her house. "Feels like forever since I've been home." She waved through the windshield at her neighbor, Mrs. Riley, who was in her front yard, weeding.

"It's been one of the longest toughest stretches in my life too. But it hasn't all been bad. Some of it has been pretty damn good."

She blinked. "It has?"

He smiled, that slow sexy smile that made her stomach jump. "Oh, yeah. *Really* good."

She cleared her throat. "Would you like to come inside with me? Maybe we can talk about the really good part?"

He leaned over and pressed an achingly sweet kiss against her lips. But it was over far too soon. "Bree, I'd love to come in and…talk. I really would. But I have an errand to run first. It's important, and I'm not sure how long it will take. An hour, maybe longer, maybe not. As soon as I can, I'll come back. Okay?"

An errand. She sighed. "Okay. If it takes a while, don't worry about the time. I'll wait. I mean, I'll be here. I'm not going anywhere." Inwardly she cringed at how desperate and needy she sounded.

She opened the Rover's door, but before she could hop

out, he asked, "Bree? You really love it here, right? Madisonville? Your job at the sheriff's office?"

"Well, yeah. I do." She searched his gaze, hoping. "Why do you ask?"

"No reason. Just thinking. Your neighbor seems really nice. Mrs. Riley, right? The one who helped you get back into your house after, well—"

"My purse and keys ended up at the bottom of the mountain?" She smiled. "Yes. She's a nice lady. Ryland—"

"I need to get going."

Her smile faded. "Right. Your errand."

"See you later," he said as she got out of the truck. "And, Bree? Be careful. Don't open your door to anyone, especially if you don't know them, or they look like Palmer. I'm telling you, that mask Kline has is incredibly lifelike."

She patted her jacket pocket. "I'm carrying. Don't worry. And I'm not opening the door for anyone but you."

Again, desperate-sounding. But his warm smile had her whole body tingling. Her pride came to her rescue, keeping her from begging him to skip his errand. As nonchalantly as she could, she waved goodbye and headed into her house.

She closed the door and flipped the dead bolt.

The unmistakable sound of a shotgun being pumped had her freezing.

"Hello there, Bree," a raspy voice called out from behind her.

Very slowly, she turned around. She blinked in shock to see Prosecutor Palmer standing in her foyer, pointing a shotgun at her chest. She'd have sworn on the stack of Bibles Ryland had once mentioned that the man standing four feet away was the real Palmer. But the voice was different, telling her this was fake-Palmer.

"Amazing, isn't it?" He turned his face left and right. "Cost a fortune in plastic surgery to get it just right."

"Plastic surgery?"

"I tried a mask at first, but it was never as realistic as I needed it to be. And since my face was destroyed in prison," he spat out, "I needed a new one. The state wouldn't pay to fix my face, to make me look human again. But they paid in the end, after I sued them for everything they were worth. Oh, where are my manners? Allow me to formally introduce myself. Liam Kline, at your service."

She dove to the side, clawing for her pistol.

He dropped down on top of her, giving her wrist a vicious twist.

She cried out and dropped the gun. It skittered across the floor.

He leaned down, his body pressing on hers, his face twisting with rage. The eyes. The eyes were off. They were brown, like Palmer's. But there was nothing behind them, an empty pit of nothingness, as if he'd traded his soul to the devil.

"You and that Ryland guy ruined everything. I was excited at first when I heard the rumors around town that UB was re-opening the Slayer case. Nothing else I'd tried had worked to make Palmer pay, and I figured this was my chance, that I could frame him as the Smoky Mountain Slayer. So I killed Rogers and planned my next steps. All I had to do was make sure someone from UB saw me the day Palmer went to Gatlinburg, thought I was him, then found the body where I'd planted his wallet. Then I'd do whatever else I could to push, keep piling on more supposed evidence to make sure they believed Palmer was the bad guy."

"Like pushing my truck off a cliff? And trying to make it look like Palmer had done it?" She inched one of her hands back toward where she thought her pistol had fallen. But the way he was pressing against her, she couldn't turn her head to look for it.

"Exactly like that. It was kind of a spur-of-the-moment thing. But I was watching from the woods when you drove up to UB in that Monroe County Sheriff's SUV. It didn't take any inside knowledge to figure out you were bringing the evidence from the Slayer case. What better way to escalate things than to kill you and frame Palmer for it? Doesn't matter that you didn't die. As long as Palmer was blamed."

He narrowed his eyes. "But after finding that body, instead of accepting the clues I was leaving that pointed to Palmer as the killer, you and Ryland got too nosy for your own good. You talked to Gerloff and figured out his connection to me. Everything fell apart after that. Revenge was the only thing I had left to live for, and you took it from me. Now you're going to pay. *Both of you.*"

A burst of white-hot pain exploded in her skull as the butt of the shotgun slammed against the side of her head.

## Chapter Twenty-Three

Ryland had proof that the entrepreneurial spirit was alive and well in Madisonville, or at least as far as Melanie Holland was concerned. She'd demanded an outrageous sum to sell Bree's painting to him. But he'd gladly paid, using his own money, not UB's, knowing how much it meant to Bree. With the painting safely stowed in the back of his Rover, he headed back to her house.

He was a block away when his phone buzzed with an incoming text message. With so much going on with the investigations right now, he didn't want to ignore it. He pulled to the curb to read the text. It was from Bree.

Ryland, I have a few more details to add to the investigation. Can you come to my house?

He stared at the text a long moment, then typed his reply.

ETA ten minutes. See you soon.

Three dots on the screen showed she was typing her reply.

Okay. See you in ten.

He quickly navigated to his favorite contacts and pressed a button.

The voice came through the phone on the first ring. "Hey, Ry, what's going—"

"Trent. Please tell me you're still at the sheriff's office."

"I'm still at the sheriff's office. Why? What's—"

"I just got a weird text from Bree. She asked me to come over to discuss the investigation."

"The investigation is over from her standpoint, isn't it?"

"Exactly. But the weird part is, she already knew I was coming back. And it wasn't to discuss the case."

"Ah. I see. So… I'm not sure I follow. What's the problem?"

"Has Kline been caught yet?"

"No. And I'd know, believe me. I'm sitting with Detective Mills right now. He'd be one of the first to hear about it."

"I don't think Bree sent that text. I think Kline is at her house, right now, with her." He glanced at the time on the dash clock. "If I'm not at her house in a few minutes, Kline's going to kill her. We have to figure out a way to save her, now."

Ryland spoke fast, bouncing ideas off Trent while keeping a close eye on the time. He didn't want to risk going past that ten-minute ETA. He could have bluffed for an even longer amount of time, but he also didn't want her alone with Kline any longer than she had to be.

Six precious minutes had flown by since Bree's, or

Kline's, text to him. After he hung up with Trent, he dialed another number in his contact list.

And prayed they would take his call.

# Chapter Twenty-Four

Bree twisted her bound hands behind the back of the chair she was tied to, desperately trying to get free without allowing her body or the chair to move enough to alert Kline.

He paced in front of her like a caged tiger from one end of the family room to the other. The dining room chair he'd dragged into the middle of the room for her to sit on faced the front door, and she had no doubt as to why. When Ryland got here, the first thing he'd see was her, tied up, a gag in her mouth. From there, it would go one of two ways. When Ryland rushed in to save her, Kline would either fire a bullet into Ryland, or he'd fire one into her. Either way, one of them was going to experience the horror of seeing the other one die before Kline finished them off.

Regret was heavy on her mind as she thought about the things she wished she could change. Like that night at Ryland's home when she'd kissed him, then went into the bedroom alone. She'd been terrified by the depth of her emotions for a man she'd just met, and terrified at the prospect of losing her heart to him with all the obstacles in their way. Now, she might never have a chance to tell him how she really felt—that she was as in love with him as she could possibly be. Two weeks or two years, didn't matter. Ryland meant everything to her. And he'd never know it. Why, oh why hadn't she told him?

Of course, she knew why. They were both consumed with their careers, neither of them even considering giving up their jobs to move the two hours away to the other's town. And she'd known him for such a short amount of time, it was difficult to trust her feelings. Were her feelings real? Were they brought on by the trauma they'd shared after her truck went over the cliff? Or were they the foundation of forever, worth giving up a career and her hometown?

She loved him. But did he love her? The fear that he didn't, a very real fear given that neither of them had spoken about their feelings, was what held her back. What would probably still hold her back even now, even if she had a chance to tell him.

It didn't matter. None of that mattered right now. What mattered was figuring out some way to save Ryland. There was no way she was getting out of this alive. But if she could do something to alert him, to warn him, maybe he would survive.

She worked and twisted at the rope around her wrists. How long had it been? She was running out of time. Ryland would be here soon.

Kline paced back and forth, back and forth, mumbling to himself. Suddenly, he stopped in front of a decorative mirror on the far wall, as if he'd been working up his courage and that was his goal all along. To get up the nerve to look at his reflection.

He stared at it a long moment, slowly turning his head this way and that. Then he roared with rage and slammed his face against the mirror. Bree let out a startled yelp behind her gag, jerking her head the other way as pieces of glass rained down on her.

"Don't turn away from me," he ordered, suddenly right in front of her, blood welling up from cuts on his face, his neck. "Look at me." His fingers curled like talons. "Do you have any idea what it's like to see the face of your enemy every time you catch your reflection? Do you?" He raked his nails down his cheeks, leaving bloody welts in their tracks. "Do you?"

She leaned as far back as the chair would allow, shaking her head no. Her wrists throbbed, something hot and wet running down her fingers. Blood, probably. But she couldn't stop. She had to get free.

He slowly straightened, eyes narrowed, blood dripping. "You'd never know it, Bree. But I was a good-looking guy before your prosecutor railroaded me into prison. I had a family, a wife, sons, a career. Palmer took all of that away. Then I was forced to pretend I liked a man I despised, a monster, who whispered sickening details about the people he'd tortured and killed every night as I lay in my bunk, trying to sleep so I could escape the hell my life had become, if only for a few hours. But there was no escape. His tales followed me into my dreams, my nightmares. And even if he hadn't told me all that, everyone in the prison knew how sick and twisted he was. Anyone who crossed him got hurt. Even the guards were afraid of him." He grabbed her shoulders. "Are you listening to me? Do you know what you've done?" He slapped her, slamming her cheek against the back of the chair.

She cried out against the gag, her cheek throbbing with pain.

Then, as if a switch had flipped, the demented monster cocked his head, studying her as a bird might eye a

worm, or a cat might eye a bird. But instead of pounc-
ing, he slowly straightened. He used the edge of his shirt
to wipe at the blood on his face, then cleared his throat
and pulled a pistol out of his pocket.

Bree tensed, watching the pistol, his finger, as he
stroked the trigger.

"I've never killed an innocent person before," he said.
"Not that you police are innocent, but you get my meaning, right?" His tone was conversational, as if they were
two friends discussing their plans for the coming weekend. "I only used the knowledge Gerloff gave me to kill
bad people, dangerous people, monsters like him who
should have been locked away, and who would have been
if not for Palmer's incompetence."

He spit the name Palmer as if it was an epithet. His
nostrils flared, and he began to pace again, his pistol
clutched in his right hand.

She twisted again, ever so slightly. One of the loops
around her wrist fell away! But not enough for her to free
a hand. She picked at the rope, working at the next loop.

He stopped pacing a few feet from her and pulled out
his phone to look at the screen.

Another loop fell away. Bree froze, hoping he couldn't
tell there was some slack in the rope where it tied her
waist to the chair.

He frowned and put away the phone. "He should have
been here by now." He raised his gun, aiming it at her
head. "Looks like I don't get that grand finale I was
going for."

"Kline! Freeze!"

He whirled around, firing shots down the hall where
the voice had come from.

Bree screamed behind the gag and shoved her feet

against the floor, using the momentum to propel herself and the chair against Kline's legs.

They both crashed to the floor, the chair hitting his shoulder.

Kline roared with rage and shoved the chair off him, throwing it, and Bree, against the coffee table. She landed on her side, the metallic taste of blood filling her mouth. She rocked the chair, ignoring the pain as she desperately tried to yank the loosened ropes free.

Kline slowly rose to his feet.

Bree looked past him, down the hall. Was that Ryland who'd tried to help her? Had he been shot? *Please, God, let him be okay. Let him live.*

Kline raised his pistol, his face mottled and red as he pointed it at her once again.

The front door crashed open, slamming against the wall with a loud bang.

Kline dove across Bree and whirled her chair around like a shield, crouching behind it with his gun thrust against her cheek. "Just in time, Beck. You get to see me kill sweet curvy Bree."

Beck? Bree twisted toward the door. Ryland stood in the opening, aiming his gun at Kline.

"Shoot her, and you won't get to talk to your wife." Ryland held up his phone, the screen facing them. "She's right here, Kline. She's on the phone. You can see her, talk to her. She wants to talk to you."

"Becky?" Kline's voice was filled with wonder and hope. "Is that really you?" He frowned. "I can't hear her. Turn up the volume."

"Move away from Bree. Come into the foyer so you can talk to Becky."

Kline shoved the gun harder against Bree's cheek. "Turn it up. Bring it closer so I can see her."

"It's as high as it goes. And I'm not going anywhere until you turn your gun away from Bree." Ryland looked down at the phone. "What's that. Mrs. Kline? You're going to hang up if he doesn't let Bree go?"

"No!" Kline lunged to his feet, but kept the gun jammed against Bree's temple. "Drop your gun. Do it!"

Ryland dropped his gun. "She's going to hang up, Kline. I had to beg her to talk to you, but she doesn't want to see this, to see what you've become. I convinced her there was still some good in you. But you're proving me wrong."

"Give me the phone!" Kline jumped over the chair.

A sound came from the hallway. Trent lurched into the opening, blood dripping from his wrist as he brought up his pistol.

Kline whirled toward him, firing.

Trent fell to the floor.

Bree screamed, but only a muffled sound came out behind her gag.

Ryland tossed the phone at Kline.

"Becky!" Kline jumped to catch the phone.

Ryland scrambled for his pistol where it had slammed against the wall when he'd dropped it.

Kline caught the phone, a twisted smile on his lips as he lifted it. He looked at the screen, then shouted with rage. Ryland lunged for his gun on the floor as Kline whirled his pistol toward him.

*Bam! Bam! Bam!*

Bree stared in horror as the gun fell from Ryland's hands. His chest heaved as his gaze met hers. Then Kline gurgled and dropped to the floor, his eyes rolling up in his head.

Ryland pushed himself to his feet, then went to Kline, kicking his gun away. He pressed his fingers against his neck, checking for a pulse. He looked at Bree and shook his head. Then he ran to her and quickly untied her.

He pulled her onto his lap on the floor and yanked the gag off over her head. "Bree, how bad are you hurt?" His hands shook as he gently wiped blood from her mouth. "Bree?" he choked on her name.

"I'm… I'm okay," she whispered, her throat raw. "That psychopath slapped me and I bit my tongue."

Ryland's mouth twitched, then he grinned and chuckled. "You bit your tongue?"

"It's not funny! It hurts!"

He threw his head back and laughed, his shoulders shaking. But he quickly sobered and hugged her to his chest. "I thought I was too late. I heard the shots. I thought—"

"Trent! Ryland, he got shot. I think… I think Kline killed him."

Ryland kissed her, a quick warm kiss that she'd have reveled in at any other time. She tugged his hands down from her shoulders.

"Did you hear me? I think Trent's dead."

He didn't seem all that concerned as he turned slightly to look down the hall. "You dead, Trent?"

"Dead sore, that's what I am." He stumbled into the family room, clutching his bloody hand as he plopped onto the couch. "That jerk shot me four times. Knocked the wind out of me." He winced as he jerked his shirt open, sending buttons flying around the room. "Think I cracked a rib too."

Bree stared at his chest. "You were wearing a bullet-proof vest?"

"Yep. It's a good thing too."

"But…your hand, it's—"

"Scraped it on a nail outside, climbing the fence from Mrs. Riley's house. Your dang gate was locked."

"Mrs. Riley?"

"Your neighbor. She gave me a spare key to your house. Came in the back door."

"Then…you're okay?"

"Did you not hear the part about cracked ribs?"

Ryland gently turned her to look at him. "Trent's like a cat. He's got about three or four more lives left in him."

"Gee, thanks for the concern, buddy."

Ryland ignored him and gently touched the side of her head.

She winced and ducked away. "Ouch."

"I thought you said you were okay."

"I am. He hit me with his gun. But I'm fine. What happened right before Kline tried to shoot you? Did Mrs. Kline hang up on him? Is that why he was enraged?"

"She was never on the phone. I called her before I came in, begged her to help, but she refused to talk to him. That was Faith on the screen."

She blinked. "You bluffed?"

"I bluffed." He grinned. "And it worked. You're alive. That's all that matters."

"You could have been killed!"

He scooped her up in his arms. The sound of sirens in the distance had him rolling his eyes. "I told them to come in silent, no sirens."

"Told you they'd manage to screw it up," Trent called out.

"You were right. For once. Come on, Bree. Let's get you to a hospital. You might have a concussion."

"What about my cracked ribs?" Trent called out.

"I'm sure Peterson will be happy to give you a ride when he gets here." He pressed a whisper-soft kiss against her lips. "We have to stop meeting like this. It's a hell of a way to start a relationship."

She blinked, then grinned. "It certainly is. Maybe you can tell me another way to start one on the way to the hospital."

"I'd rather show you." He winked, then carried her out the door.

# Chapter Twenty-Five

"It's been a month since *The Incident*," Bree said, which was what she'd taken to calling that horrible day at her house with Kline holding a gun to her head. "I can't believe Peterson still won't let me come back to work. He's punishing me for not following all his silly rules." She frowned up at the darkening sky through the windshield of Ryland's Rover. It looked like they were going to finally get some snow.

"He's not punishing you." Ryland steered around a truck hauling a trailer of horses. "He couldn't let you go back until you were medically cleared after that nasty blow to your head."

"I had a mild concussion and a few stitches. No big deal. My doctor gave me a note to return to work two weeks later. That was two weeks ago."

"Has the therapist given you a note too?"

She crossed her arms. "I'm thinking about seeing a different therapist. This one doesn't seem to like me."

Ryland chuckled. "Poor Bree. Those doctors can be so mean."

"They totally are!"

He laughed again, then slowed and turned left down a road she'd never noticed on their other trips. "At least with all that time off, you've been able to see a lot more of me."

She smiled. "True. Definitely a perk." She looked around. "Um, this isn't the way to Gatlinburg. Where are you taking us? We have another hour to go, and we won't make it to Prescott Mountain before dark if we don't hurry. I know you hate driving in the mountains at night."

"You think you know me that well, huh?"

"I do." She took his right hand in her left one. "It's been amazing spending these past few weeks with you. That's the only good part about Peterson refusing to let me return to work."

He squeezed her hand, then let go so he could use both hands on the wheel. This road was a lot bumpier than the main highway they'd been on.

"Is this a short cut?" she asked.

"Sort of." He could feel her questioning stare, but luckily, before she could ask any more questions, they reached the driveway. He slowed and turned the Rover up the long drive, glancing at her to gauge her reaction.

Her eyes widened as the beautiful vista opened up before them. He loved seeing the wonder and awe in her expression as she took in the acres of rolling hills, the thick trees that lined the massive property, the pretty little pond out front.

"Ryland, who lives here? It's incredible." Her eyes widened. "Oh my. Look at that house."

He grinned. Just as he'd hoped, she seemed just as blown away at the beauty of the two-story log cabin's honey-toned walls as he was the first time he'd seen it. He pulled to a stop in front and cut the engine.

"Daylight's a-wasting," he said. "Let's go."

"Go where?"

He hopped out of the Rover and strode to her side as she got out. "Come on. The owner gave me a key."

"A key. Why would the owner give you a key?"

"Do you ever stop asking questions?" he teased as he unlocked the front door.

"I'm a detective. It's my life's work to ask questions. But usually I'm much better at getting answers. What's going…" She stumbled to a halt just inside the two-story foyer, her gaze locked on the painting on the wall beside the knotty pine staircase. She pressed a hand to her chest, just over her heart, her eyes filling with tears. "Is that… is that my painting? The one I gave to Melanie?"

"I'm told it's an original, that there weren't any copies made."

She turned to face him, her eyes bright and misty. "Do I have to beg you to tell me what's going on? Because I'm about ready to."

He took both of her hands in his and pressed a soft kiss against her cheek. "I know that painting was sentimental to you, because it was originally your gift to your mom. I hated that you traded it to your friend to get information on the case. So I bought it back. That's the errand I had to run the day of The Incident."

"Oh, Ryland. You didn't have to do that. But thank you. That's so sweet. But why is it here? Why are we here?"

"Don't you know, Detective? Haven't you figured it out? I adore you, Bree. I love everything about you. I've never met someone who enjoyed their work the way I do, who craves the answer to every question, who refuses to give up until they follow every lead, pull every thread to see what unravels. You make me laugh at your crazy theories and leaps in logic. And then you humble me by being right most of the time. You've taught me there's more than one way to solve a case, that I should be flexible and more open to new ideas. I'm the better for having met you. And yet, the very thing that I love about you, your love for your work, is the one thing keeping us apart."

She blinked back tears and bowed her head. "You love your job too. You're talking about the commute, right? Two hours one way. You're worried that once I go back to my job, trying to maintain a long-distance relationship won't work. Is that it? You've rented this cabin for the weekend so we can have one last good memory together? And hung that painting, trying to make it special? Honestly, if that's the plan, to have one last glorious weekend together before we break up, then I'd rather you just take me home right now."

He gently tilted up her chin. "Bree, sweetheart, I didn't rent this cabin for a weekend fling. I bought it. For us. I don't want two days with you. I want forever. If that means splitting the difference between our two workplaces and moving here, then that's what I'll do. This place is almost the exact halfway point. I'm hopeful that you can handle a one-hour one-way commute to work from here. But if you don't want to move, then I'll deal with it. I'll travel an hour to work every day, an hour back. Then another hour to your place in Madisonville if that's the only way I get to see you."

Tears streamed down her face. "You would do that for me?"

"I'd do that and more. It may seem crazy after only knowing you for such a short time, but my heart knew you the first moment I saw you. You're everything to me,

Bree. I love you. I'd be deeply honored if you'd agree to move in with me, and give the new commute a chance. But like I said, if you don't want to, it's okay. I'll do the driving for both of us."

For once, she seemed at a loss for words. He gently wiped the tears from her cheeks. "Bree, what's going on in that beautiful mind of yours?"

She sniffed, and drew a shaky breath. "I'm thinking that for a detective, you don't have a clue. I've been working with a real estate agent for the past two weeks trying to find someplace near the halfway point between both of our workplaces. But I don't have the budget you have, so I haven't had any luck." She laughed, smiling even as more tears streamed down her face.

He grinned. "Then you're okay with the plan? You'll give it a try?"

She nodded vigorously. "More than okay. You silly man. How could you ever think I'd say no? The Slayer case may have been your dream case. But you're my dream man. I half fell in love with you the moment you pulled me over the guardrail, saving my life. I fell the rest of the way when I found out you'd done that in spite of your fear of heights—a fear you've yet to explain to me but hopefully will at some point. It doesn't matter. Whatever is behind it, the fear is real. And you risked everything to rescue me. You're my hero, Ryland. You'll always be my hero."

His hands were shaking as he pulled her to him and ravaged her mouth with his. They kissed and kissed, the way she'd longed to for so very long. There was nothing in their way now, nothing keeping them apart. They loved each other. All this time she'd wondered if he did, and now she knew. And it was the most wondrous feeling ever. It gave her strength, made her feel whole and happier than she'd ever been. And it gave her hope for the future, one unshadowed by the past. All because of this amazing, gorgeous man who, by some miracle, seemed to love and cherish her the same way she loved and cherished him.

When he finally pulled back, he pressed one last soft kiss against her brow. His gaze searched hers, and then, slowly, he lowered one knee to the floor.

She stared at him, her mouth falling open as he pulled a black velvet box from his pocket and opened it to reveal the most beautiful diamond ring she'd ever seen.

"Yes," she said, holding out her hand.

"I haven't asked yet," he said, laughing.

"I'm a detective. I already knew the question."

He was still laughing as he slid the ring on her finger. "Just so there aren't any misunderstandings, when you move in here, you'll be moving in as Mrs. Beck. Is that your understanding as well?"

"Mrs. Clark-Beck, maybe?" She wrinkled her nose. "That doesn't flow very well, does it?"

"As long as I can call you my wife, I don't care what your last name is."

"Now that's a name I can live with."

He laughed and scooped her up in his arms. "Welcome home, my bride-to-be. Welcome home."

\* \* \* \* \*

# MISSING AT
# FULL MOON MINE

### CINDI MYERS

For Denise and Ron.

# Chapter One

Rebecca Whitlow did not scare easy, but right now she was afraid. It was the kind of fear that took hold of her stomach and twisted, and kept her up nights with visions of everything terrible that might happen to the person she loved. When she did manage to sleep, fear filled her dreams with reminders of all the ways she had failed.

She pushed that anxiety back as she stepped into the Rayford County Sheriff's Department and looked around.

"May I help you?" A woman with short white hair and purple-rimmed glasses looked up from the desk in the center of the room.

Rebecca approached the desk. "I need to speak to someone about a missing person," she said.

"Who's missing?" the woman asked, not unkindly.

"My nephew. He lives with me." Rebecca looked around the lobby with its gray-painted walls, white-tile flooring and photographs of various men and women in uniform. "Is there someone I can talk to?"

"Have a seat and I'll get someone for you." The woman picked up a telephone at her elbow.

Rebecca moved to a row of straight-backed wooden chairs along one wall and sat, feeling a little like a schoolgirl waiting to see the principal. She hadn't done anything wrong, but she didn't know what to expect.

A door across the lobby opened and a uniformed thirtysomething man with dark curly hair emerged. He glanced toward the desk and the woman there nodded at Rebecca. She stood as he approached. "I'm Deputy Wes Landry," he said. "How can I help you?"

"My nephew is missing," she said. "He didn't come home last night, he isn't answering his cell phone and none of his friends have seen him."

"Come back here and I'll get some more information." He ushered her through the door to a desk in a room crowded with two other desks, a filing cabinet, a water cooler and many stacks of papers. He cleared some papers off a chair and indicated she should sit, then moved to sit behind the desk. He opened a notebook and picked up a pen. "What is your name and what is your nephew's name?"

"I'm Rebecca Whitlow, and my nephew is Cash Whitlow. He lives with me." She gave her address and phone number, and Cash's mobile phone number. "He's nineteen," she added. "He's a climber—a very good one. He works part-time as a climbing guide and has some professional sponsorships." She pressed her lips together to cut off the flow of words. She had so much she could say about Cash, but how much would this deputy want to hear?

Deputy Landry looked up from the pad of paper, into her eyes, and she felt the warmth and compassion of that gaze deep in her gut. He had blue eyes, the deep blue of a bird's feathers, with fine lines fanning from the corners that suggested he smiled a lot. The emotion behind the look—and the emotions it kindled in her— were so unexpected she let out a small gasp.

"Are you all right?" he asked, one eyebrow arched in question.

She looked down to her hands, clasped together in her lap. "I'm really worried about Cash," she said. "Since he moved in with me four months ago, he's never failed to come home at night, but he didn't come home last night. When I try to call him, the call goes straight to his voice mailbox. He isn't answering texts, either. I spoke to two of his best friends and they haven't heard from him." She forced herself to lift her head and look at the deputy again. It was important that he believe her, and that he take her seriously. "Because he's a climber, I worry he's been hurt, maybe in a remote location, and he's unable to summon help."

Deputy Landry nodded. "Do you know where he planned to climb yesterday?" he asked.

"No. I'm not even sure he was going to climb yesterday, though it's something he does several times a week. This morning I drove out to a couple of places I know about, but he wasn't there. His friends promised to look for him, too, but I thought it was time to get the sheriff's department involved."

"What about his job—you mentioned he works part-time as a guide. Did he work yesterday?"

She shook her head. "I called the outfitter he works for and they said he didn't work yesterday. Weekends are usually his busiest times, but I know he didn't have a client Saturday or Sunday. His boss hasn't heard from him, either."

"You say he's lived with you four months. Where did he live before that?"

"He was in California—Petaluma. He lived with his mother."

"Why did he decide to move in with you?"

"He committed himself to pursuing climbing professionally and Eagle Mountain has a big climbing community. And…and Cash's father, my brother, Scott, climbed here. Cash was only ten when Scott died, in a climbing accident. Cash wanted to live here, I think, as a way of getting closer to his father."

"What was your nephew's mood in the past few days?" the deputy asked.

"His mood?"

"Was he happy? Was he upset about anything?"

The band of tension around her head tightened. "He seemed happy, I guess. He was talking about taking a trip with some friends to Grand Teton to climb, maybe later this summer."

"So he wasn't depressed?"

"No. Why are you asking that?"

"I'm just trying to get a picture of him, that's all." He glanced down at the notepad again. "Did Cash have any history of trouble with drugs or alcohol?"

"Are you asking that because he's nineteen? Or because he's from California?"

"I'm asking because it's a question I would ask about any missing person," he said, his voice gentle.

She forced herself to relax, and to tell the truth, as much as she hated to reveal this side of her nephew to someone who didn't know him. "Cash has struggled with addiction in the past," she said. "Heroin and pills. But he completed an in-patient rehab program six months ago and I swear he's been clean since."

"Relapses aren't uncommon," Deputy Landry said.

"I know that." She forced herself to lower her voice. "It's something I'm always watching for, but I swear, there haven't been any signs. Cash is focused on climbing. It's something he has a real talent for. He can have a good future in the sport, but he knows he has to be sober to pursue that dream." She leaned toward him. "Don't dismiss him as just another addict who's off on a bender," she said. "That's not who he is. I know something is really wrong."

"I promise I take your worries seriously," he said.

His gaze didn't waver and his reassurance made her feel calmer. She sat back. "Thank you."

"Do you have a recent picture of Cash?" he asked.

"Yes." She opened her purse and took out a colored flyer. A smiling Cash stood in front of a rock face, climbing rope slung over one shoulder. "This is a flyer for a climbing clinic he taught at last month."

"Climbing phenom Cash Whitlow," the deputy read. "So he's well-known enough other climbers would recognize him?"

"A lot of them would, I think. Especially if they live around here. He's gotten a lot of attention in the media."

"So some people might be jealous of him—someone so young and I take it relatively new to the sport getting so much press?"

A chill washed over her. "Are you saying you think someone might have…hurt him?"

"I'm trying to consider every possibility," he said. "Do you have any reason to suspect foul play?"

"None. Cash has never mentioned any threats, or even anyone acting jealous of him." She bit her lip, struggling again for composure. "You'd have to know him to understand, but Cash is someone who is very hard to dislike. He's very charming and he has a sweetness about him…" Her voice trailed off, and she tried again. "You probably think I'm just a doting aunt, but if you talk to his friends, you'll see I'm right."

The deputy picked up his pen again. "Give me the

names of some of his friends and how I can reach them, if you know. That will be a good place to start."

She gave him the names she knew and where they worked or where they would be likely to be climbing, as well as the name and number of the guide service Cash worked for.

"Did he have a love interest?" the deputy asked.

"Do you mean a girlfriend?"

"Or a boyfriend?"

"He wasn't dating anyone," she said. "He's flirted with girls, but he told me he didn't have time to get serious about anyone right now."

"Does he have a car?"

"Yes. He drives an old gray Toyota Tacoma with a topper over the bed."

"How old?"

She laughed. "Old. I think it's a 1995 or 1996. But it runs well."

"Does he camp out in it?"

"Sometimes. Especially if he wants to get an early start on a climb. But if he's going to be out late, he has always called me before. And he's never not responded to my texts."

The deputy nodded. "There are a lot of areas around here with no cell service. Especially in canyons where he might be climbing."

"Yes. That's why I'm so worried. If he's hurt, he wouldn't even be able to call for help."

"Is there anything else you think I need to know about Cash?"

She thought a moment, then said, "He's a good kid, but he's just a kid. He has a reckless streak."

"What do you mean?"

"He takes risks when climbing. It's one of the things

that makes him so good—that lack of fear. But he climbs alone sometimes, which everyone—even he—agrees isn't the safest choice. He thinks he's invincible—like most nineteen-year-olds, I guess."

"I'll start with the guide shop and his friends," the deputy said. "We'll put the word out for everyone to be on the lookout for him, and we'll ask for their help checking out places he might have climbed. We'll put out a bulletin with Cash's picture and a description of him and of his car. Maybe someone will see the vehicle and that will help us narrow the search area."

"I thought I would print flyers with that information," she said. "I could post them around town and give them to other climbers."

"That's a good idea." He stood and she rose also. He handed her a business card. "If you think of anything else, or if you learn anything—and of course, if you hear from Cash, call me," he said. "Anytime."

"Thank you."

He glanced down at his notes again. "If I need to reach you, is the number you gave me the best contact?"

"Yes. But I work weekdays, eight to six, at the Eagle Mountain Medical Clinic. If for some reason I don't answer when you call my cell, you can try that number."

"What do you do at the clinic?"

"I'm the office manager."

"You're not working today?"

"I took a personal day. I wouldn't have been able to concentrate, worrying about Cash."

"I'll call you right away if we learn anything," he said.

"Thank you. I just… I feel so helpless." The words burst out of her, and she felt a hot flush on her cheeks. This officer didn't care about her personal emotions.

"Not knowing what's going on with someone you love is always hard," he said. "But remember, you're not alone now. A lot of people are going to be looking for Cash, wanting to help him. If he's out there, we'll do everything in our power to find him."

He touched her shoulder—a light brush of his fingers, but she felt the warmth like a caress. She carried the heat of that moment with her out into the lobby and back to her car. Then she sat for a long moment, collecting her thoughts, which were a tangle of worry about Cash, and confusion over why she had reacted so strongly to Deputy Wes Landry. She interacted with men all day long, some of them as handsome and masculine as the deputy, but she was usually so sure of herself—what she wanted, who she liked. But the deputy had thrown her completely off-kilter.

"Was that Rebecca Whitlow just leaving?" Deputy Shane Ellis asked as Wes was finishing up his notes about Cash Whitlow. Shane stood in the doorway of the squad room, coffee mug in hand.

"It was," Wes said. "Do you know her?"

"She works at the clinic with Lauren."

Shane's girlfriend, Lauren Baker, was a nurse practitioner, Wes remembered. "She came in to file a missing person's report on her nephew, Cash Whitlow," Wes said.

"The climber?" Shane moved to the desk across from Wes.

"Do you know him?" Wes asked.

"I know of him. There was an article about him in the local paper about a month ago. He's apparently an up and coming star in the sport. Didn't you see it?"

"Guess I missed it." Wes had sworn off newspapers

when he worked in St. Louis, where he found the reporting either sensationalized, depressing or both. Maybe small-town publications were different.

"You need to keep up," Shane said with a grin. Then his expression sobered. "So what's up with Cash now?"

"Ms. Whitlow is worried he's gone off climbing by himself and been hurt. He didn't come home last night and he's not answering calls or texts. She spoke with a couple of his friends and they haven't heard from him, either."

"He's taking a big risk, climbing alone," Shane said. "If he did fall in some of these remote canyons, it could be weeks before someone finds him."

"That's what Ms. Whitlow is afraid of." Wes shoved his chair back and rose. "I'm going to talk to Cash's boss and a few more of his friends, then put out an APB on his car with a description of him. If we're lucky, he just stayed out late with a friend his aunt doesn't know about."

"He's young, right?" Shane asked.

"He's nineteen." *And a former addict.* He'd keep that information confidential for now, but if they didn't find the young man hurt in a climbing accident or out with friends, they had to consider he was back on drugs. He might have left town altogether, gotten in trouble with a supplier or even overdosed. There was a long list of the ways someone could get in serious trouble with drugs.

"Then that's probably it," Shane said. "He'll be mortified when he finds out his aunt came to us."

"Maybe. But I'd rather do too much than too little." He knew too well the consequences of inaction.

He walked down the hall to the sheriff's office and knocked. Sheriff Travis Walker looked up from his computer screen. "Hey, Wes." Lanky and handsome in a way that recalled big-screen cowboys, Travis had recruited Wes to join the Rayford County force when he heard his friend was looking to leave the big city. He hadn't questioned Wes's reasons for wanting to quit St. Louis, merely suggested the small town of Eagle Mountain as a change of scenery where he'd have a chance to deal with all kinds of cases and work independently at a slower pace. He had persuaded Wes that this rural sheriff's department could use an officer with Wes's experience.

"Rebecca Whitlow just filed a missing person's report on her nephew, Cash," Wes said. He filled the sheriff in on the details and added, "If he is in the habit of climbing alone, then an accident seems likely, but she also shared that Cash is only six months out of drug rehab."

"We don't have a huge drug problem in Rayford County, but it is here," Travis said. "There have been a few indications of a new supplier in the area, but nothing concrete. If Cash doesn't turn up at the climbing hot spots, I can give you some names of people to question, places to look."

"Thanks. I hope it doesn't come to that."

"Let me know if you need help with anything. You're still getting familiar with people here and I'll smooth the way if you run into any resistance." Travis's family had lived in the area for several generations and the sheriff seemed to know everyone.

"Thanks. I'll let you know if I need anything." He left the office and climbed into the black-and-white SUV that had been assigned to him. He'd start at the guide shop where Cash worked part-time, then head out to Caspar Canyon, where he'd seen climbers on the sandstone canyon walls almost every time he drove past.

On his way to the guide shop, he passed Eagle Mountain Medical Clinic. Every parking spot in front of the storefront clinic was filled. Since Rebecca Whitlow wasn't working, he wondered what she was doing now. Maybe she'd gone to the print shop to order the flyers she'd mentioned. Even in her anxiety, she had the suppressed energy of someone who was used to action. She hadn't delayed in coming to the sheriff's office to report her concerns about her nephew, and she had already started the search process, talking to his friends and driving to areas where she knew he climbed. She wasn't going to sit back and let others do all the work.

That kind of personality could be both a help and a hindrance to police work, Wes knew from experience. In St. Louis he had had to deal with parents and other relatives who second-guessed his every action or who interfered with investigations. Would Rebecca be like that?

He didn't think so. Or maybe he didn't want to believe it of her. He wasn't ready to think too much about the emotions that had arisen when he'd first looked into her warm brown eyes, a mixture of sexual attraction and personal connection that wasn't the most welcome combination when dealing with someone involved in a case. Moving to a small town must have led him to subconsciously let down the barriers that kept his personal and professional lives firmly separated. The lovely Ms. Whitlow just happened to come along at the wrong time.

Well, he'd deal with it. In any case she probably had a partner who wrestled steers for a living and was insanely jealous. He wouldn't blame the man.

Wes parked in front of Colorado Mountain Guides and entered. Displays of boots, packs and other climbing gear filled the front window and crowded the walls and aisles of the small space. As Wes moved toward the counter at the rear of the store, a muscular man with a shaved head and a silver goatee emerged from a back room. "What can I do for you, Deputy?" he asked.

"I'm looking for Cash Whitlow," Wes said. "I understand he guides for you."

"You're the second man this week who's been in here looking for Cash, but you don't look as angry as the first one."

"Oh? Who was that?"

"He didn't leave his name, but I can tell you he was riled up. Don't know about what, but he threatened to kill the boy if he saw him again."

# Chapter Two

Suddenly the disappearance of Cash Whitlow sounded a lot more serious. "When was this?" Wes asked.

"Yesterday afternoon." The big man leaned close, elbows propped on the counter. "I didn't catch your name. Are you new with the sheriff's department?"

"Wes Landry." Wes handed over one of his cards. "I've been with Rayford County a couple of months." Seven weeks, but who was counting?

"Doug Michelson." The big man stuck out a beefy hand. His handshake was firm but not crushing, for which Wes was grateful.

"Back to the man who was looking for Cash," Wes said. "What time was he here, exactly?"

"A little after two o'clock. He didn't say good afternoon or how do you do or anything. He just asked if Cash was here. I told him no and he asked—demanded, really—to know when he'd be in. I told him Cash doesn't actually work in the store. When someone needs a guide, I pass on Cash's information to them and the two of them arrange things between them. I handle the payments and take a twenty percent cut. That way Cash doesn't have to handle the accounting because, let's face it, most of these rock rats aren't into paperwork."

"What did the man say—exactly?"

"He said, *Next time you see Cash, you tell him I'm going to kill him if he doesn't mind his own business.* Then I asked him for his name and he said, *Cash knows who I am,* and left."

"What did he look like?"

Michelson rested his chin on his clasped hands. "I can tell you what he looked like, but here's the thing—I don't think it was what he *really* looked like."

"What do you mean?"

"He was wearing mirrored sunglasses and a big straw hat and I think a wig. A really bad black wig, like you'd buy for a Halloween costume."

"He was wearing a disguise?" Wes asked.

"I think so, yeah."

Wes took a notebook and pen from his pocket. "Tell me what you can."

Michelson straightened. "He was a white guy, about six-two, good build, like he worked out. He had on baggy jeans and a loud Hawaiian shirt—lime green with alligators and flowers on it. I think that was probably part of the disguise, too."

"Any rings?" Wes asked. "Earrings? Tattoos? What kind of shoes?"

Michelson shook his head. "I didn't notice any jewelry or ink, and I didn't pay attention to his shoes, either. Sorry."

"Do you have a security camera that might have gotten an image of him?"

"Nope."

"What about his car? Did you see what he was driving?"

"No. He headed down the sidewalk, east, I think."

Wes made note of this. You never knew what information might turn out to be useful. "When was the last time you saw or spoke to Cash?" he asked.

"I saw him last Thursday when he stopped by to pick up a check. I spoke to him on the phone Saturday morning, about a guy who wanted to book a guide for next month when he's in town."

"Did Cash talk about going out of town or anything like that?"

Michelson shook his head. "No. He sounded his usual self. We talked about climbing, and that's about it."

"Do you have any idea where he might be right now?"

"He lives with his aunt, Rebecca Whitlow. She called here this morning first thing, asking if I'd seen Cash. She sounded kind of worried. I didn't tell her about the man who was here yesterday looking for Cash. I didn't want to upset her. Have you talked to her?"

Wes nodded. "I have. Anyone else?"

"All the local climbers know Cash, you could ask them." His expression darkened. "Why are you looking for Cash? What's he done?"

"He hasn't done anything. His aunt hasn't heard from him in a couple of days and she's worried he might have gone climbing by himself and been hurt."

"One of the first rules in climbing is to not do it alone, but it happens all the time."

"Why is that, do you think?"

"Oh, there's always a good excuse." Michelson waved his hand in the air. "A guy is anxious to do a climb and his buddy can't go. Or he wants to be the first to climb a new route and wants to keep his plan secret. Or he just likes being up there alone. I get it, but that doesn't mean it's smart."

Wes tucked the notebook and pen back in his pocket.

"Let me know if you hear anything from Cash or about him."

Michelson nodded. "Will do. And I hope you find him, and that he's okay. As aggravating as he could be sometimes, he's a good kid, and a heck of a climber."

Wes left the shop, puzzling over the man in the Hawaiian shirt and straw hat. He sounded like a character in a bad melodrama, right down to the clichéd threats. Was Cash pulling some elaborate prank on the cops? But that would mean Rebecca Whitlow was involved and he didn't want to believe that of her. Her distress over her missing nephew had seemed genuine.

He asked about the man and Cash at other businesses along the street. None of the shop owners had seen the man in the Hawaiian shirt and straw hat, but they all knew Cash and dubbed him a good kid.

"Did you know him well?" Wes asked the manager of Mo's Tavern, a white-bearded man in a flat tweed cap who introduced himself as George.

"He and his friends come in here to eat a couple of times a week," George said. "Maybe have a few beers. Not Cash—he never drank, that I saw. Except those energy drinks in a can—he likes those. But nothing alcoholic. Not that I'd serve him. I know he's under age."

Wes handed George his card. "If you see him, let me know. He hasn't gotten in touch with his aunt and she's worried about him."

"Rebecca? Sweet lady."

"What can you tell me about her?"

George's eyes narrowed. "I told you—she's a sweet lady."

"Would you say she and Cash have a good relationship?"

"What are you trying to imply?"

"I'm not implying anything. Maybe they had an argument and Cash is lying low for a few days to cool off, or he resented having to live by her rules and moved in with a friend."

George shook his head. "Nothing like that. I'd say he thinks the world of her, and she feels the same about him. I saw her at the climbing festival last month, cheering him on when he was competing, and he sent her flowers on Mother's Day—he was eating lunch in here when she came and found him and thanked him and gave him a big hug. So if you think she had anything to do with him disappearing, you need to think again."

"I'm not drawing any conclusions right now," Wes said. "Just asking a lot of questions and gathering as much information as I can."

"You should talk to Basher Monroe. He's in here with Cash a lot. They had lunch in here, just the two of them, on Sunday." His expression sobered. "Come to think of it, they had their heads together, in what looked like a pretty serious conversation."

"Any idea what they were talking about?" Wes asked.

George shook his head. "No. We were busy and I didn't have time to stand around eavesdropping."

"Know where I can find Basher?"

"He hangs out at that area along County Road Five, by the creek. There's a stretch in there with some waterfalls and sheer rock faces where people climb. Basher drives an old ambulance he's converted into a kind of camper. He lives out of it, I think."

Wes made note of this. "Thanks."

"Cash is a good kid and I hope nothing's wrong with him," George said. "I'll keep my ears open and let you know if I hear anything."

Wes returned to his SUV, mulling over all he'd heard.

Cash was a good kid. Cash didn't drink. He had a good relationship with his aunt.

But nobody had seen him or heard from him in more than twenty-four hours. As much as Wes hoped he'd find the kid staying with a friend or climbing in an area with no cell service, he couldn't help sharing Rebecca's feeling that something wasn't right with this picture. And if they were right and Cash was in trouble, the longer he went unfound, the worse things might turn out to be.

REBECCA LEANED FORWARD and clutched the steering wheel tighter as she neared her house, only to sag with the weight of disappointment as she pulled into the empty driveway. She had hoped so strongly that Cash would be there, with some story of having dropped his phone on a night out with friends, or that he'd been stranded by car trouble in an area with no service. Her relief at seeing him would have overwhelmed any embarrassment she might have felt over having to call Deputy Landry to tell him to call off the search.

Walking into her empty house now, after she had asked the sheriff's department to help, made the reality of Cash's disappearance all the more dire. She wasn't the sort of person who dwelled on worst-case scenarios or who expected disaster at every turn, but fear for her nephew had lodged itself like a bone in her throat.

All she could do now was try to swallow past that fear and work on the flyer the deputy had agreed she should make and distribute.

She had dreaded going to the sheriff, worried the authorities would dismiss her as worried over an irresponsible teen who was probably out with friends, or worse, that they would focus on Cash's history of addiction and not the strength he had shown in overcoming those problems. But Deputy Landry had taken her complaint seriously. He understood the danger Cash might be in, and while he had been concerned about Cash's former drug use (he had to be, she acknowledged), he hadn't made it the focus of his efforts to find the young man. Or, at least, he hadn't admitted so to her.

She went to the desk in the corner of the living room and switched on her laptop, then headed to the kitchen, intending to make a cup of tea. But before she could fill the kettle her gaze came to rest on the photo in a magnetic frame on the front of the refrigerator—a young man in a climbing harness festooned with coils of rope, quickdraws, sling, belays and a chalk bag, climbing helmet shoved up to reveal a tangle of messy blond curls and a grin so broad and joyful it seemed to her the very image of happiness.

Though the resemblance to Cash was strong, this young man was actually her brother, Scott, Cash's father. She had taken that photograph of him here in Eagle Mountain, up on Dakota Ridge, eleven months before he was killed in a climbing accident not far from where this picture had been taken. She had hung the photo on the refrigerator, where she could see it every day, shortly after Scott's funeral, as a reminder that he had died doing what he loved most. Though he had been taken too young, deprived of seeing his son grow up, Scott would have had no regrets about how his end came.

*But please, God, don't let Cash be taken the same way.* Rebecca didn't think she could bear it.

Instead of making tea, she left the kitchen and went down the hall to Cash's room. She had searched the room earlier this morning, desperate for some clue as to where Cash might be, but had found nothing. No drugs—which was good—but very little else. A few clothes, some climbing magazines and a phone charger. The charger worried her—did he have one in his car? No diary, no books, no computer or letters or cryptic notes about planned meetings or get-togethers. Except for a pair of slippers by the bed and dirty clothes on the closet floor, the room looked much as it had when Rebecca had used it as a guest room. "I should tell him to put some posters or pictures on the wall when he gets back," she said out loud as she moved into the room.

Talking to herself probably wasn't a good sign, but the house felt so empty. Amazing how full one active teen had made it seem in the four months Cash had lived here.

She went to the open closet and gathered up the pile of dirty clothes. Washing them would give her something to do. She checked the pockets of the pants and shook out the shirts, then froze and stared at the dark stain down the front of one of the shirts—dark brown and stiff.

With a feeling of dread churning her stomach, she brought the garment to her nose. Was that a faint metallic odor? She dropped the shirt on the bed and stared at it, telling herself she was mistaken. The stain was barbecue sauce, or ketchup.

But she worked in a medical clinic. She had seen that kind of stain too often not to recognize its origin.

But why was there a bloodstain on the front of Cash's shirt? And whose blood was it?

# Chapter Three

Rebecca left a message for Deputy Landry to call her, but she didn't hear from him until he showed up at her house after six that evening. She answered his knock, heart racing, and stood frozen for a moment, searching his face, trying to read his expression. "Have you found out anything?" she asked, torn between wanting news and fearing the worst.

"I haven't found Cash," he said. "But I have some more questions and I got your message. May I come in?"

"Of course." She stepped back and held the door open wider. A stack of the flyers she had made sat on a small table by the door and she picked up one and handed it to him. "I made these and put some up around town," she said.

The flyer featured the picture of Cash from the climbing poster, with details about his height, weight, and hair and eye color, as well as a description of his truck. *Contact the sheriff's department or Rebecca Whitlow with any information*, she had printed in bold letters across the bottom of the flyer, along with her phone number. "No one has responded yet," she said. "I'll put more out tomorrow."

"That's good." He returned the flyer to her. "You said in your message you'd found something I should see?"

"Right. It may be nothing, but I thought you should see it." She moved to the kitchen, where a plastic bag containing the bloody shirt lay on the counter. She hadn't been sure what else to do with it. "I searched Cash's room again when I got home from talking to you," she said. "I didn't really find anything, but when I gathered up his dirty laundry from the closet, there was this." She handed him the bag.

He opened it and looked inside, then pulled out the shirt.

"I can't be positive, but I thought that stain looks like blood," she said. She was jittery with nerves. What if that was just a food stain or oil from working on his truck? But it hadn't smelled like those things, and there was so much of it.

Deputy Landry pushed the shirt back into the bag. "I'll have this tested," he said. "When you last saw Cash, was he hurt?"

"No. He was fine."

"When was that?"

"At supper, Sunday. He went out again after that, but I heard him come in late—around midnight. I woke up and heard him in the hallway. I called out to him and he said hello and apologized for waking me. He slept in the next morning, and when I came home from work, he wasn't here. I texted him and he didn't answer but I wasn't worried until he didn't come home last night at all. And when he still didn't answer my calls and texts, and none of his friends knew where he was, I decided to contact the sheriff's department."

Landry nodded, and put the bag with the shirt in it back on the counter. "We've got teams out searching Caspar Canyon and other known climbing areas," he said. "Tomorrow we've arranged to have a helicopter do an aerial search."

"That's great." With so many people looking, surely they would find Cash.

"Why don't we sit down?" he said. "I need you to fill in a few blanks in the information I've managed to gather."

"Of course." She led the way into the living room, to the sofa.

She sat at one end and he settled on the other and took out his notebook. "I talked to Doug Michelson at Colorado Mountain Guides," he said. "He hasn't seen or heard from Cash in a few days, but that isn't unusual. Apparently Cash only has contact with him when someone wants to hire a climbing guide."

"I know Cash is busier with that at some times than others," she said. "But he's not really interested in full-time work. He devotes most of his time to training and climbing. It's a different lifestyle from most people, but he's able to travel and do what he loves, and he has sponsors who help with expenses and gear."

"Mr. Michelson told me a man came into his shop yesterday afternoon, looking for Cash. He described him as about six foot two inches, with a muscular build. He wore a straw hat and a loud Hawaiian shirt and had dark curly hair, but Michelson thought that might have been a wig. Does that sound familiar to you?"

She stared, trying to make sense of his words. "A wig? Was this man in some kind of costume?"

"I don't know. Maybe he was trying to disguise his appearance. Michelson said he was angry. Can you think of anyone who might have been angry at Cash and looking for him?"

"No."

"When Cash moved here from California, was he moving away from someone or something?" Landry asked.

"No. Nothing like that," she said. "He came here for the climbing." She leaned toward him, sensing there was a lot he wasn't telling her. "Why was this man angry with Cash? Did he say?"

"He told Michelson Cash would know who he was and he threatened him if Cash didn't mind his own business."

"That doesn't make sense. What would Cash have been doing that made him so angry?"

"I don't know, and neither did Michelson. You can't think of anything?"

"No." None of this made any sense. "How did the man threaten Cash? What did he say?"

"According to Michelson, he said, *Next time you see Cash, you tell him I'm going to kill him if he doesn't mind his own business.*"

Dizziness washed over her and she might have swayed. Landry leaned over and gripped her arm. "It may have been an idle threat. The kind of thing someone says in the heat of the moment."

She nodded and wet her dry lips. "Or maybe it wasn't."

"I promise you, we're taking this seriously." He stood. "I'd like to see Cash's room."

She stood also and took him to the room down the hall from her own. "I've looked through it twice now and haven't found anything except that shirt. There really isn't much to look through."

The deputy stood in the doorway and surveyed the room, his eyes traveling over the unmade bed and simple dresser. "Does Cash have a computer?" he asked after a long moment.

"No. He uses his phone. It's not here, so I'm sure he has it with him, though he left the charger plugged in, on top of the dresser.

"Is anything else missing? I don't see any climbing gear."

"He kept all that in his truck."

He nodded and moved over to the dresser, and studied the few items on top—the phone charger, some change, a half pack of gum and a tube of lip balm.

Rebecca came to stand beside him. "Deputy Landry, how long have you worked in law enforcement?" she asked.

He looked at her, his gaze warm yet unnerving, but she forced herself to meet it. "Call me Wes," he said. "We're going to be seeing a lot of each other until Cash is found. And I was with the St. Louis Police Department for fourteen years."

"All right, Wes." The name was as solid and steady as him. "You can call me Rebecca. Have you worked many missing persons cases?"

"Quite a few."

"Then you must have some instincts about these things. What do you think is going on?"

He was silent so long she wondered if she had offended him. "Please, I'm not questioning your abilities," she said. "But I need you to be honest with me."

"Something isn't right," he said. "It feels like we're missing an important part of the story. The friends of Cash who I was able to talk to weren't aware of any new places he intended to climb, and they swear they haven't seen him or his truck in the past two days. I'm still trying to locate someone called Basher Monroe.

The manager of Mo's Tavern said he was a friend of Cash's—another climber who lives in an old ambulance he's converted to a camper."

"I know the person you're talking about," she said. "Or rather, I know of him. I've never met him." She frowned. "I wasn't aware he and Cash were good friends."

"George, the manager, said they ate at Mo's pretty often."

She blew out a breath. "Cash probably has a lot of friends I don't know about."

"Then there's the man in the loud shirt and the wig," Wes said. "There's something so off about him."

"I'm sure Cash never mentioned anyone like that," she said.

"Is Cash the type to play pranks?" Wes asked. "Would he set up something like this, not meaning to alarm anyone, but as an elaborate joke?"

"No!" She shook her head vehemently. "Cash is really quiet. He's very serious—too serious sometimes, I think. He isn't the extroverted jokester. You might even call him socially awkward—about everything except climbing. He's a different person on rock or ice, competent and very sure of himself."

"So climbing is pretty much his whole focus."

"I don't want you to think he's one dimensional." She struggled to find the words to describe her nephew. "He's very focused on becoming the very best climber he can be. Partly because he loves the sport, but also as a means to do even bigger things. He and I talked about that a lot. He really wants to work with kids, maybe troubled kids, to teach them climbing and about the outdoors—maybe at some kind of camp or outdoor school. Climbing is a pathway to that."

He nodded. "You're giving me a much better picture of him. Thank you."

They returned to the kitchen and he collected the bag with the shirt. "I'll be in touch," he said. "We're going to do our best to figure out what's going on."

"I have faith in you," she said.

The words seemed to pain him, and he shook his head. "Have faith in Cash instead. He's obviously a strong young man."

*Yes*, she thought when Wes had left. Cash was a strong young man. But if she had to depend on someone, she would choose a man of experience as well as strength. Someone like Wes Landry.

INSTEAD OF GOING HOME, Wes drove down County Road Five, hoping to find Basher Monroe. The sun was sinking fast behind the trees, casting the area beneath the limestone cliffs into deep shadow. The parking area was deserted and as Wes drove slowly through the area, he saw no vehicles or people.

Past the climbing area, the gravel forest service road narrowed, with dark evergreens crowding in on either side. The road became more rutted, and Wes had to slow his speed even more to negotiate the ruts. It didn't look as if this part of the road got much use.

He was looking for a place to turn around when he spotted a break in the trees. He eased his SUV into the space, intending to back out, but stopped when his headlights flashed off something metallic. He hit the switch for his spotlight and lit up the back bumper of a vehicle—something square and boxy, like a van.

Or an ambulance. He pulled out a large flashlight and, leaving the SUV running and the spotlight on, he moved toward the vehicle. As he walked closer, he could make out the faded red stripe all the way around the vehicle, the traditional marking for an ambulance. The vehicle was nosed into a small clearing some fifty yards off the road, mostly hidden by a thick screen of brush. Wes stopped ten yards away and called out, "Hello! Anyone home?"

No answer or even movement from the vehicle. No lights shone in the rear windows, which were covered in some kind of reflective material. "Hello!" Wes called again.

Here, deeper in the trees, it was almost full darkness. Somewhere in the distance, a coyote yipped and another group answered from farther away. A branch popped beneath Wes's boot and he froze, waiting and listening, but heard nothing except his own labored breathing and the rustle of a breeze high overhead.

He reached the back of the ambulance and shone the light along the driver's side. The driver's door stood open, though he could see nothing in the blackness within. "Hello!" he called again, but without much hope he'd receive an answer. Had Basher—or whoever drove this vehicle—fled into the woods when Wes had discovered his hiding place? He hadn't heard anyone running away, but maybe the throb of the SUV's engine and the thick duff on the forest floor had obscured the sound of running footsteps.

He took a deep steadying breath and moved forward. The beam of his flashlight illuminated the empty driver's seat, the upholstery patched in several places with duct tape, more tape around the steering wheel. A passage between the front seats provided access to the rear of the vehicle. Wes leaned in and caught the funk of stale marijuana smoke and cooking grease. He played the beam of light across a counter with a propane stove, a water jug cradled in a metal rack and a small dinette. The rear of the camper seemed to consist of a bunk, blankets piled on top of the mattress.

He froze, his light trained on the bunk, as he realized there was something beneath the blankets. Or rather someone. He fixed the beam on one bare foot poking out from under the covers. "Hey!" he called. Then louder, "Basher, is that you? Wake up!"

The occupant of the bunk didn't move. A cold chill crept up Wes's spine as he continued to stare at the bare foot, the flesh so white in the bright light. He heaved himself into the vehicle and climbed over the driver's seat and into the back. By the time he reached the bunk, he knew what he would find. He used the light to fold back the corner of the blankets farthest from that bare foot.

A big man with dreadlocks wet with blood stared up at him with lifeless eyes, his mouth open in a last cry of horror.

# Chapter Four

After Wes left, Rebecca picked up her phone. She needed to let Cash's mom know what was going on, though she'd been putting off the call as long as possible. She had never been entirely comfortable with her sister-in-law. Scott's death and Pamela's decision to move back to California hadn't brought them any closer. But for Cash's sake, Rebecca had done her best to maintain contact, though their infrequent phone conversations often felt stilted.

"Hello, Rebecca." As usual Pamela's voice was cool when she answered the call.

"Hi, Pamela. How are you doing?"

"I'm fine. Did you need something?" That was Pamela—no time for polite chitchat.

"Have you spoken to Cash lately?" Rebecca asked.

"No. Why? What has he done now?"

Why did she assume Cash had done anything? "I'm worried about him," Rebecca said. "He left the house sometime after I left for work yesterday morning and no one has heard from him since. I was hoping he'd mentioned his plans to you."

"Cash doesn't tell me his plans. And I'm not surprised he didn't tell you, either. He's probably gone off with friends. He'll come back when he's out of money."

"None of his friends know where he is," Rebecca said. "I'm worried he went climbing and got hurt. Has he talked to you about exploring a new area?"

"I told you, we don't talk." Pamela's voice had a sharp edge. "Especially not about climbing. I made it clear that I didn't approve of him going to Colorado. He would be much better off going into therapy than trying to work out his daddy issues hanging from bare rock. And you haven't helped matters by supporting him in this foolishness."

Rebecca flinched. Even over the phone she felt the force of Pamela's anger. "I don't think either one of us could stop Cash once he made up his mind," she said. "At least by giving him a place to stay, I could make sure he was eating and had somewhere to sleep besides his truck."

"But you don't know where he is now, so you can't say things worked out, can you?"

"Pamela—" Rebecca began.

"I'm sorry. That was harsh. But you haven't spent the last ten years dealing with Cash. I have. You don't know how many nights I lay awake worrying about him or how many miles I put on my car driving around looking for him when he was out partying or trying to score drugs. I thought when he finally admitted he needed help and went into rehab that things would be better, but instead of going back to school and getting a job and pulling his life together, he decided to run off to Colorado and follow in his father's footsteps. Fine. I'm done tying myself into knots fretting over his foolish choices." Her voice broke, and Rebecca wondered if she was crying.

"I know you did everything you could for Cash," Rebecca said softly. "I can only begin to imagine how hard it was for you. But I don't think this time it's just a matter of Cash doing what he wants without thought for anyone else. He's not back on drugs, and since he's come here, he's been working and dedicating himself to climbing, not just as a hobby but as a vocation. He's really talented and people think a lot of him."

Pamela sighed. "That's great. But I'm not as optimistic as you seem to be. I've been burned by his behavior too many times before."

Rebecca began to pace. She didn't want to frighten Cash's mother, but maybe she needed to. "This isn't like those other times," she said. "I think something is really wrong. If you have any idea at all—if he mentioned somewhere he intended to go or something he was thinking of doing or hinted at any trouble with anyone—we really need to know about it."

Rebecca's ears rang in the silence that followed. "Pamela?" she asked after a moment. "Are you okay?"

"I'm thinking. And I'm sorry, I don't know anything. Cash knew I didn't approve of his plans, so he didn't talk to me about them."

"If Cash gets in touch with you, will you let me know?" Rebecca asked.

"I will. Though he'd probably call you before he did me. Things haven't been very good between us lately."

"You're still his mother and I know he loves you," Rebecca said. "I'll let you know as soon as I hear anything."

"You do that." Pamela ended the call before Rebecca could say more. She laid the phone on a table and hugged her arms across her chest. Pamela sounded as if she had almost given up on Cash. Rebecca wasn't ready to do that yet. When she saw him again, she was going to give him a big hug—then sit him down for a serious discussion about where his life was headed.

PORTABLE FLOODLIGHTS ringed the old ambulance, the harsh white light glaring off the crime scene techs who combed the area for evidence. The light and flurry of activity made the forest around them seem that much more dark and impenetrable.

County Medical Examiner Dr. Butch Collins, a portly fiftysomething man with short gray hair and deep jowls, emerged from the van and expertly traversed the narrow path marked out by crime scene tape to join Wes and the sheriff on the edge of the clearing. "Your victim is a fit young man who was shot twice, in the side and in the back of the head. Either of those wounds could have killed him," he said. "I'll know more when I've had time to examine him more closely."

"I only noticed the head wound," Wes said.

"It gets even more interesting," Butch said. "The wound to his side—which could have damaged any number of vital internal organs—had been bandaged some time before he died. I think the head wound occurred later or at least after the victim or someone he was with went to the trouble to bandage the first wound. He wouldn't have been capable of bandaging the first wound after he was shot in the head."

"So it wasn't suicide," the sheriff said.

"Definitely not."

"When did he die?" Wes asked.

"I can't tell you that, either. Not yet," Butch said.

"Do you have any ideas?" Travis asked.

"Rigor has already passed, so more than thirty-six hours. I'll know more after the postmortem."

"Anything else we should know?" Travis asked.

"His hands are pretty battered—busted knuckles and some cuts."

"Did he fight off his killer?" Travis asked.

"I don't think so," Butch said. "The injuries look older than that. From the position of the body, I'd say the second shot was fired after he was already in bed—possibly after he had passed out or even after he was dead."

"He was a rock climber," Wes said. "Maybe the injuries are from that."

Collins nodded. "That's good to know." He looked back over his shoulder. "We'll transport the body and see what else you find in there."

Sergeant Gage Walker, the sheriff's younger brother, joined them as Collins was leaving. Taller and more outgoing than the sheriff, Gage was the most senior member of the force and Travis's second in command. "As soon as the body is out, you and Wes search the interior," Travis said.

"Ronin shot a ton of photos with the body in place," Gage said. He nodded toward the deputy with a camera. "I'll have him stand by in case we spot anything else we want documented."

Gage turned to Wes. "How did you ever find him? Tucked back in there, that ambulance isn't visible from the road."

"I was told Basher usually kept his camper parked near the climbing area," Wes said. "I came out here looking for him and when I didn't find him there, I drove down the road, thinking he might be pulled over somewhere. I'd given up and was turning around when my headlights glinted off metal and I took a closer look."

"Huh." Gage looked back at the ambulance. "I've seen Basher parked at a couple of different climbing spots around here," he said. "And sometimes behind the guide shop or the Cake Walk Café. I think he worked there as a dishwasher sometimes. It was common knowledge he lived in the old ambulance—I never heard of him even trying to hide the fact. Why were you looking for him?"

"I heard he and Cash Whitlow were friends. I wanted to know if he had seen Cash or knew what was going on with him."

"The interior is free for you to go in." Travis nodded toward the attendants loading a stretcher into a waiting ambulance.

Wes followed Gage up to the ambulance where Deputy Shane Ellis was dusting the door for prints. "Looks like the doors and the whole cab have been wiped," he said as they stopped beside him.

"You can do the rest after Wes and I finish up in the back," Gage commented and stepped up into the vehicle.

"This is a pretty sweet setup," Gage said. He opened a door behind the driver's seat to reveal a toilet and shower. Wire shelves held back accessories and a single towel hung neatly from a hook.

Wes moved past him to the galley area, with a two-burner stove, propane refrigerator and small sink. Cabinets overhead held dishes and dried and canned food, while doors underneath concealed a water tank and on-demand water heater. It was a compact, orderly setup. Wes focused on seeing it, not abstractly but as a window into the inner workings of its occupant. What could this living space tell him about Basher Monroe?

Basher had kept his space orderly and valued his privacy enough to live alone, away from other people, while still clinging to creature comforts like on-demand hot water and indoor plumbing. A rig like this, even if he had done all the work himself, wouldn't have been inexpensive to build, so Basher had gotten the money from somewhere—family or savings, maybe.

Gage emerged from the bathroom. "There's some gauze pads and tape and other first-aid stuff dumped in the sink in there," he said.

"Dr. Collins said he had a bullet wound in his side that had been bandaged," Wes said.

"Better have all the first-aid stuff checked for prints, in case someone else was with him," Gage said. He moved to the built-in dinette. "The wide body of the ambulance gives you a lot of room. And Basher put in a pretty good propane heater. I stopped to check on him after a big storm last winter and it was pretty comfortable in here."

"How long had he been living here?" Wes asked. He opened the refrigerator and studied the contents—some leftover Chinese food, peanut butter, eggs and a few beers.

"I don't know how long he'd been in the ambulance." Gage felt under the cushions on the dinette. "He showed up in Eagle Mountain last summer and stayed. He had Colorado plates, so I always figured he came from somewhere in the area. He told me once that the police in the last place he lived hassled him about living in the ambulance, but as long as he was on public land, or in a private location with permission of the owner, we figured he had as much right to be there as anyone. He never gave us any trouble."

Wes moved to the bed, avoiding looking at the blood-stained bedding, focusing instead on the nightstand beside the bunk. He picked up the wallet he found there and flipped it open. "His real name was Benjamin," he said. "Benjamin Wade Monroe." He did the math. "He was twenty-eight, and his license gives his address as Bethesda, Maryland." How had Ben become Basher, and how had he gotten from Maryland to Colorado? Was he estranged from his family or simply indulging in an urge to explore and travel? And who had he encountered who wanted him dead?

"Huh." Gage opened the cabinets over the dinette and rifled through the contents.

Wes set the wallet aside. "I'm wondering how the van got back here. Maybe he was afraid of his killer and tried to hide back here."

"Or maybe the killer tucked the ambulance back in here to delay discovery of the body," Gage said.

Wes opened one of two large drawers built under the bunk. Gage moved in beside him and opened the other drawer. "A lot of clothes," Gage said and slid his hand beneath the stacks of T-shirts and shorts.

Wes squatted down and shone his light into the drawer, which extended deep beneath the bunk. Recognition jolted through him, and he reached back and pulled out a bright green shirt.

"Wow, that is ugly," Gage said as Wes spread out the shirt with its pattern of alligators and orange hibiscus flowers against a lime green background.

He reached into the drawer again and pulled out a black wig—the kind of wig you might buy for a Halloween costume. The kind of wig worn by the man who had come into the guide shop and threatened to kill Cash Whitlow.

BEFORE RETURNING TO work Wednesday morning, Rebecca handed out flyers about Cash at every business she could find open. At the newspaper office, reporter

Tammy Patterson promised to write a story about Cash's disappearance, and almost everyone Rebecca talked to told her how much they hoped her nephew was found safe very soon.

Clinic Director Linda Cox welcomed her back warmly. "I saw the flyer about Cash at the coffee shop," she said. "If there's anything we can do to help, let me know."

"Can I post a flyer here?" Rebecca asked.

"Of course."

She had feared she would be too distracted to focus on work, but the clinic was so busy the constant influx of patients and phone calls claimed all her attention. Before she knew it, the whole morning had passed with only fleeting thoughts of Cash.

Linda was preparing to lock the door for lunch when Wes slipped inside. "I just need a word with Rebecca," he said.

Would she ever be able to see him without her heart in her throat? she wondered as she stood to greet him. "We haven't found him yet," he said, anticipating her question. "But I wanted to give you an update before word got out around town. We've found Basher Monroe."

"Does he know where Cash is?" she asked.

"No." His expression was grim. "Basher is dead. He's been murdered."

"Murdered?" She could say the word, but the implication refused to sink in. She swallowed. "That's terrible, but does it have anything to do with Cash?"

"I don't know." He looked toward where two of the medical techs stood, talking. "Could we go somewhere else and talk? It's your lunch break now, right?"

"Yes. I usually eat at my desk."

"Get your lunch and we'll go for a drive. It's probably the only place we can talk without a risk of being overheard."

She retrieved her lunch bag from the refrigerator. "Is everything okay?" Linda asked.

"I think so," Rebecca said. "He just has more questions for me."

She had to wait while he shifted a clipboard, a small duffel and a plastic file box out of the front passenger seat of the black-and-white SUV. "Welcome to my office," he said.

She slid in, trying to avoid contact with the long gun in a holder between the seats and the laptop computer mounted on the dash. A radio squawked and crackled, and he picked up the microphone. "Unit Nine, I'll be 10-7 for the next hour or so."

"10-4, Unit Nine," a woman's voice said.

"I just told dispatch I'm taking a lunch break," he said as he started the vehicle.

"Where are we going?" she asked as he pulled into traffic on Main Street.

"Is the River Park okay? It's a nice day and there usually aren't too many people out there."

"Of course." It felt odd to think of having a discussion about murder and her missing nephew over what amounted to a picnic instead of at the sheriff's office, but the idea wasn't unpleasant.

They didn't speak on the drive to the park, but the silence between them wasn't awkward. She wasn't always comfortable with people she didn't know well, but he was easy to be with. At the park, he retrieved a small cooler from the rear of the vehicle and led the way to a picnic table by the water. "Is this okay?" he asked.

"Sure." The scene was almost too beautiful for a discussion of murder and a missing young man, but it did offer a chance to talk without being overheard.

He sat across from her and took a sandwich and an apple from the cooler, along with a bottle of water. He passed her a second bottle. "Thanks." She unwrapped her own sandwich and stared at it, not sure she could eat. "Tell me about Basher."

"It's not pleasant mealtime conversation," he said. "Don't you want to eat first?"

"Not really." She pushed the sandwich to one side and opened the bottle of water. "How was he killed?"

"He was shot. In his camper in the woods out on County Road Five. Sometime after he and Cash had lunch together on Sunday."

"Do you know who killed him? Or why?"

Wes shook his head. He took a bite of sandwich, chewed and swallowed before he spoke again. "What can you tell me about Cash's friendship with Basher?"

"Almost nothing," she said. "He might have mentioned they had climbed together a couple of times, but Basher never came by the house and I'm sure I never even spoke to him. Why? Do you think Cash had something to do with his death?" The idea was absurd—and it made her cold with fear.

"We found a wig and a shirt that matched the description of that worn by the man who came into the guide shop yesterday morning and threatened to kill Cash if he didn't do what he was supposed to do," Wes said. "Doug Michelson at the guide shop says he's sure they're what the man was wearing."

"I don't understand," she said. "Why would Basher threaten Cash like that? And why wear a disguise?"

"I was hoping Cash might have said something to you that would help us figure that out," he said.

She shook her head. "It's so…bizarre."

"It is." He took another bite of sandwich. She pinched off a corner of her own sandwich and popped it into her mouth, scarcely tasting it as she chewed.

"That whole scene you described in the guide shop," she said. "The man in the outlandish clothes spouting the clichéd threat—from the beginning I thought it sounded like playacting."

"It sounds that way to me, too," he said. "I'm wondering if someone put Basher up to it. He was known as someone who did odd jobs around town. Maybe someone gave him the wig and shirt and told him what to say."

"And then killed him so he couldn't identify this person?" She shuddered. "Why go to all that trouble?"

"I don't know," he said. "And I'm not sure that scenario fits with the time of death. We're still waiting to hear from the coroner. But I can't help think if we could figure it out, it would help us learn what has happened to Cash."

"What about that shirt I gave you?" she asked. "Have you learned anything about that?"

"Not yet. I sent it to the lab this morning, but it could be several days before we hear back."

"I was afraid you'd say that, but it's hard to be patient at a time like this."

"It's hard for me, too," he said. "And I've had plenty of practice waiting for test results and experts' reports. It never really gets easier."

They continued the meal in silence, the gurgle of the river's current soothing some of her inner turmoil. "A play has to have an audience," she said. "So who was Basher—or whoever was wearing that wig—performing for? Was it meant for Doug?"

"Or for Cash," Wes said. "Maybe the threat was real. Cash did something or said something that made someone upset. Any idea who that might be?"

She shook her head. "No. He hadn't mentioned anything like that."

"What about a drug dealer? When Cash was using, did he ever do favors or odd jobs in exchange for drugs?"

The thought made her feel sick. "I have no idea. He was living in California at the time. But I would swear he wasn't using again. I was always alert for signs and I saw nothing."

"When someone has a history with drugs, it's always something we have to consider," he said.

"Did you find drugs on Basher?" she asked.

"Only a little marijuana—nothing illegal."

She folded the wrapper around her mostly uneaten sandwich and shoved it back into her lunch bag. "I hate not being able to do more to help," she said. "I've handed out posters, and I keep calling and texting Cash's number, hoping he'll answer. But it doesn't seem to be doing any good."

"I thought I'd go this evening and talk to some more climbers," Wes said. "Doug told me some areas they like to gather in the late afternoon to climb and trade tips. Would you like to come with me?"

"Do you think that would help?" she asked.

"I do. They might be more willing to talk to you than to me."

"Of course. I'll do anything to help."

"They're going to do the aerial search this afternoon and you did a good job of distributing flyers around town. Maybe someone will have some information for us soon."

"The longer he remains missing, the further away he feels," she said. She stared out toward the rippling water. "I called Cash's mom, Pamela, last night after you left my place. I'd been putting off talking to her, hoping to have good news, but I couldn't wait any longer."

"What did she have to say?" he asked.

How to describe her sister-in-law's reaction? "Pamela has had a hard time with Cash these last few years. She had to deal with him dropping out of school, his drug addiction and his wanting to pursue climbing, even though that's what killed his father. I think at this point she's expended so much emotional energy she doesn't have anything left to give."

"What did she say when you told her Cash was missing?"

"She said she hopes he's okay and that we find him soon, but I should remember that he has always been very insistent on making his own decisions, and has never been willing to take advice from others. If he's made another bad decision this time, I shouldn't feel guilty about it." She stared down at her fists, clenched on the picnic table in front of her. "That probably sounds cold, but she isn't like that. She's just been hurt so many times, by Scott's death, then by things Cash has done. I think that attempt at distance is her way of coping."

"Do you think it's possible Cash decided to go back to California and didn't tell you because he thought you'd be disappointed?"

"No. Cash wasn't the type to worry about disappointing other people. I don't mean that as a criticism. He was like Scott that way—when he made up his mind about something, he didn't care what other people thought about the decision. He did what he thought was right for him. That could be frustrating at times, especially when his decisions—like quitting school—seemed unwise. But part of me admired that he was so confident of his own judgment."

"He sounds like a very interesting young man. I'm looking forward to meeting him."

She looked up and his gaze caught and held hers. She might have kissed him at that moment, she was so grateful that he still talked as if finding Cash alive and well was only a matter of time.

# Chapter Five

Dr. Butch Collins suggested Wes and Travis stop by his office Wednesday afternoon. "I'm going to put everything I have to tell you in my report, but I know you're going to have questions," he said. "So you might as well save us all the delay and stop by."

Collins's office very much reflected the man, with fishing gear and hunting trophies sharing space with his medical license and commendations. He stood from behind a large, cluttered desk to greet them, then invited them to sit and shuffled through the stacks of paper on his desk until he found what he wanted. He passed a folder across to Travis. "There's the report, but the upshot is, Basher Monroe was shot at two different times, by two different weapons—a 45 caliber and a 12-gauge shotgun slug." He passed over two labeled evidence bags. "The slug is the one that killed him. The wound didn't look like much from the outside, but it caused massive internal injuries."

"So he was shot by two different people?" Wes asked.

"It gets even more interesting," Butch said. "The second shot—the one in his head—was made after he was dead. He was in bed, so the killer may not have known he was dead, and thought he was sleeping. Shot him in the head and left."

"It could have been the same person who shot him earlier, come back to finish the job," Travis said.

"But he brings a different gun this time?" Wes asked.

"How long had he been dead when he was shot?" Travis asked.

"I can't be certain, but enough time had passed for Basher, or someone else, to have bandaged the first wound and Basher to have gone to bed, where he died, probably after several hours of suffering. If he had sought medical treatment immediately after he was shot, he might have survived, but he might not have. In any case, by the time the second shooter showed up, Basher's heart had stopped beating and his blood had stopped circulating."

"Is there anything significant about the bandage?" Wes asked.

Butch nodded. "An amateur job, clumsily tied, but it would have been awkward doing it himself."

"Do you think he had help?" Travis asked.

"Probably, though I can't be absolutely sure."

"Do you have an estimate on the time of death?" Wes asked.

"I'd say between noon and four on Monday," Butch said. "He was a strong man. Considering the nature of the wound, he took a long time to die."

"And you're sure he died in bed?"

"Yes."

"Anything else we need to know?" Travis asked.

"Everything I found is in my report, but nothing significant beyond what I've already told you."

Travis stood and tapped the edge of the file on the desk. "Thanks, Butch," he said.

"I'll be interested to know how this one turns out," Butch said.

"I'll be interested to know how this turns out, too," Wes said as he and Travis walked toward the sheriff's SUV.

"The preliminary forensics on the crime scene came in this morning," Travis said. "There's no indication that the killer searched the ambulance or stole anything from it, though we can't be positive about that. Maybe he stole something small and was very neat about his search. We've hauled the ambulance to our impound lot for a more thorough search, but we didn't discover any fingerprints, except Basher's on the inside of a couple of cabinets. Everything else had been wiped down. No shoe impressions or tire impressions at the scene."

"So the killer had enough time to clean up after himself," Wes said. "That's a pretty remote area, so he must have driven there. Maybe someone in the area saw his vehicle."

"There aren't any houses nearby," Travis said. "But one of the climbers leaving the area might have passed the killer. It's worth asking about."

"A man wearing a black wig and a tropical print shirt like the one we found among Basher's belongings was at Colorado Mountain Guides just after two o'clock on Monday," Wes said. "It couldn't have been Basher. He was either dead or very near death at that time."

"So, was the man who came to the guide shop looking for Cash the same man who killed Basher?" Travis asked. "Or the person who shot Basher the second time? Maybe he came to the ambulance looking for Basher, saw him in bed and thought he was sleeping, shot him, then stashed the wig and shirt in with Basher's things."

"I've asked the lab to check for DNA and hair on the clothing and wig," Wes said. "Maybe they'll find something. I'm also going to press the lab about the analysis of the bloodstain on Cash Whitlow's shirt. I'm wondering now if it's a match for Basher. I know he and Cash were together on Sunday. The manager of Mo's Tavern, George Christopher, says the two of them had lunch together there and were involved in what he described as a serious conversation. They left together in Cash's Toyota pickup. I haven't been able to track their whereabouts for the rest of the day, until about six-thirty, when Cash returned to his aunt's house. He left after supper and came back again about midnight, then left sometime after Rebecca went to work Monday morning at eight and hasn't been seen since. We have one report of the ambulance Basher had converted to a camper being parked in the parking area for a climbing area known as the Falls, off County Road Five, approximately one and a half miles from where we found the ambulance on Monday afternoon."

Travis nodded, but made no comment. Wes kept reviewing everything he knew about Basher and Cash. Had the two friends fallen out and Cash shot Basher? Then who was the other shooter who had fired the bullet into Basher's head? Was the blood on Cash's shirt from Basher or someone else? Rebecca hadn't mentioned Cash being hurt, but could he have hidden that fact from his aunt? Could the blood be his own?

Deputy Jamie Douglas met them in the hallway of the sheriff's department. "I spoke with Mary Ann Schwartz just before I came on shift," she said. "She told me she and a friend went out to the Falls about eight o'clock Monday morning and Basher's ambulance wasn't there. Mary Ann works at Eagle Mountain Grocery and she volunteered this information when I dropped Donna at work this morning. She said Basher's rig was parked near the Falls when she drove out there Sunday afternoon to meet a friend, and he usually stays parked at one spot for weeks, so she was a little surprised to see he wasn't there Monday."

Donna was Jamie's younger sister, Wes recalled. He was still putting together all the relationships between his coworkers. Jamie was married to an officer with Colorado Parks and Wildlife, and Donna, who had Down syndrome, lived with them.

"Thanks," Wes said. "So Basher or someone else moved the ambulance sometime between Sunday afternoon and Monday evening when I located it."

"So what's the link between Basher and Cash?" Jamie asked. "Could they have had an argument that got out of hand, Cash shot Basher, then freaked out and ran? Or did the same person who shot Basher go after Cash and he fled? Or he's dead, too, and we just haven't found him yet?"

"We haven't found Cash's truck or any clue as to where he might be," Wes said.

"There are a lot of canyons and gorges and old mines where a truck or a person would be easy to hide," Jamie said. "Or maybe Rebecca's first supposition is right, and Cash went climbing by himself, somewhere off the beaten track, had an accident and was unable to call for help. If that's the case, it will take more luck than skill to find him."

"Delta Farm Spray did an aerial search for us this morning with one of their helicopters," Travis said. "They focused on canyons, cliffs and peaks that might be attractive to a climber, but they didn't find anything."

"We're not getting much out of the climbing community," Wes said. "When I speak to them, they say a lot of general stuff about what a talented climber Cash was, but they all say they don't know anything about his personal life."

"Maybe we need to lean on them a little more to get at the truth," Travis said.

"I plan to go back out to Caspar Canyon this evening," Wes said. "A lot of climbers gather there after they get off work. I thought I'd take Rebecca Whitlow with me. A lot of them know her and if she asked for their help, maybe they'd be a little more forthcoming."

"We're talking about two active young men with lots of friends," Travis said. "Someone knows something about what happened."

"I THOUGHT WE'D try Caspar Canyon first," Wes said when he picked up Rebecca at her house that evening. She had changed from her work clothes into jeans and a light sweater, but he was still in his khaki uniform. "Are you familiar with the area?"

"Oh, yes. I've spent a lot of hours watching my brother, and then Cash, train and compete there and other climbing spots around here."

"Did you ever do any climbing yourself?" Wes asked.

"Some. But I never competed. I didn't enjoy it the way Scott and his friends did. Actually, I'm a little afraid of heights. I'm more comfortable cheering from ground level."

"I'm with you there," he said. He headed toward the highway leading out of town. "I'm going to let you do most of the talking today. Sometimes my uniform and badge get in the way of people telling the whole story. I'm hoping they'll be more forthcoming with you."

"All right. But what do I say? Do I just ask if they've seen Cash or know where he planned on going?"

"Those are good places to start, but there are some

things I need you to try to find out." He glanced at her. "I know it makes you uncomfortable, but I need you to ask about drugs."

"But—"

"I know you don't believe Cash was involved with drugs," he interrupted. "And you may be right. But maybe his friend Basher was. Or maybe someone else was trying to get him back into that life. We need to know."

"All right."

"Ask if anyone had threatened Cash or if he was afraid of anyone."

Every possibility he raised seemed worse than the last, but if she was going to help, she had to face that. "I hate to think something like that was going on with him and I didn't realize it," she said.

"Don't beat yourself up," he said. "We're talking about a nineteen-year-old guy. They're not into sharing feelings much, especially with an aunt."

The comment surprised a laugh from her. "I guess you're right about that."

He signaled the turn onto the Forest Service road that led into a deep, narrow canyon that was popular with rock climbers in the summer and ice climbers in the winter. The rugged canyon walls offered everything from basic beginning routes to more challenging climbs. A dirt pull-off marked the start of the most popular section of wall, and Wes turned into this and parked. Half a dozen climbers were arranged on the cliff or on the ground. Several of them turned to look as Wes pulled the black-and-white SUV into the parking area. "See anyone you know?" he asked.

"Dave Hammersmith—everyone calls him Hammer—is in the blue climbing helmet with the young woman I don't know," she said. "Garth is the man with him—I don't know his last name. And I think that's Sam Mason on the cliff on the far left. He and Cash competed in several competitions I attended."

"Good. Start with the folks you know. Take one of the flyers and start with that."

They got out of the SUV and she walked toward the trio of two young men and a woman on the ground at the base of the cliffs. They watched, stone-faced, as she and Wes drew near. "Hey, Hammer," she said, addressing the shorter red-haired young man in the blue climbing helmet.

He nodded. "Hi, Rebecca." His gaze flicked to Wes, then back to her.

"I'm trying to get out as many of these flyers as I can," she said. "Spread the word about Cash."

Hammer took the flyer and looked at it. "I saw one of these at the coffee shop in town," he said. "I was sorry to hear about Cash."

"I'm really worried he went climbing somewhere on his own and is hurt." She looked at each of them. "Did any of you ever hear him mention any area—maybe a new route or something—that he wanted to climb?"

All three shook their heads. "I've been looking for him," the young woman said. "Hammer and I even drove around some this morning, looking for his truck."

"Kaitlyn and I drove miles," Hammer said. "I'm sorry we couldn't find him. We checked everywhere we could think of."

"When was the last time you saw him?" Rebecca asked, addressing the question to all three.

"We climbed with him on Saturday," Kaitlyn said. "He was having a great day, climbing this really gnarly ridge like it was nothing. We were talking about going up to Grand Teton at the end of the summer to climb and we told him he should join us. He said he'd like that, though he was hoping to find a youth camp or something that would hire him for the season."

Garth turned and addressed Wes. "Is it true somebody killed Basher?"

"Yes," Wes said. "Do you know anyone who might have wanted him dead?"

"No," Garth said. "What happened?"

"We found him in his ambulance. Someone shot him."

Garth swore. "Do you know who did it?"

"No. Had he argued with anyone? Did he ever talk about someone being after him?"

"Not Basher," Hammer said. "The guy was super mellow. All he cared about was climbing and traveling around in that ambulance. It was a sweet life. I can't believe someone would have it in for him."

"I was wondering if maybe Basher was into drugs," Rebecca said.

"No way," Garth said. "I mean, a little pot or beer, but that's not illegal." He cut his eyes to Wes.

"You know, Cash struggled with addiction in the past," Rebecca said. "I worried he might fall back into that."

"He didn't," Garth said.

"How can you be so sure?" Wes asked.

"Because he was so focused on staying healthy," Garth said. "He was determined to be the best climber ever and for that, you have to be in top shape."

"Cash didn't even drink beer," Kaitlyn said. "He wouldn't smoke anything, either. Some of the guys gave him a hard time about it."

"Not me," Hammer said. "I thought it just showed how dedicated he was."

"Did you ever hear anyone threaten Cash or Basher?" Wes asked. "Maybe they were trespassing on private land or someone was jealous of their skills?"

All three shook their heads. "That stuff happens, yeah," Garth said. "But I never heard it happening to either of them."

Rebecca pressed several flyers into his hand. "Could you pass these out to anyone you think could help?" she asked. "And tell them to give me a call if they know anything. Even if you think it's not important, it could help."

"Sure. And I hope you find him soon and he's okay." He turned to Wes. "I hope you find who killed Basher. He was kind of an odd guy, but he never hurt anyone."

Rebecca and Wes moved on to the climbers up on the wall. One by one, as each descended, Rebecca handed him or her a flyer and asked about Cash. But none of them had seen or talked to him recently or knew anything about his plans. When there was no one left to talk to, they returned to the SUV.

She settled into the passenger seat and sighed. She had hoped speaking with Cash's friends would bring them closer to finding him, but she only felt more confused.

"Thanks for coming with me to talk to the climbers," Wes said.

"Do you really think it did any good?"

"We got a little information we didn't have before. I know some new questions to ask."

"We keep asking all these questions," she said. "I'm ready for some answers." And soon. Before Cash's time ran out.

## *Chapter Six*

"The climbers we spoke with yesterday were adamant that neither Cash nor Basher were involved with drugs, and they couldn't think of anyone who would want to harm either of them," Wes reported at the Thursday morning meeting at the sheriff's department.

"No mention of Cash wanting to leave town or having a disagreement with his aunt that might have led to him deciding to move on?" Gage asked.

"Nothing like that." He checked the notes he'd made right after their conversation with the climbers. "He talked about getting a job this summer working with kids, maybe at a youth camp."

"Trey Allerton is supposedly building some kind of youth camp on the land he leased from Sam Russell," Shane said.

"But there isn't actually a camp yet, right?" Wes asked. He had helped with the investigation of rancher Sam Russell's murder, and had visited the ranch. Trey Allerton had been questioned in that case, and in the murder of a young woman by Allerton's former business partner, but Wes hadn't personally met the man.

"Allerton has been busy talking up the project and raising a lot of money, but he hasn't done much when it comes to actual construction of his youth ranch," Shane said. "I can't see that he'd be in a position to hire employees yet."

"Go talk to Allerton," Travis said. "Jamie, you go with him." The sheriff slid back his chair and stood. "Allerton thinks he's charming. If you pretend to be impressed, he might let down his guard. He may not know anything about Cash, but I'm curious to find out if they crossed paths."

"I know the type." Jamie stood also. "I'll do my best." She turned to Wes. "Have you been to Allerton's place before?"

He shook his head. "Only to the main ranch."

"Then I'll drive. Prepare to be unimpressed."

On the way to Allerton's place, Jamie filled Wes in on what she knew about Trey Allerton. "He was in the army with Shane's fiancée's brother," she said. "That's how Shane and Lauren met—she came to us because her brother's widow went missing in this area. Or rather, she'd run off with Allerton and broke contact with everyone else. Allerton claimed to be the brother's best friend and apparently romanced the widow after the brother was killed in action. He sold her on the idea of building this youth ranch and apparently she's footing the bill for most of it from money she inherited.

"But he seems to keep associating with murderers," Wes said. In addition to his former business partner who killed a local woman, a man Allerton hired to work for him murdered Sam Russell.

"He's either incredibly unlucky when it comes to picking associates, or he's attracted to a criminal element," Jamie said. "I'll let you make your own judgment when you meet him. I'm interested in what you make of him."

Allerton's residence, as Jamie had warned, was unimpressive. The metal-sided mobile home had been painted turquoise at some point in the past, though the color had softened to a dusty pastel. The area in front of the trailer was dirt, and no attempt had been made to landscape the sagebrush and weeds that passed for a yard. "How many acres does he have?" Wes asked as he and Jamie climbed out of her cruiser.

"Sixty acres. He says there's going to be bunkhouses and cabins for the kids and staff, a stable and hiking trails, a dining hall and who knows what else."

Wes looked around at the expanse of sagebrush and cactus, a leaning barbed wire fence stretching toward the horizon. "How long has he been here?" he asked.

"Three months," Jamie said.

"Not that much time when you consider the scope of the project he's proposing," Wes said.

"Maybe not," Jamie said. She led the way to the set of wooden steps that led to the front door of the trailer, and knocked.

"Who is it?" a woman's voice called through the door.

"Deputy Jamie Douglas and Deputy Wes Landry, from the Rayford County Sheriff's Department. Is that you, Ms. Baker?"

"Trey isn't here," the woman said. "I don't know when he'll be back."

Jamie's eyes met Wes's, worry tightening her expression. "Could you open the door so we can talk to you a few minutes, Ms. Baker?" she asked.

A chain rattled and a lock turned, then the door eased open.

Courtney Baker was a petite blonde who might have been any age from twenty-five to forty. Though her features hinted at beauty, her long hair hung limp, obscuring half her face, and her T-shirt and jeans sagged on her slight frame. "Ms. Baker, are you all right?" Jamie asked. "Have you been ill?"

"I'm fine." Courtney squared her shoulders. "What do you want? I told you, Trey isn't here."

"Where is he?" Jamie tried to look past her. "And where is your daughter, Ashlyn?"

The lines around Courtney's mouth deepened. "Ashlyn is with Trey. He likes to take her with him when he's working."

"Can we come in?" Wes asked.

"Now isn't a good time." Courtney started to close the door but Wes shot out a hand to stop her.

"Wait." He held out one of Rebecca's flyers. "Have you seen this young man? He's missing and his family is very worried about him."

Courtney took the flyer and studied it for a long moment, though the fall of hair in front of her face hid her expression. At last she handed it back to Wes. "I'm sorry, I haven't seen him."

"We were wondering if Trey had talked to him about his youth ranch," he said. "Cash mentioned wanting to work with kids."

"No," she said. "I'm sorry, I can't help you." This time she succeeded in closing the door, and they heard the lock click into place.

"Something is really wrong," Jamie said when they were back in the cruiser.

"She wasn't very happy to see us," Wes said. "Do you think she's lying about having seen Cash?"

"I don't know about that, but everything about her is wrong. She's lost weight since I saw her last and she looks terrible." She stared toward the trailer. "When I first met her, she was this gorgeous, perfectly put-together woman—hair curled, nails done, clothes just so. And you saw her now. Everything about her is different."

"Maybe we caught her on a bad day," Wes said. "She wasn't expecting company."

"Did you see how she kept her hair all down in front of her face? I think she was hiding something."

"Such as?"

"I think she had a black eye. I couldn't be sure, but I thought I glimpsed bruising." Jamie gripped the steering wheel. "I have half a mind to go back up there and confront her."

"You could try," Wes said. "But I don't think it will do any good. She had plenty of opportunities to ask us for help and she didn't."

"It bothers me that Allerton has her little girl, too." Jamie shuddered. "Maybe Courtney didn't say anything because Allerton threatened to hurt Ashlyn."

"Do you think he'd do that?" Wes asked.

"I don't know," she said. "He comes across as a charming, all-American guy who just wants to help kids, but to me that always felt like an act. Like underneath the mask he's much darker."

"We could sit here and wait for Allerton and Ashlyn to return," Wes said.

"Not here." She started the cruiser's engine. "We'll park up the road a ways, where he can't see us. If he's up to something, I'd like nothing better than to catch him in the act."

REBECCA WAS WORKING the clinic's reception desk on Thursday afternoon when a handsome blond man approached, a little girl in tow. "May I help you?" she asked.

"We don't have an appointment or anything. I just

need to check my stepdaughter's vaccination records," he said. "Her mom couldn't remember if they're up-to-date."

Rebecca leaned forward to smile at the little girl, a blue-eyed blonde who shyly returned the smile. "What's your name, honey?" she asked.

"Ashlyn Baker," the man said before the girl could answer and offered her date of birth."

Rebecca typed in the information and pulled up the girl's record. Under parents' names, only her mother, Courtney Baker, was listed. "What is your name, sir?" she asked.

"I'm Trey Allerton." He grinned, a dimple forming on the left side of his mouth and the fine lines deepening around his blue eyes.

"And you are Ashlyn's stepfather?" Rebecca asked.

He leaned closer and lowered his voice. "Her mother and I aren't actually married, but since her father passed away several years ago, I'm definitely the father figure in her life."

"I'm sorry, but I can only give out medical information to an authorized person," Rebecca said. "If Ashlyn's mother will stop by, I can give her Ashlyn's vaccination records."

"I understand. I just thought I'd check as long as we were in town."

She nodded and expected him to move away. Instead, he struck a casual pose, leaning against the pillar beside the front counter. "Aren't you Rebecca Whitlow?" he asked.

"Yes."

"I saw the flyers about your nephew, Cash. I'm really sorry to hear he's missing."

"Thank you. Do you know Cash? Have you seen him recently?"

Allerton shook his head. "No, I just know of him. I saw the article in the local paper. He sounds like quite an accomplished young man."

"He is. If you see him or his truck or know anything about him, we'd appreciate it if you'd call one of the numbers on the flyer."

"Oh, I will. It's really amazing in a town this small no one has seen or heard anything."

She nodded and focused on the computer. This man's interest was beginning to bother her. Was this his idea of flirting?

"Did Cash know that young man who was murdered?" Allerton asked. "I heard he was a climber, too."

This was starting to feel creepy. "I really don't have time to talk," she said. "I have work to do."

He straightened. "Sure. I didn't mean to bother you."

The door from the back of the office opened and physician's assistant Lauren Baker entered. "Trey, what are you doing here?" she asked.

"Aunt Lauren!" Ashlyn stood on tiptoe to see over the counter and grinned at her aunt.

Lauren returned the smile. "Hey, Ashlyn." She hurried across the office and through the door leading to the waiting room. The little girl ran and threw her arms around her. Lauren gathered Ashlyn into her arms and turned to Trey. "Where's Courtney?" she asked.

"She's back at the ranch. Ashlyn and I are having an afternoon out together." He smiled at the little girl, but Lauren put a protective arm around her and took a step back.

Allerton held out his hand. "Come on, Ashlyn," he said. "We need to go."

"I want to stay with Aunt Lauren." The little girl tightened her hold around Lauren's neck.

"Aunt Lauren has work today," Allerton said. "Come on. I'll buy you an ice cream."

"You don't have to go with him if you don't want," Lauren said.

"I want ice cream." Ashlyn pushed out of Lauren's arms and hurried to join Trey.

He took the child's hand and gave Lauren a smug look.

"Tell Courtney to call me," Lauren said as he headed for the door.

He said nothing, merely left. Lauren hurried back into the office. "What did he want?" she asked Rebecca.

"He asked about Ashlyn's vaccination records. He said he was her stepfather."

"He is most definitely not her stepfather." Lauren's voice was brittle. "I hope you didn't tell him anything."

"Of course not. He isn't listed on her records as authorized to receive any information."

"Sorry. I wasn't implying you don't know your job. Trey Allerton just makes me so angry."

"He's your sister's boyfriend?" Rebecca asked.

"Sister-in-law. Courtney is my brother's widow. Trey Allerton was in the army with my brother, Mike, though I never heard him mention the man. He showed up one day and poured on the charm and Courtney fell for it. Now he has her living in a trailer on some ranch land he leased, financing his dream of building a camp for troubled youth—though so far no one has seen evidence that he's doing anything more than fundraising at this point. I can't believe Courtney let him take Ashlyn off alone. I wouldn't trust him with my pet cat—and she has claws to defend herself."

"Ashlyn didn't seem upset about being with him," Rebecca said carefully.

"Ashlyn is barely three years old," Lauren said. She shook her head. "Why would Trey need to know about her vaccination records?"

"I'm not sure if that wasn't just an excuse to talk to me," Rebecca said. When Lauren stared at her, she flushed. "He was asking a lot of questions about Cash, and about Basher Monroe."

"You need to tell the sheriff," Lauren said.

"Why?" The idea alarmed Rebecca.

"Trey Allerton has a history with them. Two people he associated with were murderers. If he was asking about Basher, maybe it's because he knows something."

Gail, one of the techs, stuck her head into the office. "Lauren? Dr. Mezaluna is on line three," she said.

Lauren left and, after she checked that no one was waiting for her, Rebecca dialed Wes's number. The call went to voice mail. She left a message for him to call her, then tried to focus on the billing information she needed to enter into the computer. The visit from Trey Allerton had been upsetting, though she couldn't articulate why. He was probably one of those people who got a thrill out of being close to tragedy, as long as it wasn't their own.

JAMIE MANEUVERED THE cruiser behind a stand of pinion trees alongside the road, a few hundred yards and slightly uphill from Trey Allerton's driveway. "We'll be able to see Trey when he gets home," she said. "He drives a black F-150." She lowered the windows before switching off the engine.

Quiet enveloped them. A warm breeze carried the

scents of dirt and sagebrush. "Not much traffic up here," he said.

"There are some hiking trails near an abandoned mine at the far end of the road," Jamie said. "But they don't get a lot of use. A young couple live in a yurt about a mile farther on, and there's an old guy who lives on some mining claims past them, and that's about it."

"What's the guy mining?" Wes asked. "Gold? Silver?"

"I don't know," Jamie said. "Supposedly there's still some of each around here, plus a lot of rare earth minerals—the stuff they use to make cell phones and computers. But there must not be enough to make it worth putting in all the effort to get to it. I think Martin Kramer is just one of those eccentric people who march to a different drummer. He's kind of a grouch, really, but he isn't hurting anyone."

"I guess it's not a bad life, if you like your own company," he said. He had never aspired to be a hermit, but there were times when he saw the beauty of being alone.

"How do you like Eagle Mountain?" Jamie asked.

"I like it," he said. "I enjoy the outdoors, and the slower pace."

"I imagine it's a lot slower than St. Louis," she said.

Slow was exactly what he had been hoping for when he moved here. Or rather a more reasonable pace, with time to devote to each case and enough hours off to recuperate. "I'm not bored," he said. "I like the variety of the work and I'm enjoying getting to know the area."

"I like that about this job, too," she said. "What did you do with the St. Louis police?"

He didn't really want to talk about this, but he supposed the questions were only natural. "I worked Vice my last four years there," he said.

She wrinkled her nose. "I get that it's really important work, but I'm not sure I could stand always dealing with the worst side of people. Still, it must have been pretty satisfying to put some of those criminals away."

He shifted in his seat. "It was." And very frustrating when some of them managed to escape justice time after time. "What more can you tell me about Trey Allerton?" he asked.

She shrugged. "You probably already know everything I know. He's leasing this land from the Russell Ranch and is raising money to build a camp where troubled or disadvantaged youth can spend time in the outdoors. I gather Courtney is financing most of it, though Trey has mentioned *investors* without naming names. He can be very charming, so maybe he has raised a lot of money, though as you can see, no signs of construction yet."

"What do you know about Courtney Baker?" Wes asked.

"Shane is the one to ask about her," Jamie said. "His fiancé, Lauren, is Courtney's sister-in-law. Her late husband was Lauren's brother. She apparently inherited a lot of money and was living a comfortable life in Denver and left it all to live in that junky trailer out here in the middle of nowhere."

"Maybe she wanted a complete change," Wes said. He could relate to that, though he hadn't opted for quite so rustic an existence.

"And maybe Trey Allerton is a really great partner and intends to go through with his plans for his youth camp, and I'm just overly suspicious," Jamie said. "But something about him doesn't feel right to me."

"Cop sense," Wes said. After so much time on the job, some people developed a sixth sense about crime.

"I guess." She ran her palms along the steering wheel. "Do you feel that way about people or situations sometimes?"

"Sometimes," he said. "But I haven't always been right." Being wrong about those intuitions could be disastrous.

The staccato blast of distant gunfire made them both sit up straighter.

"It's not hunting season," Jamie said.

"Maybe someone target shooting," Wes said.

Another burst of gunfire. Jamie started the cruiser. "Maybe we'd better check it out."

"Yeah." He reminded himself he wasn't in the city anymore. Rural people might be shooting at a predator or sighting in a hunting rifle.

But he wouldn't soon forget the sight of Basher Monroe shot in his bed. Murder happened even in peaceful places like this, as much as he wished it weren't so.

# Chapter Seven

Jamie turned in at the first driveway on the left, and bumped the cruiser to a halt in front of a green-sided yurt. As she and Wes waited, listening for more gunfire, a young man in brown cargo shorts and a faded black T-shirt came around the side of the yurt and moved toward them at a leisurely pace.

Jamie rolled down her window. "Hey, Robby," she called. "We thought we heard gunshots."

Robby, a man in his twenties with short reddish hair, stopped beside the driver's side window. "That was probably just Mr. Kramer," he said.

"What's he shooting at?" Wes asked.

"Probably nothing." Robby leaned down and looked across at Wes. "Mr. Kramer is kind of an eccentric old guy. He's paranoid about someone trying to steal his gold. We've learned if we go up there, we need to stop away from the house and honk the horn to let him know it's us."

"Does he have a lot of gold?" Jamie asked.

Robby shrugged. "Who knows? We've heard rumors that he does, but I suspect those may have been started by him. Anyway, he has a tendency to shoot at anything that moves. He's convinced they're coming for his gold. I don't know if there's some real mental illness, or dementia, or what's going on, but Becca and I try to keep an eye on him. We check on him at least once a week and Becca bakes for him, or we take him produce from our greenhouse. When he's not ranting about people trying to steal from him, he's really an interesting guy. He used to be an engineer in Ohio, and he's traveled all over the world."

"He's lucky to have you two for neighbors," Jamie said. "What about the folks in the trailer down the road?" She nodded toward Allerton's place. "Do you see much of them?"

"Nothing," Robby said. "We went down there to introduce ourselves and take them some fresh produce and the man told us they preferred to keep to themselves and didn't like unannounced visitors. He wasn't mean about it or anything, just very straightforward—*we're busy and don't have time to socialize.* I guess that's their right. We still wave when we pass one of them on the road, but they don't wave back."

"That's an odd way to behave," Jamie said.

"Yeah, well, some people really do move off-grid because they want to be completely alone."

Wes took out one of the flyers about Cash Whitlow and passed it over to Robby. "Have you seen this young man around?" he asked.

Robby studied the flyer and shook his head. "I haven't. Do you think he was climbing around here?"

"We don't know," Wes said. "Do people climb near here?"

"I don't think so," Robby said. "But I don't know much about the sport."

He tried to hand back the flyer but Wes waved him off. "Keep it. Show it to your wife. Maybe she's seen him or his truck."

"I don't think so, but I'll show it to her."

"I think we'll drive up to the Full Moon Mine and make sure everything is all right," Jamie said.

"Be careful," Robby said. "I don't think Mr. Kramer likes law enforcement any more than he does anyone else."

Robby watched as Jamie turned the cruiser and headed out the drive again. "Those two didn't exactly hit the jackpot with their neighbors," Wes said.

"I'm surprised Courtney Baker would be so standoffish," Jamie said. "Lauren described her as very friendly and outgoing, and you'd think she would welcome company up here so far from town."

She slowed as the cruiser climbed a hill, then rounded a curve, and stopped at a sign that read Full Moon Mine. No Trespassing. Owner is Armed. "This is the place," she said and turned into a narrow rutted drive.

When they were in sight of a cabin, she stopped and tapped her horn. A few second later, a figure emerged from the cabin, and she inched the cruiser forward.

Up close, the cabin was more of a shack, constructed of rough-hewn logs, stood on end, the bark peeling off in long strips. The man who stood in front of the structure had a gray beard, but an erect posture, and wore dirty canvas trousers and a faded plaid shirt.

Jamie stopped the vehicle and rolled down the window. "Good afternoon, Mr. Kramer," she said.

"What do you want?" Kramer barked.

"We heard gunshots," she said. "Is everything all right?"

Kramer stalked toward them. "A man's got a right to protect himself and his property," he said.

"What happened?" Jamie asked. "Why were you shooting?"

"I was shooting at a two-legged varmint who's been

trying to rob me blind," he said. He bent low and looked in at Wes. "I don't recognize you. Who are you?"

"I'm Deputy Wes Landry. Who is this person who's trying to rob you?"

"If I knew that, I'd march down to the sheriff's office and file charges," Kramer said. "But he's a sneaky devil. He comes around at night or when I'm working in the mine."

"And he was here just now?" Wes asked.

"Maybe. I thought I heard something. The other night was a full moon and I got a good look at him."

"What does he look like?" Wes asked.

"He was young. Young enough to be fast. He was wearing one of those sweatshirt things with a hood, the hood pulled up so I couldn't see his face, and jeans."

"What night was this?" Wes asked.

"Monday. After midnight. I got an alarm set up in the mine so I can hear when anyone but me goes in there and it went off. This wasn't the first time he was in there, just the first time I got a look at him."

"And you shot at him?" Jamie asked.

"I did. He ran away. And he'd better not come back. Next time I might not miss."

"Next time, call us instead of trying to take matters into your own hands," Wes said.

"Phones don't work up here, or didn't you know that?" Kramer said. "By the time I got to where I could call you people and got back here, the thieves would have robbed me blind."

"Do you think more than one person is involved?" Wes asked.

"Maybe." Kramer stuck out his lip in a caricature of stubbornness.

"What have they stolen from you?" Jamie asked.

"They took a bucket of ore samples and an old copper kettle I use for heating water. They broke the lock on my cabin door and rummaged around, but they didn't find where I hide the real valuables. But they keep coming back to try again."

"How many times have they been here?" Jamie asked.

"Two or three. Four, if that was them I heard today."

"How do they get here?" Wes asked. "Do they come in a car or truck?"

"I don't care if they come in a spaceship, they're trespassing," Kramer said.

Wes took a steadying breath. Questioning Kramer was like trying to pin down quicksilver. "If you had a vehicle description, it might help us find these people," he said.

"Well I don't," he said. "And I don't have time to wait around for you people to solve my problems. I can take care of myself."

"Mr. Kramer, please don't do anything rash," Jamie said.

"I know what you think," he said. "You think I'm a senile old man who's seeing things that aren't there. But I'm not a fool. These are real people and I've got real bullets in my gun that will take care of the problem sooner or later."

"What kind of ammo are you shooting?" Wes asked.

"Bird shot. Not that it's any of your business." He took a step back. "Now get out of here and leave me alone."

Wes sensed that Jamie wanted to argue, but she pressed her lips together and shifted into Reverse. Neither of them said anything until they were on the Forest

Service road again. "Do you think someone is really stealing from him?" she asked.

"I don't know," Wes said.

"We should have asked to see the broken door lock," she said.

"He would have probably said he already fixed it."

"So you think he's lying?"

"Not lying. But maybe exaggerating. Or misinterpreting what's going on."

"As bad as it is to think of him terrified of figments of his imagination, I hope real people aren't involved," Jamie said. "If he doesn't kill someone shooting at them, they're liable to hurt him shooting back."

"I'd like to know if he always shoots bird shot or if he uses slugs, too," Wes said.

"You're thinking of Basher Monroe," Jamie said. "But lots of people have shotguns."

"Yes, but Kramer has a reputation for using his."

"The camper where Basher died is a long way from here," Jamie said. "From the description of his wounds in the autopsy report, I don't see how Basher could have been shot at Kramer's place and gotten back to that ambulance before he was dead."

"Basher was a young strong guy, who maybe didn't realize he'd been hurt as badly as he was," Wes said. "And if he had someone to help him get back to his ambulance…"

"Someone like Cash Whitlow." Jamie nodded. "It's something to think about."

"In the meantime, we'll report this to the sheriff," Wes said. "He may want to add some extra patrols up this way."

Jamie slowed as they neared Allerton's trailer. A

black Ford pickup sat in the driveway now. She turned in and parked behind the truck. "Let's see what Allerton has to say for himself," she said.

Wes knocked on the door this time, but no answer and no sounds from within the trailer. He tried again, harder this time. "Mr. Allerton, we need to speak to you," he called.

A moment later, the door eased open and a small blonde girl looked out. "Trey says he's taking a nap and can't talk to you right now," she said.

Jamie knelt until she was eye level with the child. "Hello, Ashlyn," she said. "We met once before. My name is Jamie."

Ashlyn stared at her, wide-eyed.

"Can we speak to your mom?" Jamie asked.

"She's napping, too," Ashlyn said. "I'm supposed to be napping, too, but they sent me to answer the door."

Jamie looked up at Wes. They could insist that the child go fetch an adult, but they couldn't compel Trey or Courtney to talk to them.

Wes handed Ashlyn one of his cards. "Give this to Trey and ask him to call me," he said.

Ashlyn took the card and nodded. "Okay."

"Ashlyn, close the door now," Courtney called from the far end of the trailer.

"I have to go now," Ashlyn said and shut the door.

Jamie and Wes returned to the cruiser. "Some days, no one is glad to see you," she said as they headed back to town.

And some days, Wes thought, everyone you met was hiding something. But he didn't know enough about these people to determine if discovering their secrets would help him to figure out what had happened to Basher Monroe and Cash Whitlow.

REBECCA PACED HER living room, unable to settle. Wes hadn't returned her call, and she couldn't decide if this was good news—he had nothing to report and he wasn't concerned about Trey Allerton—or if it meant he didn't *want* to talk to her. He was probably busy with other cases and didn't have time to hold her hand. She was supposed to trust that the sheriff's department was doing their job, and Wes would let her know when he had something to report.

But she wasn't the type to sit back and wait. And, truth be told, she wouldn't mind a little hand-holding from the handsome deputy. She hated to admit that—having romantic thoughts about a man right now struck her as inappropriate. But Wes had made her feel less alone in her distress over Cash's disappearance, and that translated into some pretty warm feelings for him.

Did that make her pathetic or just human?

A knock on the door startled her, and she hurried to look outside. A sheriff's department SUV sat at the curb, and Wes stood on her doorstep. She fumbled open the locks and opened the door. "Hello!" she said, smiling in welcome.

"Sorry to stop by so late," he said. "I've been out of phone range all day and just got your message."

"It's not that late." She held the door open wider. "Please, come in."

In the brighter light of her living room, he looked weary, with the slightly slumped shoulders and dull eyes of someone who has worked too many hours and slept too few. "Can I get you some coffee, or water, or something?" she asked.

"I'm okay."

She followed him farther into the room. "Do you have any news?" she asked. "Please, sit down." She sat and he lowered himself to the opposite end of the sofa.

"No news. I spent the day following up some leads and getting nowhere."

"That sounds frustrating."

"All part of the job. I got your message. What did you want to tell me?"

"Something odd happened at work today. I don't know if it means anything or not, but a man came in, Trey Allerton. Our nurse practitioner, Lauren Baker, said I should speak to you about him."

At the name Trey Allerton, Wes sat up straighter. "What did he want?"

"He had a little girl with him, apparently his girlfriend's child, and said he wanted to check her vaccination records. Of course, we couldn't give him that information without the girl's mother's permission, which we didn't have on file. But I really think that was an excuse to talk to me."

"Why do you think that?"

"He knew who I was. He said how sorry he was to hear about Cash, and asked if we had had any sightings or any theories about what had happened to him. His behavior just struck me as…odd." She felt a little foolish telling him this. It wasn't as if Trey Allerton had really done anything. "I don't know. Maybe he's just one of those people who likes to get the inside scoop on breaking news."

"Trey Allerton was one of the people I was trying to track down today," he said.

Her breath caught and she leaned toward him. "You

think he had something to do with Cash's disappearance? Or with Basher's murder?"

"He's leasing part of a ranch in the mountains outside of town and says he plans to build a camp for disadvantaged youth. I wondered if maybe Cash had tried to get a job with him. You mentioned Cash wanted to work with young people, and his fellow climbers said he had talked about getting a job at a camp."

"What did Mr. Allerton say?"

Wes shook his head. "I wasn't able to speak with him. The first time I went by his place, he wasn't there. So Deputy Douglas and I waited and after we knew he was home, we went back. But he refused to come to the door. He sent his girlfriend's daughter to tell us to go away."

"Can he do that—refuse to talk to a law enforcement officer?"

"At this point I don't have any evidence tying him to a crime. I showed his girlfriend, Courtney Baker, the flyer you made, and she said she had never seen Cash before. Though what you've told me does give me one more reason to try to pin Allerton down."

"I can't imagine why he wouldn't talk to you, unless he is hiding something." She hugged her arms across her chest. "I'm even more creeped out about him now."

Wes's expression hardened. "Did he threaten you or do anything to make you uncomfortable?"

"No. He was perfectly polite. Maybe I was just picking up on Lauren's dislike of him. She's definitely not happy that her brother's widow took up with him."

Wes nodded. "Let me ask you about something else that happened today. It probably doesn't have any connection to Cash, but I need to ask."

"All right."

"There's a gold mine up the road from Trey Allerton's place—the Full Moon Mine. It's operated by a man named Martin Kramer. He says someone has been stealing from him. He described a tall young man in a hoodie and jeans, though he admits he never got a good look at the man's face. Do you think Cash would do something like that?"

"No! Cash doesn't steal. Why would he?"

"Maybe he heard the rumors that Kramer has gold stashed up there."

"Cash doesn't steal," she said again.

"Addicts will do things they wouldn't normally do, including steal to support their habits."

"Cash isn't an addict." She stood. "How many times do I have to tell you that?"

"I believe you," he said, remaining calm. "But I have to consider the possibilities, and ask all the questions, even the hard ones."

She took a deep breath, trying to smother her agitation. "Even when Cash was at his worst, I never heard of him stealing," she said. "I know that doesn't mean he didn't, but even if he was back on drugs—and he's not—but if he was, why target a miner in the middle of nowhere? Why not steal from me or burgle a home or business in town?"

"I agree Kramer seems an odd target," he said. "But I've learned that people sometimes do odd things." He stood. "I've kept you long enough. I'd better get going."

The thought of him leaving left her even more bereft. "You don't have to leave," she said, then, more boldly, "Stay. I could fix us something to eat. Have you had dinner?"

His smile erased most of the weariness from his face and made her feel lighter. "That would be great."

"Come into the kitchen and let's see what I can find," she said.

What she found was chicken and vegetables and tortillas, which she transformed into fajitas while he helped by chopping lettuce and tomato, shredding cheese and setting the table. "I'd offer you a beer or wine," she said as she carried the meal to the table, "but I don't have anything on hand."

"Water is fine." He took his seat and waited until she was settled before he lifted his water glass. "To the chef," he said.

She solemnly clinked her glass to his, then busied herself making her fajita. It had been a long time since she'd sat across the dinner table from a man. Well, a man other than Cash, who would always be part boy to her. Eating with Wes was different, from her constant awareness of his presence to an awareness of her own movements. She wouldn't have said she was self-conscious around him, simply more conscious of herself as a woman responding to the companionship of this man.

"How long have you lived in Eagle Mountain?" he asked after a moment.

She had to think a moment to find the answer. "Twelve years," she said. "It's hard to believe it's been that long."

"What brought you here, and from where?" he asked.

"From California. The San Diego area. I grew up there. And how I got here is a story you've probably heard a dozen times—I followed a love interest. Things didn't work out with him, but I liked it here and I stayed. What about you? How did you end up with the sheriff's department?"

"The sheriff and I have been friends for a long time," he said. "Since college. I was a few years ahead of him in school, but we shared a lot of the same interests. We kept in touch and he knew I was looking for a change, so he let me know the department was expanding, if I was interested. I was, so…here I am."

"What were you looking for a change from?" she asked. "Or is that too personal a question?"

"I was burning out, working Vice in a big city." He laid down his fork and gave her his full attention. "My last case was a sex-trafficking case. There were children involved. It didn't end well." His voice was even, but she sensed the turmoil behind the words.

"That's terrible," she said. Terrible for him. Terrible for the children. Terrible for a world in which that could happen.

He picked up his fork again. "It was. And now I'm happy to be here, though I imagine some people think of it as running away."

"Some people are wrong," she said.

He chuckled. "You sound so sure of that."

She looked down at her plate. "I guess any job working with the public, you get to see the good and bad sides of people," she said. "Medical practices are privy to people's darker sides, too. In addition to physical ailments, we handle a lot of mental health problems. If you were burned out on your job, you were harming your own health, which meant you couldn't be very effective for others. Now you're here, where I hope you're feeling better, and you've been a big help to me, at least."

"I haven't done anything to help you," he said.

"You've listened and you've believed me, and you're doing everything you can to find and help Cash. Just knowing all that helps me."

He leaned over and covered her hand with his own. "You're an easy person to want to help."

The weight and warmth of his hand, and the strength behind it, filled her with such heat, and a tingle of longing curling up from her middle. She started to turn her hand over, to entwine her fingers with his, but he straightened, pulling his hand away, and resumed eating.

They finished the meal in silence, the absence of conversation not awkward, but humming with tension. She wondered if he was as aware of it as she was.

When the meal was done, he helped collect the dishes and put them in the sink. When he started to turn on the water, she stopped him. "I'll do that later," she said. Then she left her hand on his arm and looked into his eyes, silently asking what he wanted next.

His eyes met hers, then his gaze shifted to her lips. She leaned closer, willing him to kiss her. His eyes darkened, and his grip on her arm tightened. She held her breath, waiting and wanting.

Then he took a step back. "I'd better go," he said, avoiding her gaze. "Thank you for dinner. I'll keep you posted on the case."

And then, before she could protest, he was gone. She stared after him, listening to his footsteps cross the floor, then the door close behind him.

The case. He meant Cash's disappearance. Maybe Basher's murder, too. The thing that had brought them together. Was it now the thing keeping them apart?

*Chapter Eight*

Wes returned to Trey Allerton's trailer the next morning, determined to talk to the man, but as he passed the gates for Russell Ranch, a black Ford pickup, with Allerton behind the wheel, passed him. Wes pulled onto the side of the road, then turned to follow the truck. He debated switching on his lights to pull the truck over, but decided confronting Allerton at his destination might be more effective.

The destination turned out to be Mountain States Bank. Allerton parked at the curb and went inside the bank. Wes found a space a little down the block. When Allerton emerged from the bank fifteen minutes later, Wes was leaning against the driver's door of the truck. "Hello, Trey," he said. "You and I need to talk."

"I don't have anything to say to you." Allerton stopped in front of Wes, keys in hand. Short of shoving the deputy out of the way, Allerton wasn't going to get into his truck. "Move, so I can leave," he said.

"I just have a few questions." Wes straightened and took one of the flyers about Cash Whitlow from the pocket of his uniform shirt and unfolded it.

"I've had enough of your questions," Allerton said. "For some reason the sheriff's department has decided I'm guilty of every crime that happens in this county when I haven't done anything wrong. I'm fed up with your harassment."

"I just want to know if you know this young man." Wes held out the flyer.

"I don't know anything about anyone," Allerton said. He tried to move around Wes, but Wes sidestepped to block him.

"Rebecca Whitlow says you were in the medical clinic yesterday, asking about Cash," Wes said.

"I was in the medical clinic with Ashlyn, not that that's any of your business. I'd seen those flyers around town and, like any decent person, I told her how sorry I was her nephew is missing, and that I hope he's found soon."

"Your concern struck her as more than casual," Wes said.

"I can't help what she thinks."

"Cash was talking about getting a job working with young people, teaching them to rock climb," Wes said. "I thought maybe he applied for a job with the camp you're building."

"You know as well as I do that I'm not ready to hire anyone yet."

"So, Cash didn't come to you asking about a job?"

"No. I don't know the guy. I haven't had anything to do with the guy."

"What about Basher Monroe?"

"What is this—throw out every random name on your books and see if it sticks to me? I never heard of him, either."

"Basher was murdered Sunday," Wes said.

"And that has nothing to do with me. None of the deaths you've tried to associate with me have anything to do with me. You people need to do your job and actually investigate crimes instead of making me your convenient universal suspect."

Wes could have left it there, but who knew when he'd have Allerton in this position again? Might as well keep going. "When we spoke to your girlfriend yesterday, we were concerned about her," he said. "She looked like she had a black eye."

Nothing in Allerton's expression changed. "She fell. The ground is pretty rough around our place and she was chasing Ashlyn." He shrugged. "It happens. She'll be fine."

"The deputy with me said it looked like Mrs. Baker had lost weight.

"Courtney looks fine to me. Did she tell you something was wrong?"

"No."

"Then nothing is wrong. And I think we're done."

"Not quite. Your neighbor, Martin Kramer, says someone's been stealing from him," Wes said. "Have you had any trouble at your place?"

"No. And I wouldn't put much stock in anything Kramer said. He's delusional. Or maybe just senile."

"What do you mean?" Wes asked.

"He sees things that aren't there. Or rather he shoots at things that aren't there. He's always firing that shotgun of his at figments of his imagination. I've tried to talk to him about it, but he just shoots at me."

"Have you heard the rumors about him hoarding gold at his place?"

"All he's hoarding are rocks. Everyone knows if those mines really had any gold, the big companies would have taken it out years ago. But hey, if you're looking for a murder suspect, you ought to talk to Kramer about your missing climber. Maybe he shot him."

He shouldered Wes out of the way and jerked open the door to his truck. Wes let him go.

Allerton had an explanation for everything, and Wes had nothing really linking Allerton to any of his cases. Was Allerton right, and the sheriff's department had fixated on him as a convenient suspect? By focusing on him, were they missing out on someone less obvious but truly guilty?

SATURDAY AFTERNOON, Rebecca drove out to Caspar Canyon, an area of rocky cliffs streaked with vermillion and purple from minerals in the rocks. Once a month local climbers gathered here to trade tips and tricks, try out new gear and look for new, ever more challenging routes in what they had termed the Canyon Clinics. Newcomers to the sport came to be tutored by the pros, and professional climbers dropped in to brag about recent conquests and catch up with friends. Cash had been a regular at the clinics, and Rebecca hoped someone there would know more about his activities in the days before he had disappeared.

She hadn't spoken to Wes since their dinner Thursday. She told herself he would contact her if he had any new information about Cash, and she needed time to let her feelings cool off. Clearly he wanted to keep things between them professional. And she respected that, even if part of her longed for more. She hadn't been involved with anyone for more than a year, and she'd been fine with that—until she met Wes. How inconvenient that he also happened to be the deputy investigating Cash's disappearance.

She parked and walked up to the cliff area, and approached a group of climbers. "I wanted to make sure you all had seen the flyer about Cash," she said, handing out copies.

"I was sorry to hear about him," a girl with long red braids—Rebecca thought she went by Zippy—said.

"Do any of you remember him talking about going away?" Rebecca asked. "Or maybe he talked about climbing in a new area? Someplace off the beaten path? I'm worried he went climbing alone and got hurt."

They all shook their heads. "I never heard anything like that," Zippy said. "He wasn't a big talker anyway, but he was really good about helping other people, you know, showing them techniques or suggesting routes."

"And you don't recall seeing his truck parked anywhere recently?" Rebecca asked. "Maybe it didn't really register with you as unusual at the time."

More head shaking. "We're keeping an eye out for him," a young man with an acne-scarred face and a shaved head said.

"Thank you," Rebecca said. "Tell everyone you know about Cash. The more people who are looking for him, the more likely we are to find him."

She turned away, only to almost collide with a tall young man in ragged cargo pants. "Sorry," he said, stumbling back. "I was in a hurry to get to you before you left. Are you Cash's aunt Rebecca?"

"Yes. Do you know something about where Cash might be?"

"I was hoping you knew something." He stuck out his hand. "I'm Payson Fritsch. Cash is a friend of mine. He's been teaching me so much about climbing."

"It's good to meet you, Payson." Rebecca didn't remember Cash ever mentioning Payson. She was beginning to realize how much about her nephew she didn't know.

"I can't believe he just disappeared." Payson shoved his hands deep into the pockets of his shorts and rocked back and forth. He had short-cropped brown hair and beautiful dark brown eyes, with lush lashes Rebecca envied. "We were supposed to meet up here today. He said he was going to show me a new route up the falls." He nodded over his shoulder, toward a trickle of water down the canyon wall. Slick rock showed the path the more forceful waters took during spring runoff.

"So Cash didn't give any indication that he planned to go away somewhere?" Rebecca asked.

Payson shook his head. "No way. I can't believe he's just...gone." He looked as if he might cry.

Rebecca's heart went out to the young man. He looked so forlorn. She tried to find some way to comfort him. "So many people are looking for him," Rebecca said. "I'm really hoping he'll be found soon."

"He was just such a big help to me." Payson wiped at his eyes. "I had a chance to get a job working on this ranch and I was so nervous about the interview that Cash went with me. And Basher—Basher went, too. Cash thought it would be good to have him along because he's so big and kind of intimidating. I guess Cash had a bad feeling about the whole setup from the start."

"When was this?" Rebecca asked.

"Last Saturday." He shook his head.

"Did you get the job?" she asked.

Payson shook his head. "It was just too weird, you know? Cash and I talked it over after the interview and we decided I should probably try for something else. So I got a job at a T-shirt place in town."

"What was weird about it?" she asked.

"First off, the guy who was going to hire me—he said his name was Bart Smith—didn't want to meet at the ranch. We had to meet him at that old, abandoned gas station up on the highway. I'd only talked to him on the phone before that, and when Cash and Basher and I got to the place, the guy—or, at least, I guess it was the guy—was waiting for us. Only he was wearing this really cheesy black wig and a loud Hawaiian shirt. It had, like, alligators on it." He shook his head. "It looked like some kind of costume, not something a rancher would wear."

Rebecca felt cold all over. "How did you find out about this job if you'd never met the man before?"

"He had this card pinned to the bulletin board outside the coin laundry over on South Fifth," Payson said. "I called the phone number on the card and we set up this meeting at the gas station. He said it was more convenient for him."

"Do you still have the card?"

"Sorry. I threw it away."

"What was the job?"

"Just doing odd jobs on the ranch. He said I'd be cutting firewood and clearing brush, and he might want me to ride along when he went to collect money from people who owed him. I thought that was a little weird but, whatever." He shrugged.

"But you decided not to take the job. Why?"

"I just got a bad vibe from the dude—the wig and the loud shirt, and he wore these mirrored sunglasses he didn't take off the whole time we were talking. And then he said he'd pay me eight dollars an hour to work, but I could make more by doing extra jobs for him—but he wouldn't say what the extra jobs were." He stared at the ground and shuffled his feet. "I might still have taken the job, to try it out, you know, if Cash hadn't said it was a bad idea. He said he thought maybe the guy was involved in drugs and he was worried those *extra* jobs might involve selling drugs or something. He said nobody wears a disguise like that unless they have something to hide. Basher agreed that the guy was probably shady."

"And you're sure Cash or Basher didn't know this Mr. Smith?" Rebecca asked.

"No way. They were as weirded out by him as I was." He frowned. "You don't think Smith had anything to do with Cash's disappearance, do you?"

"I don't know," she said. "But I think you should tell the sheriff's department about him and have them check him out."

Payson's eyes widened. "You want me to talk to the cops?"

"One cop. Deputy Wes Landry. He's a good guy." She took out her phone. "Give me your number and I'll have him call you."

"Do you really think it will help Cash?"

"I do."

He gave her his number and she recorded it in her phone. "Thanks for telling me this," she said. "Sometimes it's little things like this that make all the difference." Or so she had heard on TV and read in countless mystery novels.

"Sure. I wish I could do more."

He moved away and she was headed back to her car when someone behind her said, "Hello, Rebecca."

The voice still had the power to stop her in her tracks. She took a deep breath, trying to calm her racing heart, before she turned around. "Hello, Garrett," she said.

Garrett Stokes was a blond beach bum turned rock rat, with the lean, muscular physique of a climber and a ready grin, though he wasn't grinning now. He had been her brother Scott's best friend and frequent climbing partner.

He had also been the man Rebecca had thought she would marry, until it became clear that Garrett had no interest in settling down with one woman, much less her.

"I heard about Cash," he said. "Is there anything I can do?"

A memory flashed through her head of a younger Garrett carrying Cash on his shoulders as the little boy giggled and urged him to run faster. Her heart twisted a little at the thought. They had all been so happy then, before Scott died and her relationship with Garrett withered away. "Have you spoken to Cash lately?" she asked. "In the past couple of weeks?"

"He and I climbed over in Post Office Basin last week," Garrett said.

She blinked. "He never said anything about that to me."

"He probably didn't want to upset you. He knows I'm not your favorite person."

"Oh, Garrett—"

"It's all right, Becca. I probably deserve whatever your feelings are for me. Anyway, Cash was in a good mood. Full of big plans."

"What kind of plans?"

"He told me he had decided to focus on getting a job working with kids. He was stoked about the idea."

"But you don't know any more?"

Garrett shook his head. "Sorry. I don't."

"Did you know Basher Monroe and Cash were friends?" she asked.

"Yeah. I used to see them together a lot. Basher was

a good guy. I heard somebody shot him in that ambulance of his. Did they find out who did that?"

"I don't think so. The manager of Moe's Tavern said Basher and Cash had lunch the day before Basher died. The day before Cash disappeared."

"Huh. Strange timing. Do you think Cash knows something about Basher's murder and is hiding from the killer?"

"I don't know what to think." She wanted someone to make things clear to her—to give her the information that would suddenly reveal all the answers.

"Yeah, well, we're all keeping our eyes and ears open. I'll let you know if I find out anything."

"Thanks." She started to turn away, but he put his hand on your shoulder. "Let's have dinner together," he said. "You look like you could use some cheering up."

She shook her head. "I'm not in the mood."

He took his hand away, all the warmth gone from his eyes. "I take back what I said earlier, about deserving whatever you felt about me. I was never as bad as you made me out to be."

"Garrett, I don't want to have this discussion."

"You were always focused on what I was doing wrong, not what I was doing right." He took a step back. "I've got news for you, Beccs—nobody is perfect, not even you."

He turned and stalked away, leaving her torn between wanting to swear at him and wanting to cry. She hadn't wanted him to be perfect—but she had hoped for a man for whom she wouldn't always be second place in his life.

# Chapter Nine

Cash woke to a darkness blacker than any he had ever experienced. He sat up, wincing at the pain in his thigh, and unwrapped the emergency blanket from around himself, the tinfoil-like material crinkling loudly with each movement. He pressed the button to illuminate the display on his watch: 2:54 a.m. Too early to get up and try to go anywhere.

He lay back on his makeshift mattress of pine boughs and closed his eyes again, his mind replaying the events of the past few days.

The first thing had been that weird interview with Payson and Basher and the man in the bad wig and the alligator shirt, Bart Smith. Cash had had bad vibes about the guy from the beginning, which was one reason he'd suggested Basher come along. Basher wouldn't hurt a flea if he didn't have to, but he was big and strong and looked intimidating.

Cash didn't think it was a coincidence that Bart Smith's initials were B.S. What kind of employer refuses to meet a potential employee at his place of business? Cash had been ready to walk away as soon as he saw the guy's disguise, but he hadn't wanted to embarrass Payson any more than he had to, so he'd stayed to hear the man's spiel.

More bad vibes there. All that talk about extra pay for extra work, but a refusal to say what the work entailed had every nerve in Cash's body saying no. A person with this much to hide was into something bad. Probably drugs. Basher had thought so, too. A ranch in the middle of nowhere was probably the perfect place to manufacture and/or distribute illegal drugs. The man had probably pegged Payson as a naive kid desperate for money, which was sort of true. But the man hadn't figured on Cash having his friend's back.

After Payson turned down the guy's offer, he and Cash and Basher left, but Cash, who was driving, insisted on circling back around and trying to follow the man.

"What are we doing?" Payson asked.

"I want to see if I can figure out who this guy is." He pointed ahead of them, to the smear of mud across the license plate of the white RAV4. "You can bet Bart Smith isn't his real name. And why didn't he want us to know where he lived?"

He kept his truck well back of the RAV4, and was doing a good job of keeping the guy in sight until they turned off on County Road 361. All of a sudden the RAV4 disappeared. Cash guessed the guy had realized he was being followed and turned off into the brush, but even after driving up and down the road three times, they weren't able to figure out where.

The next day Cash had lunch with Basher and told him his plan. "I'm going to find out who this guy is and what he's up to," he said.

"Why do you care?" Basher, who had already eaten all his lunch, stole a French fry off Cash's plate.

"Because—I'm always saying how I want to help kids, you know?"

Basher nodded. "You help them by teaching them to climb, turning them on to how great the sport is."

"Sure. But if we're right and this Smith character is dealing drugs, think how many more kids I'll help by putting him away."

"Who are you now, the DA?" Basher laughed at his own bad joke.

"I'll take my evidence to the sheriff and he can take care of Smith," Cash said. "But I can't just walk into the sheriff's department with a story about a guy with a bad wig. I need evidence."

"How are you going to get evidence?" Basher asked.

"I'm going to drive out to County Road 361 and see if I can find the guy," Cash said. "When I find him, I'm going to watch him. I'm bound to see something suspicious." He shoved back his chair. "Want to come with me?"

"Sure." Basher took out his wallet to pay for lunch. "I don't have anything better to do."

It hadn't taken long to determine there were only four houses on County Road 361: The Russell Ranch, a faded old single-wide trailer, a yurt and someplace called the Full Moon Mine.

Cash started at the ranch. He pretended to be selling magazine subscriptions. A pregnant woman with a toddler clinging to her legs answered the door. She had long brown hair and a harried look on her face. In the course of trying to sell her nonexistent magazine subscriptions, he learned that she and her husband had only recently taken over operation of the ranch. Her husband showed up about that time and one look told Cash he was too short and stocky to be the man in the wig, so he said goodbye and moved on to the trailer.

A pale blonde woman answered the door here. She

would have been really gorgeous if she hadn't looked so tired and sick. She said her husband wasn't around and they didn't need magazines. Cash decided to save time and asked her about her neighbors. Did she think they needed magazines?

"I don't know much about the young couple in the yurt," she said. "Though they're always friendly. But if I were you, I wouldn't go near Mr. Kramer at the Full Moon Mine."

"Why is that?" Cash asked.

"Because he shoots at visitors."

At Cash's blank look, she continued, "He has a shotgun and he shoots at anyone who comes by. He's very paranoid and convinced that everyone is trying to steal from him. He's dangerous, so I'd stay away if I was you."

He thanked her and returned to his truck, where Basher was waiting. He told Basher what the woman had said. "Kramer is our man, I'd bet anything," Cash said as he put the truck into gear and backed out of the driveway.

"Because he's a grouch with a gun, you think he's a drug dealer?" Basher asked.

"He's hiding something," Cash said. "Why else shoot at someone just for turning in your driveway? That's the kind of thing drug dealers do."

"You're the expert."

Cash ignored the comment and drove past the yurt and its accompanying greenhouse, chicken yard and pig pen. Like the trailer, this place looked too poor to belong to someone who was raking in cash from drugs.

He stopped at the sign for the Full Moon Mine, but didn't turn in. "What are you going to do now?" Basher asked.

"We can't just drive up there," Cash said. "If he is Smith, he'll recognize us from the interview with Payson."

"That, and he's liable to shoot us," Basher said.

"We're going to have to sneak in there," Cash said. "Figure out what's going on and take pictures, so I'll have proof to show to the cops."

"I don't know about that," Basher said. "Why don't we drive on out to the old quarry and climb the cliff there? Garrett told me he was out there last week and found a sick new route up the north side."

Cash shook his head. "If you don't want to help me, I'll take you back to your camper and I'll come back out here by myself."

"I didn't say I didn't want to help." Basher squinted up the driveway. "But if you're going to snoop around, you'd be better off doing it after dark. It's a lot harder to hit someone with a shotgun when you can't see them."

So they'd ended up driving out to the quarry after all, and messing around, then Cash went home to eat until almost dark, when he picked up Basher and they drove back to the mine. Cash parked past the end of the road, up above the mine, and they hiked back in the fading light. They lay on their stomachs on a ledge behind Martin Kramer's shack and watched him hauling buckets of rocks from a hole in the hillside that Cash guessed was the entrance to his mine. "I wonder what's underneath all those rocks," he whispered to Basher.

"A mine would be a good place to hide drugs," Basher said. "How are we going to get a closer look?"

"We wait until he's inside and sneak down there. My phone doesn't get a signal up here, but the camera works. We'll take some pictures of what we find and leave. Easy."

"Easy," Basher repeated.

The first part was simple enough. They waited until it got dark and Kramer was inside his shack, then they crept down to the mine entrance and went in. They kept their lights off until they got inside. Cash had been hoping to find lockers or shelves or some kind of containers filled with illegal drugs, but there were only a bunch of five gallon buckets full of rock. "What's with all this rock?" He picked up a gray chunk about the size of his fist. It was rough and heavy, but it didn't look like anything special.

"I guess that's the ore he's taking out of the mine," Basher said.

"It doesn't look like it's worth anything," Cash said. "I thought the mines around here were supposed to have gold and silver in them."

"I don't know what gold and silver looks like when it's still in the ground," Basher said. "Maybe this is it?"

They moved a little farther into the mine. "There's probably a passage, or another room, or something back here," he called over his shoulder. "Or maybe there's an underground lab." Why hadn't he thought of that before? This place would be perfect for a lab.

"What do you think you're doing?" A light blinded them and an angry voice roared.

Cash couldn't see anything in the glare of that light, but he assumed the person shouting at him was Kramer. He thought the old man was standing in the entrance to the mine, trapping them. Cash was trying to think of something to say to convince the old guy not to kill him when Basher grabbed his arm. "Come with me," Basher muttered. "Now!"

Then he dragged Cash after him as he charged directly at the old guy. Basher almost knocked Kramer over as they ran past. Cash had never run so hard in his life, legs pumping, lungs straining to take in enough oxygen. Kramer fired off a blast from the shotgun behind them, then another. Basher yelped and Cash stumbled. "It's okay!" Basher said. "Go! Go!"

They didn't stop running until they reached Cash's truck. Cash jammed the key in the ignition and the engine roared to life. He raced out of there, the tires kicking up gravel, the truck fishtailing around curves. He didn't care that he was driving way too fast. He would have welcomed being pulled over by a cop, but of course there were no cops out here in the middle of nowhere after dark.

He didn't slow until they were in town. "That was wild," he said and looked over to Basher.

Only then did he realize his friend was hurt. Basher lay back against the seat, his face gray, eyes closed, one hand pressed to his side. Cash slammed on the brakes and pulled to the side of the road, just past the grocery store. "Basher! Are you okay?"

Basher opened his eyes, then lifted the hand from his side and looked down. Cash stared at the dark wet patch spreading across Basher's T-shirt. "Dude, did he shoot you?" he asked.

"I don't think it's that bad," Basher said. He clapped his hand back over his side. "Just take me back to the camper."

"If you're shot, I need to take you to the hospital."

"No! No hospital!"

He sounded like he meant it, but come on! "If you won't let me take you to the hospital, we should at least go to the sheriff's office," Cash said. "That old guy can't go around just shooting at people."

"Except we were trespassing on his property after

dark," Basher said. "The cops will probably want to lock us up, not him."

"Basher, come on."

"No!" The anger behind the single word made Cash shrink back. "No cops and no doctors," Basher said. "Just take me to the camper. I'll be fine."

So Cash took him to the old ambulance he had transformed into a pretty awesome camper. Basher groaned as he slid out of the truck, and Cash came around and helped him limp into the camper, where he sank onto his bunk. "Let me see," Cash said, pointing to Basher's side.

Basher pulled up his shirt to reveal an angry puncture wound, red and seeping around the edges, though it had almost stopped bleeding. "I thought there'd be lots of pellets from a shotgun," Cash said.

"I guess just one pellet got me. Help me strip off this shirt. I'm just going to go to bed. I'll be fine in the morning."

"Should we maybe clean it up and bandage it?" Cash asked. "In case it starts bleeding again?"

"Sure. We could do that. The first-aid kit is in the bathroom."

Cash found the first-aid kit and, with a lot of swearing from Basher, managed to clean up the wound and tape some gauze over it. It seemed to be bleeding more now, but Basher insisted he was okay. "I just want to get some sleep," he said.

"Okay." Cash stood. "I'll check on you in the morning, see if you need anything."

Basher reached out and grabbed Cash's arm, hard enough to hurt. Cash tried to wrench free, but Basher held tight. "No cops," he said. "Don't tell anybody about this. Not even your aunt."

"Why not?"

Basher winced. "I can't risk having my name in the paper. You know how they always print that sheriff's report that lists all the calls they went on. There are people—bad people—that I don't want seeing my name in there and coming after me."

Was Basher delirious or something? "What are you talking about? What people?"

"Just some people I used to know. In Colorado Springs."

"I thought you were from Maryland."

"I'm from Maryland, but I spent some time in the Springs. It doesn't matter. I just can't risk anyone seeing my name in the paper and coming looking for me. Understand?"

Cash didn't really understand, but he nodded.

"Promise you won't say anything to anyone," Basher said.

"I promise," Cash said.

Basher lay back on the bunk and closed his eyes. He looked pretty awful, but maybe he was just tired. "I'll be fine," Basher said. "See you later."

Cash left him to sleep and went home, managing to slip in without running into his aunt Rebecca. It wasn't until he got into his room that he realized he had blood all over his shirt. He stripped off all his clothes and hid them at the bottom of the pile in his closet. He'd deal with them later. He took a shower and went to bed. Basher didn't answer the text he sent the next morning, but Cash figured he was either asleep or had gone in to work the early shift at the café. Cash decided to go by himself to spy on Kramer again.

Big mistake. Now he was hurt, too. His truck had disappeared and he'd lost his phone. Had that really been almost a week ago? That's what his watch told him, but he had no memory of much of that time. Aunt Rebecca was probably really upset with him by now. And really worried. He hoped she hadn't called his mom, but he was sort of hoping she had contacted the sheriff. He liked to think that somebody was looking for him.

He hoped they were. He didn't know how many more days he could last up here on his own.

# Chapter Ten

"Next up, we've got some updates on the Basher Monroe murder investigation," Travis addressed the gathered deputies Saturday morning. "Wes, let's start with the analysis of the blood found on the shirt belonging to Cash Whitlow."

"The state lab says the blood found on the shirt is a match for Basher Monroe," Wes said. That wasn't the news Rebecca wanted to hear.

"How much blood are we talking about?" Deputy Dwight Prentice asked.

"Several ounces," Wes said.

"So we're not talking a cut finger," Gage said. "It's enough to put Cash with Basher at or near the time he was first shot, since the ME's report says the second shot—the head wound—didn't really bleed."

"Did Cash shoot Basher?" Jamie asked.

"The blood on Cash's shirt wasn't a spatter pattern," Wes said. "And in any case, the ME said most of Basher's blood loss was internal bleeding. I talked to Dr. Collins again after I got this report from the state lab, and he said the external blood loss from Basher's wound was blood seeping out, not gushing. In his opinion, in order for blood to soak into Cash's shirt, he either had to lay in a pool of blood that had already seeped out of Basher or be positioned right up against him."

"So, maybe when he was helping Basher into his bunk at the camper," Gage said.

Wes nodded. "Something like that. I'm wondering if Basher's death is somehow related to a conversation Jamie and I had with Martin Kramer on Thursday. He told us someone had been trying to steal from him—a young man in a hoodie. Kramer admitted to firing on the man with his shotgun. He said he only had birdshot in the gun, but what if he was lying about that?"

"When did this occur?" Travis asked.

"He said it was Monday," Wes said.

"That doesn't match up with Basher's time of death," Gage pointed out.

"But if Kramer heard that Basher had died from a gunshot wound, he might have put two and two together and lied to protect himself," Wes said.

"You and Jamie question Kramer again," Travis said. "And talk to Rebecca Whitlow again. Maybe Cash mentioned wanting to climb on those cliffs above the Full Moon Mine."

"Yes, sir." Wes hadn't exactly been avoiding Rebecca since their dinner Thursday evening, but he had thought it a good idea to put a little distance between them, to try to rein in his feelings. She was a beautiful, interesting woman and under other circumstances, he wouldn't have hesitated to act on the attraction that simmered between them. But working a case that involved someone you cared about complicated things in so many ways. His last relationship had ended badly when the woman he was seeing became part of the investigation. She'd expected more of him than he'd been able to give. What if Cash Whitlow was never found?

Would Rebecca blame him and end whatever developed between them?

But he couldn't avoid her altogether. He'd promised
to tell her about the lab results on the bloody shirt she
had found, and now he needed to quiz her about Cash's
familiarity with the area around Kramer's mine.

"Dwight, you talk to every business in town that sells
ammunition," Travis said. "See if any of them sold 12-
gauge slugs to Kramer. The rest of us will keep pressing the local climbers for information about Cash. If
Kramer was firing at anyone who approached his place
and Cash and Basher were up there for whatever reason,
there's a chance Basher isn't the only one who was hit
by one of his shots."

REBECCA WAITED UNTIL she was home to call Wes. "Hello,
Rebecca," he answered. "What can I do for you?"

He sounded glad to hear from her—or was she reading too much into a simple greeting? "I spoke to some
more climbers this morning," she said. "I learned some
things you need to know."

"I need to talk to you, too," he said.

*About Cash?* she wanted to ask, but stopped herself.
Why else would he sound so grim? She tried to brace
herself for the worst. "All right. Do you want me to
come to the sheriff's department? Or you could come
here." Whatever he had to say, she would rather not hear
it in a public place.

"I can come to you. About 12:15?"

"All right." She was grateful he didn't make her wait
much longer. Even so, by the time he arrived she was
jittery with nerves. She tried to determine how bad his
news might be by the expression on his face, but he revealed nothing. She supposed law enforcement officers

were schooled in not showing their emotions. "Come in," she said, then as soon as she closed the door, "What did you need to talk to me about?"

"We got back the results of the lab tests on the shirt you found," he said. "The blood on it is a match for Basher Monroe."

All the air left her lungs and she sank onto the sofa. "How?" she asked.

"We don't know. It's possible Cash was with Basher when he was shot."

"Cash wouldn't have shot Basher." She looked up at him, silently pleading for him to believe her. "He wouldn't. Cash isn't violent. He doesn't own a gun. I don't think he's ever shot one." Maybe she was wrong about that. There was so much she didn't know about her nephew.

Wes sat down on the sofa, only a few inches from her. "It's possible Cash got the blood on his shirt when he tried to help Basher."

"Yes. That has to be it. He would try to help his friend."

"Did he say anything about meeting up with Basher on Saturday?"

"No. We hardly talked that day. And I tried to give him privacy and not be overly nosy about his comings and goings."

"Did Cash ever talk about climbing in the area at the end of County Road 361?"

She frowned. "No. Is that a new climbing area? I'm not familiar with it."

"There are some cliffs there. They're not very accessible, but maybe that would be an attraction for him— some place no one else was climbing."

"I never heard him talk about it. Why? Do you think he was there?"

"It's near Martin Kramer's place. And remember, I told you he said he saw a young man in a hoodie and jeans in that area a few days ago," Wes said.

She sank back. "That description could be anyone."

"We're following up on everything, no matter how small."

"Of course." She smoothed her hands down her thighs. "I appreciate it."

"You said you had something to tell me about?" he prompted after a moment.

"Oh, yes." She tried to bring her mind back to the present, to pull away from the dark pit of imagining all of the terrible things that might have happened to Cash. "I went out to Caspar Canyon this afternoon and met a climber you really need to talk to. His name is Payson Fritsch and I have his phone number."

"Why do I need to talk to him?"

"He was with Cash last Saturday. Cash went with him to meet a man called Bart Smith. Smith was wearing an obviously fake black wig and a shirt with alligators on it."

"Was it Basher Monroe?"

"No. Basher Monroe was with them."

"How did they know Smith?"

"They didn't know him. Payson told me he had seen a card tacked up at the coin laundry, advertising for help to work on a ranch. He called the number and this Bart Smith told him to meet at the old gas station out on the highway. You know, the one that's been closed for years?"

Wes nodded. "I know the place. Why not meet at the guy's ranch?"

"Apparently Cash thought that was suspicious, too, so he and Basher went with Payson to meet the guy. I guess Cash has been mentoring Payson, and maybe he was protective of him. Payson said they asked Basher to come with them because Basher was big and intimidating." She shook her head. "I had no idea. I mean, I thought Cash told me everything, but I'm finding out there's so much I don't know."

"What about Smith?" Wes prompted.

She sighed. "Apparently he offered Payson the job, but he also offered extra pay for extra work—but he wouldn't say what the work was. The guys didn't like the sound of any of it, so Payson turned down the job. Cash told Payson he didn't think Smith was the man's real name and that wearing a disguise and refusing to give details meant the man had something to hide. Cash thought he might be involved in drugs or something."

Her eyes met Wes's. "I'm wondering if Cash got involved with this man somehow—not using drugs again, but maybe he confronted the man about preying on kids like Payson?"

"I'll talk to Payson. And we'll try to track down Smith."

"Now I'm really scared for Cash." Rebecca buried her face in her hands. "I just feel so helpless and alone." She fought to keep back tears. She needed to be strong, for Cash.

Wes put his arm around her and drew her close and she leaned against him, saying nothing, taking comfort from his strength.

The buzz of his phone shattered the stillness between them. "I'd better get that," he said and shifted away.

She stood and went into the bathroom, determined to pull herself together. Maybe Cash had gone climbing in that area Wes was talking about. And maybe they would find him soon, and he would be all right.

When she emerged from the bathroom, Wes was waiting for her. "They've found a truck," he said. "We don't know for sure yet, but it sounds like it could be Cash's."

"Where is it? Who found it?" *Why isn't Cash with it?*

"It's in a ravine in the national forest. A wildlife officer found it. That's all I know. I'm going out there now to take a look."

"Let me come with you."

She hadn't realized she had gripped his arm until he laid his hand over hers. She pulled away and stood straighter, forcing herself to appear calm and rational, though inside she felt anything but. "I can identify the truck, and tell you if any of Cash's things are missing."

"It might not even be Cash's truck," he said. "Apparently the license plates are missing. We'll have to check the vehicle ID number."

"I'll know his truck. And if it isn't his, I'll know that much sooner. We all will." *Can't you see how sitting here doing nothing is making things that much worse?* But she didn't want to beg him to take her.

"All right." He took his keys from his pocket. "But try not to get your hopes up."

Hope was the only thing keeping her going right now. That, and the belief that he was doing everything he could to help. One day she would find the words to tell him how much that meant. One day, when Cash was found and life could move forward again.

"THE LICENSE PLATES are missing, but the description fits the one on the bulletin we received." Wes stood with wildlife officer Nate Hall in a narrow canyon below

Dakota Ridge, contemplating a gray Toyota Tacoma that lay on its side up against the trunk of a cottonwood tree, the roof caved in and the front quarter panel smashed. Every window in the vehicle was broken, and a tree branch poked through the roof of the camper top.

Getting to this spot had required a two-mile hike from the end of a narrow Jeep road, then a steep climb down. Wes had tried to persuade Rebecca to wait for him in the parking area, but he hadn't been surprised when she refused, and she hadn't balked when confronted with the climb or the wrecked truck, which didn't look as if anyone in it could have survived. She had only turned a little paler and pressed her lips tightly together before taking a deep breath and saying, "That's Cash's truck. I'm sure of it."

"This is Rebecca Whitlow, Cash Whitlow's aunt," Wes said to Nate. He walked closer to the wreck and peered into the camper. A tangle of ropes and what might have been a sleeping bag were visible in the dim interior. He looked back over his shoulder at Nate. The big blond was responsible for enforcing game laws across a wide swath of the county. "How did you ever find it out here?" he asked.

"A hiker saw the ruts of the tires veering off the old Jeep road up top and got curious," Nate said. "He spotted the truck from the ridge and reported it when he got back within phone range. I was supposed to be in this area today checking on some cameras we have out as part of some research into the local lynx population, so I agreed to check it out. The hiker was smart enough to note the GPS coordinates, so I didn't have any trouble locating the wreck."

Rebecca picked her way over to stand beside Wes. "That looks like climbing gear in the back," she said.

"And Cash has a sleeping bag like that." She looked around them, at the stacked boulders and old tree trunks piled up like children's toys. "But where is Cash?"

Wes took her elbow and encouraged her to come with him, away from the vehicle. They rejoined Nate. "We'll get the VIN to verify, but I'm sure she's right," he said. He looked up the slope to the craggy ridge. "How far is it up there?"

"Three hundred yards or so," Nate said. "You can see the path the truck took coming down by the broken bushes." He pointed, indicating the scar of broken limbs and dislodged rocks that marked the truck's trajectory.

Wes studied the ground around the vehicle, which looked undisturbed. The driver's side of the Toyota was wedged tight against the trunk of the cottonwood, and a large boulder would have made it difficult to open the passenger door wide enough to exit. Yet there was no one in the cab of the truck.

"No sign of the driver," Nate said. He cast a wary glance at Rebecca but continued, "No blood, no cut seat belts and no key in the ignition."

Wes looked up the slope again. "So how did the truck get down here? Did someone push it over?"

"That's what I think," Nate said. "You'll want some forensics guys to look at those tracks. Maybe they'll find some shoe impressions. But once you get off the Jeep trail, there's a pretty good incline. If someone was parked on the side of the trail, it wouldn't take that much to start the truck rolling toward the edge."

Rebecca gasped.

"If Cash Whitlow wasn't in the truck, where is he?" Wes asked.

"I've already called for a search," Nate said. "There's

nothing to indicate he was in the vehicle when it went over, but this is pretty rough territory, so…"

He left the sentence unfinished, but Rebecca completed the thought. "But he could be out here anywhere, under fallen leaves or rock fall or brush."

"If he is, we'll find him," Wes said. He believed they would do everything in their power to do so, but was he overestimating their capabilities? This was difficult terrain, with wild animals. What if Cash had crawled away somewhere to hide? The more he thought about it, the more monumental the task seemed. But a lot of police work was about confronting monumental tasks, creating a whole picture out of tiny fragments. The challenge appealed to him most of the time.

Wes was taking more photographs of the scene when a forensics team and the search-and-rescue crew arrived. "We're almost positive this is Cash Whitlow's truck," he told the SAR captain, a rangy bearded man who introduced himself as Tony Meisner. "We don't have any evidence that he was in the truck when it went off the cliff, but we need to make sure."

Meisner nodded. "We've done these kinds of searches before. With luck, we'll find him or some indication of where he might be."

Forensics would comb the area as well, then arrange to get the mangled vehicle out of the canyon. "It could take a few days," Gage, who was heading up the team, said. "It's going to take some maneuvering."

Rebecca, who had taken up a position nearer the truck, rejoined him. "Search and Rescue is going to comb the area," Wes said. "They've had experience with this kind of search before."

She nodded. "Everyone is working so hard. I wish there was more I could do."

"We'd better go and leave them to it," he said.

She followed him back the way they had come. The climb up was harder, not merely because of the steepness, but because they had to leave this place with so many questions still unanswered.

# Chapter Eleven

Wes drove Rebecca home. They didn't say much on the drive. She stared out the side window and tried to imagine what had happened to Cash. Was he out there, alone and hurt? Or was he already dead?

Wes parked at the curb in front of her house and they sat in silence for a moment. "Do you want to come in?" she asked, then before he could answer she shook her head. "Of course not, you have to get back to work. I know you have so much to do." She opened the door and started to climb out of the cruiser.

"I can come in for a few minutes," he said. "I want to take another look at Cash's room."

Right. This was all about the case.

She unlocked the door and they went inside. Stopping only to drop her purse on the table by the door, she led the way back to Cash's room. As spartan and cold as the last time Wes had seen it. "There's so little of his personality here," she said. "Nothing to tell us what he was thinking or feeling."

"He may not have planned this out." Wes picked up one of the books on the dresser, then set it down again. "We just don't know."

"Come on." He took her arm and guided her out of the room. "We're not going to find anything here."

"I've been going over and over all this in my head," she said as they moved toward the living room. "We know that last Saturday afternoon Cash and Basher and Payson met with Bart Smith. The next day Basher and Cash had lunch together at Moe's Tavern. Sometime after that on Sunday, Basher was injured, probably by the shot that eventually killed him. Cash got Basher's blood on his shirt and left the shirt here, before leaving the house again Monday morning. Basher died Monday afternoon. And sometime after he left here on Monday, Cash's truck ended up in that ravine." She shook her head. "If Basher was hurt, why didn't Cash tell anyone about it? Why didn't he tell me when he came home Sunday night? And what was he doing out there near that ravine anyway?"

"Maybe he went to climb."

"It's not a place for climbing. The cliffs are more clay than rock, or too obstructed by trees, or not vertical enough. And Cash's climbing gear was in the back of the truck. I can't be certain it was all there, but I think it was. You said you didn't think Cash was in the truck? What makes you think that?"

"The keys weren't in the truck's ignition," he said. "The truck was wedged between a big cottonwood and a boulder. If someone was in there, they wouldn't have been able to open the doors to get out, and the way the roof was smashed, he wouldn't have been able to crawl out the windows, either. There wasn't any obvious blood, and no sign that the seat belt had been cut or broken. Search and Rescue is out there going over the area, but I think if Cash had been thrown from the vehicle on the way down, we'd have found him or some indication that he'd been there."

She put a hand over her mouth and dropped to the sofa. "Where is he?" she asked. "What's happened to him?"

He sat beside her, his arm strong around her. She leaned into him, and breathed in his scent. All this worry had left her with little energy for anything else. And no more willingness to continue to fight her attraction to this man. She lifted her head and met his gaze, and saw her desire reflected back to her. She slid her hand around to the back of his neck and gently pulled his mouth to hers.

He kissed her with the intensity of a man who had decided that he, too, was done with holding back. His lips were firm but tender, and she responded hungrily, greedy to taste and feel. She leaned into him, pressing her breasts against the hard wall of his chest—*body armor*, she thought, and smoothed her hands across the muscles of his biceps. After so much time holding back, she felt reckless. He was the first to pull away. "This could be a really bad idea," he said.

"Or a really good one." She crawled into his lap, straddling him, and kissed him again.

He cupped her face in his hands and looked into her eyes. "You've had a rough day," he said. "You're emotionally vulnerable now and…"

"And I want this." She splayed her hand across his chest, over his heart. "I want to be with you. Nothing complicated. Just that."

The doubt she had seen in his eyes fled, and he pulled her close once again. "Give me a minute to call in to the office," he said.

"I'll wait in the bedroom."

Wes dialed the sheriff's direct line at the office, but instead the office manager, Adelaide Kincaid, answered the phone. "I need to take a couple hours personal time," he said.

"Oh? Is everything all right?"

"Everything's fine. Just something I need to see to."

"So you're signing out of your shift two hours early? I'll make note of that, but what should I put as the reason?"

This was exactly the kind of grilling he'd been hoping to avoid. "Just note that it's for personal time. I'll be back on shift Monday. Or sooner if I'm needed."

"Will do, Deputy."

He hung up before Adelaide could question him further. And before he could overthink this whole thing and leave. But he didn't think he was strong enough to do that. He'd wanted Rebecca almost from the moment they met and if she wanted to be with him now— for sex, or comfort, or for whatever reason—he wasn't going to deny them that.

She was waiting for him in the bedroom, still dressed but seated on the edge of the bed. Her eyes met his when he walked into the room and he felt the impact of that gaze to his core. She held up her arms. "Come here."

He had thought she would kiss him again, but instead she began undoing the buttons of his uniform shirt. Her fingernails scraped against the rough surface of his body armor. "Let me help," he said and reached down to unbuckle his duty belt, then laid it carefully to one side. She finished unbuttoning his shirt, then he stripped it off and removed the body armor as well.

"You must feel ten pounds lighter now," she said.

"Just about." He slid his hands beneath her T-shirt, trailing his fingers across the soft silk of her stomach, then moving up to slide his thumbs under the band of her bra. She reached back and unfastened the strap, then peeled off bra and shirt together, revealing full breasts that he had to stare at a moment before reaching for her once more.

They fell back on the bed together, wriggling out of their clothes and laughing—over the awkwardness of the moment, with a little nervousness, and with a lot of joy. When at last he pulled her, naked, on top of him, he was ready to put aside thoughts of everything and everyone but her.

There was always an urgency with a new lover, that desire to see everything, do everything, feel everything. But he was old enough to know the value in taking things slow. They'd only have one first time. It didn't have to be the best, but it ought to mean something. Would she think he was overly sentimental if he told her that? After all, men weren't supposed to be so focused on feelings—said who?

Then she straddled him and his mind finally shut up and instinct took over. They set about discovering each other—the soft gasp she gave when he pulled the tip of her breast into his mouth, and the lightning bolt of need that rocketed through him when she wrapped her hand around the length of his erection. She liked when he feathered kisses over her belly, and he growled with pleasure at the feel of her fingernails raking lightly down his back. The low chuckle in the back of her throat when he stroked the satiny skin at the top of her thigh sent a quiver through him, and when she wrapped her legs around his waist and pulled him tight against her, he wanted to shout in triumph.

He loved her with his hands, and with his mouth, and finally with his whole body, sliding over and into her as she gripped his hips and kept her gaze steady on his eyes, saying so much without a single word. He kept watching her, making note of what pleased her, and what filled her expression with a kind of awe, and then release as her climax shuddered through her. This time he did shout as his own release followed. He felt needed and powerful and...whole. For the first time in a long time.

REBECCA WOKE TO dim light, aware of movement on the bed beside her. Wes was sitting up on the side of the bed, reaching for his pants. "Do you have to go?" she asked, then immediately regretted the question. She would not be a clinging woman. And he had a life apart from her, and a job that made demands on him at all hours.

"I don't have to go," he said. "But I thought I might fix us something to eat."

They made sandwiches, her in her robe, him clad only in his uniform trousers, a very pleasant sight across the kitchen table from her. He had messy hair and a five-o'clock shadow and looking at him, she couldn't stop smiling.

"I want to tell you why I left St. Louis," he said when all that was left of their meal was a few crumbs and some crumpled napkins.

Her first instinct was to protest that he didn't have to, but that wasn't right. If he wanted to tell her, she wanted to know. "All right."

He stared down at his hands, flat on the table in front of him. "I had a case. A tough one. I was working Vice and we were trying to track down the head of a pedophile ring. We had caught some of the people he was peddling kiddie porn to, but we needed to locate the man making the films. I thought we had a good lead, and I followed it for months—but I was wrong. And in the time I wasted, that many more kids were abused by that scum."

"I'm sure you did your best," she said, wishing she could find better words to lessen the pain behind his words.

"But my best wasn't good enough. When that happens—it makes you start questioning your job. Maybe you're not the right person to do this, if your best falls so short."

She waited, forcing herself to remain silent. To give him time. He looked older, the light over the table deepening the grooves on either side of his mouth, hooding his eyes so she could no longer read his expression. She felt privileged, seeing him like this—a strong man allowing himself to be vulnerable.

"We were working the case of a missing child," he said after a moment. "When we spotted the girl in one of the films, we tracked down her mother. That's how she and I got involved." He shook his head.

When he said nothing more, she couldn't bear it. "What happened?" she asked.

"We finally caught the guy. It took too long and too many people were hurt before it was over."

"What happened to the daughter?"

"She died. She killed herself."

"Oh." She put one hand to her mouth, trying to stifle the cry, and another over her heart, where pain stabbed for this child and this woman she didn't even know. And for Wes, carrying all of this with him.

"The mother blamed me for not saving her."

"Wes—"

"Yeah, well, I blamed myself, too."

"It's a terrible thing to happen." She tried to choose her words carefully, not wanting to resort to cliché, but unwilling to remain silent. "But you're only one man. You can't make the whole world right. And you did find the man. Think how many children you saved because you did stop him."

He nodded. "You're right. It's what I try to live with now, but I don't think I'd be human if I ever completely shook the guilt."

"So you decided to come to Eagle Mountain." She was anxious to shift the conversation to what she hoped were happier times.

"I wanted out of Vice. Away from the kind of crime I like to imagine only happens in big cities. I know that's foolish. Some of the people we arrested for buying those kiddie porn films were from small towns. I know no place is immune."

"But Eagle Mountain doesn't have a vice squad," she said. "Things are a little…tamer here. Most of the time."

He nodded.

"What do you think, now that you're here?" she asked. "Are you bored because it's not the fast pace you're used to?"

"No. I was ready to have a job that didn't consume my whole life." He shifted, the chair creaking. Maybe it was just the angle of light as he changed position, but he seemed less burdened now. "Since I've moved here, I've gotten back into fly fishing and photography. I go hiking, and I'm getting to know people in town."

He leaned across and took her hand.

She held his hand and his gaze. "I'm not going to blame you if you don't find Cash," she said. "Or if you don't find him alive." She had to face that possibility.

His grip tightened. "Grief changes people," he said. "You might not be able to help yourself."

"I won't blame you."

"Don't make promises you don't know you can keep."

"And don't worry about something that hasn't happened yet. That will never happen." She stood and pulled him close. "None of us can predict the future, so let's just be grateful for what we have. Let's enjoy now. I intend to enjoy it a lot."

She took his hand and led him back to bed. Whatever bad happened tomorrow or next week, she would have this good to balance it. She knew life didn't really work that way, but it was a nice thought, and she was determined to hang on to every good thing she could. She would hang on to Wes, as long as he would let her, and not worry about ever having to let go.

"GOOD MORNING, DEPUTY," Adelaide greeted Wes when he arrived at work Monday morning. "Did you enjoy your afternoon off?"

"It was fine." He started past her, but she stopped him.

"Deputy Landry, could you come here a moment?" she asked.

He turned toward her. "Yes?"

She crooked her finger, motioning him to come closer. When he reached her desk, she leaned toward him and spoke in a low voice. "Just a word of advice. It's always good to remember that this is a small town. People notice things."

Why did he suddenly feel like a kid caught out playing hooky by the principal? "What are you getting at?"

"Unless you want the whole town knowing you spent Saturday afternoon and evening at Rebecca Whitlow's house, it would be a good idea to park around back."

He wasn't one for blushing, but now his face burned. "I wasn't—" he began. Wasn't what? Wasn't skipping out of work early to make love with the woman whose missing nephew he was supposed to be looking for?

"Shh." Adelaide put a finger to her lips. "We're all adults here. It's just a good idea to be discrete.

He blew out a breath, part relief and part exasperation. "Thanks. I'll keep that in mind."

At his desk, he started sifting through the various bulletins and reports that had come in since yesterday. He was reading through a bulletin about a string of thefts in a neighboring county when Gage added a new report to the pile. "You'll want to read this one," Gage said.

"The FBI found a match for Basher Monroe's prints."

"Oh?" Wes picked up the paper.

"Basher's real name isn't Benjamin Monroe," Gage said. "It's Bradley. Benjamin is his younger brother."

Wes stopped reading and looked up. "What else?" Gage obviously wanted to tell him.

"Benjamin hasn't had so much as a traffic ticket," Gage said. "Bradley, on the other hand, was in and out of court and local jail in Colorado Springs on a string of petty theft and drug charges." He leaned over and tapped the paper. "It says here that the last time he was charged, he made a deal to testify against his supplier, but skipped town before he could do so."

"Was he running from the supplier, the cops or both?" Wes asked.

"I don't know, but his murderer may have been settling an old score. Or maybe he was back to dealing. Maybe Cash Whitlow was in it with him."

*Chapter Twelve*

"If you're calling about my brother, I haven't seen or spoken to him in at least eighteen months," Benjamin Monroe, reached at his office in Maryland, said after he and Wes exchanged hellos.

"What makes you think I'm calling about your brother?" Wes asked.

"You're a sheriff's deputy from Colorado. Last I heard, Bradley was in Colorado, and he's had his share of trouble with the law. It's one of the reasons I've distanced myself from him."

"When was the last time you saw your brother?"

"Thanksgiving, year before last. He came home for a few days. He said he was going to make a fresh start, stay away from drugs and out of trouble. He talked about fixing up a camper and doing some traveling, but then I didn't hear from him again, so I thought maybe that didn't work out for him."

"You weren't worried when you didn't hear from him?"

The man on the other end of the line let out an audible sigh. "Bradley was a grown man, from a good family, with a good education. He had all the same advantages I did, but he repeatedly made bad choices in his life. You can only worry about someone like that for so long before it's too exhausting. My parents might not say that, but it's true for me. When Bradley ran out of money or needed real help, I figured he'd call. But you're calling instead, so tell me what's wrong."

"I'm sorry to have to tell you that your brother is dead, Mr. Monroe."

A heavy silence greeted this news. Wes waited, and Benjamin finally cleared his throat. "What happened?"

"He was murdered. Shot in the ambulance he had converted to a camper."

"Shot?" Another throat clearing. "What happened? I mean, who would shoot him? When did this happen?"

"Monday, the twenty-second. Were you aware that your brother was using identification that belonged to you? That's why it took us a few days to determine his real identity and track you down."

"My...my driver's license!"

"You knew your brother had your driver's license?"

"No. I thought I'd lost it. Right after that Thanksgiving, the last time I saw him. I was doing some shopping and thought it had fallen out of my wallet. I replaced it right away. But Bradley had it?"

"He did. Though he went by the nickname Basher."

"Basher, huh?"

"Did you and your brother look alike?" Wes asked.

"We did. When we were children, people sometimes mistook us for twins. And when I was in high school and he was in college, I'd sometimes use his ID to get into clubs while I was still underage. I suppose that's where he got the idea of using my driver's license. I'm sorry, what town did you say you were calling from?"

"Eagle Mountain. It's a small town in southwestern Colorado."

"Last I heard, Bradley was in Colorado Springs. What was he doing in Eagle Mountain?"

"This area is popular with rock climbers. Basher was part of that community. You mentioned your brother's previous run-ins with the law. What can you tell me about those?"

"Surely you've accessed his record by now."

"I'd welcome any information you can provide. The records don't go into a great deal of detail."

"Bradley has been involved with drugs off and on since college. Probably before then, but his first arrest for possession happened when he was a junior in college. After that, he become more heavily involved and dropped out of school. My parents paid for in-patient rehab and then they persuaded a friend in Colorado Springs to hire him. They thought removing him from his former friends and suppliers would help him stay clean, but it didn't work that way. He fell back into using, and then apparently selling drugs. My parents spent a great deal of money trying, mostly successfully, to keep him out of jail. He had just gotten out of jail that Thanksgiving when he came home to visit. He said this time he was really going to stay clean. I didn't believe him, but my parents wanted to. I'm sure they gave him money—and then we never heard from him again. Do you think his death had anything to do with drugs?"

"The toxicology report showed no drugs in his system," Wes said. "And we didn't find any illegal drugs in his camper."

"Wow. That almost makes this harder to take. But if he really was clean, why didn't he stay in touch? Not hearing from him, not knowing where he was—it hurt my parents so much."

"Mr. Monroe, do you think it's possible your brother was hiding from someone?"

Another long pause. "Mr. Monroe?"

"Maybe. I don't know. I mean, my impression is there are some pretty nasty people involved in drug trafficking. And you say he was living in a small town, using my name instead of his own. That sounds like someone who might have been hiding."

"Were you aware that the last time he was arrested, he agreed to testify against the people who were supplying him with drugs to sell in exchange for a more lenient sentence?"

"No, I didn't know that. We never talked about his criminal activities."

"So you don't know who his suppliers were?"

"No. Maybe the police in Colorado Springs have an idea."

"I'll be talking to them," Wes said. "One last question—did your brother ever mention a man named Bart Smith to you?"

"No. That name doesn't sound familiar. Like I said, we never talked about that part of his life. I didn't want to know."

"Thank you, Mr. Monroe. If I have more questions, I'll be in touch."

"What happens now?" Monroe asked. "I mean, to Bradley...to his body? My parents will want to know."

"I'll contact you again when we release his body and belongings," Wes said. "I'm sorry for your loss. If you or your parents have any other questions or think of anything that might be helpful to our investigation, you can reach me at this number."

He ended the call, then stared down at the notes he had made while he had been talking to Monroe. It sounded as if Basher had kept his promise to stay out of trouble and stay clean. He had no more encounters with the law—not even a traffic ticket—for the past eighteen months, and no one they interviewed had mentioned anything about drugs. But Basher Monroe had behaved like a man in hiding—using his brother's driver's license, having no fixed address and taking the kinds of low-wage jobs that didn't involve background checks. That seemed to point to the person he was hiding from having found and killed him.

But it didn't explain him being shot twice, at different times. And it didn't account for Cash Whitlow's involvement. Had Cash merely been in the wrong place at the wrong time, or was he somehow more deeply involved?

REBECCA WELCOMED THE distraction of a busy Monday morning at the medical clinic. When she arrived at work, she collected six messages from the answering service and others quickly followed, along with three people who showed up to see the doctor or nurse practitioner whenever they could be worked in. As well as regular appointments, she had the weekend's mail to open and emails to be answered or forwarded to other staff members for answers. Sometimes these mornings overwhelmed her, but today she was grateful for a reason not to think about Cash.

Or about Wes. Thoughts of him did steal into her mind from time to time, but they weren't stressful thoughts. Not at all. How was it that in the middle of such a terrible situation she had found such happiness?

"Now what—or should I say who—put that smile on your face?" Carlotta, one of the med techs, teased as she deposited a stack of reports on Rebecca's desk.

Rebecca focused on the reports. "I was just daydreaming."

"Must be some daydream." Carlotta walked away, laughing.

Rebecca's lips curved in a smile once more. It had

been a long time since she had been involved with anyone. She had forgotten how much fun new relationships could be.

She decided to eat lunch at her desk while she caught up on paperwork. With the front door locked and the phones forwarded to the answering service, she would have an hour and a half to make serious headway through the stack of papers and files. She had just set a cup of soup and a fresh mug of coffee beside her desk when her cell phone buzzed, indicating a new text message. Her heart jumped, and she fished the phone from her pocket, hoping the caller was Wes.

CASH. The name glowed bright at the top of the text.

I'm okay. Sorry to worry you. Have some things to deal with. Talk later.

Heart racing, she read the message through twice, then hit the call button. The phone rang twice before an electronic voice said, "You are being transferred to a voice mailbox."

"Cash! Cash! Pick up please. This is Aunt Rebecca. I got your message. Cash, please tell me what's going on."

She ended the call, then sent a text with the same message. She held the phone, staring at the screen, willing him to reply. But…nothing.

She jumped up and ran into Linda's office. "I have to go," she said. "I just heard from Cash and I need to tell the sheriff."

Linda stood and came around the desk. "Is he all right? Are you all right?"

Rebecca thrust the phone at her. "This is all he says. My call back went straight to voice mail and he hasn't answered my text. I need to let Wes know. Maybe they can trace the call or something and find him."

"Of course. Go. Tell them. And I'm glad he's all right."

Rebecca nodded and left the building. She didn't bother with her car but walked the few blocks to the sheriff's department, continually glancing at her phone, praying for a reply. But the phone remained still and silent.

She burst into the lobby of the sheriff's department. "I need to see Wes. Deputy Landry."

Adelaide Kinkaid rose from behind her desk. "Rebecca, what's wrong?"

"I heard from Cash. He says he's all right." She held out her phone. "I need to show this to Wes. Maybe they can trace the call."

"Deputy Landry is on a call right now..."

"It's okay, Adelaide." Wes moved toward them. Gently, he took the phone from Rebecca and slipped his arm around her. "Come into my office."

"I tried calling and texting, but he hasn't answered," she said. "But that's his phone number."

He sat her down, then took his seat across the desk from her and scrolled through the messages on her phone. She sat on the edge of the chair, tensed, until he finished making notes and laid the phone down. "Can you trace it?" she asked. "Can you figure out where he is?"

"We can try," he said. "Do you have any ideas where he might be?"

She shook her head.

"Maybe he said something—an offhand remark that didn't connect for you until now."

She bit her lip, trying to come up with anything that

would help. "He mentioned climbing in Grand Teton some day. But if he was going to do that, he wouldn't have left his truck and his climbing gear behind. And how did he get to wherever he is without his truck? Or most of his clothes?"

"It could have been an impulsive decision. He got a chance to go with someone else and did."

"Except that none of his friends are missing."

"Maybe it was someone he just met. Or someone he knew before, who was passing through the area."

"Then what was his truck doing wrecked at the bottom of that ravine?"

Wes leaned across the desk toward her. "I know there's not much to go on, but does that message sound like Cash to you? Are the words ones he would use?"

She frowned. "Yes. I mean, it doesn't *not* sound like him. Do you think it isn't him?"

"Anyone who found the phone and was able to unlock it could pull up the contacts and send a text like that."

"But they'd have to know how to unlock it. It's fingerprint technology, right?"

"There are ways to get around that."

She sat back, deflated. "Are you saying you don't think Cash sent that text?"

"We don't know. But it might not be."

She nodded, trying to let this sink in. After a moment, she said, "I can think of one reason he might have left town suddenly, without telling anyone. Maybe he was afraid. Maybe he knows who killed Basher and he's hiding from them. It would explain why he wrecked his truck. He pushed it into that ravine so that whoever was after him would think he's dead."

"Yes," Wes said. She could see on his face that he

had considered this possibility also. He picked up the phone again. "We'll get to work trying to find a location this text was sent from."

"Have you found out any more about Bart Smith?" she asked.

"No, but we're working on it."

"Of course." She stood. "I should get back to work, too."

He stood also and moved around her toward the door, but instead of holding it open for her, he shut it firmly, then turned to her. "Come here," he said, reaching for her.

She moved into his arms and laid her head on his shoulder. This was what she needed right now. To be reminded that she wasn't in this alone. "I'll let you know as soon as I know something," he said.

That was enough. Not everything she wanted, but for now, it was enough.

## Chapter Thirteen

Wes spent the rest of the afternoon working with Cash's cell phone provider to track down the location from which the text message to Rebecca had been sent. While he waited to hear back from them, he contacted the Colorado Springs Police Department. He was transferred to several people until he was finally forwarded to Detective Mike Paredo. "I remember Brad Monroe," Paredo said. "An educated kid from a good family who got sucked under by addiction. Too many of these kids end up dead before their life has really started."

"The tox report on Monroe came up clean for drugs," Wes said. "And there's no indication he's been using since he moved here a few months ago. But we're wondering if his death is linked to something that happened to him before. I understand the last time he was arrested in Colorado Springs he had agreed to testify against his supplier."

"And you think the supplier came after him as payback. It could happen."

"Who was the supplier?" Wes asked.

"Don't know," Paredo said. "We were counting on Monroe to tell us that, but he disappeared. What was he doing in Eagle Mountain?"

"Working odd jobs and rock climbing, living in an

old ambulance he'd converted to a camper. Using his brother's ID and going by the nickname Basher."

"That sounds like he was hiding, all right," Paredo said. "From us, and maybe from his old drug connections, too. Maybe one of them did track him down. These people don't take kindly to anyone who cooperates with the law."

"Does the name Bart Smith ring any bells for you? I suspect it's an alias."

"No. How does this Smith figure into this?"

"We know that Monroe and a couple of other climbers met with a man by that name a couple of days before Monroe died. He had supposedly advertised for someone to do menial labor on a ranch he owned, but at the interview he brought up some extra unspecified work he'd be willing to pay more money for. He was wearing an obvious disguise—a fake wig—and was evasive enough that at least one of the young men suspected he was involved in something illegal, possibly drug trafficking."

"Huh. It sounds interesting, but I can't help you out."

"Have you heard of any players in the local drug scene who have moved out of the area?" Wes asked.

"No. But I'll do some looking around and let you know if I hear of anything. Do you have new activity on your side of the state?"

"Not that I'm aware of, but maybe someone was getting ready to open up a new operation here. Maybe Monroe didn't recognize him because of the disguise, but he recognized Monroe and decided to shut him up before he put two and two together and got in the way."

"It's a good theory, but try proving it. These guys learn to cover their tracks pretty well."

"I worked Vice for twelve years in St. Louis," Wes said.

"Then you know. Good luck to you, Deputy. I'll let you know if I find out anything that might be useful."

At six o'clock, after consulting with Travis, Wes decided to bring Payson Fritsch in for questioning. Payson agreed to stop by the station *just to talk*, though when he arrived, he was fidgeting and pale. Most people were nervous around law enforcement, especially when a serious crime was involved. Wes didn't think the young man was guilty of anything, but he had a sense there was more Payson hadn't told them.

Wes led him to an interview room, where Travis joined them, and Wes went through the formalities of establishing time, place and who was there for the recording. Payson's eyes widened when Wes recited the Miranda warning. "I'm not in trouble, am I?" he asked. "I haven't done anything wrong."

"We just have some more questions for you," Wes said. "And we want to make sure we have everything on the official record. I'd like you to tell me everything that happened last Saturday, from your first encounter with Cash Whitlow and Basher Monroe to your last."

"Um, okay." He clasped his hands and rested them on the table in front of him. "So I go to Caspar Canyon where a bunch of us go to climb on Saturdays, about ten o'clock. Cash was there, and Basher. They were getting ready to climb this cliff face that kind of slants back over the water. A little challenging, but those two make it look easy. Cash was on the ground while Basher climbed, so I started talking to him, and I told him about this job I'd seen advertised—this guy looking for someone to work on his ranch. I've been looking for some part-time work and Cash knew that. I showed him the index card I took from the laundry bulletin board, with the guy's phone number."

"Why did you take the card from the bulletin board?" Wes asked.

"I didn't want anyone else seeing it and getting the job before I even had a chance."

"Do you still have the number? On your phone?"

"Uh, yeah. I guess so." He pulled his phone from his pocket and scrolled through. "I think it's this one," he said and handed over the phone.

Wes passed the phone to Travis, who wrote down the number and returned the phone to Payson. "All right," Wes said. "Go on with your story."

"So, I showed Cash the card and told him I had an interview with this guy, Bart Smith, in a couple of hours. Cash was pretty interested. He asked if he could come with me to talk to the guy." He fell silent, looking conflicted.

"Did it strike you as odd that Cash wanted to go along?" Wes asked.

"Well, yeah. I thought maybe he wanted to poach the job. And he's older than me and really outgoing and friendly. I figured Smith would want to hire him and not me. I told him I didn't think it looked good for me to bring a friend on a job interview. Like I was a kid or something." He wet his lips. "Could I have some water?"

"I'll get it." Travis left the room and Wes and Payson waited in silence until he returned with a bottle of water.

"Thanks," Payson said. He uncapped the bottle and drank half of it, then said, "Cash asked me where the ranch was and I said I didn't know—that Smith wanted me to meet him at the old gas station out on the highway.

"Then Basher finished his climb and came over and the three of us started talking. They asked me what I'd be doing at the ranch, and I said chores and stuff, but that Smith said I could earn extra money doing extra work. I thought that sounded pretty good, but Cash and Basher didn't like the sound of it. They said they thought they should come to the meeting with me.

"At first I said no again. But Cash said I needed to be careful. All this secrecy—Smith not wanting to tell me where the ranch was, meeting me at such an out of the way place and the offer to pay extra for extra work—but not saying what that work was—Cash said that might mean Smith was up to something illegal. Like drugs."

"Cash specifically mentioned drugs?" Wes asked.

"Yeah. And Basher said he thought the same thing. I felt pretty dumb for not having seen that before. So I said maybe I should call the whole thing off, and just not show. But Cash said no, we needed to know who this guy was, so we could warn other people. We'd bring Basher because he's a big guy and that would be good in case Smith got any ideas about taking advantage of me." He looked down at his thin arms. "I'm strong from climbing, but some people think I look pretty scrawny." He shrugged. "Anyway, they made it sound exciting. Like an undercover investigation or something. He and Basher were all up for it, so I went along with the idea."

"So what happened at the meeting? First, how did you get there?"

"Cash drove in his truck. We got there and at first it didn't look like anybody was there. Then this guy comes out from behind the station. We all kind of stared at first, because he looked like a joke. He had on this really fake black wig and a big straw cowboy hat and this Hawaiian print shirt with green alligators and pink flowers—it was just wild. But he acted like everything was normal. He walked up and shook our hands, introduced himself as Bart Smith. He didn't ask why Cash and Basher were there, just said he was glad to meet us.

"Cash and Basher let me do the talking. It went pretty much like a regular interview. Smith told me he was looking for someone to do manual labor on his ranch—clearing and burning brush, repairing fence, digging out rocks. He said he'd pay eight dollars an hour, which isn't bad for that kind of work, and I could set my own schedule, which was great. Then he said if I was interested, there'd be other work I could do for more pay. I asked him what kind of work and he said I'd have to wait until he was sure he could trust me before he told me more. I told him I'd think about it and let him know, we all shook hands again and then we got in Cash's truck and left."

"Where did you go?"

"Not far. I thought Cash was going to take me back to my car, but instead he drove down the highway a ways, then turned around and went back to the gas station. We were just in time to see a white SUV leaving the place. Cash said we should follow it and see where it went."

"Smith was driving the SUV?"

"I don't know. The windows were tinted and we couldn't really see the driver, but who else would it be, coming out of that abandoned gas station? And there was mud smeared all across the license plate, so you couldn't read it. Cash pointed that out and said it was clear Smith had a lot to hide."

"So you decided to follow the vehicle?"

"Cash decided. I was just along for the ride. I thought if this guy really was up to something illegal, he wasn't going to be very happy to have us following him. But Cash stayed pretty far back and the driver of the SUV never acted like he noticed us."

"Where did you end up?"

"We drove through town and out again, and the SUV turned onto County Road 361. Cash slowed way down, to put some more distance between us and the SUV, then he turned, too. But the guy must have turned off somewhere along the road pretty quick, because we drove up and down the road a couple of times and never did see the SUV again."

"Tell me more about the SUV. What kind was it?"

"I don't know. I mean, I'm not really into vehicles. It was just an SUV—a smaller one. White and kind of dirty. Like a lot of cars around here."

"What happened when you didn't find the SUV on County Road 361?" Wes asked.

"We came back to town and Cash dropped me off at my car. And that was it."

"You didn't hear anything from Cash or Basher again? No texts? Did you see them at all the rest of that day or Sunday?"

"No. I didn't think anything about it, until I heard that Basher was dead and Cash had disappeared." He leaned across the table toward Wes. "You don't think I'm in any danger, do you?"

"Has anyone threatened you?" Wes asked.

"No. Nothing like that. It's just kind of freaky that both of them are, well, gone now, and I'm still here."

"What did you think of Smith?" Travis asked. It was the first time he had spoken to Payson.

Payson shrugged. "I thought he was kind of a blowhard. I mean, it was hard to take anyone serious in that costume he was wearing, and it was an awful lot of drama for a job on a ranch. Why not just have me come to the ranch and talk about the job? If he did have some special *extra* work for me to do, why not wait until I'd worked for him a bit and we knew each other better be-fore he offered it up? Why all the playacting?"

Why, indeed. "Thanks." Wes shook Payson's hand. "You've been a big help. If we have more questions, I'll be in touch."

"I can go now?" Payson stood.

"Yes. Thank you."

Wes walked Payson to the door, then returned to the interview room where Travis waited. "That number he has for Smith is a Colorado Springs exchange," Travis said.

"If Smith is up to something illegal, would he be dim enough to give out a number that could be traced?" Wes asked.

"Payson didn't think he was too bright."

"Yeah, but maybe that's part of the act. Doug Michelson at Colorado Mountain Guides said the man who came to his shop looking for Cash sounded like he was playacting, too."

"So, was that man—Bart Smith—the same man who killed Basher Monroe?" Travis asked. "And he planted the wig and the shirt in Basher's camper."

"Why? Cash and Payson know Smith and Basher aren't the same person because Basher came with them to the interview with Smith."

"He's already eliminated Basher, and maybe Cash, too," Travis said. "I'll have Shane do a few patrols in the area around Payson's place. He's on duty tonight."

"It's almost as if Smith is trying to draw attention to himself," Wes said. "But why? Because he wants to keep us from looking at something else?"

"Let's call his number and see who answers." Travis took out his cell and punched in the number.

"The number you have dialed is not a working number. Please hang up and try again."

Travis pocketed the phone again. "He ditched the number," he said.

Down the hall a phone rang. "Sounds like your phone," Travis said.

Wes hurried to answer. "Deputy Landry."

"Deputy, we traced the text you sent over to us," a woman's pleasant voice said. "It was placed from Colorado Springs. Downtown."

Colorado Springs. Basher was from Colorado Springs, and Bart Smith's no-longer-working number was a Colorado Springs exchange. What was the connection to Eagle Mountain?

# *Chapter Fourteen*

Rebecca tried to stifle her disappointment when she didn't hear back from Wes all afternoon. She felt untethered without her phone, and more helpless than ever as she waited for other people to figure out where Wes might be. Questions played on an endless loop in her mind: Had Cash sent that message? Why would he have taken off the way he had? Was he in some kind of trouble?

It was after nine o'clock when someone knocked on her door, startling her. When she peered out the security peep, she was surprised to see Wes. She hurried to unlock the door and open it. "Hey there. I didn't see your car." She looked past him toward the curb, which was empty.

"I parked around back." He moved past her into the house, bringing the aroma of late summer: warm jasmine and pine.

"Why did you do that?" she asked.

"Because someone pointed out to me that if I'm going to spend so much time over here, I might want to be a little more…discrete." He pulled her close and kissed her, and the fierceness of her response to him still surprised her. She had never thought of herself as passionate, yet he brought out that side of her.

When they finally parted, he said, "Sorry I'm so late. There have been some developments. Nothing big," he hastened to add. "Just new information." He led her to the sofa and they sat.

"Did you find out anything about Cash's phone?" she asked.

"The text was sent from Colorado Springs."

"So... Cash's phone is in Colorado Springs?"

"Probably. Has he been there before? Does he have friends there he might have visited?"

"I don't think so. I think the only place in Colorado he's been is here. He drove here from California when he moved in, but I'm sure he didn't stop over in Colorado Springs. He's never talked about knowing anyone who lives there, though it's possible he knows climbers who have come here to climb. Maybe a client he guided?"

"What about his mom? Would she know?"

"I can call her and find out. But you still have my phone."

He took the phone from his pocket and handed it to her. "We're done with it now," he said.

She scrolled through her contacts and found Pamela's number, then glanced at the time. Only a little after eight o'clock at Pamela's house. "Hello, Rebecca," Pamela said. "You must be a mind reader. I was just thinking about calling you."

"Oh? Why is that?"

"I got a text from Cash this afternoon. As I expected, he decided to hare off somewhere and didn't bother to tell anyone. He says he's fine, not to worry." She laughed. "Didn't I tell you? It's so typical of him not to think about anyone but himself."

"Yes, he sent me a message, too." Rebecca met Wes's

eyes. Should she say something about the possibility that the text hadn't come from Cash at all?

"Oh, good. When he decides to show up at your place again, you're welcome to read him the riot act on my behalf."

"Do you know if Cash has friends in Colorado Springs?" Rebecca asked. "Has he ever been there?"

"Why? Is that where you think he is?"

"I don't know. Someone mentioned it as a possibility."

"Huh. Well, I don't think he knows anyone there, but you know Cash. Maybe he met someone and they hit it off, and the next thing you know he decided to visit him. Or her." She sighed. "To be that young and carefree again."

"Let me know if you hear from him again," Rebecca said. "I'll do the same."

"Will do. You have a good evening."

She ended the call and Rebecca laid the phone on the coffee table. "Did you hear most of that?" she asked.

"I did. We've contacted police in Colorado Springs and we'll ask them to look for Cash."

"Why would he be in Colorado Springs? And without his truck and gear?"

"Basher Monroe was from Colorado Springs," Wes said. "Or at least he was there for a little over a year before he moved to Eagle Mountain."

"But Basher is dead. Why would Cash go there now?"

"I don't know. It's just a connection we're looking into. It might not mean anything."

"What about the search here?" she asked.

"Search and Rescue didn't find anything, and they did a thorough sweep of that ravine and the area above.

We didn't find anything of particular interest in the truck, either."

"I want to go back out there and look for myself," she said. "I know I probably won't find anything, but I have to see for myself. I have to know I at least tried."

"Don't go by yourself," he said. "If you wait until Wednesday, I can go with you."

Waiting would be hard, but she didn't really want to conduct a search on her own. "All right," she said. "Is there anything I can do in the meantime?"

"Keep trying Cash's phone," he said. "And give yourself credit for already doing everything you can." He put his arm around her. "Patience is a lesson I have to learn over and over. It doesn't seem to get any easier."

"And we can't control other people." She sighed and leaned her head on his shoulder. "It's probably just as well we can't. I have enough trouble running my own life without having to be in charge of someone else's."

THE NEXT DAY, Wes returned to County Road 361. As he drove slowly down the gravel road, studying the landscape and the few residences, he wondered if Bart Smith lived or worked here, or if he had merely turned down this mostly deserted road because he realized he was being tailed and needed to evade his followers.

He decided to reinterview every person who lived on the road, and check for any white SUVs. He began at the end, with Martin Kramer. "I'm looking for a man who may go by the name of Bart Smith," Wes said. "Caucasian, six feet to six-four, broad shoulders and muscular." It wasn't much of a description. Thanks to the wig and sunglasses, they had no idea of Smith's hair or eye color.

"That description fits a lot of people," Kramer pointed out.

"Does anyone who lives around here fit that description?" Wes asked.

"I'm six feet tall," Kramer said. "And I'm strong enough."

This was true. Though Wes thought of Kramer as older—he was clearly in his sixties—he had an erect posture, and beneath the loose flannel shirt and baggy canvas work pants he wore was the hint of muscles. He would have to be strong to haul the buckets of rock that dotted the area around his shack.

"What's your phone number, Mr. Kramer?" Wes asked.

"There's no phone signal up here," Kramer said.

"Does that mean you don't have a phone? No means of communicating with the outside world?"

"I didn't say that. I've got a cell phone, but I don't even turn it on up here. It wouldn't do any good."

"What's the number?" Wes asked.

Kramer stuck out his lip, and Wes was sure he was going to refuse to answer the question, then he rattled off a number. Wes didn't recognize the exchange. "Where's that from?" he asked.

"Ohio. Where I used to live. And what's it matter to you?"

"Have you ever lived in Colorado Springs?"

"No. Why are you asking?"

"Just curious." Wes looked around the cluttered homestead, with its piles of old timber and many orange-and-white plastic buckets of rocks. No sign of any white SUVs, just a gray pickup. "Have you had any more trouble with trespassers?"

"No. I guess I scared them off."

"Let me know if anyone else bothers you."

Kramer turned away. "I have to get back to work now."

Wes moved on to the young couple in the yurt. Robby Olsen was mucking out the chicken house when Wes arrived, the stinging ammonia odor of the manure making Wes's eyes water. "Hello, Deputy," Robby said, wheeling a wheelbarrow full of bedding and manure out of the chicken run. "What can I do for you?"

Wes described Bart Smith. Becca Olsen walked over from the vegetable garden to join them. "Robby is six-two," she said and smiled at her husband.

Wes wouldn't have described Robby as broad-shouldered, but he was wiry, his arms corded with muscle as he propelled the full wheelbarrow forward. The young couple seemed innocent enough, but what better cover for illegal activity than a homestead in a remote area? "I'd really love a tour of your place," he said. "If you have time."

"Of course." Becca's smile was warm and open. "It's not fancy, but we're pretty proud of it."

Over the next half hour, Wes toured the yurt they called home, with its loft bedroom, woodstove, propane refrigerator and range, and solar-powered well. A separate washroom held a shower, laundry and composting toilet. He tromped past the chicken house, pigsty, goat barn, greenhouse and garden patch, a tool shed, wood shed and equipment storage. The Olsens drove a blue Volkswagen Jetta and a tan Chevy truck. They ended the tour back at Wes's cruiser.

"What are you really looking for, Deputy?" Robby asked, his tone not unfriendly. "You can see we don't have anything illegal around here."

"We received a tip that someone out this way was involved in illegal drug activity," Wes said. This wasn't entirely true, but close enough. "The tip was very vague—I don't know how credible it is, but I have to check it out."

"Of course," Becca said. She pressed her lips together and gave her husband a worried look.

"What are you thinking?" Wes asked.

"I hate to think anyone here is involved in that kind of thing," she said. "But the truth is we don't know our neighbors that well. Except for Lindsey and Micah Carstairs at the Russell Ranch. They're friendly, and I don't think they're involved in anything like that at all. But the couple in the trailer and Mr. Kramer—we just don't know them."

"Have you heard any more gunshots at Kramer's place?" Wes asked.

"Not lately," Robby said. "Things seem to have really calmed down. And Trey and Courtney keep to themselves and are pretty quiet. I don't think they're up to anything illegal, either." He frowned at his wife.

"I didn't say they were," Becca said. "Just that we don't know. And the one time I went over there to introduce myself and give them some vegetables from the garden, they made it pretty clear they didn't appreciate visitors." She shrugged. "I'm just used to people who are a little friendlier."

"Any increase in traffic on this road lately?" Wes asked.

They both shook their heads.

"Thanks. Let me know if you think of anything else that might be helpful."

"We will," Becca said. "But I hope your tip is wrong. We haven't had any trouble out here and we want it to stay that way."

Next stop was Trey Allerton's trailer. There was no sign of any vehicles parked there. Courtney Baker answered the door. She looked healthier today, with no bruises, her hair and makeup done. "What can I do for you, Deputy?" she asked. She wasn't smiling, but she wasn't hostile, either.

"Is Trey here?" Wes asked. Allerton, he knew, was the right build for Bart Smith, though, as he was quickly realizing, that didn't make him unique.

"He isn't," she said. "He went out of town on business for a few days, though I expect him back any time now."

"Where did he go?" Wes asked.

She hesitated, then said, "He went to Colorado Springs. He lived there before we moved here, and he still has friends there. But then you probably already know that."

It was probably in the file they had on Allerton, though Wes hadn't studied that. "What's his phone number?" Wes asked. "I just have a couple of questions. He could easily answer them over the phone."

She rattled off a number that was not the one for Bart Smith, but Wes made note of it. "One last question," he said. "What kind of vehicle does Trey drive?"

"A Ford pickup. Why?"

"What color is it?"

"Black. What is this about?"

"Just filling in some blanks. Thank you for your help." He looked around. "Where is your car?"

"We don't need more than one vehicle, so we got rid of the other one."

"You're not worried about being stranded here by yourself?"

"I can always ask the neighbors if I need help."

"So you're all right here, by yourself?"

"I'm fine," she said. "I enjoy the peace and quiet."

"And your daughter—how is she?"

At the mention of her daughter, Courtney suddenly looked older, more drawn. "Ashlyn is with Trey. He thought the trip would make a nice treat for her."

"And you didn't go with them?"

She shook her head but didn't elaborate.

"But you're okay with her going with him?"

"Of course." She took a step back. "I have to go." Without waiting for a reply, she shut the door. He heard the lock turn.

He moved slowly away, his unease growing.

Back at the station, Jamie was at her desk. "I stopped by Trey Allerton's place this morning and talked to Courtney Baker," he told her. "She looks much better than the last time we saw her."

"That's good," Jamie said. "Maybe she really did fall down, but I think it's worth keeping an eye on her."

"I do, too. Allerton isn't home right now. She said he went to Colorado Springs for a few days."

"Maybe that's why she looks better." She shook her head.

"She told me they had sold her car, so with Trey in Colorado Springs, she's there by herself with no transportation and no phone."

"That doesn't sound good," Jamie said.

"I asked her about it and she said she was fine, that she could ask the neighbors if she needed help," Wes said. "Which I guess is true, but it's still a long walk to any of her neighbors' houses. She also told me her daughter, Ashlyn, went to Colorado Springs with Trey."

"I really don't like the sound of that," Jamie said. "Who sends a three-year-old off with a man who isn't related to her?"

"Courtney says Allerton is like her stepfather."

"Still." Jamie shook her head. "I checked Allerton's file after we saw her last and there's nothing in there about inappropriate behavior with children. Not even a hint. But it still feels off to me."

"I think I'll contact the Colorado Springs PD again and ask them to do a welfare check," Wes said. "If they can find Allerton. I don't know where he's staying. But Courtney did give me his phone number. The police can start there."

And having the local police department contact Allerton would let him know he was being watched. Maybe it would make him less likely to step out of line. Or the Colorado Springs PD might catch him up to something illegal or find some evidence that tied him to Basher Monroe or Cash Whitlow. It was a long shot, but so much in solving crime came down to luck. Wes felt they were overdue for some luck when it came to this case.

# *Chapter Fifteen*

Cash woke to light and cautiously sat up. His thigh, where the bullet had struck him, didn't hurt as much as it had, and he no longer felt feverish. But his stomach growled loudly. He had eaten the last beef jerky in his pack a long time ago. Day before yesterday? He had lost all track of time. But he needed to get out of here and find something to eat. And water. He was so thirsty. And he needed to let someone know where he was and that he needed help. If he could figure out how to get back to the road, maybe he could walk to a house, where someone would help him or at least let him use the phone to call Aunt Rebecca.

The ceiling in this cave was too low for him to stand upright. He had to walk hunched over to the entrance, then he had to inch along a narrow ledge before he reached a place where he could climb down a series of rock slabs. How had he ever made it up here, injured? He guessed he'd been desperate enough to do anything.

Once he was on fairly level ground, he tried to get his bearings. He had no idea which direction he had come from that night. He'd simply been running, trying to get away from the old man who had shot at him and Basher. He had thought the old man wouldn't expect him to come back so soon, and alone. But he'd been wrong about that. Cash had been lucky to get away alive. He hoped the fact that the old guy had shot at him and at Basher, on two different occasions, would be enough proof that he must have something to hide for the sheriff's deputies to investigate. No way would someone be that protective of a bunch of worthless rocks.

Cash had intended to circle back to his truck and drive for help, but then the truck hadn't been where he'd parked it. What had happened? Had he gotten turned around and been wrong about the place he had left it? If he could find the truck, he could drive back to safety. But nothing about this area looked familiar. There was no road or even a trail to follow, just rocks and stunted trees.

His watch said he'd been away from home two weeks. Had it really been that long? He had been really out of it for a lot of that time and even now, walking out in the open, he was dizzy and unsteady on his feet. Maybe it had been more than a day or two since he'd eaten the last of the emergency supplies he'd had stashed in his pack. He really needed to get something to eat, and some water, before too much longer. How long did it take a person to starve to death or die of thirst? Did being shot shorten that time? He didn't know how much blood he had lost, though the side of his pants was stiff with it.

*Don't think about dying,* he told himself. He focused on walking downhill. After a while, he came to a stream and lay on his stomach beside it and drank and drank. He tried not to think about what might be in that water. He'd heard pretty much every body of water around here was contaminated with giardia, but he couldn't be picky right now. He sat up and pulled his water bottle out of his pack and filled it. He searched again for something to eat, but there wasn't anything. He'd taken all the ibuprofen from the first-aid kit, too. He wished he had his phone. He must have dropped it when he was running away from that miner.

His aunt Rebecca would be worried about him. Maybe by now she had even reported him missing. Which meant someone would be looking for him, but how would they know where to look? Rebecca had no idea where he had intended to go that day. Maybe Basher was feeling well enough now to talk to her.

He zipped up the pack, then froze. What was that noise, way off in the distance? It sounded like an engine. Maybe a Jeep or an ATV. That meant he was close to the trail. He pulled the pack onto his shoulders and stood, then closed his eyes and tried to zero in on the direction the sound was coming from. Then he set out walking.

He had almost given up on reaching the trail when he came upon it. He hadn't been able to hear the vehicle for a long time now, and figured it was a small miracle that he hadn't ended up walking in circles, the way lost people apparently did in the woods. He felt like crap, and kept stumbling over rocks or roots, but seeing the trail sent a surge of energy through him. He turned onto it and headed right—downhill. He would have run, but he didn't have the strength, so he settled on walking, eyes straining for some sign of civilization—a vehicle, a house, another person. Even a sign letting him know he was headed in the right direction would have been good.

He walked for what felt like at least an hour when the trail gradually began to widen. Soon the area began to look familiar. He stopped beside a wide, graveled area. The parking lot where he had left his truck. The lot was empty. Cash walked around it, staring at the gravel as if it might provide some clue as to what had happened to his truck. How did a whole truck simply disappear?

Finally he gave up and set off down the road. As he neared the Full Moon Mine, he moved off the road into the shelter of some trees, watching the driveway that led up to the old man's shack. The last thing he needed was the man with the gun seeing him out here. He'd probably decide to finish him off.

He stayed off the road until he could see the roof of a yurt ahead. He'd stop there and ask for help. But he didn't approach the yurt directly. Instead he crept up on it, hoping to get a feel for whether or not it would be safe. He didn't know these people. If they were the type to shoot trespassers, he wanted to know before they pulled out a gun.

An old tan pickup was parked on one side of the yurt, and some chickens scratched around in the dirt in a pen not far from the front door. But he didn't see any people.

There also weren't any no-trespassing signs or anything else to discourage visitors, so he decided to take a chance. He emerged from his hiding place behind a rock and walked up the driveway toward the front door. "Hello!" he shouted, in case someone was working in the barn or one of the sheds scattered around the place. But no one answered.

"Hello!" he called again.

Chickens clucked and scratched, and somewhere an animal—a goat or a sheep, maybe?—bleated. He leaned forward and tried to peer into the yurt. It looked deserted. He knocked again and tried the door. Locked. They probably had food in there, but he wasn't going to break in, even if he could figure out how.

He walked away from the yurt, toward the chickens. They probably laid eggs. Could he eat one raw? He decided he was hungry enough that he could do that, but only if he had to.

He moved past the chicken house to a plastic-covered greenhouse. The heat wrapped around him as he stepped through the door, along with the earthy scents of compost and greenery. Tomatoes shone red among the vines crowded along one side of the structure. Cash plucked one and bit into it like an apple, the juice running down his chin. He moaned—he had never tasted anything so good.

After the tomato, he picked a handful of green beans and ate them raw, along with a cucumber, some lettuce and another tomato. Not the most filling meal he had ever eaten, but it was food and it tasted good.

He thought about staying right here and waiting for the people who lived here to return. But how long would they be gone? What if it was several days? He decided he'd better move on.

The road was dusty, the sun glaring off it so bright he had to squint. His head throbbed and his leg ached, and despite the vegetables he had just eaten, or maybe because of them, his stomach hurt.

He couldn't think about all that. He had to keep going. He had to find help. The sound of tires on gravel made him freeze. He looked over his shoulder to see a vehicle approaching—fast, from the direction he had just come. Was it the old miner? Or someone else? He stepped to the side of the road, torn between hiding and asking for help. The vehicle was really moving now, rocks pinging off the undercarriage, dust rising in a huge cloud around it. Cash dove behind a clump of bushes as it roared past.

From here on the ground, he couldn't tell who was driving. He lay there for a long time, panting, but finally forced himself to his feet and kept going, staggering down the road.

He reached the driveway of the house trailer. There were no cars out front, and the place looked deserted, but he limped up the steps and pounded on the door. No one answered. He pounded harder. "Help!" he shouted. "Somebody, please help!"

He pressed his ear to the door, listening, but heard nothing. He wanted to sink down to the steps and cry. Or maybe he should try to break in and find food and water. He tried the door, but it didn't budge and he didn't have the strength to kick it in or any tools to open it.

Defeated, he turned away and kept going. There was a ranch at the end of the road. Surely someone there would be able to help him.

He hadn't gone far before he heard another vehicle approaching. This time he didn't try to hide. If he lay down in the ditch again, he might not have the strength to get up. Instead he raised his hands in the air and waved.

The vehicle—a dirty white SUV—stopped in the middle of the road. The passenger window lowered and Cash limped over to it. A man with a big black mustache, a hat pulled low over his forehead, looked at him from behind dark sunglasses. "Please," Cash said, "I need help. Could I use your phone to call my aunt?"

"I don't have a phone," the man said. He sounded annoyed. But Cash couldn't worry about that. The man had stopped, so that was something.

"Then could you give me a ride into town?"

"What are you doing out here?" the man asked.

"My name is Cash Whitlow. My aunt Rebecca works at the medical clinic in town."

"I didn't ask who you are. I asked what you're doing."

Yeah. Not friendly. Well, he didn't have to be Cash's buddy. He just had to help him. "It's a long story, but a friend and I were…we were hiking…and this crazy old man started shooting at us. One of the bullets grazed me." He half turned and showed the tear in his jeans where he could feel the wound seeping something sticky and damp.

The man stared at him. "Get in," he said.

Cash didn't hesitate. He climbed into the passenger seat. "Thanks a bunch, mister," he said as the man shifted into Drive. "You can drop me off at the clinic right in town."

But instead of turning back toward town, the man kept going back the way Cash had come. "Uh, you can just take me to town?" Cash said.

The man didn't say anything.

"Where are we going?" Cash asked. He put one hand on the door release, then heard the lock click into place.

"I have something I need to do first," the man said. He glanced at Cash. "Don't worry."

Cash sat back and tried to remain calm. To think. He felt sick to his stomach, whether from fear or the pain in his side or from all those raw vegetables he'd eaten earlier, he didn't know.

The truck bumped along the road, every jolt sending fresh pain through Cash's body. The driver didn't look at him or say anything. His silence made Cash even more nervous. "Thanks for giving me a ride," Cash said. "What's your name?"

The man didn't answer. The guy was seriously creeping Cash out.

At the sign for the Full Moon Mine, the truck slowed. Cash held his breath, willing the driver not to turn in here. Were he and the old man with the gun working together? Had Cash chosen the exact wrong person to ask for help?

Then the SUV sped up again and they passed the driveway. "You said you were hiking with a friend," the driver said. "What happened to him?"

What should he say? He'd already lied about what they had been doing. "He was shot, too, but he managed to get away. I ended up lost."

"Some friend."

Cash wanted to protest that it hadn't been like that, but why bother? He couldn't really explain what he'd been up to, just in case the old miner and this guy were partners, or friends, or something.

"What were you really doing out here?" the man asked.

"I told you, we were hiking."

"I recognize a lie when I hear one. I bet you were snooping around. Poking your noses into something that's none of your business."

"What are you talking about?" Cash asked. "Why would I care about anything anyone out here is doing?" Unless they were doing something illegal. So was this guy partners with the old miner? Or did he have his own illegal activity he didn't want anyone to know about? "Where are we going?" he asked again. "The road stops up here just a little way."

"I know."

Cash was still trying to figure out what was going on when they reached the parking area. The driver turned in. "Get out," he said.

Cash got out. What else could he do?

By the time he'd eased out of the SUV and shouldered his pack, the driver was standing at the back bumper of the vehicle. Cash yelped when he realized the man was holding a pistol.

"The thing you need to realize—" the man said and raised the pistol "—is that we don't like trespassers around here."

Cash didn't wait for the man to fire. He turned and ran into the woods. Gunfire echoed loud behind him, but he kept running. Pain seared through him with every footfall, tears streaming down his face. He didn't want to die. Why were all these people trying to kill him?

## Chapter Sixteen

Rebecca had asked for and received a half day off on Wednesday. "Is everything all right?" Linda asked when she made the request.

"Cash's truck was found in a ravine off the Jeep trail above County Road 361," Rebecca said. "I need... I need a couple of hours to take care of some things related to that." Some people might point out that it wasn't absolutely necessary for her to go back to the area where the truck had been found, to search for a young man who might very well be safe in Colorado Springs. But she needed to go for her own peace of mind.

"Oh, Rebecca." Linda's face filled with concern. "I'm so sorry."

"Thank you. They didn't find Cash with the truck, so I guess that's good. I'm still holding out hope."

"So am I." Linda leaned forward and squeezed her hand. "Do you need to go now? We'll manage, I'm sure."

"No. What I need to do can't be done until this afternoon." When Wes had time off as well.

She returned to her desk. As usual, the clinic was busy. They treated a boy who had fallen off his skateboard and broken his arm, and a woman with strep throat. Rebecca was entering some patient information when a bearded man in a dirty flannel shirt and canvas trousers walked up to the window. "I don't have an appointment, but I think I need stitches," he said. He held up his arm, wrapped in what looked like a dish towel, blood seeping through the fabric.

"Of course." Rebecca stood. "I'll get someone to see to you right away, Mr...?"

"Kramer. Martin Kramer. And no, I've never been here before. I don't get sick." He said the words as if health was merely a matter of refusing to give in to illness.

Rebecca summoned Gail, who took one look and escorted Mr. Kramer to an empty exam room. Rebecca followed, clipboard in hand. "While Gail is taking a look at your arm, I'll fill out the paperwork," she said. Not only did this allow her to get the information they needed without delay, talking to her would help distract the patient while Gail washed and assessed the wound.

She learned that Martin Kramer was sixty years old and had good health insurance through his former employer in Ohio. "What is your address, Mr. Kramer?"

He rattled off a PO box in town.

"What is your physical address?"

"I'm at the Full Moon Mine, 1162 County Road 361."

Rebecca stopped writing, her pen digging into the form. County Road 361. Near where Cash's truck had been found. This was the man Wes had told her about—the one who had complained of someone in a hoodie trying to steal from him. A young man who might have been Cash.

"How did you do this?" Gail asked. She had finished unwinding the towel to reveal a six-inch long cut seeping blood.

"I was transferring ore from one of the mine tunnels, loading it into buckets," Kramer said. "I reached into one of the buckets and cut my arm open on a big shard of glass."

"What kind of glass?" Gail asked. "A broken bottle?"

"This was more like window glass. A big, jagged piece." He shook his head. "I don't know where it came from or how it got into that bucket."

"You're lucky you didn't slit your wrist open."

He winced as she began cleaning the wound. "Do you know when your last tetanus vaccination was?" Gail asked.

"No."

"Then you'll need another one." She laid a gauze pad over the wound. "You hold that there—tight, please. Our nurse practitioner will be in in a moment to stitch you up. Rebecca will finish getting your information."

She left the room and Rebecca moved closer to Kramer. She couldn't stay too long or someone might get suspicious, and she couldn't risk the nurse practitioner, Lauren Baker, overhearing what she had to say. "Mr. Kramer, my nephew, Cash Whitlow, is missing," she said. "His truck was found in a ravine off County Road 361. Not far from where you live."

"I've seen the posters about him. What's that got to do with me?"

"I was wondering if you had seen him. Or his truck. It's a gray Toyota Tacoma."

Kramer shook his head. "I'm too busy working to pay attention to whoever drives up and down my road. And if anybody comes on my property, I make it clear they need to leave."

Someone tapped on the door. "Mr. Kramer?" The door opened and Lauren moved in. "Oh, Rebecca. I didn't know you were still here."

"I was just leaving." She scooted past Lauren, out of the room. Kramer would need to sign the forms before he left, but that could wait.

She couldn't say why she felt so disappointed over the encounter. There was no reason Kramer should have had any contact with Cash, but so few people lived on that road she had hoped he might have some information that would link Cash with that area. An area where Cash really had no reason to be.

She returned to her desk and began entering Kramer's information into the computer. She was almost done when another man approached the check-in counter, this one more familiar. "Hello again," Trey Allerton said. He flashed his movie-star smile and held up a flyer. "I hope you'll let me put one of these up on your bulletin board." He nodded to the board in the waiting room filled with announcements of local activities.

"What is it?" she asked and held out her hand.

"I'm going to be hosting a weeklong camp for local students next month," he said. "I'm trying to get the word out."

"What kind of camp?" The heading on the flyer was for Baker Youth Ranch. "You run a youth ranch?"

"We don't have permanent facilities yet, but we'll have tents, and plenty for the kids to do. And this will be at a very reasonable cost."

"I'll have to ask the clinic director," she said, setting the flyer aside. "If she okays it, we'll put it on the board."

"Be sure and let her know I'm accepting donations to underwrite the cost," he said. "Perhaps the doctors would like to contribute."

"I'll let them know."

"Any news about your nephew?"

She studied him. His expression was one of genuine concern, but she didn't trust this man. Then she remembered that he lived on Country Road 361. "The sheriff's department found Cash's truck in a ravine not far from where you live," she said. "A gray Toyota Tacoma. You didn't happen to see it driving around there, did you?"

"No. What would Cash have been doing out there?"

"I don't know. I think he and a friend might have driven out there to look for a man they knew. Someone named Bart Smith." She had almost forgotten about Smith. Why hadn't she asked Kramer about him?

Allerton's expression didn't change. "Never heard of him, and I know everybody on that road. Not that there are many people to know. Why were they looking for Smith?"

"I don't know."

"Young people are so impulsive," he said.

"What do you mean?"

"Just that it's not unusual for them to make sudden decisions. You know, let's take a road trip to the beach or let's climb this peak that hasn't been climbed before. I'll bet your nephew did something like that. He's probably on a beach a thousand miles from here, not even thinking about how he's worrying everyone."

"If that's so, how did his truck end up at the bottom of a ravine?"

Allerton shrugged. "Maybe his impulse wasn't to take a sudden vacation but to get involved with something he shouldn't have."

The hair on the back of her neck rose. His tone was still light and conversational, but the words chilled her. "What kind of thing do you mean?"

"I'm just speculating," he said. "I don't know anything. But maybe they found this Mr. Smith and he wasn't too happy that they had followed him."

"You're frightening me," she said.

"I don't mean to do that." He nodded toward the flyer. "I'd appreciate you putting that out for me. Thanks."

He started to turn away when Martin Kramer, arm bandaged, was escorted out of the exam room by Gail. "She says I have to go to the hospital to get checked out for tendon damage," Kramer grumbled. "You've got to call over and let them know I'm coming."

"Mr. Kramer, what happened to you?" Allerton called.

Kramer scowled at Allerton. "None of your business."

"It looks like you hurt your arm," Allerton said. "You need to be careful, messing around in that mine."

"I don't need your advice," Kramer said. "I need people to leave me alone." He leaned across the counter toward Rebecca. "The more I think about it, the more I believe someone put that glass in that pile of rock. They knew I'd be moving that rock eventually and this was tucked in where it was hard to see, but could do a lot of damage. I'm lucky I didn't bleed to death out there."

Rebecca wasn't sure how to respond to this. She picked up the phone. "I'll call the hospital now." She leaned over and closed the window in Allerton's face. He was still staring at Kramer, his expression amused. "Mr. Kramer, do you know anyone named Bart Smith?" she asked while she waited for someone to answer her call.

He shook his head. "No. Who is he?"

"It's not important." Someone picked up at the hospital and she informed them the clinic was sending over a patient. She had just hung up the phone when the window slid open and Allerton leaned in again, as if he had been waiting for her to finish the call. "Kramer, do you want me to take you to the hospital?" he asked. "You probably shouldn't drive in your condition."

"I drove all the way here, didn't I?" Kramer barked. "I don't need your help."

"I'm just trying to be neighborly."

Kramer mumbled something under his breath that wasn't very complimentary to Allerton. "Thank you, Mr. Allerton," Rebecca said. "I think Mr. Kramer will be okay." She closed the window again.

Kramer signed the forms she slid toward him. "Everything out my way was nice and quiet until he moved in." Kramer jerked his head toward the window. Allerton was gone, but Rebecca understood his meaning.

"Is Mr. Allerton not a good neighbor?" she asked.

"He doesn't know how to mind his own business. He's always stopping by to check on me. But I know he really just wants to nose around, see what I'm up to. And he's always going on about this youth camp he's going to operate. Not about the kids he wants to help so much, but about how expensive it is to build a project like that, and don't I want to make a donation? He's one of those people who always has their hand out, but once they get money from you, all they want is more. He's hit up everybody in the county and must have collected a dump truck load of cash by now, but he hasn't done one thing to that worthless piece of land he leased from Sam Russell that I can see. Well I can tell you one thing—he'll never get a dime out of me, no matter how hard he tries."

He left, and Rebecca returned to entering his information into the computer. But her encounter with Allerton had shaken her. Had Cash and Basher found Bart Smith? Had Smith killed Basher? Was Cash dead, too?

The thought made her feel hollow and cold. She had meant it when she told Linda she wasn't giving up hope. But the longer Cash remained missing, the harder it was to believe he was all right.

"WE TRACKED ALLERTON to a motel on the north side of town where he was staying, but he checked out yesterday," Detective Paredo with the Colorado Springs Police Department said.

Wes cradled the phone against his shoulder and made a note of the name of the motel. "Any luck locating Bart Smith?" he asked.

"He's not in our records, none of the motels I talked to while looking for Allerton had heard of him, and no one I talked to knows anyone by that name. Of course, it could be a new alias."

"What about Allerton? Is he in your records?"

"He's never been charged with anything. His name came up in connection with a couple of things—an assault and a fraud case—while he was stationed at Fort Carson. But only peripherally. He knew the people involved—that kind of thing."

That fit with the pattern Allerton had shown here of associating with the wrong people.

"What about Martin Kramer?" Wes asked. "Does that name ring a bell?"

"No. Who's Kramer?"

"He has a gold mine up here. A neighbor of Allerton's."

"I'll run a search on him for you, but I've never heard of him. I did check out your missing person—Cash

Whitlow. We don't have anything on him, either. A dead end on the phone, too."

"Yeah, the phone company told me no more calls or texts are being sent from that number. No signal, either."

"Whoever had it probably destroyed it," Paredo said.

"Maybe so."

"Sorry I couldn't be of more help," Paredo said.

Wes hung up the phone and looked up at Gage, who had walked over to lean against his desk. "We should ask Trey what he was doing in Colorado Springs," Gage said.

"He'll say he was visiting friends."

"Or raising money for his youth camp. That's his full-time occupation these days." Gage stretched, cracking his knuckles. "I'd love to take a look at his bank accounts, figure out where all that money is going."

Wes wasn't interested in Trey Allerton. Not unless he could be tied to Basher Monroe's murder or Cash Whitlow's disappearance. "Have you had any luck tracking down Bart Smith?" he asked.

Gage shook his head. "I talked to every landlord in town, and every retail business. Nobody knows him. No business made a credit card sale to that name and no one rented lodgings to him."

"I'm convinced Bart Smith isn't his real name," Wes said.

"There's another possibility," Gage said.

"Oh?"

"Maybe Payson Fritsch made up the whole story."

Wes nodded. That kind of thing happened all the time. "Did Payson strike you as the typical attention seeker, though?"

Gage shrugged. "Maybe it started out as a joke between the three of them."

"If that's so, it's a joke that got way out of hand, considering Basher is dead."

"Speaking of that, we got forensics back on the bullets that were in Basher. Just like Doc Collins said—a 12-gauge slug and 45 ACP. Common loads. Martin Kramer bought some of each at the hardware store here in town, but—and this is interesting—Trey Allerton purchased a box of 45 ACP a couple of weeks ago."

Allerton again. What was with the guy? Wes stood. "I'm taking Rebecca back out to the area where Cash's truck was found," he said. "I doubt we'll find anything, but she insisted on taking another look and I wasn't about to let her wander around out there by herself."

"Good idea," Gage said.

The two of them walked together to the lobby, where Adelaide appeared to be arguing with a familiar figure. "Trey, what are you doing here?" Gage asked.

Trey Allerton's expression brightened when he saw them. "Deputy Landry," he said. "Courtney told me you stopped by to see her yesterday."

"She said you were in Colorado Springs," Wes said. "Did you have a good trip?"

"I did." He held out a single sheet of paper. "I want to put this poster in your window."

"I've tried to explain to Mr. Allerton that we don't allow businesses to advertise on sheriff's department property," Adelaide said.

"It's not exactly a business," Allerton said. "It's a benefit to the community—a weeklong camp for local youth."

"Which you are charging for," Adelaide said.

"A very reasonable fee. And I'm asking local businesses and organizations to donate to underwrite the expense, if the sheriff's department would like to contribute."

"I didn't think you had any facilities to host campers yet," Gage said.

"This will be in tents," Allerton said. "It's a good way to publicize what we're doing, get locals familiar with the project and invested in it. This kind of thing can be good for the whole town."

"How's the fundraising coming?" Gage asked.

"It's a process. Would you like to make a personal donation? We can always use funds."

"Not right now," Gage said.

Wes returned the flyer. "Better find someplace else to hang this."

Adelaide sniffed and returned to her desk.

Allerton opened his mouth as if to protest, but Wes cut him off. "I'm glad you stopped by. I wanted to ask if you knew Basher Monroe."

"The young man who was killed? I read the story in the paper. But no, I didn't know him."

"I thought you might have," Wes said. "He used to live in Colorado Springs, too."

Allerton shook his head. "I didn't know him. But that's not surprising, really. I was in the military at the time. I didn't interact much with the locals."

According to Detective Paredo, that wasn't true, but Wes didn't contradict him.

"How's the search for Cash Whitlow coming?" Allerton asked. "I stopped by the clinic just now and his aunt Rebecca told me you found his truck not far from where I live."

"We did," Wes said. "Do you have any idea how it might have ended up there?"

"Rebecca said he and a friend were out there looking for someone they knew."

"Bart Smith. Do you know him?"

"No. It sounds like a fake name, doesn't it? Initials B.S." He chuckled.

"Fake or not, Bart Smith may have murdered one young man and be involved in the disappearance of another," Wes said. "If you know anything that could help us find him or Cash Whitlow, you need to tell us."

"All I know is what I told Rebecca. Young men can be impulsive. Maybe Cash and his friend got involved in something that wasn't their business."

"Such as?" Gage asked.

"I wouldn't know," Trey said. "But it doesn't take a genius to figure out that it would be relatively easy to hide all kinds of illegal activities in these remote areas. I mean, look at my neighbor, Martin Kramer. Do you have any idea what he's really up to in that mine of his?"

Had Allerton changed subjects in order to divert attention? "Do you think Mr. Kramer is involved in something illegal?" Wes asked.

"He just seems overly protective of his property to me. And if there's really gold in these old mines, why isn't everyone out digging it up? I think the mine would make a great cover for other kinds of businesses—drugs or smuggling or something."

"It sounds like you've given this a lot of thought," Wes said.

"It's pretty natural to wonder about your neighbors isn't it? Especially when one of them threatens you with a shotgun every time you pull up in the driveway."

"Maybe you need to stop visiting him," Gage said.

"Except maybe he's just a lonely old man in the early stages of dementia," Allerton said. "If that's the case, I feel I have an obligation to check in on him." He waved the flyer. "I'd better get going. I want to post as many of these as possible."

"Thanks for stopping by," Wes said.

"Not at all," Allerton said. "Oh, and Deputy?"

"Yes?"

"You might want to have a talk with Rebecca Whitlow. When I spoke with her today, she asked a lot of questions about her nephew. She seemed to think I knew something. I'd hate for her to go snooping around the neighborhood, thinking she was helping her nephew, only to end up in trouble herself. I mean, she's a really nice lady, but probably a little naive about how dangerous some people can be."

"Do you have any particular dangerous person in mind?" Wes asked.

Allerton's expression remained guileless. "No one in particular, but she really needs to be careful."

Gage waited until Allerton had exited before he said, "Nice of him to be so *concerned* about his neighbor and about Rebecca."

Right. That hadn't sounded like concern to Wes. It had sounded like a threat.

# Chapter Seventeen

Rebecca was waiting out front when Wes arrived to pick her up. "How are you doing?" he asked as she climbed into the front seat of the sheriff's department SUV.

"I don't know," she admitted. "I'm excited to be doing something other than sitting around worrying, but I know, realistically, that we probably won't find anything. And a couple of things happened at work this morning that are a little, well, unsettling."

"Oh?" Though his eyes remained on the road as he drove, she sensed that he was focused on her. "What happened?"

"Martin Kramer came in to the clinic. He's the miner you were telling me about, isn't he? He lives on Country Road 361."

"Yes. Why was Kramer at the clinic? Or are you allowed to say?"

"I can't imagine you'd have reason to tell anyone else. He cut himself on a piece of window glass. Lauren, our nurse practitioner, sent him to the hospital to make sure he didn't have tendon damage."

"Was he repairing a broken window or something? He made a complaint last week about someone trying to break in at his place."

"He said the glass was in a pile of rock he was transferring into five-gallon buckets. It was a pretty bad cut. He could have sliced an artery and bled to death."

"That seems a strange place for a piece of glass. Did he say how it got there?"

"He told me he thinks someone may have put the glass there, intending to hurt him. I thought maybe he was being paranoid. He'd already talked about warning off anyone who came to his place."

"He is paranoid," Wes said. "But sometimes people feel that way because they really are being persecuted."

"I asked him about Cash, and about Bart Smith, but he said he didn't know anything about them. How could all three of them have been out there and nobody saw them? There aren't that many people who live out there."

"Kramer is something of a hermit," Wes said. "I don't think he engages with a lot of other people if he can help it."

"Yes, that's the impression I got. He told me how much he doesn't like his neighbor Trey Allerton."

Wes glanced at her. "He specifically mentioned Allerton?"

"I think that was just because Allerton was at the clinic this morning, too. He dropped off a flyer about a kids' camp he's hosting. He didn't know Bart Smith, either, and he said Cash was probably off on a beach somewhere, oblivious to how worried I've been."

Wes nodded. "Allerton brought his flyer by the sheriff's department, too."

"Did he ask you for a donation?" she asked.

"I think he asks everyone for a donation."

"Kramer says he thinks all the money he collects goes into Allerton's pocket."

"He hasn't spent much on this so-called kids' ranch of his," Wes said. "But maybe he needs a lot of money before he can really start work. I don't have any idea what's involved in a project that size. For now, he says he's going to put the kids in tents."

"I wouldn't trust my kids to someone with no experience, no infrastructure and I'm assuming no staff—would you?"

"No. But a lot of people find Allerton very charming."

Trey Allerton was good-looking. And he exuded a kind of charisma. But she had always been leery of people who found it so easy to mesmerize others. "Do you think he's right?" she asked. "Do you think Cash is relaxing on a beach somewhere—or in Colorado Springs?"

"The police in Colorado Springs are looking for him, but so far they haven't found him," Wes said. "If he's staying with friends and staying out of trouble, there's no reason they should know he's there."

"I keep calling his phone, but I never get an answer."

Wes's jaw tightened, but he didn't say anything. He turned onto County Road 361 and she sat forward, studying the landscape as they passed. She wasn't sure what she was looking for, but she couldn't shake the belief that the clue to what had happened to Cash was somewhere on this road.

A young woman, belly round in the late stages of pregnancy, was walking back from her mailbox at the entrance to the Russell Ranch. She waved as they passed. "That's Lindsey Carstairs," Wes said. "She and her husband, Micah, are leasing the ranch. They both grew up in the area and have good reputations. I spoke to them about Cash and Basher, and about Bart Smith, but they didn't know anything."

"Everyone says they don't know anything," she said. "But someone has to know, don't they?"

"That's how a lot of criminal cases are solved," Wes said. "Someone who knows something comes forward. The key is finding that someone."

"Which is why I'm here today," she said. "I want to find that someone."

Wes slowed as they neared Trey Allerton's trailer. Allerton stood outside his door, watching as they passed. Wes lifted his hand in a wave, but Allerton didn't return the gesture. "I guess he's not feeling very charming today," Rebecca said.

"He thinks the sheriff's office is harassing him," Wes said. "He's been on the periphery of several of our cases, so he's been questioned a number of times."

"But he hasn't done anything wrong?"

"He hasn't been charged with any crime," Wes said.

"That's a very diplomatic answer."

He laughed, and her mood lifted at the sound. He drove past the yurt. "We've questioned the Olsens, too," he said. "They seem sincere in their desire to help, but they didn't have anything to tell us."

"When I think about it, I don't pay attention to every vehicle that drives down my street," she said. "And I don't know all my neighbors, though I do know most of them. They've been in the clinic at one time or another. But if someone wanted to keep to themselves, I probably wouldn't notice."

"Most people are too involved in their own lives to notice what's going on with others," Wes said. "It's not a bad way to live, though it makes investigations more difficult. There's nothing we like better than finding the nosy neighbor who knows what everyone else is up to."

"Too bad you don't have someone like that here."

The sign for the Full Moon Mine loomed ahead. "I'm tempted to stop by and see if Mr. Kramer is all right," she said. "Even though he complained about Allerton doing the same. He said Trey was just snooping. I can always claim a professional interest." He slowed as they neared Kramer's driveway. "Let's stop and talk to him a minute."

The SUV bumped and rattled up the driveway and came to a stop a hundred yards from a shack constructed of rough sawn lumber and sheets of corrugated metal. Wes waited a moment, then honked the horn. "When I was here before, Kramer didn't waste any time warning us off," he said.

"I don't see a vehicle," she said. "Maybe he's not back from the hospital yet."

"I'll just check around." He unfastened his seat belt and reached for the door handle. "Let me get out first, and make sure the coast is clear."

He opened the door and slowly eased out of the vehicle, then stood beside the SUV, looking around. He walked up to the shack and knocked. "Mr. Kramer! It's Deputy Landry. Are you all right?"

Rebecca could stand it no longer. She got out of the vehicle and hurried toward him. "I don't think he's here," she said.

Wes tried the door, but it didn't budge. "I think you're right." He nodded to their right. "Let's make sure he's not up at the mine."

A narrow gravel path led up the hill from the shack. Rebecca followed, and they picked their way around several orange plastic buckets of rocks, an overturned wheelbarrow and various rusted pieces of what she guessed was old mining equipment. At last they reached a rough timber shed over the dark hole in the side of the mountain. A sign proclaimed this to be Adit #1, Full Moon Mine. Estab. 2016.

Wes cupped his hands to his mouth. "Mr. Kramer!"

Silence enveloped them, so complete she might have believed she had suddenly lost her hearing, except she could make out the soft sigh of her own breath and the click of rock against rock as Wes shifted his feet. He knelt and touched something on the ground. "Blood," he said. "There's a trail of it back toward his shack."

How had Rebecca not noticed the bloodstains on their walk up the path? Now they seemed obvious—dark splotches in the gray gravel. But she had been looking for a complete man, not his blood. "It was a bad cut," she said. "He was smart enough to bandage it up tightly—not so easy to do for one person alone."

"I'm going to take a look inside." He took a flashlight from his utility belt and switched it on.

Rebecca followed him into the mine tunnel. Though she could remain upright in the narrow passage, Wes had to stoop. Kramer would have had to do so also. About twenty yards inside, the passage opened into a kind of room, a large pile of fist-sized rocks on either side. "This is where he cut himself," Wes said and played the beam of light over a larger bloodstain. Then he shifted the light to a piece of glass, about the size of a sheet of paper torn from a notebook. He knelt and looked at it more closely, then handed Rebecca the light. "Hold this so I can take a closer look," he said.

She did as he asked and he pulled a pair of thin gloves from his pocket and put them on. Then he picked up the glass by one corner and held it up. It glinted in the light, and she thought she could make out the thin stain of blood across one corner. "This isn't ordinary window glass," he said.

"It isn't?" That's exactly what it looked like to her.

"Look at this edge." He pointed to the longest edge. "I'm not positive, but it looks to me as if it's been filed, so that the edge tapers." He gingerly touched the edge. "It's razor sharp."

"Could it have broken that way?"

"I don't see how." He held the glass in one hand and fished in his pocket with another and took out a thick plastic bag. He deposited the glass in this, then took out a pen and wrote on the label on the bag. "I think I'll have the lab take a closer look at this," he said.

"Do you think Mr. Kramer is right?" she asked. "Someone deliberately planted that here?"

"I want to find out." He stood and took the flash-light from her, and shone it around the room. "Kramer has been working here five years. It's hard work. Why would he keep doing it if it didn't pay off?"

"Maybe he keeps going because he's convinced he'll strike it rich someday," she said. "Isn't that what keeps gamblers placing bet after bet, even after they've lost almost everything?"

"Maybe," Wes said. "Or maybe Kramer really has found gold and someone else knows it and is trying to steal from him."

They returned to the SUV, and Wes locked the glass in its evidence bag in a box in the back of the vehicle. Then he turned around and they headed back to the county road, and up the hill to the point where the road narrowed. A sign announced that only high-clearance, narrow wheelbase, four-wheel drive vehicles were al-lowed past that point.

Wes swung the SUV into the parking area to the left. Rebecca stared at the empty gravel lot. It looked famil-iar, yet also foreign. With the trees closing in around them and no more houses or driveways for reference, it was easy to lose track of where you were. "How far are we from where Cash's truck was found?" she asked.

"It's right below here." He got out of the SUV and she followed him to the edge. Bright yellow paint on the ground marked a pair of ruts from a vehicle. "This is where the truck went over," Wes said.

She stared at the faint impressions in the dirt and gravel and tried to imagine what had happened. "The parking area stops ten feet from the edge," she said. "How did Cash's truck get from there to here? Did he just drive? Maybe he didn't see the edge in the dark or thought he was farther away?"

"Maybe." He took her arm and led her away from the tracks. "But the forensics team think the truck might have been pushed over."

His grip on her arm tightened. "But we don't think Cash was in the truck when it went over," he reminded her.

"Then where was he?" The question came out as a wail, and she struggled to regain her composure. "None of this makes sense to me," she said.

"It doesn't make sense to me, either. Let's walk a little way up the trail and see what else we can see."

He didn't let go of her arm, and she didn't try to pull away. The warmth of his hand and the strength of his grip steadied her. She didn't have to go through any of this alone.

The trail itself was a rutted red dirt path, approximately four feet wide, stunted juniper trees and large boulders scattered on either side. The air at this elevation was cool and crystal clear, smelling of warmed granite and cedar, like an expensive men's cologne.

Wes studied the ground as they walked, slowly, down

the middle of the road. "What are you looking for?" she asked.

"I'm not sure," he said. "Anything odd or different."

*Like bloodstains*, she thought, but didn't say so out loud.

Wes put up his hand, a signal for her to stop. Then he knelt and stared at the ground. Without changing her position, she tried to see what he was looking at. "Is that a footprint?" she asked.

"Part of one." He indicated what she could now see was the impression of the front half of a tennis shoe. "Someone stumbled and fell," Wes continued. He pointed to a rounded impression two feet ahead of the partial shoe print. "Here's his knee where he caught himself." He leaned forward, and so did she, her heart starting to beat faster when she saw the next clue. "And here's where his hand went down." He took out his phone and focused it on the spot. "I don't know how clear a photo I'll get in this dappled light, but it's such a clear impression, we might even be able to get finger-prints off of it. We'll definitely want to get a forensics team up here to make an impression."

The shutter of the camera clicked, a tiny sound in the vast empty space, and then sound exploded around them. Shards of rock flew up from the ground inches from where Wes knelt. A scream tore from Rebecca's throat and then Wes was shoving her to the ground. She flattened herself to the rough dirt, Wes's weight heavy on top of her, as another shot hit close to them. And another still.

# Chapter Eighteen

Wes grappled to free his pistol from its holster, even as he tried to keep his body over Rebecca's. She lay still beneath him, unmoving except for the involuntary shudders that coursed through her every few seconds. She was shaking with fear. He might have done the same, but he didn't have time to be afraid. He was too busy processing everything that was going on. The shots were coming from behind them, back toward the parking area. Had someone followed them here? How had he failed to notice them, if that was the case?

He freed the weapon at last, and scanned their surroundings for the best place to shelter. He flattened his body over Rebecca again, and pressed his lips to her ear. "On the count of three, I'm going to roll off of you and I want you to drag yourself over behind that boulder," he said. "Do you see it, just ahead?"

"Yes," she whispered.

"Good. Are you ready?"

"Where are you going to be?" she asked.

"Right behind you."

"All right. I'm ready."

The shooter had stopped firing for the moment. But that might only mean he was moving closer, into a better position to finish them off. "One," Wes said. "Two. Three."

He levered himself off her and she dragged herself forward, scrambling on her knees. Another shot rang out and she stifled a cry but kept going. Wes didn't bother answering the fire. He had already assessed that their assailant was using a semiautomatic rifle. One with much greater range than Wes's Glock.

He followed her and they crouched behind the boulder. "Are you all right?" he asked.

"I'm terrified. But I'm not hurt." She sat on the ground, her back to the stone, while he leaned over her, staring in the direction he thought the shots had come from, but seeing nothing. Everything around them was utterly still and silent. "Who's shooting at us?" she asked.

"I don't know." Was it Kramer? Maybe he had seen them at his place and followed them here, though so far he had shown an inclination to fire only on people he deemed trespassers, and then his weapon of choice was a shotgun. It could be Bart Smith. Or someone else entirely.

Wes leaned around the boulder, and immediately another shot sent him diving for cover. Rebecca gripped his arm. "Don't do that!" she said.

He nodded but didn't answer, willing his heart to slow.

"What are we going to do?" she asked. "He has us pinned here."

He tried his shoulder-mounted radio, but raised only static. He might have better luck on the unit in the SUV. Though the police radio, like cell phones, didn't always work in these remote locations, a series of repeaters placed on peaks around the county had improved service of late. If they could get to the SUV, they would radio for help or even drive away.

"Let's see if we can move parallel to the road, back toward where we're parked," he said. He pointed behind them. "There, in that thick brush. If we can get on the other side of that, it will provide more cover."

She nodded. "Go now," he urged, and she darted forward, keeping low. No shots came. Had the shooter not seen her or was he taking advantage of their inattention to move even closer?

Wes followed Rebecca, and held back a tangle of branches while she wriggled her way in and through a tangle of vines. From here, they were able to keep a screen of shrubs, stubby trees, downed logs and other forest debris between them and the roadway. Wes worried the shooter was tracking them through the sounds of their movements. Dried leaves crackled and twigs popped underfoot, no matter how stealthily they tried to move.

They stopped when they were in sight of the SUV. It sat, undisturbed, where they had left it, but getting to it would require crossing the open roadway and the barren gravel parking area. "How are we going to get there without being shot?" she whispered.

"Let's wait a minute and see what happens." He strained his ears for any sign of movement around them.

"Maybe—" But he never heard what else she had to say. The back windshield of the SUV shattered as another shot echoed, this one sounding much closer to them. Two more shots shredded the back tires. So much for that avenue of escape.

The shooter knew exactly where they were, and he was coming closer.

Rebecca stared at Wes, wide-eyed, her fist over her

mouth, as if stifling a scream. "We have to get out of here," he said. He pointed back the way they had come. "We'll run. Stay in cover if you can, but moving quickly is even more important. Zigzag from side to side and stay low to make yourself a smaller target. And don't stop. We need to put as much distance as we can between ourselves and whoever is shooting at us."

She lowered her hand and nodded. "All right."

"You go first." He wanted to put himself between her and the shooter. "I'll follow."

She frowned, but he didn't wait for her to debate him. "Go," he said and nudged her.

She went. Together, they crashed through the woods on a zigzagging course. The shooter fired after them, but they kept going, darting between trees. He spotted a narrow trail into deeper undergrowth and tugged her arm, indicating they should take it, and she veered onto it, ducking beneath a curtain of vines, around a fallen ponderosa pine and up a slope carpeted with moss.

His lungs burned and his side ached by the time she stopped in the shelter of a rock outcropping. She leaned against the rock and pressed her head to the rough surface, eyes closed, panting. He pressed his back to the same rock and stared up at a triangle of darkening sky showing through the canopy of leaves. "I haven't heard any more shots in a while," he said.

"Do you think he followed us?"

They would have been easy to track. They weren't trying to hide their path. But he had no sense that they were being pursued. "I don't think so," he said after a moment.

She hugged her arms around her shoulder. "It's getting colder," she said.

Even in summer, nights at this elevation held a chill.

They needed to find shelter. He had emergency gear in the SUV. If they could make their way back to it, maybe they could get help at the yurt or at Russell Ranch. He trusted the Olsens and the Carstairs enough to go to them.

Rebecca straightened and brushed her hair back off her forehead. "Which direction do we go from here?"

He stood up straight also and looked back the way they had come. Or the way he thought they had come. Though he had felt as if they were bulldozing through the woods, on a path anyone could follow, he realized with a start that he could make out no sign of their passage. It was as if the forest had closed over their tracks.

"Wes?" she asked.

He took her hand and squeezed it. "I don't know where we are," he said. On top of everything else, they were lost.

CASH HEARD THE gunshots from his hiding place, under a rock overhang on the side of a hill. He hadn't been able to make his way back to the cave he had used before, but had found this sheltering overhang just before dusk. He woke from a fitful sleep, shaking with the visceral memory of the old miner firing at him and Basher, of Basher going down and the nightmarish hike back to the truck.

And then the next day, when he had come back to the mine and been shot himself. He had thought it was the miner wanting to finish him off, but now he wasn't so sure. The man in the white SUV who had driven him back to the parking area. Had that been Bart Smith? Or someone who was working for the old miner? Or someone else who simply wanted Cash dead?

He had run until he had fallen, too exhausted to get

up, but he had made himself get up and dragged himself to this shelter. He didn't know how long he had lain here. The place where he had been shot was oozing blood and pus now, and his fever raged.

Was he going to die? When he was climbing, he never thought about death. Clinging to a rock face in the most precarious position, he always felt incredibly alive. But now, alone in these woods, hurting and hungry, death haunted him.

The shots sounded far away. Was it hunters, after a deer or the man with the big mustache? Was it the miner?

He struggled to sit up. Were the shots getting closer? He couldn't tell. He should move to a better hiding place. But where? And he couldn't keep hiding like this. When he had first retreated here, he had told himself that by now Aunt Rebecca would have reported him missing. People would be looking for him. All he had to do was wait for them to find him.

But what if they weren't looking? He couldn't stay here much longer, without food and water, waiting.

He forced himself to a standing position, though he had to hold onto the wall of the overhang to keep from falling over. Though he was some ways up the hill, he couldn't see much from here, except the tops of trees. Sometimes he could see deer moving through the woods below, and once he had watched a porcupine undulating its way up the trail, its lush cape of quills quivering with each step.

Then he saw the people—the woman first, then the man behind her. Was he following her? Was this the shooter?

But no. She stopped and waited for the man, then they embraced. They were together. A couple. Out hiking? He opened his mouth to shout, then remembered the shooter. He was still out there. If Cash drew his attention, would he kill these strangers, too?

Instead, he waited, watching. They were headed this way. When they were near enough for him to speak to them without shouting, he would do so. He'd warn them about the shooter. Though, surely, they would have heard the shots.

The man had dark hair, and was clean-shaven, so he wasn't the man who had given Cash a ride. And he wasn't the old miner. This man was younger.

He focused on the woman again. Something about her was familiar, but he only caught glimpses of her as she moved between the trees.

How long since the shooting had stopped? Since before he saw the man and woman? He felt as if he were trying to move through fog, drifting in and out of awareness, unable to keep track of time. He forced himself to focus on the man and woman again. They were definitely getting closer.

He was getting dizzy, standing so long, so he sat and watched the couple move up the slope toward him. He could only see the tops of their heads now. And the man's hand. He carried a gun. Had he been the one shooting?

Cash drew back. Maybe he should go back under the overhang and hide. Let these people pass.

But the woman was with this man. No woman had been with Bart Smith or the miner or the man with the mustache. And she didn't have a gun that he could see.

They were directly below him now, on the same path he had followed to this place. "Hey!" he said.

But the sound was barely a squeak. He hadn't used his voice in so long. He swallowed and tried again. "Hey!"

Only slightly louder. Frustrated, he picked up a rock and threw it. It landed right at the man's feet. He looked up, weapon raised. Cash raised his hands. "Don't shoot!" he pleaded.

"Cash!"

The woman was the one who said his name. He shifted his gaze, and looked into the astonished face of his aunt Rebecca. "Cash," she said again, and ran up the trail toward him.

# *Chapter Nineteen*

Rebecca rushed forward to embrace Cash. It was really him. Safe. Alive. She stepped back to look at him more closely, and fear gripped her anew. "What's wrong?" she asked. "What happened to you?" He was so thin and pale, not at all the vibrant young man she knew.

"I'll tell you in a little bit." He looked past her at Wes. "Are you a cop?"

"Deputy Wes Landry, Rayford County Sheriff's Department." Wes stepped forward and offered his hand.

Cash took it, but released it quickly. "We have to get out of here," he said. "There's a guy out here who's trying to kill me."

"Who is trying to kill you?" Rebecca's gaze shifted to his leg, and the bloodstained jeans. The shock of the sight made her queasy. "Cash, you're hurt!" She gripped him harder, as if he might vanish if she released her hold on him.

"It's not safe out here," Cash said, speaking to Wes. "There's a kind of cave back here." He pointed along the ledge. "We can talk there. Or we could just head for your car." He eased out of Rebecca's grasp. "That would be better. Let's just get out of here."

"Do you know how to get back to the parking area from here?" Wes asked.

Cash shook his head. "I'm so disoriented. I don't know where I am most of the time." He licked his cracked lips. "Do you have any food on you?"

"I'm sorry. No," Wes said.

Cash looked past him. "I heard gunshots. Was someone shooting at you?"

"They were," Rebecca said. "But we never saw who. Cash, what is going on? What have you gotten yourself into?"

Wes took her arm. "He's right. We're too exposed here. Let's go to this cave and figure out our next step."

She wanted to demand Cash tell her everything, right this second, but the memory of those bullets, so close to them, propelled her forward. They followed Cash along the ledge to a rock overhang that formed a shallow cave. She wrinkled her nose at the stench of unwashed body and sickness. Cash sank down onto the floor and pulled a foil emergency blanket around him, his face drained of color.

She knelt beside him. "We've been looking for you for days," she said. "I've been so worried."

"I never meant to worry you."

"We found your truck in a ravine," Wes said. "Below the parking area. And your phone sent a couple of texts from Colorado Springs."

Cash closed his eyes. For a moment Rebecca thought he had passed out. She leaned over and took his hand and cradled it in both of hers. His fingers were ice cold. "I'm okay," he said. He looked up at Wes. "I wondered what happened to my truck. I came back to the parking area and it was just…gone. And I thought I must have dropped my phone, running through the woods."

"Running from what?" Wes sat on the other side of Cash, facing him.

Cash sighed. "It's a long story. Let me think a minute how to tell it."

"Payson Fritsch told us some things," Wes said. "About the meeting with Bart Smith, and about how he and Basher Monroe and you followed Smith to County Road 361."

"That's how it started," Cash said. "Smith was acting so strange. Basher and I were sure he was involved in something illegal. Probably drugs." He looked Wes in the eye. "You probably already know I had trouble with drugs. Basher had, too, so we knew a little bit about the kind of people who prey on others and get them hooked. I didn't want that happening to someone like Payson, or even younger kids, so I decided we should check this out."

"You should have gone to the sheriff with your suspicions," Rebecca said.

"I didn't have any proof," Cash said. "I wasn't going to confront him or anything, just follow and see where he went." He rubbed the side of his neck. "How is Basher? Didn't he tell you any of this?"

Rebecca's throat tightened. She squeezed Cash's hand. "Honey, Basher is dead," she said. "Someone shot him."

His face twisted. "He told me he wasn't hurt bad. He told me all he needed to do was rest. I never should have left him."

"Who shot Basher?" Wes asked.

"That old miner. Or at least I think it was him." He pulled the emergency blanket more tightly around him.

"What happened?" Wes asked. "How did Martin Kramer come to shoot Basher?"

"I'll see if I can remember everything straight. So much has happened."

Rebecca listened, enthralled and horrified, as Cash took them through everything that had happened since she had seen him last and how he and Basher had decided Martin Kramer was the most likely person to be masquerading as Bart Smith.

Cash hunched forward, his face more animated. "It was the perfect setup. You could be doing anything down in that old mine. Later, toward dark, we came back and parked at the parking area at the start of the Jeep trail and hiked back to a place above the mine entrance. We had a good view and figured we'd watch for a while, but the place looked deserted, so we decided to go down and look closer. But this old guy came out with a shotgun and we ran away. Only Basher was shot."

He fell silent and Rebecca squeezed his hand again. "The wound didn't look that bad," Cash said. "It wasn't even bleeding much."

"Just one wound?" Wes asked. "Kramer shot Basher once?"

Cash nodded. "In his side. Why? Is that important?"

"Basher was shot in the head also," Wes said. "But after he was dead. Do you know anything about that?"

"No! That…that's sick." He cradled his head in his hands. "I should have stayed with him, but he insisted he would be fine on his own."

"Did anyone follow you back to Basher's place?" Wes asked.

"No. At least—I don't think so. I mean, I was pretty freaked out and focused on Basher, so I guess someone could have." He shook his head. "I don't know."

"What happened next?" Wes asked.

"Right. Well, I went back home—to Aunt Rebecca's house. I took a shower, and changed clothes, and spent most of the night tossing and turning, thinking about everything. The more I thought, the more I was sure there was something not right at that mine. Drug dealers get really paranoid because they know if anyone finds out what they're doing, they could end up in prison for a really long time or even dead. So I decided to make one more attempt to get some proof that the old guy was up to no good. Then I could bring that proof to you guys."

He told them about approaching the mine a second time and getting shot himself.

He looked down at the wound in his thigh. "I tried to find my truck, but it was just…gone. Then I realized I must have dropped my phone. I was scared, and I'd lost a lot of blood. I still had my pack, so I decided I'd better find someplace to hide. I found a cave—not this place, but another deeper cave. I holed up in there. I had some water and some energy bars and stuff. I kept drifting in and out. But finally I started to feel better and decided to try to make my way to a road or a house. Someplace I could call for help." He met Rebecca's gaze. "I knew you'd be worried. I figured you'd have people looking for me."

"I did," she said. "Lots of people looked for you. I don't understand why they didn't find you."

"There's a lot of territory out here," Wes said. "It's hard to cover it all. How did you end up here?"

As he told them about leaving the cave and searching for help, Rebecca could scarcely believe all he had been through. "Finally a white SUV stopped for me. I asked the driver to take me to the medical clinic where Aunt Rebecca works, but instead he took me back to that same parking area. He ordered me out of the truck, then he pulled out a big pistol. I didn't have any choice but to run again."

"What did he look like?" Wes asked. "Did he give you a name?"

"I can't be sure," Cash said. "But now that I've had time to think about it, I wonder if it was Bart Smith. Payson told you about the cheesy disguise Smith was wearing, right? The wig and the wild shirt?"

Wes nodded.

"I think this guy was wearing a disguise, too. Instead of a wig, he didn't have any hair at all—but I think it was one of those bald cap things actors use. I thought I could see the line below his hat. He had a big mustache, too. Really big, like a cartoon mustache, really black, with curled up ends. He had on dark glasses and his cheeks were really full and he spoke with a lisp like he had something stuffed in his cheeks. And he was wearing leather gloves so I never saw his hands. He didn't tell me his name or say much of anything, really. Except, when we got to the parking area, he said I needed to learn they don't like trespassers around here."

"When was this?" Wes asked.

"Yesterday," Cash said. "I ran blindly until I couldn't run anymore, then I realized I was really lost. I found this place to hide out and tried to think what to do next. I kept hoping someone would find me—someone who didn't want me dead."

"You say he threatened you with a handgun," Wes said.

"Yes. I thought maybe he was the one shooting at you just now."

"Those shots didn't come from a handgun," Wes said. "And it wasn't a shotgun, like the miner, Martin Kramer, shot Basher with. This was a rifle."

Cash buried his head in his hand. "Maybe there are three of them. Maybe they're working together."

Rebecca slid her hand up his arm. Whereas his fingers were icy, the rest of him was hot to the touch. "Cash, I need to look at that gunshot wound," she said.

"What are you going to do about it?" he asked.

"I haven't worked in medical clinic for eight years without learning a little bit," she said. "I want to see it."

He said nothing, but lay on his side and shoved off the emergency blanket. Rebecca steeled herself, then pushed down the bloody pants and studied the angry swelling at his thigh. "It's infected," she said.

"I figured," he said.

She pressed gingerly around the wound and he flinched. She gave up and covered him again. "We need to get you out of here," she said.

"You should stay here with Cash while I try to make it back to the truck," Wes said. "I can try to radio for help. If the radio doesn't work, he can head to the Olsens' place at the yurt."

"How are you going to make it back there?" she asked. "And if you do, how are you going to find us again?"

He pulled out his phone. "I was stupid not to think of it before," he said. "The internal GPS will work without cell service. I can figure our location with it and use the information to get back to you. And there's internal mapping software that will help me find the truck. It's not precise, but it should be enough. If I get back to the road, I can make it from there on my own."

She opened her mouth to protest they should all go together. But Cash clutched her arm. "Let him go," he said. "I don't think I have the strength to walk out of here and I'm scared I'll die if you leave me alone."

"You're not going to die." She gripped his hand again. "Of course I'll stay with you."

"Come see me off," Wes said and held out his hand. She took it and he pulled her to her feet and they walked together out onto the ledge.

Once outside, he unholstered his pistol and pressed it into her hand. "Take this, but don't use it unless you have to."

She looked down at the weapon, heavy and cold against her skin. The thought that she might need this sent a tremor through her, but she forced back the fear and slipped the gun into her pocket. "All right."

Wes pulled her close and kissed her, hard. "I love you," he said.

And then he was gone, his words and the emotion behind them leaving her lightheaded. "I love you, too," she whispered, even though she knew he couldn't hear.

WES HALF SLID down the steep slope they had climbed to reach Cash's shelter, praying that what he'd once been told about the GPS on his phone would work in real life. Cash had looked to be in pretty bad shape; he didn't have time to waste.

He worried, too, about the person who had been shooting at them earlier. Whoever it was might track them to that cave, where Rebecca and Cash would be trapped. Try as he might, he couldn't sort out the different players in this drama. There was Kramer, who he was convinced had fired the shot that killed Basher Monroe. A ballistics test would prove that, and Kramer had admitted to firing on trespassers before.

But who was Bart Smith? A bizarre alter ego for Kramer? Someone working with Kramer? Another shady associate of Trey Allerton, who had a record of palling around with murderers?

He forced himself to focus on the map on his phone,

though walking a straight line in this terrain proved difficult. He repeatedly had to detour around fallen trees, impenetrable thickets, or brush, or large rock outcroppings. But he pushed forward, moving as quickly as he could, the knowledge that Rebecca and Cash were depending on him keeping him going.

After an hour of walking, he reached the Jeep trail. The trail itself showed as a thin blue line on the map on his phone. He broke into a jog and a few minutes later, the parking lot was in sight.

His SUV listed to one side like a foundering ship, the back windshield spiderwebbed, spilling pellets of green safety glass across the bumper. Wes approached cautiously, every nerve alert. The sight of the wrecked SUV emphasized how isolated he was in this spot. But after watching the wrecked vehicle for several minutes, he decided he was spooking himself. He couldn't waste any more time. He dug out his keys and hit the button to unlock the door, then slipped inside and picked up the radio microphone.

Static crackled from the speakers when he first turned it on. He held the microphone close and spoke loudly. "This is Unit Nine. Do you copy?"

More static, but he thought he could almost make out a voice. "This is Unit Nine," he repeated.

No answer. He tried several more times, then tossed the mike down on the seat in disgust. Maybe someone on the other end had heard him, but he couldn't count on it. He needed to get moving again. If the Olsens were home, he'd send them to town for help while he took food and water back to Rebecca and Cash.

He slid out of the SUV and slammed the door behind him, sending another cascade of broken glass to the ground. He turned to walk away, just as Martin

Kramer stepped from behind a tree and pointed a shotgun. "Don't move another muscle!" Kramer ordered.

Wes eased both hands into the air. "What are you doing, Mr. Kramer?"

"I came to get back the gold you stole." Kramer took a step forward. "And don't lie to me or I'll blow you away."

# Chapter Twenty

Rebecca sat with Cash, the weight of Wes's pistol heavy against her hip, tension tightening every muscle. She wanted to ask Cash how he was feeling, but she also wanted him to sleep if he was able. So she remained quiet, listening to him breathe, reminding herself that as long as she could still hear him, then he was still with her. He still had a chance.

"Tell me about the cop." Cash's voice was raspy but startling in the silence.

"Do you mean Wes?" She shifted to face him. His eyes were closed, the blond beard fuzzing his jaw and the lines of pain around his eyes making him look much older.

More like his father, she realized with a start.

"Yeah. How'd you meet him?"

"We met when I reported you missing."

"Huh. Then I guess you can thank me later."

Now he sounded like Scott, that breezy sarcasm that had driven her crazy when he was alive, but that she had missed so keenly when he was gone. "Wes has been a big help," she said.

"He loves you, you know."

Had Cash heard their whispered exchange outside

the cave? No, that wasn't possible. "What makes you say that?" she asked.

"I can tell. The way he touched your shoulder."

"How old are you again?"

"Old enough to know love when I see it. I'm happy for you. I never could figure out what you were doing alone."

"Because that would be the worst thing ever," she said.

"Yeah, well, I heard about you and Garrett. For what it's worth, I think he regrets dumping you. Though you should count yourself lucky. He and Dad may have been friends, but they're nothing alike. And that's not just my opinion—everyone says so."

She shouldn't have been surprised. The climbing community was tight, and there were no real secrets. She was curious about what people had said about her and Garrett, but she didn't want to know enough to hear it from Cash. That was all ancient history now, anyway. "You're right," she said. "Garrett is nothing like Scott." She put her hand on his arm. "But you're so much like your dad."

He turned his face away. Talking about his father had always been hard for him, though she suspected Cash thought about Scott all the time. She certainly did.

"If I get out of here alive, I'm going to go back to California and go to college," he said. "I'll study counseling, or teaching, or something where I can make a difference. I'll still climb and teach climbing, but I want to do more."

"You're going to be okay," she said.

"Without me in the house, maybe your cop can move in," he said.

"Cash!"

"I'm just saying."

She laughed. In spite of everything, she laughed and felt lifted up by the release of tension. None of them knew what the future held, but it was so freeing to envision a positive tomorrow, instead of one where all the worst things happened.

"Someone's coming," Cash said and shoved up onto his elbows.

At first, she didn't hear anything, then she made out a sound like someone breathing hard and shoes scraping the loose rock on the slope leading up to their shelter. Heart thudding, she stood and slipped her hand into her pocket, touching the grip of the Glock.

"It's too soon for Wes to be back," Cash whispered.

She nodded and moved carefully toward the opening of the overhang. Whoever was out there moved closer. Rebecca slid the Glock from her pocket and steadied it with both hands.

The man came into view—a big man, with broad shoulders. He wore a black-knit beanie pulled down low, and if he had hair, it didn't show. Big dark glasses obscured his eyes, and he had a bright bandanna knotted around his throat and an extravagant black mustache. He grinned and held up his hands. "Hey now, don't shoot! I'm here to help."

"Don't come any closer," she said.

"I wouldn't dream of it." He slowly lowered his hands. "But I ran into a friend of yours—a sheriff's deputy—and he told me you and that lost climber were back in here and needed help, so I came to see what I could do."

"He's lying. That's the man who tried to kill me."

Rebecca glanced around, to where Cash leaned

against the opening of their shelter. He had to cling to the rock to stay upright. "Cash, go back—" she began.

Then the breath was knocked from her as the stranger tackled her. He knocked the Glock from her hand and straddled her, crushing her with his weight. "I know you're only trying to protect the kid," he said. "I can appreciate that. So I'll do you a favor and I'll kill you first, before I shut him up for good."

"We haven't done anything to you!" she protested.

"That kid knows things I can't let become public knowledge," the man said. He drew a pistol from his side and pointed it toward Cash. "Don't try anything, unless you want your poor aunt to have to watch you die."

WES WATCHED KRAMER CAREFULLY. The older man's face was red, his eyes glittering with excitement—or rage. "I don't know what you're talking about," Wes said. "I haven't taken anything that belongs to you."

"Don't lie to me." Kramer kept the shotgun fixed on Wes. A ballistics vest probably wouldn't do much good against a shotgun slug fired at this distance. "I got home from the hospital and I could see your tracks in my driveway. And you were foolish enough to leave one of your cards where I had the gold stashed."

"I did stop by your place," Wes said. "I'd heard you'd been hurt and I wanted to check on you." Better to leave Rebecca out of this. "And I wanted to hear more about your accident. I think you're right that someone planted that piece of glass where you were likely to hurt yourself."

"You probably planted it there. That woman at the clinic—the one who was asking so many questions—probably let you know I had to go to the hospital, and you took the opportunity to swoop in and take everything I've worked for over the last five years. I'm not going to let you get away with it." He pumped the shotgun, the *ka-chunk* of the barrel sending a chill through Wes. "Now, hand it over."

"Put the gun down, Kramer," Wes ordered. "You've got bigger things to worry about than some missing gold. One of the young men you shot has died and the other one is in bad shape. You could be facing a murder charge."

"It's not murder if a man's defending his own property," Kramer said. "I told you I'd been having trouble with people coming around my place, trespassing and causing trouble. You didn't do anything about it, so I had to. Besides, how do you know I'm the one who shot them?"

"We'll match the slugs to your shotgun," Wes said.

"Or maybe you won't be around to do that." Kramer brought the shotgun to his shoulder.

"Don't shoot!" Wes spoke loudly, freezing Kramer. "I'll give you back the gold," he added, when Kramer lowered the shotgun.

"I knew you were lying," Kramer said. "Where is it?"

"It's in the back of the SUV here." It took everything in Wes to turn his back on a man with a shotgun aimed at him, but he was counting on Kramer being more focused on the gold.

"What happened to your vehicle?" Kramer asked. "Looks like somebody shot it to pieces."

"I thought you did that," Wes said.

"Not me. I just got here a few minutes before you did. Now quit stalling and give me that gold."

Wes opened the rear lift gate of the SUV, sending a shower of broken glass over himself and the surrounding gravel. Glass crunched under his feet as he leaned into the vehicle and grabbed the first thing that came to hand—a duffel bag filled with tools for dealing with traffic accidents—flares, cones and other supplies. It was heavy and awkward, but he mustered every bit of energy to drag the bag from the vehicle and swing it toward Kramer. He hit the older man square in the chest, knocking him off balance. The shotgun slid to the ground and Kramer stumbled backward. Wes kicked the gun out of the way and leaped on the older man.

Kramer struggled out from under the duffel and grappled with Wes, grunting with the effort. Though he was almost thirty years older than Wes, years of work in the mine had hardened him, and anger added to his strength. The two rolled on the ground, Wes dodging a punch for every one he landed. He was dimly aware of the edge of the ravine somewhere beyond the front bumper of his SUV, and the still-cocked shotgun nearby as well.

Kramer swore and cuffed Wes hard on the side of the head. Wes shook off the dizziness and twisted one arm behind Kramer's back. He managed to flip the older man over and straddle him. From there he was able to restrain Kramer's hands behind his back. The older man continued to thrash beneath him, filling the air with abuse.

Wes climbed off Kramer and stood. "I don't have your gold," he said. He picked up the shotgun and carried it with him to the front of the SUV, and reached for the radio mike again. "Dispatch, this is Unit Nine. Officer needs assistance." He'd keep sending that message until someone answered or he'd rested enough to march Kramer to the nearest telephone.

CASH STARED AT the man with the gun—the same man who had given him a ride, then tried to shoot him—Bart Smith, or whatever his real name was. Looking for him had started this whole sorry escapade. Having him show up now, when he was so close to getting out of this alive, was too much.

Anger rose in his throat—a rage stronger than the fatigue and weakness that made even standing up a challenge. He clenched his fists at his side. He wasn't going to let this man—this stranger who Cash had done nothing to—ruin his life and his aunt's life. "What kind of idiot are you!" he shouted. "Why do you want to kill two people who never did anything to you?"

Aunt Rebecca's eyes widened and she shook her head, probably trying to warn him not to make this man any angrier than he already was. But Cash didn't care. He had had enough. "You're sick, you know that!" he said. "Why hurt someone you don't even know?"

"You're just an innocent kid, right?"

*Bart* smirked. "But you know enough about me and my business to put me away for a long time. And I can't let that happen." He aimed the pistol at Cash. "I should shut you up first, then deal with your aunt."

"Wes, no! Get back!" Rebecca shouted and waved her hands, staring over Bart's shoulder. Cash turned to look and saw nothing. Bart turned, too, and it was enough for Cash to take his chance. He charged the bigger, older man, driving his head into Smith's stomach, and knocked him off balance. Rebecca picked up the pistol she had dropped earlier and fired. The bullet missed Smith and Cash, but it apparently made Smith think twice about dealing with her. He shoved Cash off him and leaped from the ledge outside their shelter to the ground below, and took off running. They could hear him crashing through the woods for a long time after he disappeared from sight.

Rebecca sank to her knees, still clutching the gun in both hands. Cash crawled to her. "Are you okay?" he asked.

She nodded but said nothing, still clutching the gun.

"I think you can put the gun down now," Cash said. She was making him nervous, her finger hovering so near the trigger.

She nodded. "Right." And she slowly lowered the gun to her lap.

They sat side by side on the dirt floor of the rock overhang. Cash prayed Smith wouldn't return. He didn't know if he had the strength to stand. It was taking everything he had not to pass out.

They didn't say anything for a very long time. An hour, or maybe longer. Cash wasn't doing a good job of keeping track of time. He had fallen asleep, or maybe lost consciousness, when Rebecca nudged him. "Someone's coming," she said in a harsh whisper.

He raised his head. Someone was definitely walking toward their shelter, and not even trying to be quiet about it. "Rebecca! It's Wes!" a man shouted.

She cried out and dropped the gun, then stood and stumbled toward the opening of their shelter. Wes climbed over the side and gathered her to him as she sobbed against him. "It's going to be okay," he said. "Help is right behind me. It was Kramer shooting at us, and he's under arrest and on his way to jail now."

"It wasn't Kramer," Cash said. "It was Bart Smith. He was here. He tried to kill us, but Aunt Rebecca shot at him and he ran away."

Wes looked from Cash to Rebecca. She nodded. "He was wearing the same disguise as the man who picked up Cash and tried to shoot him. He said Cash knew things about him that would ruin him, and that he was going to kill us both."

"But I don't know anything about him," Cash said. "I don't even know who he really is."

"What's this about Kramer?" Rebecca asked.

"He was waiting at my SUV and held a gun on me. He accused me of stealing his gold. There was a bit of a struggle, but he's under arrest now."

"Are you all right?" She clutched at his shoulders.

"I'm fine." He looked at Cash. "They're sending a helicopter to get you out of here," he said. "It should be here soon. I've got some fellow deputies arranging a landing spot not far from here."

"Thanks." Cash lowered himself to the ground again. Running at Smith had taken everything out of him. That chopper couldn't get here soon enough.

He closed his eyes and drifted off, though he had a fleeting impression of his aunt Rebecca and Wes, kissing as if they might never stop.

WES HATED TO leave Rebecca to deal with Cash on her own, but he had to get to work putting together the pieces of the case. "Go and do your job," she urged him. "It's more important to me that you find the people who hurt Cash than that you sit with me in a hospital waiting room."

"Keep me posted." He kissed her again, then whispered, "I love you."

"I love you, too," she said and the words made him feel a foot taller than he had before.

When he returned to the scene, Gage caught him up with developments so far. "Kramer has contacted a lawyer and we're waiting to question him, but he's had plenty to say about his stolen gold. Seems he's been stashing away the proceeds from his mine for several years and has accumulated a small fortune. He alternates between believing you stole it or that Cash and his friends—he doesn't say who that might be—spirited it away."

"Cash says he and Basher never got close enough to see much of anything," Wes said. "They thought Kramer was manufacturing or distributing drugs."

"No sign of that," Gage said. "And no sign of your mysterious bald-headed, mustachioed attacker, either. We were able to get a tracking dog on loan from the Colorado Bureau of Investigation, and they're out with a team, trying to find him, but no luck so far."

"I want to talk to Trey Allerton," Wes said.

"I agree," Gage said. "He has a habit of being on the periphery whenever anything bad happens around here."

Allerton was more affable than usual when he answered their knock that afternoon. "I was thinking about calling the station and asking what's with all the cop cars going up and down the road all afternoon," he said.

"May we come in?" Wes asked.

In answer, Allerton held the door open wide.

Courtney Baker was sitting on the sofa with her daughter, Ashlyn, in her lap. "Is something wrong?" she asked when Wes and Gage entered.

"Martin Kramer has been arrested for the murder of Basher Monroe." Wes had debated which topic to lead with and had decided on this one.

"I'm not surprised," Allerton said. "The old guy threatened to shoot anyone who set foot on his property."

"We've determined Kramer fired the shot that killed

Basher Monroe, but someone else shot Basher in the head, after he was already dead at his camper," Wes said. "Do you know anything about that?"

"No. Why would I? I never met Basher Monroe."

"Kramer says someone stole a cache of gold he'd been saving up," Gage said. "Do you know anything about that?"

Allerton laughed. "So the old man really had gold? Are you sure he's not making that up?"

"Did you know about the gold?" Gage pressed.

"No way. And I still don't believe he ever found enough to amount to anything. Though I guess from the crime scene van I saw headed his way, y'all think Kramer is hiding something."

"Cash Whitlow was found this afternoon," Wes said. He watched for a reaction from Allerton, but the handsome face remained impassive.

"Dead or alive?" Allerton asked.

"He's alive," Wes said. "He's expected to make a full recovery."

Courtney looked up. "That's so wonderful. I'm glad."

"Yeah, good to hear," Allerton said. "Of course, I imagine he's pretty traumatized. Bound to be."

"We're looking for another man who attacked Cash," Wes said. "A big guy, bald, with a thick black mustache."

Allerton shook his head. "I don't know anyone like that."

"Maybe you've seen him. He picked up Cash when he was walking down this road yesterday, and pursued him again this afternoon."

"I was gone all day yesterday and most of today," Allerton said. "You can ask Courtney."

"We were together all day yesterday and today,"

Courtney said. She didn't look at Wes or Gage, focused instead on her daughter. "We didn't get home until a little while ago."

Allerton stood. "Sorry we can't be of more help," he said. "But it's getting late, so I'll say good night."

Wes wanted to press him, but doubted he'd get anything more. "What do you think?" he asked Gage when the two of them were back in Gage's SUV, headed to town.

"I think we don't have any evidence against Allerton. We'll keep looking for Bart Smith, but for now we'll have to content ourselves with a resolution to the murder of Basher Monroe and Cash Whitlow home safe." He glanced at Wes. "Not a bad day's work."

It wasn't, but Wes hated loose ends. Unfortunately there were almost always loose ends in any case.

It was after eight o'clock by the time he got to the hospital in Junction, where Cash had been flown for treatment. He found Rebecca with Cash in a private room on the surgical floor. Despite having undergone surgery to remove a shotgun slug from his thigh, and treatment for exposure and an infection, the young man already looked better. "Hey," he answered Wes's greeting, almost shyly.

Rebecca stood and embraced him. "Cash is doing so well," she said.

"Good to hear it," he said.

"So are you here on business or pleasure?" Cash asked, then grinned at Rebecca.

"A little of both." He held up a folder he'd brought with him. "Can you look at a few pictures for me? See if you recognize anyone?"

"Sure." Cash sat up a little straighter, wincing only a little.

Wes looked at Rebecca. "Any reason I shouldn't do this? Do they have him on heavy-duty pain meds?"

"No pain meds," Cash said.

Wes's surprise must have shown, because Cash added, "I didn't want to risk getting hooked on opiates again. I'm okay with over-the-counter meds. I feel so much better already than I did in the woods. I got to eat a bowl of soup for dinner. Tomorrow I might graduate to real food—a hamburger."

"Fair enough." Wes slid the folder onto the tray table in front of Cash. "Just tell me if anyone looks familiar." He had pulled together photographs of men who fit the description of Bart Smith, with and without hair, with and without a mustache. A photo of Trey Allerton was in the mix, too."

Cash studied the photographs for a long while. Rebecca stood beside him, looking over his shoulder. Finally he pushed the folder away. "Sorry," he said. "I don't recognized anyone."

"No need to apologize." Wes turned to Rebecca. "What about you?"

She shook her head. "None of them are the man I remember."

He nodded and closed the folder. "We're not having any luck finding Bart Smith," he said. "He may have left the area. Until we know for sure, we're going to be keeping a close eye on both of you. If you see anyone acting suspicious, or you feel threatened, or just uneasy, let me know right away."

"That's good," Cash said. "But when I get out of here, I've already decided I'm going back to California. I figure you'll do a good job of looking after Aunt Rebecca, and you'd probably just as soon not have me around, cramping your style."

"Cash!" Rebecca's cheeks flushed pink.

Wes put his arm around her shoulders. "I promise to take good care of your aunt," he told Cash.

Cash nodded.

A nurse came in. "Time for a wound check," she said.

Rebecca walked with Wes into the hallway. "I'm sorry we haven't found Bart Smith," he said. "We'll keep searching, but we'll need to get lucky to track him down. So far we haven't come up with any hint of who he really is or where he might be hiding. Search and Rescue are pretty sure he's not still in the woods. The search dog led them to a place where a vehicle had been parked. They think he probably drove away in it."

"It's okay," she said. "You know who killed Basher Monroe, and you found Cash. That's what matters most."

"You found Cash. If not for you, I probably wouldn't have gone back out there to look for him again."

She glanced back at the closed door to Cash's room. "I think Cash saved my life," she said. "I pretended you were coming in order to distract Bart Smith, or whoever he was, and Cash ran at him, knocking him over. Then I fired your gun. I didn't come close to hitting him, but he ran off anyway."

"He's a remarkable young man. And you're a remarkable woman." He tugged her toward an alcove at the end of the hallway, where they would have more privacy. "I meant what I said about protecting you. Not just now, but for the long-term. For forever."

Her breath caught, and she search his face. "What are you saying?"

He took a deep breath. Was he being rash? Rushing her? "Rebecca, will you marry me?" he asked. "I don't have a ring, and I didn't plan an elaborate proposal, I'm just saying what's in my heart. I love you, and I want to be with you. Forever."

"It's what's in my heart too," she said. She kissed him, very lightly, then drew back. "Yes."

"It's not too soon?" he asked. "We haven't known each other very long."

"I've been waiting for you for years," she said and kissed him again. "What took you so long to get here?"

He could have told her that they both needed to go through all the things they went through to get to be the people they were today, able to promise to love each other and mean it. But he didn't waste the words. He only held her tight, and promised himself that he was going to stop wishing to change the past and focus on the future. With this woman, in this place.

Exactly where he was supposed to be.

\* \* \* \* \*

# MILLS & BOON

## THE HEART OF ROMANCE

---

## A ROMANCE FOR EVERY READER

---

**MODERN**

Prepare to be swept off your feet by sophisticated, sexy and seductive heroes, in some of the world's most glamourous and romantic locations, where power and passion collide.

**HISTORICAL**

Escape with historical heroes from time gone by. Whether your passion is for wicked Regency Rakes, muscled Vikings or rugged Highlanders, awaken the romance of the past.

**MEDICAL**

Set your pulse racing with dedicated, delectable doctors in the high-pressure world of medicine, where emotions run high and passion, comfort and love are the best medicine.

*True Love*

Celebrate true love with tender stories of heartfelt romance, from the rush of falling in love to the joy a new baby can bring, and a focus on the emotional heart of a relationship.

*Desire*

Indulge in secrets and scandal, intense drama and plenty of sizzling hot action with powerful and passionate heroes who have it all: wealth, status, good looks…everything but the right woman.

**HEROES**

Experience all the excitement of a gripping thriller, with an intense romance at its heart. Resourceful, true-to-life women and strong, fearless men face danger and desire - a killer combination!

---

To see which titles are coming soon, please visit

## millsandboon.co.uk/nextmonth

# LET'S TALK
## *Romance*

For exclusive extracts, competitions
and special offers, find us online:

facebook.com/millsandboon

@MillsandBoon

@MillsandBoonUK

**Get in touch on 01413 063232**

For all the latest titles coming soon, visit
**millsandboon.co.uk/nextmonth**

# JOIN US ON SOCIAL MEDIA!

Stay up to date with our latest releases, author news and gossip, special offers and discounts, and all the behind-the-scenes action from Mills & Boon...

 millsandboon

 millsandboonuk

 millsandboon

*It might just be true love...*

# MILLS & BOON
## *Desire*

Indulge in secrets and scandal, intense drama and plenty of sizzling hot action with powerful and passionate heroes who have it all: wealth, status, good looks…everything but the right woman.

# MILLS & BOON

## MODERN

# Power and Passion

Prepare to be swept off your feet by sophisticated, sexy and seductive heroes, in some of the world's most glamourous and romantic locations, where power and passion collide.

# MILLS & BOON
## MEDICAL
*Pulse-Racing Passion*

Set your pulse racing with dedicated, delectable doctors in the high-pressure world of medicine, where emotions run high and passion, comfort and love are the best medicine.

# MILLS & BOON
*True Love*
## Romance from the Heart

Celebrate true love with tender stories of heartfelt romance, from the rush of falling in love to the joy a new baby can bring, and a focus on the emotional heart of a relationship.

Celebrate their love with a fairy-tale style
wedding - complete with the pitter-patter of
tiny feet, as two single dads and a bride-to-be
discover the emotional heart of a relationship.